ONE CHILD IN BERLIN

STELLA BLED BOOK THREE

A.W. HARTOIN

One Child in Berlin

A Stella Bled Thriller Book Three

ALSO BY A.W. HARTOIN

Afterlife Issues

Dead Companions (Afterlife Issues Book One)

A Trunk, a Canoe, and all the Barbecue (Afterlife Issues Book Two)

Old Friends and Fedoras (Afterlife Issues Book Three)

The Trouble with Tinsel (Afterlife Issues Book Four)

Fun Ivy (Afterlife Issues Book Five) coming soon

Mercy Watts Mysteries

Novels

A Good Man Gone (Mercy Watts Mysteries Book One)

Diver Down (A Mercy Watts Mystery Book Two)

Double Black Diamond (Mercy Watts Mysteries BookThree)

Drop Dead Red (Mercy Watts Mysteries Book Four)

In the Worst Way (Mercy Watts Mysteries Book Five)

The Wife of Riley (Mercy Watts Mysteries Book Six)

My Bad Grandad (Mercy Watts Mysteries Book Seven)

Brain Trust (Mercy Watts Mysteries Book Eight)

Down and Dirty (Mercy Watts Mysteries Book Nine)

Small Time Crime (Mercy Watts Mysteries Book Ten)

Bottle Blonde (Mercy Watts Mysteries Book Eleven)

Mean Evergreen (Mercy Watts Mysteries Book Twelve)

Silver Bells at Hotel Hell (Mercy Watts Mysteries Book Thirteen)

So Long Gone (Mercy Watts Mysteries Book Fourteen)

Short stories

Coke with a Twist

Touch and Go My Book

Nowhere Fast

Dry Spell

A Sin and a Shame

Stella Bled Historical Thrillers

The Paris Package (Stella Bled Book One)

Strangers in Venice (Stella Bled Book Two)

One Child in Berlin (Stella Bled Book Three)

Dark Victory (Stella Bled Book Four)

A Quiet Little Place on Rue de Lille (Stella Bled Book Five)

Her London Season (Stella Bled Book Six)

Double Duet (Stella Bled Book Seven)

Paranormal

It Started with a Whisper (Son of a Witch Book One)

Angels and Insects (Son of a Witch Book Two)

Young Adult fantasy

Flare-up (Away From Whipplethorn Short)

A Fairy's Guide To Disaster (Away From Whipplethorn Book One)

Fierce Creatures (Away From Whipplethorn Book Two)

A Monster's Paradise (Away From Whipplethorn Book Three)

A Wicked Chill (Away From Whipplethorn Book Four)

To the Eternal (Away From Whipplethorn Book Five)

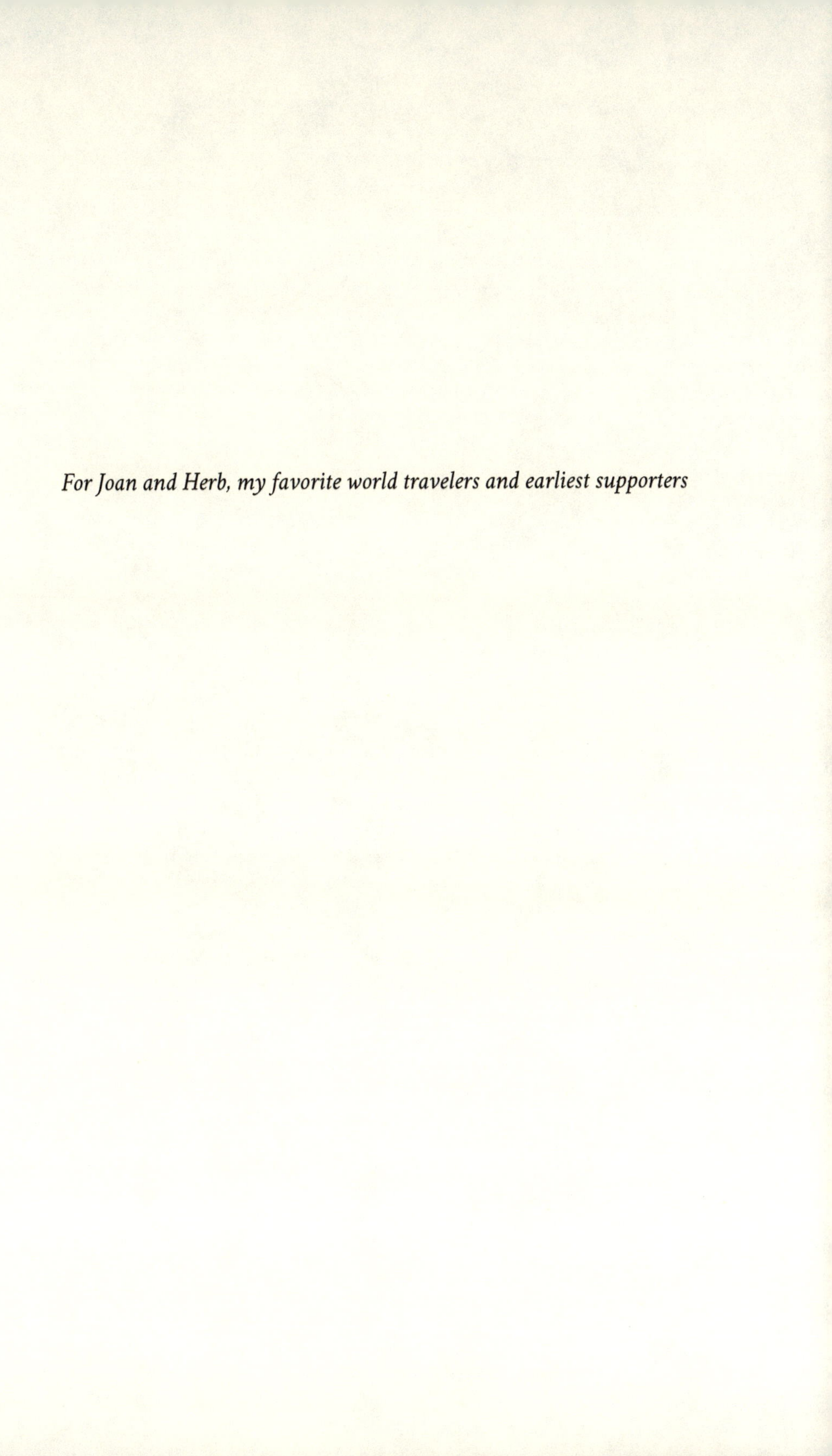

For Joan and Herb, my favorite world travelers and earliest supporters

PROLOGUE

It was a gift from God. A sign of *his* bountiful mercy and because of it they would survive the Dachau internment camp and go on to fight for the inevitable defeat of the Nazis. Michael Haas could find no other explanation and he believed it with all his heart. His friend, Adam Stolowicki, did not.

Adam could not find God in Dachau and he had tried. He'd prayed for months, given service where he could, and looked for a sign that God knew he was there, that *they* were there. But after a year, he'd lost too much, including his name and profession along with his clothes, weight, and hair. Not to mention the friends, too many to count, who had died in ways he couldn't bear to remember.

There were days when he could not recall his real name and when he did, it seemed unimportant that he was Abel Herschmann, a historian and travel guide. He had become someone else entirely. If Michael had known, he would've said this was a gift, too. That the real Adam Stolowicki had died in that dirty, freezing boxcar so that Abel Herschmann might live to fulfill a purpose.

That was certainly what Jakob thought. The old man gave him Adam's name and instructed Abel on who he now was, a bricklayer from Warsaw and a communist. As far as Abel could tell, if God was in Dachau he took the form of an elderly man with gout and severe arthritis. It was Jakob who delivered the gift that Michael was so sure came from God.

"Do you hear them?" whispered Michael.

"No. Not yet," said Abel.

"Maybe we should start now."

"No. It will be suspicious if we go out early. They'll ask questions."

Michael nodded, his head rubbing against Abel's shoulder in the bunk they shared with three other men. The other men were recently arrived from Poland and were still sleeping, having talked late into the night about escape. They didn't yet understand there would be no escape. The SS guards would see to that and, if they didn't, their fellow prisoners would. An escapee left a death sentence for his fellows still in the barrack. Abel carried the scars of one man's failed attempt on his legs and buttocks, but he survived the beating well enough. Others hadn't.

Michael, who had already been weak from an illness, had gotten an infection. His legs were swollen and weeping fluid. There were several doctors in the barracks and they'd done what they could, but Michael wasn't improving and was so weak Abel had to support him while walking. Hiding that from the guards wasn't easy. Abel lived in fear that Michael would be noticed or collapse during roll call and he'd be sent to the infirmary. Abel would sooner have him shot in the head.

"God forgive me, but I miss Jakob," said Michael.

Abel smiled. "We all do. Hope left with him."

"Don't say that. God is with us." He patted the badge on his chest. "He gave us the best chance."

"Yes," said Abel.

"You must believe," insisted Michael.

A door banged open and the Kapo came in yelling and hitting their bunks with his truncheon. The Poles jolted awake and one fell off the bunk with a yelp, only to be given a swift kick and a torrent of screaming about being clumsy.

Abel climbed off the bunk and looked over at Dr. Fleck, who

quickly moved between Abel and the Kapo. He and several other men shielded Abel as he hauled Michael off the bunk.

One of the Poles sneered and moved away. "What is wrong with him? Send him to the infirmary."

Ludwik, a usually quiet biologist, made a fist and said, "If Michael goes, so will you."

The Pole's eyes narrowed, but he shut his mouth before he headed out into the icy morning air.

"Thank you, my friend," whispered Michael. "You'll see. It won't be long now."

Abel held him under the arm as casually as possible and helped him to the door. "You can do it."

"I will because I know that Jakob will find my family. Help is coming. I feel it."

"Yes. Now quiet. Save your strength."

"You must believe."

"I believe," said Abel automatically as he helped Michael out of the door and down the block alley to the square. It was more crowded than ever since Germany invaded Poland. Abel had heard a guard complaining about the smell. He'd said that the camp should only have six thousand prisoners and it now had nineteen thousand. Abel could well believe it. Many of the men who had been arrested after Grynszpan killed the Nazi in Paris had been released, but the Germans always found more men to imprison. Czechs from the Sudetenland and then Czechoslovakia itself. Now Poland.

"Who's next?" Abel wondered aloud without much interest. He was where he was. A year in hell had taught him that nothing would change it.

A guard came charging by, yelling, "Go on there, you stinking Jew!" He raised his baton and cracked a man on the shoulder with it. "What did you say? What did you say?"

More guards came, passing Michael and Abel, and concentrating on the barracks that held the Jewish prisoners. Grief and guilt washed over Abel, making his heart feel like it was twisting in his chest and wringing out his soul.

Michael squeezed his arm. "It is a gift from God."

Two Jewish prisoners went down and were savagely kicked as Michael and Abel shuffled by.

"It's unfair," Abel whispered.

"It is God's will that we live." Michael sounded strong. His eyes sparkled with fervent belief or perhaps it was the fever Abel could easily feel through the thin fabric of his ragged shirt. "It is."

Abel nodded, but he knew it was Jakob's will that he and Michael lined up with the communists and not the Jews. How the old man had done it wasn't clear, but Abel was sure that it was him.

When the first wave of Czechs came into the camp, Jakob had been designated for release, but while he was waiting, the guards decided to make him useful and assigned him to help process the influx of prisoners. Thousands were flooding in and the system they'd so carefully designed was overwhelmed.

Abel hardly saw his dear friend for the next few days, except for a glimpse of him bent over a desk, carefully filling out paperwork and another when he was being escorted out of his barracks with his meagre possessions. The Kapo, who wasn't as harsh as the others, allowed him to shake Abel's hand.

"I will see you again, my Leopold," said Jakob, referring to his son who had died at Dachau and in whose name Jakob had saved Abel.

"I hope so," said Abel.

Jakob's eyes sparkled under his shaggy brows. "I know so."

The Kapo forced him away before he could say more, but Abel had the strongest feeling that the old man was up to something and a few hours later he was proved right when his Kapo came to get him, yelling about mistakes and idiocy. He and Michael were hit and kicked all the way to the Shunt Room, where prisoners were processed when they arrived. It was the first place where Abel had been beaten without knowing why, and it wasn't the last.

After they'd gone inside and been shoved through a door to the long room where prisoners were stripped and cataloged, an SS screamed in their faces and waved paperwork around. Michael and Abel looked at each other in confusion, but all was revealed when the officer ran out of steam. He told them that they were not specific when they were brought in with the filthy Jews and had been cataloged incorrectly. He seemed to think this was a kind of crime, but exactly why wasn't clear.

The officer slashed at them with a razor and demanded that they remove their striped pants. They did, shaking so hard that the knocking of their bony knees was audible. Abel fully expected to be cut, possibly slashed to the bone, but, like a miracle, it didn't happen. The officer flung the razor at him and ordered him to remove his badge from his pant leg.

Utterly confused, he and Michael removed the red triangle stitched over the yellow triangle. When they tentatively placed them on the desk, the officer threw up his hands and yelled, *"Dummkopf!"*

He pointed at a couple of punchcards on the table, screaming about "the machine" and then waving the handwritten paperwork in their faces.

"Do you want to be a dirty Jew? Do you want to be with the scum?"

Abel and Michael just stared at him, mute. There was no right answer, experience had taught them that, and there they were standing in front of a mad man with their genitals barely covered by their shirts.

Another guard came over and Abel recognized him as Weiß, some sort of assistant to the camp commander. The tiniest sigh of relief escaped from Abel's lips. Weiß could not be considered kind or just by any stretch of the imagination, but he wasn't irrational or unpredictable as many of the guards were.

"What is this?" Weiß glanced with disdain at their shaking thighs and the yellow triangles on their pant legs, denoting them as Jews.

"These stupid fools can't understand a simple order," snapped the guard and then quickly stiffened when he saw Weiß's irritation at his tone. "They were classified wrong and told no one."

"Impossible," declared Weiß and he turned away.

"But the cards," said the guard. "My orders…"

Weiß turned back and eyed the punch cards on the table. "What about the cards."

"They say they are Jews, but the papers say no." The guard handed the paperwork over to Weiß, who glanced through it swiftly.

"Who punched the cards?" he asked.

The guard named several SS and hastily said, "It was a simple mistake, but these dogs did not tell us. These asshole communists let us put them with the Jews." He sneered. "Maybe they like the smell."

Abel knew this was the time to speak, but he found he had no voice. Fear had taken it. But Michael, a man of both extraordinary courage and faith, said in a clear voice with no hesitation or tremor, "We are not Jews." He sneered identical to the guard and said, "The smell is worse than you know."

"It says here you were arrested in Vienna on the tenth of November last year and brought in with Jews," said Weiß.

"Yes," said Michael. "We were arrested while watching a synagogue burn. At first they thought we were Jews, but we had our identification."

"Why were you arrested?"

Michael shrugged.

"Why did you allow the yellow triangle to be sewn on your pant leg?"

"No one was interested in what we said." He pointed at the punch cards. "They said the card was law."

Weiß nodded and tossed the paperwork on the table. "Remove the yellow and sew on the red, tip up." To the guard, he said, "Double check all the other cards punched from their group and put them in the correct barrack."

Weiß walked away and the guard began yelling about how slow they were. His face went red and spittle hit their hands as they cut the threads that held their Jewishness fast to their fate, amazed that neither Nazi thought to take a look under the hem of their shirts.

After they sewed on their red triangles, tip up, they put on their pants, careful to conceal themselves, and walked out into a spring day that was suddenly fresh and hopeful. They got their thin blankets and tin cups and took themselves to the new barrack on a different block away from the Jews, asocials, and criminals to the section where polit-ical prisoners were housed.

No one questioned their inclusion. The badge was everything.

Later that afternoon when they'd been assigned a new work detail out of the dreaded gravel pit to a painting crew, Abel found his voice. "How can we…"

"Live?" asked Michael. "By the grace of God. It is *his* will."

"But to deny our faith," said Abel.

Michael gestured to a man lying next to the electrified fence. The body with its yellow triangle had been there for three days, shot a dozen times for wandering too close to the fence line. "Do you want to end up like him?"

"We can still end up like him. We all can," said Abel, thinking of his mother. She was a faithful woman, kind and proud of who she was. She'd taught her son to be the same. What would she say to her son with his red triangle? Would she be joyful at this small chance or ashamed? Abel honestly didn't know.

"It is a gift from God," said Michael, his eyes lit with hope. "We will take his gift and find a way to get out of here. When the time comes we will make them pay for what they do and they will suffer as we have, as our people have."

"If you say so," said Abel.

"I don't. *He* does. God has given us this chance. He changed our paperwork. He showed it to the guards. How else could this be? Once you are categorized, it is over. But not for us. God gave us this. How else could we go from being Jews and political prisoners to only polit-ical? Now we will get more food. We won't be worked to death in the pit or beaten as much. They don't shoot the red triangles as fast." Michael grabbed Abel's arm with tears in his eyes. "We're going to live."

As Michael spoke of the paperwork, a memory sparked in Abel's mind. Jakob's face. His eyes. The old man's certainty that they would see each other again. The use of his son's name. Leopold was like a talisman to Jakob. He used it rarely and only in moments of hope and triumph. Jakob had been doing paperwork. He had done this for them.

Abel felt nauseated when he realized it. His dear friend had been days or hours away from release, if he had been caught… The retribution didn't bear thinking about.

"Adam," said Michael, "you will not deny the gift. He has done this for us."

"*He* has done this for us. I will not deny it." Abel smiled. "God forbid."

"We can do it. We can get out. Being communists is easy. We are after all."

"Yes," said Abel. "We are communists."

What was another lie on top of the first one, the big one, the one where he stole a dead man's name and lived because of it? Clearly, he could lie. He always could, although he didn't think it was lying exactly. As a Jewish boy among gentiles, Abel had learned early and well how to fit in and not make a fuss. His father called it being wallpaper. It was okay, he said. It meant you were still in the room. His parents worked hard for him to be in the room.

"She would be joyful," said Abel.

"Who?" asked Michael. "Your girl? The American?"

"What? No. My mother."

"You're thinking of your mother?" Michael rolled his eyes. "I'm thinking of my wife and how she will reward me when I get out of here."

In an impetuous moment weakened by hunger, Abel had spoken of Stella, the wife of his friend and the main reason he could endure the pain. She was out there somewhere. Seeing her again was a reason to live, but he had only mentioned her once, and once was all it took with Michael. He never forgot anything, names, what people said or did. Nothing. Abel had no doubt that he knew each and every guard's name that had beat him or Abel or anyone else. If Michael ever got out, he would not forget and if it took fifty years, he would find them and mete out a punishment worthy of the crime.

"I'll help you find your Stella as soon as we win the war," said Michael with a rather sleazy smile.

"I told you she's married."

Michael slapped him on the back. "I promise you will see her again. We will survive, kill the Nazi scum, and find your American." His friend's eyes twinkled. "God wills it."

Promises in Dachau were practically impossible to keep. Every day was a defeat. Merely surviving to see another morning was the only victory allowed. As Michael stood next to him for roll call, Abel could see his legs buckle and Michael caught himself just barely as they were counted. Abel began to pray that the count would be correct. That the SS would not miscount on *accident*, requiring punishments for those who stood silent and shivering, unable to correct or protest the vicious creature bellowing at them.

For once, the count was going quietly and Abel paused his prayer. Only for a moment, but that was enough. Up ahead in a Jewish block, a guard began screaming about a prisoner's expression. The guard doing their count stopped and turned to watch with a gleeful smile on his face.

Abel started a different kind of prayer. "One hundred and twenty-six. One hundred and twenty-six. You're on one hundred and twenty-six. Please God. One hundred and twenty-six."

The Jewish prisoner went down and their guard turned back to them, laughing. "Fucking dog. That will teach him." He looked at the guard next to him. "Where was I?"

"One hundred and twenty-six," prayed Abel.

The second guard shrugged. "One hundred and twenty-something."

The first guard smiled. "One hundred and twenty it is."

A tear of anguish rolled down Abel's cheek. He couldn't stop it or wipe it away. It would be noticed and, in a moment of clarity, he knew he didn't care. Michael would die. It was certain. It could either be for Michael's collapse that would come any minute, and the beating it would set off, or for the miscount for which they would all be punished. If Michael wasn't beaten to death, he would definitely be sent to the infirmary where his legs would be experimented on. Death was coming and Abel decided it could come for him, too. If Michael couldn't live, then he didn't want to either.

The guard finished the count and it was wrong. Then the bastard called out to his compatriots with a broad smile and the other guards left their sections to join in the fun. Michael wavered, but Abel wouldn't let him fall. His last friend, his only hope.

"Don't," whispered Dr. Fleck. "They'll only kill you, too."

"I want to die," said Abel as Michael's legs buckled.

Abel grabbed him and lowered his friend to the sharp gravel. The guards were swift and the first strike was on his shoulders, sending a burst of pain up into his brain. The rest were a blur, but then they stopped. Someone was saying a number. Abel couldn't focus on it. He kept his body over Michael's, shielding him as the other prisoners stood stiff in their rows.

A number was yelled out again and a guard grabbed Abel. Cursing, he pulled him back and examined the number on his pant leg. *"Nein!"*

"Check the other one, you fool," said a voice. It was Weiß, calm as always. The sight of Abel's blood spattering the gravel had no effect on him.

The guard grabbed Michael's leg, causing him to yelp in pain. "Ja."

They pulled Abel away and double-checked Michael's number. They agreed with some disappointment that he was the one they were looking for. Michael had passed out and Weiß smacked him until he responded. "It is your lucky day, communist scum."

Michael blinked at him without comprehension.

Weiß yanked up his pant leg and saw the oozing wounds. "Scheiße," he muttered and then jabbed a finger at Abel. "You. Help him to the Jourhouse."

Abel stayed on his hands and knees, not comprehending himself. "Now!"

The guards yanked him to his feet and Weiß got in his face. "You are a lucky man twice now. Do not try my patience."

Abel nodded slowly.

"Get your friend to the Jourhouse. He's being released."

"Released?" whispered Abel.

Weiß leaned in and said in Abel's ear, "Someone paid for the privilege of having this dog back. Perhaps someone wants you as well?"

Abel couldn't think of anything to say. Paid? A bribe. It must be. Abel had heard that bribes were possible, but Michael wasn't wealthy. Where had the money come from?

"No ideas?" asked Weiß. "A pity. I would enjoy a boat to go with my Mercedes." He slapped his baton in his palm. "Take him away before I up my price."

Abel staggered over to Michael and somehow managed to get him to his feet, whispering, "You must walk. I can't carry you."

A smile flickered on Michael's lips. "You've carried me long enough. Soon I will carry you."

"Shut up," yelled the guard. "Our count was wrong. Who's missing? Speak up, you dogs!"

"Recount," ordered Weiß. "There's too much blood on the gravel already."

Abel half-dragged Michael out of the formation as the guard started over again. His bellows were high-pitched, a sound the men had come to fear as a precursor to pain.

"I told you," said Michael. "Not long now."

Abel didn't answer. All his strength went to carrying his friend across the square past thousands of men who didn't dare look at who was leaving.

"Take him to the gate!" yelled a guard and he pointed at the black iron in the Jourhouse with its taunt barely visible in the dim morning light. *Arbeit Macht Frei.*

Underneath were several people in shadow. At least one was a woman. Abel could hear her weeping. They weren't coming to help. A guard stood in front of them, his weapon a warning. Abel had to get Michael there. Fifty yards, but it seemed like a mile or more.

"Adam?" Michael grasped at his arm.

"Almost there," Abel choked out.

"Tell me."

Not much farther. He could get Michael there. To the gate. To safety. He didn't care what happened after that. Only Michael mattered. Abel would die, but Michael, faithful Michael, would live.

"Tell me."

"What?" asked Abel.

Sunlight came over the buildings and the people's faces lit up in hope and agony at their slow, painful walk. Michael stopped and gripped Abel's arm, sending stinging pain up to his shoulders.

"Hurry up there, you dogs!" The guard pointed his rifle at them.

"Come on, Michael," said Abel. "You're going to live. It's God's will."

"You believe?"

"I do. I believe."

Their eyes met and Michael said again, "Tell me."

"I did. I believe," said Abel.

Michael reached up and put a weak hand on Abel's shoulder. "No, my friend. Tell me your name."

The guard started toward them, his boots crunching on the gravel.

"For God's sake, Michael. Come to us!" cried out the woman.

"Tell me who you really are," said Michael.

"Adam—"

"In God's name, tell me and I will come for you if it takes me to my dying breath. Tell me." His bloody hand came to rest on Abel's cheek. "I know you're not a red triangle. If you believe, believe in me."

The guard stuck his rifle in Michael's back and barked an order that Abel didn't really hear. He only saw his friend and despite the fear, he uttered the name he hadn't spoken in a year. "Abel Hershmann."

The guard dragged Michael backwards to the gate, but his friend was smiling and Abel saw his real name whispered on Michael's lips.

Then he was gone, carried out under the iron words and pushed into a waiting car. Gone. Saved.

The guard thrust his rifle at Abel, eyeing the blood on his face and clothes. "You want to go to the infirmary?"

"No," said Abel. "I want to live."

CHAPTER 1

*W*ind whipped through the mourners, carrying away the rabbi's words and a couple of hats. No one chased them and a few ravens perched on the statue of Diana, Goddess of the hunt, took note, cawing loudly, but they didn't chase them either since the hats were sensible black in light of the occasion and hardly a prize for a thief with an eye for worth.

So the hats were left to tumble away through the formal English garden past the Italianate landscape only to disappear into the topiary garden where they would be trapped by the ornamental hedges and retrieved later.

The Rabbi finished and there was a moment of silent reflection that no one announced but that everyone understood was necessary. The only sound was the insistent wind and the ravens. Stella Bled Lawrence stood as still as everyone else, but her blue eyes weren't cast down. She read the words on the memorial over and over again, waiting for the peace a memorial was supposed to bring. But as she suspected, a year had changed nothing. Neither did the memorial. Of course, the marble monument wasn't for her, although her opinion had been asked. She did approve of the design, a whimsical represen-tation of a section of the Bodleian library, Abel's favorite place in the world. There was a desk and an empty chair with stacks of books on ten foot high shelves in a protective curve around the missing student of history. Abel's memorial dedicated a year to the day that he died, beaten to a pulp and thrown into a boxcar bound for Dachau. No. Stella didn't feel comfort, not an ounce, but she prayed that the gesture, lovely as it was, would help someone.

The Earl of Bickford, lord of the manor and buyer of memorials, moved first, respectfully taking the hand of Rabbi Hertz and thanking him for the beautiful and moving service. At the earl's signal, the mourners began moving, speaking in low tones and wiping eyes. Abel had brought in quite a crowd. With satisfaction, Stella glanced around at the people a gentle Jewish historian from Vienna brought to a great English estate in the dead of winter. That was a testament to his worth and meaning, more than any memorial, in her eyes. There were several members of the aristocracy beyond the members of the earl's family, a Duke and several other lords. A whole cadre of dons from Oxford came. Practically the whole village of Bickford had walked the frigid distance to pay their respects, not to mention every single member of the Bickford staff and the Rabbi's family and congregation. All had known Abel and valued him. Stella hoped that he knew that they were there and that she wasn't through. A memorial hadn't ended it for her.

As the area cleared, one mourner stayed, standing directly in front of the stone carrell and not speaking to anyone. Viscount Finley, better known as Albert. His mother, Agatha, Countess of Bickford hesitated before returning to the house and looked for a sign from her son that she should go to him, but none came. She glanced at Stella, nodded, and took her husband's arm when he offered it. So the Bickford family left one member behind, because it wasn't different for Albert either.

Stella waited a few minutes and then approached him, her kitten heels crunching loudly on the pea gravel as the wind died down. Albert didn't react, so she put a hand on one shoulder, the one that was slightly lower than the other, and came to stand next to him. The scars on his face from the beating he'd received from the SS had faded, but the damage to his hand, shoulder, and back would never heal completely. He would not be joining the fight against Germany. Although he'd rarely alluded to any sadness or regret about that, Stella knew it pained him.

"It was a beautiful service," she said because that's what people say at a memorial.

"Yes," said Albert. "I can't believe it's been a year."

"I can."

He turned to her, his face ragged in grief. "So can I."

Stella hugged him and took his hand, not the damaged one. It pained him too much. "Nicky wanted to be here, but he couldn't get a pass."

"I understand flight training is intense," said Albert.

"It is." The little seed of worry that sat next to Stella's heart grew. Nearly every day she heard of another training accident. At the rate they were going she wasn't sure there'd be any pilots left to fight.

"Try not to worry. It hasn't been much of a war so far."

"A Phoney War? Right. That's what they'd like us to believe. We're losing people. I keep thinking about the HMS Courageous."

"It's not phony. Just the quiet before the storm," he said. "Stella, does Nicky know what you're doing?"

She smiled at him and asked, "Attending Abel's memorial? Of course."

"You know what I mean."

"I do."

"Word to the wise. My father did some things during the Great War that my mother found out about later. She wasn't best pleased."

"I tell him what I can," she said.

"It won't be much?"

"No."

Albert sighed and turned to look at the back of Bickford House. The mourners were swarming up the curving back staircases to attend the luncheon that had already been laid out. Lord and Lady Bickford were standing at the enormous doors with Smith the butler welcoming each and every person to the house. "I envy you and them," said Albert, a muscle twitching under the scar tissue. "I would like to be useful."

"You've done a great deal for the estate. All the open fields have been plowed and are ready for grain production. You've organized the county home guard and—"

"It's not like the SIS though, is it?" asked Albert.

It was the first time Albert or indeed anyone in the Bickford family had referred to the Secret Intelligence Service or that Stella had accepted an invitation to serve the British government as an operative. Neither had the earl's involvement in the spy agency. Stella had been in training for nearly a year and she still had no clear idea of his rank or station other than it was high and unofficial in that he didn't have a title, but she knew people answered to him and he was making decisions.

"No, but just as necessary," she said. It was no good pretending. That was just an insult. The earl was a spymaster. She was a spy or would be in due course. Albert was growing grain and making sure everyone used their blackout curtains. It wasn't enough for him. How could it be after Abel's death and what happened to him in Vienna?

Albert reached up and touched the ropey scar on his cheek. "This isn't why, you know? They wouldn't allow it, even if I was whole."

"No?"

"No. I would get a regular commission in the Navy or army. They'd do their best to keep me out of the fray." He laughed. "They wouldn't succeed, but they would try."

"Because you're the heir?" she asked.

"Yes. The heir has to be protected."

"But your father…"

Albert's eyes were trained on his father, a slight man who did not in any way cut an imposing figure. A perfect spy, Stella suspected. "He wasn't the heir. His brother, Albert, my namesake, was. My father was a third son. He could do whatever he wished."

"Third? The war, I assume."

He nodded. "Albert was killed in Gallipoli and the second son, William, was killed in Amiens in an accident. He was a translator and it was unexpected to say the least. When my father became the heir, he refused to take a staff position. It didn't protect his older brother, so I don't know what the point was anyway."

Albert and Stella watched his mother welcome the last of the mourners, smiling and shaking every hand. The earl followed them inside, but Agatha didn't. She stayed at the balustrade, looking out at them by the memorial. Stella could feel her motherly concern even at such a distance.

"I think she's relieved in a way that I can't go," said Albert. "Not that she wanted this to happen to me."

"Of course not," said Stella. "Your brothers are going?"

"As soon as possible. Arthur will be joining Nicky soon. He's been assigned to train on Spitfires, too. Freddie has opted for the Navy. That leaves me. Here. Being a farmer."

"I wouldn't be so sure," said Stella.

Albert raised an eyebrow. "What do you mean?"

"I have an idea."

"Do you?"

"Let me think on it," she said. There was more to war than combat and spies. Stella knew that much from her father and Uncle Josiah. There had to be a better place for Albert than behind a plow. He'd suffered more at the hands of the Nazis than almost anyone and he deserved a chance to defeat them in a way that left a mark. "Are you coming in?"

"In a moment," he said. "I just want to say goodbye. I never have. Not really."

Stella looked at the memorial. Goodbye. No. She wasn't ready.

"Can you go see to Cousin Gaspard for me? Someone ought to be looking after him and I'm…I can't just now."

Stella glanced at Bickford House. "I will. He's so sad. I forget sometimes how lucky I am to have my family. He's the last of his."

"Can you talk to him?" asked Albert.

"About Abel? I have. We've written," she said.

"No. About staying here, not going back to Greece. Father thinks Greece is a prime target. Abel would want him protected."

That was very true. Gaspard was another kind of heir, but Albert didn't know that and it wasn't Stella's place to say. "I will. He should stay here." She started to the house, but Albert stopped her.

"He said he was going to look for his hat." Albert turned back to the memorial and Stella scanned the grand Bickford gardens, eventually spotting someone walking in the topiary garden between two conical trees.

She touched Albert's arm. "I'll see you inside."

He nodded and she left him there in his grief, glancing up at Agatha still standing at the door of Bickford House. Smith was putting a fur cape over her shoulders and pressing a steaming cup into her hands. The lady barely noticed and shook her head at the butler's urging for her to come inside. Stella waved and she nodded. Albert's mother knew he wasn't all right.

Cousin Gaspard, as he had come to be known to those who weren't actually his family, walked out of the topiary garden with his black bowler hat firmly pushed down on his head and carrying another couple hats in his hands. He saw her and changed his direction into the gusting wind to meet Stella halfway.

"Did Albert send you?" he asked.

Stella turned up the collar on her mink coat and nodded. "He's worried about you."

"I know," Gaspard offered his arm and Stella took it "I'm returning to Greece."

"Are you sure? It's likely to be invaded."

"You say that like Britain isn't."

She sighed and squeezed his arm. "It feels safer for some reason."

"Because you never made it to Greece," he said.

Her head jolted upright and she looked away.

"I'm sorry," he said hastily, his Austrian accent growing stronger, reminiscent of Abel's soft tones. "It wasn't an accusation. Truly it wasn't."

"I'm the one that's sorry. If I hadn't pushed to go to Vienna. If—"

Gaspard stopped walking next to the Diana statue and the ravens hopped over to her extended bow to cock their heads and stare with beady eyes. "Don't do that. No ifs. Ifs will haunt you and stop you from living. I know."

"But your cousins." Her throat tightened and burned. "Venice."

"No buts either. I loved Susanne and Raymond-Raoul. I mourn them. I will always feel their loss, but it's not your fault. I know that. You should know that, too."

Stella did know that. In her head. Her heart was another story. She'd insisted on going to Vienna on the eve of the Kristallnacht. No one could've predicted what would happen when the Nazis decided to seek revenge for something the Jewish population couldn't control. That Abel would be swept up in the mass arrests. That he was carrying his family's greatest treasure and would entrust it to Stella. She couldn't have anticipated that he and Albert would be beaten as a consequence of the Nazis' rabid pursuit of Johannes Gutenberg's diary and its secrets. And when they failed to catch Stella and Nicky, their attention would focus on Abel's remaining family members, the Sorkines, who never had the book but were searching for it in Venice. They would be murdered in a frustrated rage by the SS officer Peiper. She couldn't have known, but somehow she felt she should've, that it should've been different.

"I haven't given up hope," said Gaspard, a sad smile in his soft brown eyes. They were the only physical resemblance to his cousin Abel. He was short and stocky where Abel was tall and lean. Gaspard's face was rounded and soft with a bulbous, perpetually red nose and prematurely grey hair that was retreating from his forehead at an alarming rate. He was the very opposite of Abel in every respect, except his gentle intelligence, brown eyes, and lilting Austrian voice. For Stella, it was almost unbearable to hear. Guilt blossomed in her chest with every word.

"They're gone, Gaspard. The earl confirmed it," she said.

"Yes, but Lucienne is still out there. I know everyone assumes she's dead, that Peiper got to her, but I haven't. Until I see some proof that she's gone, I'm going to continue to hope. You can't deny me that."

Stella swallowed hard and nodded, although she had no hope at all for the young college student, Lucienne Sorkine, who had never returned to her family apartment in Paris or to the Sorbonne where she studied the classics. The family money hadn't been touched and no effort to contact Abel, her parents, or Gaspard was ever made. Where was Lucienne if not six feet under?

"I want to thank you for writing, Stella," he said. "You didn't have to."

They started walking up the long path through what Agatha called her love garden filled with flowers that symbolized passion, attraction, fidelity, and everlasting love.

"I wanted to," she said. "You're Abel's cousin. He always spoke so highly of you that I wanted to know you."

"In my experience, people avoid grief if they can."

She looked up at the house. "Have they avoided you?"

"I wasn't speaking of now," he said.

"Oh." Stella had never asked how there happened to be so few members in Abel's family, but she had wondered.

"Can I tell you about my family?" Gaspard asked.

"I wish you would."

Gaspard's story was short but unbearably sad. The family had always been a small one, intentionally in an attempt to stay unseen. Jewish descendants of the great Gutenberg would not be welcomed into German society or any society in their opinion, so they kept their numbers small and the diary hidden for five hundred years. Gaspard's grandfather had changed that. He had three children instead of the normal single offspring, thinking he lived in an age of civility. He was wrong, but his children, one boy and two girls, grew up healthy and safe. Those children became the three branches. Abel descended from Simon and was his only child. Simon's sister, Suzanne Charlotte, like her brother, was less optimistic than her father and had one child, Lucienne. But Gaspard's mother, Adele Eliza, married a Belgian Catholic and his opinion was different.

"My father was optimistic about the future. We were not raised as Jews. My mother converted to Catholicism."

"We?" Stella asked.

"I had four brothers and sisters."

Had. What a terrible word.

"What happened, if you don't mind me asking?" she asked.

Gaspard told her frankly that his father had died in the Great War while Gaspard was at boarding school. His mother sent for him to return home, but when he arrived their small village was a place he didn't recognize, silent and empty. In the five days it had taken for Gaspard to receive his mother's message and come home, the Spanish flu had swept through killing over sixty percent of the villagers, including his mother and all his siblings.

"No one would speak to me," he said. "They weren't unkind, but to lose one's entire family in the space of a week, what could they say?"

"How old were you?"

"Nine."

Stella hadn't thought the Sorkines' and Abel's deaths could get any worse, but they certainly had. "Did you go to your cousins?"

"I did, splitting my time between Paris and Vienna, but Vienna became my home eventually."

A familiar flame of anger burst to life in her chest. So much had happened to so many. Gaspard was suffering as Albert continued to suffer and she'd spent the last year in training. The war had started and she was still studying.

"I didn't tell you this to hurt you, Stella," said Gaspard. "I want you to know what your letters have meant to me and that I'm not alone. You're my family now, you and Albert. We three that truly loved Abel."

They started up the curving stone stairs to Agatha, who was still standing there, watching over her firstborn.

"Did Albert tell you?"

"That Abel was in love with you?" He chuckled. "No. He didn't have to. My cousin's letters were full of you, every little detail from the color of your eyes to your curiosity and your never-ending knowledge of beer. He loved you. I knew from the start. If I had to have guessed the one person he would've entrusted the diary to, it would've been you."

"I don't know what to say," said Stella.

"There's nothing to say. It's a fact."

Stella took his arm and held him back. "Now that we're together, just the two of us alone, I want to tell you where—"

Gaspard shook his head. "No. I don't want to know where you put it. It's safe. That's enough for me."

"But it's your family's property," she said.

"And you think that SS went after my young cousin and killed her. If he comes for me, it's better that I don't know anymore than Lucienne," he said.

"You've put a lot of faith in me."

"Abel loved you."

Their eyes met and she asked, "What if he shouldn't have? Ever think of that?"

"Abel was an excellent judge of character, having an excellent character himself."

She bit her lip and said nothing.

"He knew you were married, Stella, and that would never change. He admired Nicky and considered him a dear friend. There's nothing wrong in it."

Wasn't there? Stella had felt for Abel, but as a friend. To have such love be right in front of her and never acknowledged seemed terribly sad but perhaps that's how Abel wanted it.

"How is he?" asked Agatha when they reached her.

"Fine, I think," said Stella. "He wanted to say goodbye."

Agatha's generous bosom rose in a deep sigh. "He'll never say goodbye. Abel meant the world to him. He was his only friend beyond his brothers." Her eyes hardened and she focused on Gaspard. "I hope you're not going back to Greece any time soon. He needs you."

Gaspard jerked back. "Lady Bickford, I...I..."

"No. Don't Lady Bickford me. I know you have a life there, but right now we need you here."

"Well..."

"Then it's settled," she said.

"Ma'am, I really have to—"

Agatha narrowed her gaze at him. "Go back to some Godforsaken island so the Italians can attack you?"

"The Germans are going to attack *you*," said Gaspard.

"And we need every man to repel them."

Gaspard didn't look like he was capable of repelling a mosquito and, from his expression, he knew it.

"You're a mathematician, aren't you?" Agatha asked.

"Yes, but I don't see how that—"

She took his arm and shooed Stella toward the door. "Go in and get warm, my dear girl. We'll stay out here and discuss the impending invasion."

It was startling to hear Agatha say it as if the invasion was a forgone conclusion. It would happen and the only question was what was to be done about it. Stella went for the door, dazed and unsteady. In her mind there would be no invasion. It would be stopped before it started. That Agatha assumed it wouldn't put everything in a different light. Stella trusted the countess's perceptions more than the politicians or the papers certainly. The daughter of a textile magnate, Lady Bickford had grown up much like Stella had on a factory floor with the real people as she called them. Agatha knew the world and didn't shy away from it. There were no rose-colored glasses on her dressing table. She didn't aspire to the aristocracy or to marriage in general, but George had worn her down after three years of courtship with a promise that she would have the run of her life and his. A promise that had not always been kept but certainly gave the appearance of it.

Smith opened the door for her and took her coat and hat.

"Thank you, Smith," she said. "Do you think you can get Lady Bickford inside? It's absolutely freezing out there."

"No, ma'am."

"Cousin Gaspard could use some help."

"I don't doubt it." The butler remained as imperious as ever, but Stella knew him as a kind man who was doing his level best to appear otherwise.

"I guess I'll join the…everyone else," she said. "Do you know where the pub owner is? Mr. Thompson."

"Mr. Thompson is in the dining room, ma'am, but Lord Bickford requests your presence in the small library."

"Now?" she asked.

"Yes, ma'am."

Stella hesitated as she looked out into the great hall with its distinctive flying staircase, tapestries, and enormous paintings. Quite a few mourners were milling around, taking the rare chance at seeing the Bickford House treasures and Stella would much rather have joined them. Being called to the small library was much like being called to her father's office. She had the sneaking suspicion she was about to be told off.

"Do you know what it's about?" she asked.

"I couldn't say, but," Smith lowered his gaze to hers and said quietly, "I believe there is some urgency."

She frowned. Urgency? When she'd arrived the day before the earl had been relaxed and calm.

"Did something happen?"

"A telegram came right after the memorial. His lordship read it and asked to see you immediately upon your return."

Stella bit her lip.

"Ma'am?"

"Uh-huh."

"His lordship is waiting."

"I guess I'd better go."

"Yes, ma'am."

"I don't want to."

Smith couldn't suppress his smile. "As Lord Albert says, it's best to rip off the plaster."

"If you say so."

"I do."

Stella took a breath and headed for the small library, knowing no good could come of it.

CHAPTER 2

oby, one of Bickford's many footmen, stood guard next to the small library's door, presumably to keep mourners from wandering in. He didn't usually stand there and wouldn't for much longer. Bickford, unlike most other great estates, had always kept a full staff and would continue to do so until the servants joined the war effort or were called up. Toby was to be trained as flight crew and reported in three weeks to Exeter where Nicky was stationed. Stella's handsome husband had promised to look after the shy twenty-year-old and Toby's mother, an assistant cook, found some comfort in that.

"Is he in there?" asked Stella.

"Yes, ma'am," said Toby.

"Any yelling, cursing, or throwing of books?"

Toby broke from his training and deep dimples popped out on his plump cheeks. "No. His lordship doesn't yell, except for at the races."

"I have a feeling I'm walking into something," she said.

Toby glanced around and since no one was looking, he bent over to her. "You are, but I don't know what. He got a telegram and he's pretty upset. He sent a message back and asked to see you straight away."

"I guess I better go in."

"Good luck," Toby said with a cheeky wink and opened the door.

Stella stepped into the smoky library and blinked at the blue haze. The earl looked up from behind his desk, a cigarette in hand. The earl smoked a lot, but she'd never seen him in a cloud before, and she took it as a bad sign.

"Ah, Stella, there you are." The earl stood up, waved at the smoke, and snubbed out his cigarette. "This may have gotten out of hand, this smoke. Come sit down."

Stella was still wary, but the earl seemed happy to see her. It didn't last long though. They sat in a pair of armchairs in front of a blazing fire. The small library was nothing like the large one that the mourners were no doubt ogling in wonder that very moment. The small library was really more like an office. It was only one story with floor-to-ceiling bookcases in lovely walnut, but the books on the shelves were well-used ledgers, created over the many years of the estate's long life. The earl had piles of paper on his desk and a few metal filing cabinets were wedged in wherever they fit.

Stella sat impatiently as the earl tossed another log on the fire, though it didn't need it. Sparks flew out and she watched them die one by one on the surround while the earl poured a generous whiskey. "It's a bit early, but I have cause. Would you like something?"

A knock echoed through the room and the earl smiled. "Never mind. Come in!"

Mrs. Hart the housekeeper bustled in with a tray. It held a small chocolate pot and a single cup. "There you are, Mrs. Bled Lawrence. Absolutely freezing. Not a day to celebrate Mr. Hershmann's life, but we don't get to choose, do we." She set down the tray, cracked open a window, poured a cup of hot chocolate, tucked a lap blanket over Stella's legs, and left without the earl or Stella saying a word.

"It is generally assumed that you are always cold and want hot chocolate," said the earl with a smile.

"It's a good assumption," said Stella, sipping the marvelous concoction.

"Drink up. That won't be going on for much longer."

"What do you mean?"

"Rationing," he said with a frown. "It hasn't been publicly announced, but it will start after Christmas, probably early in January."

Stella did as she was told, which was rare, and the earl noted it.

"You know that I received a telegram?" It wasn't really a question. The servants would, of course, inform her. Stella had easily become a great favorite with both the family and the staff.

"I heard. Has something happened? Please say it's not the start of the invasion," she said.

The earl stiffened. "There will be no invasion, no matter what my esteemed wife says. We are preparing and we will be ready when those krauts give it a go. They won't get far. You have my word on that."

Stella noted that no one had thought the Germans would go as far as they already had, but it seemed impolite to point it out. "So what did you want to talk to me about?" she asked instead.

The earl swirled his whiskey. "Well, Glamour Girl, you're aware that we have a new chief?"

Stella smiled at her code name, even though it'd been given to her to imply that she was little more than fancy, but didn't matter what they called her as long as they did. "Yes, I heard."

"And Sinclair has died," he said.

"I didn't know that." Stella struggled to think what this had to do with her. Her training had gone swimmingly, but she'd never been in the field, officially anyway, and she doubted if Hugh Sinclair had known her name.

"Stewart Menzies is running the show and he's a good man for the job."

"I had heard you might be in the running," said Stella.

"Glad you keep your ear to the ground, but no I was never going to be the new 'C'. I'm best in my usual position."

Which is what?

The earl didn't elaborate, but said, "Have you met Menzies?"

"No. Does he deal with people like me?"

"Low man on the totem pole? No, not typically."

Stella sipped her hot chocolate and the earl sipped his whiskey.

"Is there a problem with Menzies?" she asked finally.

"Not as such, but he's an Etonian through and through."

"Didn't you go to Eton?" Stella asked.

The earl smiled. He had attended Eton as had his brothers and Albert and his brothers. It was a family tradition, but according to the earl there were Etonians and there were men who went to Eton. Stella understood this was important. Why was less clear.

"Menzies favors what he knows. What he understands. When he has a problem he looks to those he believes are the problem solvers."

"Etonians?"

"The upper class. Men specifically."

Now they were getting down to it. Stella was a lot of things. A man wasn't one of them.

"He's not enamored of the Americans either," said the earl.

"Swell."

"Roosevelt's doing what he can, but the isolationists are holding him back."

Stella downed the rest of her cup and poured another out of the long skinny spout of a pot that was probably two hundred years old. "Are they going to fire me because I'm a woman?"

"And an American. No, not yet," he said. "Menzies thinks what we do is a business best left to men, well-educated, well-bred men. British men."

Stella clunked her cup on the saucer, splashing the thick liquid onto the highly polished silver tray. "But I've done everything you've asked of me. I speak German in three dialects. I speak Swabian. Nobody speaks Swabian. Plus, I've mastered French. I've got a little Czech and Polish, too. I'll perfect them. It won't be long."

"You've impressed everyone along the way. There is no dispute."

"Well then." She crossed her arms.

The earl picked up a file from a small table beside his chair and opened it. "Your Morse code is rated excellent. Weapons training. Personal combat, etc."

"What about the other stuff?" she demanded. "Can any of Menzies' men do that?"

"That, my fiery little American, is where we have Menzies over the proverbial barrel. Your added skills are impressive." He leafed through the pages. "A short nursing course, sewing, cleaning, typing and shorthand. What made you think of learning cooking?"

"If I'm to pass as an ordinary German girl, I should be able to make German food. I've read Göring's Nine Commandments."

"You have me at a disadvantage," he said with eyebrows raised.

Stella straightened up and recited in a singsong voice, "To the German woman: Take hold of the cooking pan, dustpan and broom and marry a man."

"And did you? Embrace the cooking, that is?"

"I make a swell Dampfnudeln," she said.

A broad smile stretched across the earl's thin face. "Would I like it?"

"I don't." She wrinkled her little nose. "It's awfully doughy, but I'm assured it's right."

"How did you learn the recipe?" he asked.

"My handler introduced me to some refugees, Leo and Magda Popper."

"Jews?"

She nodded. "They got out just before the Kristallnacht and they've been giving the government intelligence ever since."

"They will probably be classified as enemy aliens," the earl noted sadly.

"I hope not. They're lovely and they've taught me everything. I can clean the German way, make odd, lumpy desserts, knit, garden, and properly care for uniforms and medals. All the things the Nazis think a prospective bride should know. I've got my tradecraft down pat."

"I can see that, but it isn't enough," he said.

"Because I'm a girl? The Germans won't be expecting a girl. That's the whole point."

"There are a few reservations, despite your skills."

She cocked her head to the side. "Oh, really? Do tell."

"This is from your latest evaluation. 'Stubborn about judging right and wrong. Will make choices contrary to superior's orders. Impulsive. Obsessive. Possibly uncontrollable in the field.'"

Stella's mouth had dropped open and she closed it with a snap. "They don't like me at all, and I thought I was doing so well."

"They do like you very well. Your training has gone better than anyone expected."

"Except that I'm an impulsive, uncontrollable nitwit."

"No one would ever call you a nitwit." He hid his amusement by pouring more whiskey. "Do you deny it?"

"Which one?" she asked.

"Any or all?"

Stella thought about it. She didn't think she was obsessive, but Nicky definitely did. He'd said as much. "I don't know."

"It's not all bad news."

She rolled her eyes. "What's the good news? That I look swell in a skirt?"

"No." He looked down at the paper. "Shows enviable clarity of thought. Brave beyond all expectations for a young woman. Calm and thoughtful under pressure."

"How can I be both 'calm and thoughtful under pressure' and 'impulsive'?"

"Hard to say, but you've managed it."

"So what are we going to do?" she asked.

"We must show Menzies your value. Sinclair believed in you. So will Menzies, given the opportunity."

"Fine. How do I do that? I'm not technically done with training. They wanted Czech and Polish fluent."

"That was a delaying tactic. Your training is done as of today." He raised his glass. "Congratulations."

"Well, bully for me."

"You're practically British already," he said.

"Let's not go that far. My mother would have a fit," she said.

"Francesqua would have a fit if she knew where you were going."

Stella leaned forward. "Where am I going?"

The earl explained her mission. SIS had several operatives in place in Berlin. They needed a courier to take over money for bribes and instructions for bringing one agent out. "It's a critical time for us. Two of our agents have been arrested."

"When?" Stella asked sitting up straight.

"Yesterday."

Her eyes widened. "News travels fast. Are they dead?"

"Not yet, but we expect the latest attempt on Hitler's life to be blamed on them," said the earl. "As I said, we still have people on the ground in Berlin and we need to support them."

"And all I can do is take money?" she asked.

"It's not much, I admit. But see what you can make of it."

"How long do I have in country?"

"I talked them into two weeks. If you show your contact that you've got real value…"

Stella slumped. "I can't make solid connections in two weeks."

The earl leaned forward and held out his glass. "I'm betting that you can."

THE EARL SIPPED his whiskey and explained the plan simply with no extra words or flowery explanations. He would've been a marvelous 'C' in Stella's estimation.

Two aliases had been developed for her before Sinclair's death. The earl had the basic details, but she would be given the complete dossiers in London along with her kits to include money, clothing, and, what the earl called, extreme measures, weaponry and the like.

The first alias was Charlotte Sedgewick, an English nanny working for a French family, the Barbiers. The second was Sophie Weber, a German girl from Munich who'd recently lost her fiancé to an industrial accident.

"That fits nicely with my extra training," said Stella.

"It does indeed." The earl swirled his whiskey and she waited. A feeling that there was more to this assignment grew ten-fold in her stomach. She'd had many meetings with the earl in the last year. Her actual handler was James Park-Welles, a middle-aged man who spoke seven languages and had an encyclopedic knowledge of the continent and the Nazi hierarchy but few interpersonal skills. Park-Welles wasted no time on chat. He was the nuts and bolts of her job. The earl was the glorious paint job required to do it. At his direction, she'd assumed the role of devoted, if somewhat brainless, wife of the dashing Lt. Nicky Lawrence. The earl made sure she appeared in the papers, looking glamorous and pointless with heavy makeup that changed the look of her face and her hair done a certain way so it looked a good deal shorter than it was. She attended society dinners and toured the Cotswolds. Nicky squired her around when he had the time and there were several photos of her gazing up at him in his Spitfire with dimwitted adoration. Nicky wasn't thrilled with her decision to join the SIS, but he knew he had no choice in the matter, just like she didn't in his choice to join the RAF.

Between silly photo shoots and dress fittings, Stella studied her languages ten hours a day. She was given native speakers to converse with so she could perfect her accent. It didn't take long. She wasn't called Miss Myna for nothing. The earl or Agatha would ask her to visit Bickford House every six weeks or so under the guise of visiting the ailing Albert or the earl would turn up out of the blue and meet her in a pub or at Nicky's airfield. He always knew where she was and what she was supposed to be doing, even though it varied widely from day to day. The one thing that remained consistent was the earl's manner. He never hesitated or delayed telling her what was going on. He knew she didn't want to have tea with the Archbishop of Canterbury, a kind but tedious man who thought it was his duty to educate her on pretty much everything British. Touring a dairy farm wasn't high on her list and neither was visiting the many places Jane Austen lived, but he always just came out with it. Go there. Tour that. And she did.

This time he hesitated. He delayed. When someone knocked on the library door, he said, "Later." That wasn't like him at all.

"When should I leave for London?" asked Stella when the waiting became unbearable.

"Immediately."

He swirled the drop left in his glass and Stella looked over at the cold, congealed chocolate in her cup.

"And that's all for London? I get my packet, memorize and go."

"No. I've decided we need some reinforcements."

Stella sighed but only on the inside. She knew what this meant. He didn't trust her to go alone. She was getting a partner, someone to baby step her through her first assignment like she really was a nitwit. "Fine."

"It's not what you think. You will proceed to Berlin alone, but there's a stop in London I'd like you to make. Unofficially."

"How unofficially?" she asked.

"Completely off the record and it could cause a problem down the road."

Stella folded her hands in her lap. "All right. Let's have it."

The earl wanted her to dine at the Admiralty with Lord and Lady Churchill. Stella was rarely astounded, but that did it. Park-Welles had been absolutely clear that she was to stay away from politics at all costs. Because she was a Bled and was seen as representing the famous brewing family, the invitations came and it took some doing for Stella never to meet Chamberlain, the Prime Minister, any member of cabinet or the government. The Prime Minister wanted to meet her. Stella was a famous socialite, a Bled, and now a Lawrence on top of it. Her connection to United Shipping and Steel alone was considered worth the time, but the earl and Park-Welles wanted her clean. No one must ever think she could be a spy.

"Why in the world?"

"We need an insurance policy. I don't want to put any more pressure on you than you already have, but Menzies may try to pull you even if this assignment is successful," he said.

"Why would he do that?"

"We may have done our job too well. Menzies sees how you've spent this last year. He reads the papers like everyone else."

"So he does know my name," she said.

The earl frowned. "You're surprised?"

"I guess I didn't think he'd have time to follow a socialite's activities."

"Well, he has and it's not a good thing."

"Has he read my evaluation? Does he know what I know?"

"He has and he does, but Menzies is a man. He's...visual. He sees you and the package you present is hard to shake. Can you do the job like a man? Like an Eton man? It's an open question and I don't want to take any chances."

"So I have to convince Winston Churchill that I'm up for the job, is that it?" she asked.

The earl laughed and relaxed the tiniest bit. "Not Winston. Definitely not. Clemmie. We want Clemmie."

Stella stared at him. *Clemmie?*

"Don't call her that. She won't like it," he said and then seeing her confusion, "Clementine, Lady Churchill. She's the one we need on your side. Winston will love you. He does enjoy a pretty face, but he'd put you to work buttering up Roosevelt or that bastard Kennedy. There's nothing to be done with Kennedy. He's all for appeasing Hitler. To hell with the Jews."

Stella stared at him in shock. She knew little about Kennedy, but she never imagined that he wouldn't care what happened to the Jews after the Kristallnacht. It was inhuman.

"It's true," he said.

"I believe you, but what can Lady Churchill do for me?"

"Everything. Clemmie is more powerful than people realize. When Winston becomes PM and he will, it will be because of her. If you can get her on your side, Winston will be on your side. No question."

"But I can't...how would she know anything about it? She's not in government service," said Stella.

"She most certainly is. Clemmie knows everything. Winston keeps no secrets from her. None at all. She softens him, contains him, advises him. There's a reason the staff hates when she goes on one of her holidays. Winston is practically unmanageable without her. Smile. Play the flirt with Winston. Show *Clemmie* who you really are. She'll understand. If Clemmie wasn't a woman, she'd be PM."

"Is she making decisions?"

"As much as any good advisor does. Clemmie doesn't have the power, but she has a lot of control." He smiled at her. "I, for one, am glad she's on our side."

"I'll get her on my side then."

"It'll be a test. Never forget that she's probably the smartest person in the room, except perhaps for Winston."

"I'll remember, but how will I know if Lady Churchill will help?"

"Oh, you'll know," he said.

Stella watched the earl continue to swirl his one remaining drop of whiskey. He wasn't done. That glass told her so.

"What was in the telegram?" Stella asked.

A smile broke out on his face. "I thought you might forget."

"Not a chance."

"What do you think was in it?" he asked.

"I have no idea, but there's something you're not telling me. Sinclair may have just died, but he's been sick for a long time. Menzies has been 'C' for awhile now."

He nodded. "Yes, that's true."

"But you're rushing me out the door today, on the day of Abel's memorial. Something else must've happened."

The earl set down his glass and steepled his fingers, looking at her over their tips. "I have a personal mission that I want you to do for me."

"In London?"

"In Berlin."

"Fine by me."

He reached back and picked up a second folder. "I want you to memorize the details. You won't be taking this with you."

"No problem." Stella took the folder and opened it. She couldn't have been more surprised at what she saw inside. A picture of a baby topped the slim stack of paper, a little girl about eighteen months old sitting on a cushion and holding an oversized floppy rabbit in one hand.

"Her name is Anna Wildholz. She's just turned two and she's missing."

Stella studied the photo, noting everything from the child's eye shape to hair color, curly and light brown by the look of it. Then she put the photo aside and found another underneath it. A photo of a family at a picnic, casual and smiling.

The earl leaned forward and pointed at the two people seated on a blanket with little Anna. "That's Anna's mother Lotti and her father, Joseph Wildholz. Standing behind them is Anna's nanny, Gertruda Hoppe. She's the one that matters for your purposes."

Stella studied Gertruda's face and figure until she was certain she could recognize the woman on sight. "All right. Who are they to you?"

The earl swallowed and showed the first emotion he had all day. "Anna is the granddaughter of my dear friend, Henry Brooke, the Viscount Alanbury. Lotti is his daughter and my goddaughter."

She looked down at the photo. *Missing.*

"Jewish?"

"No. Well, Henry isn't. Lotti married Joseph who is or was. He converted shorty before the wedding five years ago."

"So where are Lotti and James?" Her stomach flipped as she asked the question. Jewish, formerly or not, in Berlin. It couldn't be good.

"Joseph was arrested for fraud six months ago. Trumped up charges, of course. It was an attempt to seize his family's business, which he'd just inherited, Wildholz and Sons Furriers."

Stella wanted to yell and stomp her feet. Why didn't they get out? Leave. Go. They had to know what the SS was up to. They were in Berlin, for crying out loud.

As if the earl could hear her questions, he said, "They thought they were safe. Joseph converted. Lotti isn't Jewish. And his family has always been highly respected."

"The Nazis don't respect anyone," she said.

He nodded sadly. "I told Henry that. He wanted them out. He tried. But that factory, it was Joseph's birthright. All the money was tied up in it. He didn't want to be the failed fool that married an English heiress, converted, and lost everything. Joseph was proud. He thought he could outlast the current insanity."

"Is he still alive?"

"I don't know. I suspect not. They arrested Lotti three months ago when she tried to flee the country with Anna and Gertruda. She has a British passport, but they still arrested her."

"You can't do anything? She's your citizen," said Stella.

"They charged her with black market trading of controlled goods. Lotti couldn't find the black market if you put it on a map for her."

"What happened to the baby when Lotti was arrested?"

The story sounded fairly simple and that Anna had every chance. She'd been left in the family home with the servants, in the care of her loyal and Aryan nanny, Gertruda, who continued to work for the family after it was outlawed. Anna's grandfather arranged for her to be put on a Kindertransport. Charitable organizations were arranging for Jewish children to leave Germany, Austria, and The Netherlands for safety in Britain. Because Anna was only half Jewish she wasn't allowed on her assigned transport two months ago. Gertruda was able to contact the viscount through the British embassy shortly before war was declared, but it was too late for a transport out of Germany. The high command had shut them down so the viscount arranged for Gertruda to take Anna to The Netherlands in October. They were still operating Kindertransports there and Anna was supposed to be on a transport leaving on October twenty-second, but she wasn't on the ship when it landed. For the last two weeks, the viscount and the earl had been frantically trying to find out what happened. So far they knew Anna's slot had been filled at the last minute by another child because Anna failed to appear. No one in The Netherlands had heard from Gertruda or anyone else about the child. They were able to discover that the train tickets purchased for the trip to Amsterdam weren't used, but that was where the trail ended.

"You think they're still in Berlin then?" asked Stella.

"We have no indication that they're not," he said.

She watched him carefully and then said, "You have no information about Berlin since the war started. You have no idea where Anna and Gertruda might be."

The earl's shoulders slumped ever so slightly. "That's true. Our lines of communication were effectively cut the moment war was declared and our embassy staff left."

"But you have people in place and they're gathering intelligence. Why not send a message two weeks ago? You have those lines."

"Our government has no interest in the Jewish situation. All resources are to be used to win the war. Period. No exceptions."

"There are always exceptions. Always."

He nodded. "You are my exception."

CHAPTER 3

The telephone rang on the little table next to Stella's bed. She glanced at the clock and then picked it up. "Hello?"

"Mrs. Bled Lawrence, your car has arrived," said the hotel concierge.

"Thank you. I'll be right down."

Stella hung up and spritzed herself with perfume before rechecking her lipstick for the fifteenth time. It was showtime, still safe in London, but she'd rather have been in Berlin. Impress Clementine Churchill. Say just the right thing at just the right time to a woman who was not easily impressed. The earl and countess described her in detail in an effort to be helpful, but all Stella got out of it was that Clemmie was old and tough like her grandmother as well as being reserved like her mother, Francesqua. It was not a good combination. Her grandmother was the original tough nut and how do you get to know someone who doesn't want to be known?

She put on her shoes, mink, and hat, one chosen by Agatha with exotic feathers and made to garner attention. Agatha, like Clementine Churchill, knew everything about the proper way to get things done. Grabbing her beaded handbag, Stella went out into the hall of the grand Savoy Hotel. You'd never know a war was on there. There'd been champagne and caviar in her room on arrival. The only differ-ence from the time she'd spent there a few months ago with Nicky was the presence of gas masks and blackout curtains. Plenty of food. Plenty of wine. Plenty of guests and not a single one was down in the mouth. If she stayed a couple of days, she'd have to pinch her leg to remind herself of what Agatha said. The invasion was imminent. What shows were sold out in the West End wasn't so important, but you'd never know that from the other guests. They had no concerns beyond having the best lobster in town or perhaps oysters were a better choice. Stella wanted to smack a woman who complained about having to carry a gas mask because it would distract from her look. The word "gas" meant less to her than if someone dared cancel her next manicure.

Stella bypassed the elevator, where she was sure to be boxed in with carefree guests. She just couldn't bear the joviality. Her slim shoulders felt weighed down, burdened beyond belief. She had to convince Clemmie not only for herself, but for the other women in the ranks. Agatha clued her in on that. They needed the women in the game. Winston was old-fashioned. Women on the front line wouldn't be his first choice, so Clemmie was the way in. And beyond that, was doing her job. She'd have to do it better than a man to be considered almost equal. Not to mention finding one child in Berlin. It all seemed impossible and part of her wanted to drink champagne like the rest of the idiots and forget all about it.

"Mrs. Bled Lawrence," called out a voice.

Stella cringed and turned to see the elevator operator, Mr. Temple, standing in the open door, his hand on the cage. "Can I help you?"

"Thank you, Mr. Temple," she said. "I thought I'd just take the stairs."

His eyes crinkled. "There are no other birds in the cage, ma'am, if I might say so."

She flashed a smile at the operator's perceptiveness. "I do have these shoes." She held out a high heel that caused pain with every step.

"They are some shoes, ma'am." He held out an arm and welcomed her.

Stella hustled onto the lift and he quickly closed the cage.

"You have a car waiting, ma'am?"

"I do. I wish I didn't," she said as she impulsively sat on the little lounge at the back. It would wrinkle her dress, but she didn't care.

"That's too bad," said Mr. Temple. "We have a very popular cabaret on today. The ladies dance with gas masks."

"That's popular?"

"It's fun to forget."

She hadn't considered that. Maybe the champagne had a purpose. "I'd like to forget."

"We all would, but we can't. Mr. Lawrence's training is proceeding well?"

"Yes, it is and I'm to have dinner at the Admiralty."

"That'll be a treat," he said in a way that made Stella think it wouldn't.

"The new Mrs. Churchill is here every other day. Perhaps she'll be there."

Stella's heartbeat quickened. She hadn't been briefed on that. "There's a new Mrs. Churchill?"

The elevator stopped and Mr. Temple said, "Mrs. Randolph Churchill. She's very popular and the papers say the life of the party." He opened the cage and gave Stella a sly wink. "Maybe you'll get lucky."

She slipped a generous tip in his hand and said, "I'm feeling better already."

"I thought you might." He touched his forehead and she stepped into the grand foyer filled with people coming for dinner, a show, or who knows what. The famous Thames foyer was full to the rafters and she bypassed it, going out the doors before anyone could stop her or ask a question or request a picture. That happened surprisingly often. No one took her picture in St. Louis. She was just another Bled. Uncle Josiah was the real headliner. People hung about just to see what he might get up to.

A doorman hurried over to open the door for her. "Mrs. Bled Lawrence, may I assist—"

"Mrs. Bled Lawrence!" A chauffeur came to attention next to a limousine and gave her a broad smile.

"Oh, Thompson," she said. "I'm so glad it's you."

Stella thanked the doorman and Thompson tucked her into the car in a flash. They drove out of the Savoy court onto their private drive, passing two limousines coming in. It was so narrow she didn't think they'd squeak by, but they did and headed into the darkened city.

Stella had been in London several times since the blackout started, but it never failed to unnerve her. Such a big, alive city cast into the dark. Thompson drove at the required twenty miles an hour, but Stella thought it might still be too fast. People were getting killed in traffic accidents in record numbers. The little shields fitted to the car's headlamps allowed the driver to see the road directly ahead but not much else.

Thompson slammed on the brakes, throwing Stella to the floor. "Bloody hell!"

Someone yelled and she heard a thunk.

"Did you hit someone?"

"No, thank God!" exclaimed Thompson. "Are you all right, Mrs. Bled Lawrence?"

Stella crawled back onto the seat and examined the slit in her periwinkle evening gown. Where it had been fashionably cheeky, now it was downright daring. She had a big run in her silk stockings and a scrape on her knee. "I'm fine. It happens."

What would Lady Churchill think? Agatha said she never put a toe out of line just like Francesqua. Stella's mother would be seriously displeased if someone showed up at a one of her dinner parties disheveled and showing way too much leg.

"It happens too much. Hitler's killing us and the bombing hasn't even started yet," said Thompson in frustration. "Sorry, ma'am. I shouldn't have spoken like that to you."

"Speak however you want. I'm just glad to see you. It's nice to see a friendly face."

He glanced in the rearview mirror, his friendly face concerned. "You need a friendly face, Mrs. Bled Lawrence?"

"Stella, please, and yes I do. Somehow I got roped into dinner with the Lord Admiral."

Thompson whistled. "You're coming up in the world."

"Dinner with politicians? I don't know about that."

"Old Winnie's the one to get us through, not The Coroner."

"The Coroner?"

"Chamberlain. That man hasn't had an original thought in three decades. He's too old and too scared. We need a go-getter."

Stella didn't point out that Chamberlain wasn't much older than Churchill because Thompson slammed on his brakes again and Stella barely held on to her seat.

"Son of a bitch! She stepped right out in front of me. Look at the curb, woman. Don't glare at me. I didn't do it."

A middle-aged woman dashed past the car, jumping onto the curb that had been painted in a checkerboard pattern so that people would see it.

"I guess the paint's not working."

"Sorry, Mrs.—Stella," said Thompson. "It's working. I can't imagine what it'd be like without it. This night's darker than usual. A lot of clouds."

"I'll be glad to get out of London," she said.

"Me, too."

Her heart sunk. "You've been called up then?"

"I have." He flashed a grin at her. "Don't look like that. I'm what you call skilled or so they say. I'm going in the army as a driver. I'll be driving the great and good, if they can find any."

She laughed. "Did Lord Bickford have anything to do with that?"

"My mother more like. I'm sure Lady Bickford had her hand in."

Thompson was native to the village of Bickford and had known the family all his life. His father owned one of the two pubs and his mother was a talented seamstress that did all the repair work on the estate's vast linen collection. Her embroidery was extraordinary.

"Your parents must be relieved."

"They are, but I don't know if that's doing my bit."

"Someone has to drive," she said.

"And someone has to fight," he said grimly. "Mr. Lawrence isn't even one of us and he's going to fight."

"Yes, but I'll tell you a secret, I wish he wasn't. I wish none of it was happening," said Stella.

"Hitler would have it no other way," said Thompson.

"Truer words have never been spoken."

Thompson drove behind a grand building into a dark courtyard with several other cars parked. Their chauffeurs sat in the dark. Stella had to squint to see the imposing building. It had a kind of square dome. That was all she could really make out. "Is that it?"

"That's it. The Admiralty House."

"How will I see to get in?" she asked.

Thompson parked and said, "Here comes someone. He'll take you." Thompson got out and rushed around to open Stella's door.

A uniformed man with a red flashlight came from the dimly lit doorway and asked, "Mrs. Bled Lawrence?"

"Yes," said Stella.

"We've been expecting you. Right this way."

She turned to Thompson. "I don't know when I'll be done."

"I'm not going anywhere. Ready when you are," said Thompson.

Stella thanked him and followed the man with the flashlight. When she glanced back, Thompson was leaning on the limousine lighting a cigarette. She waved and he touched the brim of his hat. Good luck, he was saying. She hoped she didn't need it.

STELLA FOLLOWED the servant to an unprepossessing door tucked in a corner instead of the grand entrance under the pediment with all the columns. They went into a warmly lit entrance hall with buttery yellow walls and an elegant staircase that went up and split into two, forming an oval like a well-formed tulip. Despite the fact that it was after business hours, the place was a hive of activity. Officers dashed up and down the stairs and back and forth across the small hall, reading telegrams and papers as they narrowly avoided multiple collisions.

"Right this way, ma'am," the servant said with a glance at Stella's ripped dress as they went for the tulip and squeezed past two women who were exchanging files, red-faced and aggravated. They frowned at Stella and pursed their lips but said nothing beyond something about a meeting conflict in the morning.

Stella reflexively glanced down at their disapproval and a lump formed in her throat. She hadn't realized her knee was bleeding, the split had grown and there was absolutely nothing she could do about it. A clock was chiming. She was just about to be late and something told her that Lady Churchill wasn't a fan of late. She got her handkerchief out of her handbag but could only get a moment to press it to her knee as they hurried up the stairs.

"We will go directly to the dining room as Lady Churchill is awaiting you there," he said.

"I'm not late, am I?" she asked.

"No."

There was more yes in that no than Stella had imagined possible, but she shook it off. It wasn't her fault it took forever to go anywhere in the blackout and that people kept trying to get themselves flattened by limousines.

On the second floor, they walked past a mirror on the way to the dining room and that, more than the servant's tone, gave her pause. It wasn't just the bloody knee or the split in her slit. Stella was a wreck and she wanted to call the whole thing off, claim a sudden, killer headache, a family emergency, or some other distraction. The chances of her successfully winning over the immaculate Lady Churchill had gone from slim to none. Stella's hair, so carefully done by one of the Savoy's girls, had been knocked out of its pins. Half was out of its coil and the other half in. Her hat hung off the side of her head and, worst of all, her perfect lipstick was smeared off her lip up onto her nose. She, Stella Bled Lawrence, was starting her very first assignment with a clown nose.

"I think maybe I ought to—"

The servant whipped open a door and sharply gestured for her to enter another hall. She went in and before she could say, "Never mind," and skulk out in shame and horror, he plucked the hat off the side of her head and slipped her coat from her shoulders.

Another servant waited outside a door, and after a sly and blatantly amused glance at her, he opened his door.

"I…um…" Stella frantically rubbed the lipstick on her nose.

"The dining room, ma'am," said the original servant and he took her coat away.

The second servant cocked his well-groomed head at her and she swallowed hard. Stella knew she'd faced worse, much worse, but at that moment she couldn't remember ever dreading anything quite so much.

Somehow her legs moved. She didn't know how, but they walked her right in through that door and into a room that was distressingly full of people, none of which was the slightest bit disheveled, and every single one turned to look at her.

"Mrs. Nicolas Lawrence of New York, New York," announced the servant.

Stella gazed at the array of surprised faces and never felt more out of place in her life. There were only two women, the statuesque, silver-haired Lady Churchill and another woman, a young and buxom blonde. The rest were men in suits and uniforms, all with bags under their eyes and a nervous tension to their shoulders. The First Lord of the Admiralty, Winston Churchill, wasn't there.

"Are you just back from the war or has combat come to the capital without my knowing it?" asked a friendly face from across the room.

It took Stella a second, but she beamed at him "Mr. Rhodes, what a pleasure."

Ambassador Kennedy's attaché hadn't changed in the year since Stella had last seen him when he accompanied them to Bickford House. He was still slim, and dressed in a suit designed not to be remembered. "Mrs. Bled Lawrence, I forgot you were still in England. If I may…"

Mr. Rhodes came around the table and began a bewildering

barrage of introductions and Stella found herself nodding and smiling, fully aware that there was still a bloody handkerchief in her hand when they came to Lady Churchill and the girl next to her.

"Our esteemed hostess. Lady Churchill, may I present Stella Bled Lawrence?"

They shook hands and Lady Churchill's chilly reserve did not crack. "It is my pleasure, Mrs. Lawrence. May I—"

"What happened to you?" The blond girl stepped up, her blue eyes twinkling. "Mr. Rhodes is right. You look like you've been under attack."

Lady Churchill smiled and relaxed. "This is my daughter-in-law Pamela. She is nothing if not observant."

"Stella, may I call you Stella?" asked Pamela.

Stella smiled, warmed through and relieved. "Please do."

"Did you have an accident?"

"Nearly. Two, in fact."

And something happened, Stella had a flash of Nicky standing in his commander's dining room telling to hilarious effect about a near miss on the runway between his Spitfire and a flock of sheep who were very certain who was supposed to be where, and she used it. She told the story of a harrowing drive through blacked-out London where every other person's desire was to be run over and had everyone laughing or, in the case of Lady Churchill, smiling.

"What's all this ruckus?" Winston Churchill, the man the earl believed would save England and thus the world, walked in, carrying a little brown poodle and an empty glass, with a stub of a cigar clamped between his teeth. He was shorter, rounder, and happier than Stella imagined.

The poodle yipped and he said, "No one asked you, Rufus."

"Winston," said Lady Churchill, "Mrs. Lawrence was telling us about her journey to us through the blackout."

The Lord Admiral saw the red-stained handkerchief in her hand and reddened. "Bloody Nazis. Killing us every way they can."

He insisted she be tended to by Pamela, who cheerfully took her into a drawing room with surprisingly comfortable furniture and nautical paintings covering the walls. Pamela helped her fix her hair, bandage her knee, and pin her dress so it wouldn't rip further when she sat down to dinner.

"Well, you've made a good impression," she said.

"Have I?" asked Stella.

"Your story was roaring. We need a good laugh. It's all work here all the time."

"I saw all the activity downstairs."

"And upstairs. Inside and out," said Pamela. "It never stops. Winston works like no man alive. There will be a staff meeting after dinner." She leaned in. "Those lazy bastards at Number 10 can hardly stand it. No coming in at eleven now and leaving early, not with Winston here. If Hitler isn't shaking in his jackboots, he should be."

"Lord Bickford told me he's formidable," said Stella.

"That's an understatement." Pamela grinned at her. "So you married that handsome devil, Nicky Lawrence. Some girls have all the luck."

"You're here."

"I am and I'll do my duty, don't you worry about that," said Pamela.

Stella had no idea what she was referring to, but she didn't doubt Winston Churchill's daughter-in-law was up to something. "Everyone will have to do their duty and more if Germany is to be defeated."

Pamela's eyes, usually filled with mirth, showed a glimmer of sharp intelligence. "You've never been here before."

"Here" could mean anything, but Stella was fairly certain she wasn't referring to the Admiralty. "No. Not even close."

"You're not political."

"No."

She smiled at her conspiratorially. "I bet you will be."

"Pamela, dear," Lady Churchill called from the doorway. "Do come back in."

The girls returned to the dining room and were seated across from each other between men of the government and the Navy. Pamela was in her element. She flirted shamelessly in the absolute best way, giving each man she spoke to a reason to like her and trust her. Stella had never given one single thought to what a courtesan would be like, but she was sure Pamela fit the bill, skillfully giving each man what he wanted and boosting his confidence by giving him what he needed. A useful skill and one Stella could use. No one had ever trained her to flirt. Francesqua Bled was the opposite of a flirt and so was Uncle Nicolai's wife, Florence. It occurred to Stella that she'd spent most of her life with men, her father and uncles and the men at the brewery. She never flirted. It would've been counterproductive. Her father, the stern Aleksej Bled, would've had her out of the brewery before she could get a full swish of the hip. But now she wasn't in the brewery and as she watched Pamela she knew what skill she needed to get information from the kind of men that sat in those chairs and it wasn't sewing or making a Dampfnudeln. Those would help, but there was nothing like Pamela's rapt attention or the skillful way she enticed a man to say too much about his day.

Stella could feel Lady Churchill watching her quietly while holding court at the table and effortlessly making sure everyone was well-fed and looked after. Even Rufus the poodle was given a plate.

It wasn't until a dessert of pears and Stilton was served that Churchill turned his piercing gaze on Stella. She was a nobody in the political world and to the English in general, but she was astonished to find him knowledgeable about Bled Beer, St. Louis, her family, and their opinions. He came at her with questions about brewing, American politics, and isolationism. She answered them or deflected them as best she could and Lady Churchill watched, judging and to Stella's mind, calculating. Just what she couldn't say. The earl wouldn't have told either of the Churchills anything about who she really was, what she was actually doing at a wartime table, or where she was going next. The request for her dinner invitation had gone through "channels" and the earl had not specified how it would come about, only that it would.

"The Americans must pick a side," bellowed Churchill and Rufus yipped.

"Now Winston," said Lady Churchill, "Mr. Rhodes doesn't control that."

"But he knows. Roosevelt knows. That fool Kennedy is working against us every day. He must be replaced." He glared at Mr. Rhodes, who calmly looked back and speared a piece of cheese.

"Miss Bled!" Churchill chomped on a pear slice and eyed her expectantly.

"Yes, sir?" Stella used a Pamela technique, emphasizing the "sir" and dimpled at him.

"Are the American people with us?"

"This American is."

He guffawed and slapped the table. "Quite right."

"The American people are watching what's happening," said Mr. Rhodes.

"Watching? What good is that?" Churchill asked. "The Hun is coming over the barricades and you plan on watching?"

"The ambassador as well as the administration believe that the Reich is satisfied. They will not make a move toward France. They won't—"

"They won't? They won't? You didn't think they'd take Czechoslovakia or Poland."

"The High Command insist that a counterattack was necessary," said Mr. Rhodes.

"Miss Bled," said Churchill. "You've been to the enemy, haven't you? What is your opinion? Will the Hun be satisfied with a little when he can have a lot?"

The entire table, as well as the servants standing at the ready, looked at her. What should she say? Mr. Rhodes was there. This was hardly in keeping with her carefully constructed image of a socialite.

Stella glanced at Lady Churchill and knew it wasn't a moment to evade. There would be no intervention on her behalf if she did. "The Nazis will never be satisfied. They don't know what satisfied is."

Questions came from all sides and Stella revealed where she'd been a year earlier, leaving Abel and the book out of it.

"Beasts!" Churchill declared, "The whole lot of them. Beasts!"

"But as Ambassador Kennedy has said, this has nothing to do with us," said Mr. Rhodes. "The American people don't want another war."

"No one wanted another war, but the Nazis require their 'Lebensraum'." Churchill pounded the table. "Do you think they will stop at Poland?"

"My government is betting they will."

"They won't." Churchill pointed at Stella. "This slip of a girl knows it."

"You are against everything the Reich does."

"Hitler says I am going around Europe trying to set something on fire. Poland is alight. It is not just nor a counterattack."

"Sir," asked Mr. Rhodes. "Isn't there any good in the Nazis? They've brought—"

"No. None at all. If Hitler invaded hell, I'd be against it." Churchill jolted out of his chair, snatched up his cigar, and stomped to the end of the table. He kissed Lady Churchill's hand and said, "Delightful dinner, Clemmie. The consommé was perfection."

"Thank you, Winston." Lady Churchill rose amid a barrage of commands about a briefing in the boardroom and the company dispersed. Pamela met Stella at the door and they exchanged cheek kisses.

"We should have lunch or do some shopping," said Pamela.

"We should."

"Before Christmas though, to be on the safe side." She winked and Stella smiled. Everyone knew about the rationing, except maybe the people it would most effect. "Give your flyboy a kiss for me. I'm famous for my kisses."

Stella couldn't help but laugh. Pamela was the effervescence needed in a world ready to go at it in another war. They walked out and Pamela took a look at Stella's hand. "Gorgeous rings, darling. He has good taste in jewelry, too. Harry Winston?"

She held up her hand and caught Mr. Rhodes watching her. "Yes. How clever of you to know."

"I know good jewelry and—"

"Mrs. Churchill," interrupted a servant, "there's a call for you in the library."

"Oh, bother," said Pamela. "I was going to ask if you wanted to go dancing at the Savoy. You never know who we might meet."

"Pamela, dear," said Lady Churchill.

Pamela gave them a grin and flounced off for the library with the eyes of the remaining men on her. A servant brought Stella her coat and hat, and Mr. Rhodes offered to walk her out.

"Thank you very much for having me, Lady Churchill. It was a lovely dinner," said Stella.

The older lady smiled. "It was a pleasure to make your acquaintance and I hope we will see you again soon."

Was that the sign? The earl said there would be a sign that Clementine approved of her. He insisted that Stella would be able to tell one way or another.

"I hope so, too."

"Lady Bickford speaks very highly of you," said Lady Churchill.

Stella buttoned her coat and set her hat on her head where it was meant to be. "That means a lot to me. Lady Bickford has been very kind while Nicky has been in training."

"In my experience, Agatha always takes the right course and makes sure George does, too."

"Like most great marriages I've noticed," said Stella.

"Winston found you very entertaining," said Lady Churchill. "He needs interesting young people around him."

"It was my pleasure."

They shook hands. Stella's felt hot and sweaty in Lady Churchill's cool one and Mr. Rhodes offered his arm as the two of them went down the stairs. "That was a long goodbye."

"Was it?" asked Stella. "I thought dinner went fast. My mother's dinner can go on for hours."

"It's wartime and there's always another meeting."

"Late at night?"

"And early in the morning." Mr. Rhodes laughed. "Winnie's got them running. The ministry isn't happy."

"Why not? They're at war, for crying out loud," she said.

"The Navy doesn't like the interference in professional matters."

"Isn't the Lord Admiral in charge of the Navy?"

"Winnie will be in charge of everything if he has his way," said Mr. Rhodes.

A servant opened the door and they stepped out into overwhelming darkness.

"I think that would be a good thing," said Stella.

"You take your opinion from Lord Bickford."

She turned up her collar at the cold. "And you have yours from Ambassador Kennedy."

"I work for the ambassador. Who do you work for, Mrs. Lawrence?"

"Nobody, I'm happy to say." She fought the urge to step on his foot or spit in his eye. Good in the Nazis? What a thing to ask.

"We're not going to war if Kennedy has anything to say about," said Mr. Rhodes.

"It's a good thing he doesn't then. What do you have to say?" she asked. "You yourself?"

Mr. Rhodes sighed. "I think that if the Brits are counting on us, we can count them out."

Stella whirled away from him, rushing toward the limousine where Thompson dropped his cigarette and rubbed it out with his toe.

"Mrs. Lawrence," called out Mr. Rhodes. "I'm only telling you the truth. You should get out of here while you still can."

Thompson opened the limousine door for her and she slid inside without answering. There was no answer. She feared he was right.

STELLA SLIPPED OFF her rings and rubbed a thick layer of cold cream on her face, feeling more sad and lonely than she had in months. Nicky was at his base or flying over the Atlantic and there was no one to talk to about the dinner that may or may not have been successful. What would happen next was an open question. The earl said she'd be contacted with instructions and until then she'd have to wait, tour the museums or take Pamela up on shopping, but she didn't want to shop or see anything. She wanted to go and do. She hadn't talked to another American in months and when she did it was all appeasement. Appeasement wouldn't bring back Abel or the Sorkines. It certainly wouldn't help Karolina and Rosa.

She plucked a tissue out of the box and wiped her fingers clean. Tears splattered the glass on the dressing table and she couldn't stop the images and the sounds. Rosa von Bodmann lying dead on the Venice train station floor. Karolina's wails as they dragged her away. She could smell the briny air tinged with the grease of the trains. The sisters had been caught up in the events in Venice when Nicky and Stella did their level best to find the Sorkines. Rosa died as a result and Karolina had been arrested. They sent her back to Germany, charged with ridiculous crimes. The earl tried to track her, working through diplomatic channels, but the most he had come up with was that she'd been sent to Lichtenburg, a camp that originally held both men and women but switched to only women a couple of years ago.

Stella held onto hope until the earl had unexpectedly met her while she was traveling in Derbyshire on her way to see more sites associated with Jane Austen, a convenient cover while she studied German and French. He appeared at her elbow at Chatsworth House as she gazed at a portrait of Georgiana, Duchess of Devonshire, who was its mistress at one time.

"She's nothing to our Cecily, is she?" the earl asked as if he'd been there all along.

"She's beautiful, but it seems like that's all she had."

"Like I said, nothing to Cecily."

They walked through the great house and discussed the art, which pieces the Bleds would particularly enjoy and details of the artists' lives. Little nothings like that until the West Sketch Gallery emptied of visitors and the earl said, "We've lost her."

"Karolina?" Stella asked.

"Yes. Lichtenberg has been closed and the prisoners transferred to a new camp called Ravensbrück. My contacts say there's no sign of Karolina being moved."

"But they don't know for certain," said Stella.

"I think they do." He let that sink in for a moment as her eyes stayed fixed on a portrait of a child by de Vos. "It's been six months and she wasn't a young woman. Conditions are harsh. We tried, Stella, but I don't believe they would've let her go under any circumstances."

"If I paid those taxes or bribed the right person…"

"I let it be known that I would pay her debt in exchange for her release," said the earl.

Stella turned to him, her eyes filling. "You did?"

"I got nothing back. Nothing. They know you and I are connected and you escaped by the narrowest of margins. They won't forget or forgive that."

"Do you think that hurt Karolina?"

The earl's stiff upper lip quivered and he shook his head. "No, my dear girl. I don't. She was lost the moment they arrested her."

"Like Abel," she said.

"And so many others."

So many others. Stella tossed her tissue in the trash and went to the little writing desk. The Savoy thought of everything. Lovely embossed stationery with envelopes and a tortoiseshell fountain pen was waiting for her to do her duty and write the required thank you note. Stella hated thank you notes. They were redundant. She'd thanked Lady Churchill in person, but that wasn't enough. Clementine was of her grandmother's ilk and would no doubt expect a note. Stella's grandmother's good opinion often hinged upon a well-written note, so she sat down and penned one, adding a tiny detail about Agatha and hoped for the best before she stuck on a stamp and began the other letters she owed.

First her mother. Francesqua needed regular reassurance that all was well. Stella was eating, healthy, and not pregnant. Because if she was to become pregnant, either she had better be on a ship home or Francesqua would be on a ship to England.

Next was Florence to whom she poured out her sorrow and homesickness. She would understand and never judge or send an impatient note for her to come home and be like everyone else.

Florence assumed without being told that Stella wasn't coming home until it was over. The two girls, for Florence, although a mother of two, wasn't that much older than her niece, had developed a communication system where Stella let her know where she was and what she was doing through literary and art details. Florence's letters back, mentioning Millicent and Myrtle and the brewery, were so well phrased that Stella knew that Florence knew what was happening beyond what Uncle Josiah had told her when he returned to St. Louis after delivering the news of Abel's death to Bickford House. Stella had written a long letter to Florence telling her everything and had received a letter of love in return. "Wherever you are, know that we are here and will always be."

Stella finished her letters and rang for a bellhop to come for them. A young man appeared minutes later, received a generous tip, and said they would be posted immediately, so Stella was able to go to bed with a heavy heart and a clear conscience having done her duty.

CHAPTER 4

Stella waited and waited, but the much anticipated knock on the door to say she must go somewhere at such and such a time didn't happen, so she stayed lounging in bed for the first time since she'd begun her training because staying in bed did not drill French verbs into one's head or the peculiar Swabian twang onto one's tongue. Park-Welles had been very clear about that, but, since he wasn't around, Stella happily ordered breakfast in bed.

The tray arrived so fast that Stella thought the kitchen staff must have an extra sense when it came to American guests. She had pancakes with real maple syrup, fluffy scrambled eggs, and thick streaky bacon. The coffee came in a silver pot with an ornate handle and all looked perfectly normal until she picked up her crisp linen napkin. Underneath was a buff-colored envelope with Stella's full name and The Savoy written underneath. She flipped the envelope over and found the back blank. Neither the earl nor Park-Welles had mentioned a letter. Her contacts were usually done in person.

The smell of hot coffee won out and she poured a cup before slitting open the mysterious envelope with her butter knife. She pulled out a fat note folded in half and when she did, a photo fell on her lap. Stella propped it up against the coffee pot, mystified as to its meaning.

It was a picture of a low walking bridge with thick trees on either side and London in the background. There were people on it, but it was taken far enough away that they were unrecognizable so probably incidental to the meaning.

Stella thought it looked vaguely familiar, but she couldn't quite place it. The note wasn't so difficult. Admiralty House and its address were at the top in bright blue ink. The sight of it made Stella catch her breath. Lady Churchill. She thanked Stella for her kind note and invited Stella to come for dinner when she returned from her travels.

When she returned from her travels. That was the sign. She'd done well. Clementine was on her side, but the note didn't explain the photo. It was hardly remarkable either in composition or subject. A snapshot really.

Stella sipped her coffee that *was* remarkable in its well-brewed goodness and took a closer look at the photo. There must be something there that she was supposed to see. Nothing on the back, but, when she searched the front inch by inch, she found 10 a.m. written in the trees on the right. It wasn't difficult to see once you knew it was there but otherwise practically invisible.

So it was the bridge at ten. A quick glance at the clock told her that she better get a move on and she bolted down her carefully-prepared breakfast in under ten minutes, wrapping up a pancake for the ducks, and then chose her clothes carefully. She had to be Stella Bled Lawrence at the hotel and then she must be an ordinary Londoner out for a walk at that bridge wherever it was.

Her blue suit of Cheviot wool was just the thing, good quality but not so the average person would notice. Next she chose her brown coat and Agatha's hat. The hat said Stella with all those exotic feathers, but it'd been designed for them to be easily removed. Then the hat was an everyday going to the market sort of hat. Perfect. To her coat she added a gift from Nicky, a stunning Harry Winston brooch made to resemble a bow tie. It was extravagant to the extreme in platinum and covered with white diamonds in various cuts. Nothing said wife of shipping magnate more than that brooch, not even her new rings compared. Nicky gave it to her as a sort of congratulations for not dying in Venice and she'd never worn it, except the night he gave it to her. She had to. He was so pleased to give it to her, but she didn't deserve it. She seriously doubted she ever would.

The brooch, a pair of diamond earrings, and her grandmother's hatpin completed the look of luxury she was expected to have. She almost left, but then rethought leaving the photo and note there or taking it with her. She didn't have a fireplace to burn them and it would take some time to flush them successfully, so she stuffed them in an envelope and addressed it to Florence before heading out with her gas mask box bouncing against her hip and a pancake in her handbag.

"Mrs. Bled Lawrence," said Mr. Temple at the door of the waiting elevator, "going out early today?"

"Yes, indeed," said Stella. "I've hardly exercised at all lately. I need to get out and walk."

He ushered her into the elevator and closed the cage and door. "It's a good day for it. Nice and clear." Then he frowned. "Jerry might like that tonight though. Please be ready to go down to the air raid shelter, ma'am."

"I will, don't worry about that. I wouldn't want to be caught up here if they bomb us."

The elevator slowly went down and Stella saw the worry on the older man's face. Did he have a good shelter to go to? Was it close enough? Unanswerable questions really. He wouldn't know until it was too late. Just then, it was plan and hope, so there was no use harping on it.

"Mr. Temple, my husband mentioned a spot in a park that he saw once when I wasn't with him. I thought I might walk there because he liked it so much. I don't think it's far, a low foot bridge in a park. Lots of trees and ducks. It's right here in the city."

The operator brightened. "Oh, I'd lay a bet that he was talking about St. James' Park. The Blue Bridge. It is a lovely spot and not far at all. Fifteen minutes if you're slow."

"I'm sure you're right," she said. "How do I get there?"

Mr. Temple gave her simple directions and she had to be on the right track. Clementine and presumably SIS wouldn't make it hard. When they stopped on the main floor she thanked and tipped him. He tried to refuse but she insisted. Money was such a small thing for her and now that she knew its worth, having been broke after Abel gave her the book and in Venice, she gave people as much as she could without raising eyebrows.

"Have a pleasant walk, ma'am," said Mr. Temple, "and do take a brolly with you. It could rain no matter what the sky says."

She thanked him and accepted an umbrella from a bellhop who rushed up. She gave him Florence's letter to post for her and tipped him nicely, too, making the young man flush with pleasure. In a moment, Stella was outside in the morning chill with rosy cheeks, trotting beside noisy traffic in the city she'd come to love and admire. No one panicked when instructions were given about air raids, shelters, and the like. The Londoners simply went about their business, calmly accepting that the storm was coming and that they must weather it. She wondered if Americans would take it so well.

Once she was well away from The Savoy, Stella took a little detour into an alley where she removed the feathers from her hat, the striking hatpin, her brooch and earrings. They got stowed in her handbag before she ventured back onto the street, looking much more normal.

The walk to St. James was short and she made it in twelve minutes, heading into the park past a memorial to the last war with five life-size bronze figures standing watch on it. The sight made her hurry along past casual walkers, most without their gas masks. She supposed they weren't worried like she was. But if the Nazis could figure out a way to gas the British civilians with no harm to themselves, she had no doubt they would do it. The Sorkines' senseless deaths had taught her that there were no limits to the Reich's rage and she wanted to pull people aside and lecture them, but she'd just be a crazy girl in the park, saying that the sky was falling. No matter that the sky was most certainly falling.

Happily, the path led her straight to the bridge and she slowed down once it got reasonably close, checking her watch. Five until ten.

Her heart was pounding, but she must not show it so she meandered a little and went to the right, down another path to look at the bare trees and some flower beds.

Then, exactly at ten, she stepped onto the bridge and walked to the center, pulling out her napkin and the pancake tucked inside. Several people walked past as she hooked her umbrella on the railing and leaned over to toss some crumbs to the ducks. They churned up the water in great excitement and she laughed, almost forgetting why she was there.

Then seemingly out of nowhere, a man appeared at her elbow. "Feeding the ducks is a nice touch and right on time, too."

She glanced over, barely long enough to register that he was tall, thin, moderately well-dressed with what the British called a toff's accent and a truly ridiculous pencil thin mustache.

"I do my best," she said.

"And your best is all we ask."

She tossed out a few more crumbs to the waiting ducks. "And…"

"And you will proceed directly to Tophams Hotel in Belgravia. Third floor. Room six."

"A hotel?"

"We can't send you to Boodle's or White's, can we?"

Stella bit back a retort. Men's clubs. If that was what they used for meetings, no wonder she was on the outs. "Fine. If that's it then…"

"I wish you the best of luck, Mrs. Bled Lawrence."

Stella controlled her breath. Her name. Her real name. She tore off a generous chunk of pancake and offered it to the agent. He took it and she said, "They told you my name or you recognized me?"

He chuckled and his voice completely changed. No longer the toff, he became a man from the middle class. A man from Wickham Place. "Oh, Miss Myna, I don't forget a face. You should know that."

She tossed another chunk far out into the stream and laughed as the ducks went mad chasing it. "Mr. Bast, you do have a way of turning up out of nowhere."

"It's a gift and speaking of gifts, I have one for you."

Something dropped into her coat pocket. Not particularly heavy, but she definitely noticed it. "To what do I owe the pleasure?"

"They decided to limit you. I disagree," said Mr. Bast. "Have a lovely walk and thank you for sharing your pancake."

"You're welcome," she said in a Parisian accent and was rewarded with a hint of a smile before he turned away and strolled off the bridge greeting other walkers with his reassumed toff's accent.

Stella finished tossing out her pancake, leisurely, while her mind raced. Limit her? What did that mean? Keeping her to courier or something else? Did the earl know?

Once she finished, she tucked the napkin in her pocket discretely touching Mr. Bast's gift. Flat metal with a hinged top. A cigarette case. It had to be. Stella had learned to smoke during her training. Even though Germany unofficially banned it for women, plenty of women smoked and Park-Welles thought she should have experience with it. Stella disliked everything about smoking, but she was sure Mr. Bast was up to something interesting.

She smiled as she walked off the bridge and out of the park to hail a taxi.

"Where to?" asked the driver.

"Tophams Hotel in Belgravia. Posthaste, if you please," Stella said in her own toff's accent. The marble-mouthed drawl was as fun to use as it was easy to imitate.

The driver wrinkled his nose and shoved the gearshift into position muttering under his breath, "Bloody posthaste. Bloomin' toffs."

She arrived at Topham's Hotel, posthaste as requested, but tipped little as befitting the wide gap between her assumed persona of toffee-nosed git and the driver's tobacco-stained grit.

He screeched to a halt in front of her hotel and did not open her door, although she stubbornly waited a good two minutes for him to do it while he glared through the windshield, tapping his stubby fingers on the wheel.

Stella finally sighed and got out, the very vision of put-upon and he screeched off again. She thought she heard a few *bloodys* through the glass and congratulated herself on being thoroughly upper-class obnoxious. It really was fun. Perhaps that was why so many people did it.

"Good afternoon, ma'am," said the doorman, rushing out to assist her. "I apologize. I did not see you arrive. Welcome to Topham's."

"Thank you very much," she said, nose in air. "I'm merely meeting a friend."

"Very good, ma'am."

She went in past simple columns into what looked like a row house, except for the hotel name painted on the portico. The lobby was nicer than she expected and the girl at the desk welcoming. Stella told her the same thing as the doorman, still using her accent, and went up the stairs to the third floor. It was empty and she found the room easily down the end of the corridor. There was a tray of breakfast dishes outside and the smell of kippers rose off it, making Stella wrinkle her nose involuntarily. Fish for breakfast was a tradition she couldn't understand.

She knocked and received a sharp, "Come in."

Inside the small, uninteresting room was plenty of interesting. No bed, dresser, or wardrobe filled the space. Instead, there was a table, filing cabinets, and two desks. Her handler, Park-Welles, sat at one, doing a crossword puzzle. Puzzles were the only thing Stella had ever seen him do for fun, if you could call it that. Park-Welles had a stopwatch and he timed himself relentlessly, noting each puzzle and time in a little notebook, though for what purpose Stella couldn't guess.

She stood there waiting as she had so many times before. His pen raced across the paper, scratching wildly, and then he picked up the stopwatch and clicked the knob. There was no squeal of triumph or moan of defeat. Park-Welles didn't do things like that. The only noise she'd ever heard him utter was a slight squeak during a French lesson three months into her training. He squeaked, politely excused himself, and went to the bathroom, where he stayed for six hours vomiting with the flu. He came back the next day and resumed their lesson like nothing had happened. That flu was the best thing that happened during Stella's training. She went to a pub and learned about cider instead.

Park-Welles noted his time in his notebook, straightened his glasses, and looked over at her with his usual expression of slight dissatisfaction, but it didn't bother Stella. She'd long since given up trying to get him to look any other way.

"Ah, GG. You're here." It was almost like he was surprised, but Park-Welles didn't do surprised either.

"I'm here as instructed," she said.

"Shall we get started?"

"Sure. Why not?"

He nodded, having long since given up on correcting her tendency to ask a question that wasn't really a question, and went to the table where a series of articles was laid out. The first was a folder labeled GG. He handed it to her.

"Read and memorize. You will not be taking it with you."

Stella sat in his chair, propped her feet up on the table because she hoped it annoyed him, although it was impossible to tell, and opened the file.

Pretty simple for the most part. Stella had two aliases, one for traveling through England, France, and The Netherlands, Charlotte Sedgewick, and one for Germany, Sophie Weber.

Charlotte was a British nanny for an aristocratic French family, the Barbiers. She was to have an educated accent but not aristocratic. She'd taken her A levels, but had not gone to university. Charlotte was the daughter of an archdeacon, who had six children and little money.

Sophie was a shop girl from Munich, where she was the only child of a widowed housekeeper. She was twenty years old and her fiancé had died of pneumonia. She was in Berlin looking for work to help her mother and had all the usual qualifications of a girl her age in Hitler's Germany, membership in the League of German Girls, minimally educated but physically active in hiking and gymnastics.

Stella had to smile at the details. "Did you do these?" she asked Park-Welles, who was holding his stopwatch.

"Are you done?"

"Yes."

He clicked the button and noted the time in the notebook he kept on her. He loved to time her memorization of verbs, which he knew she hated but did it anyway. "Excellent. Yes, I was instrumental in developing your aliases."

"My favorite food is Dampfnudeln?"

"Yes." Perhaps he did have a sense of humor after all. "You won't forget."

She rolled her eyes. "I won't forget any of it. Test me. I know you want to."

Park-Welles did test her with the stopwatch. She had two hesitations on the first go round—that counted as a mistake—and one on the second. None on the third, fourth, fifth, or sixth. He tested her accents, her knowledge of the Church of England, Nazi ranks, and anything else he could think of.

"Very well."

"You look disappointed," she said.

"Not at all. You are prepared," he said. Of course he could've said she was amazing and ready to chat up Hitler himself but that wasn't Park-Welles. She'd do, just barely.

He stood up and went over to the table, standing stiffly next to a somewhat battered suitcase made of cardboard covered in canvas. "Are you ready for your kits?"

"Do penguins come from the North Pole?" she asked.

He reached out and then withdrew his hand. "No. You aren't ready."

Stella took her feet off the table and slapped her file on the desk. "I'm ready. I just wanted to see if you were paying attention."

"Very amusing. Do not be amusing there. Germans have no sense of humor." That seemed to be the prevailing opinion, but it was one of the few things that Stella doubted about her training. Abel was Austrian and he had a sense of humor, quiet and wry, but it was definitely there. Cousin Gaspard was very sarcastic when the mood struck him. Austria wasn't Germany, but they weren't far off. The

Poppers were very funny, but maybe he thought, as Jews, they didn't count.

"Do you hear me?" he asked.

"I hear you. I'll be dull as dishwater."

Park-Welles looked as though he doubted that very much, but he didn't say anything and started handing over her equipment. Two sets of identification and the suitcase were the main things. He showed her how the suitcase had a built-in false side and how to pop it open. Inside were rows of Reichsmarks that she was supposed to hand over to her contact.

"Who's my contact?"

He handed over another file and she memorized it quickly. There wasn't much to it.

"We have an agent in the American embassy?"

"You're surprised?"

"A little."

"You're here, aren't you?" asked Park-Welles.

"I see your point."

So it was Lester Nimitz, a secretary to an attaché. He was able to get messages out via the embassy pouches without detection and had been operating for nearly a year. His description left something to be desired: short and homely with a constantly red nose and an ill-fitting brown suit. That was half the men in London. But she could find him in a bar near the embassy called Leon Klaus and he would be drinking Fanta. Stella had some lines from Shakespeare to exchange to confirm his identity. Once she had, she'd drop the money and return to London.

"They gave you two weeks," said Park-Welles with a frown.

"Maybe I'll need two weeks."

"*You* won't need two days. In and out was my recommendation."

That was almost a compliment and Stella got a little warmer toward a man who was mostly iceberg. "I'm supposed to get the lay of the land and make some connections."

"I'm aware." He went through the rest of her kit, stationery with Deutsches Reich stamps, a copy of *Gone with the Wind* in German, dull serviceable clothing, German manufacturer tags for Sophie and French for Charlotte. Stella was to sew on the appropriate tag at the right time. Makeup was frowned on in the Reich so she only got a compact and a few cheap cosmetics. The compact had a false bottom with a coded message in it. She was to hand the message over with the money and Lester would send it in the pouch to confirm their contact and the drop. She was well-versed in coded messages, including poem codes, but they didn't trust her to do it and she flushed as Park-Welles continued on about the boarding house they were sending her to. The matron was suspected to be sympathetic to the British, according to an operative.

"What about a weapon?" Stella interrupted.

"You don't need a weapon."

"Says who?"

"You are there to contact, drop, observe, and leave. Nothing more."

"What if I make a good connection?"

"You have two weeks," he said. "This is not negotiable. You'd do well to follow orders and return on target." He gave her her tickets, boat and train, both ways. "Here are your ration cards. Do not lose them or give them away. Replacements will raise questions."

Stella tucked the ration cards in the ugly German handbag she was issued along with her passports. "Anything else?"

He picked up a pair of chunky black shoes. They were Sophie's and Stella felt sorry for her. "These have compartments in the heels. Something we're experimenting with." Park-Welles grasped the right heel, twisted sharply left and then right. The heel popped off the shoe and he held it out to her. It was completely hollow.

"That's pretty nifty. What am I supposed to put in there?"

"Nimitz may pass you something he doesn't want to risk in the embassy packet. You can put it in there or if you do get something from the many connections you'll make in two weeks, you can use them for that."

She glared at him. The man had trained her for nearly a year and had no faith that she could do the job he'd taught her to do. She was supposed to be put in place and observe, long term and moving around the enemy as one of them. None of this in and out stuff.

Park-Welles picked up a key, clunky and old. "Lastly and against my better judgement, this is your most valuable weapon."

"A key? How about a Mauser or a Luger. The Walther P-38 is very nice. You trained me to be a crack shot."

"Not on this trip. You won't need it. You will raise no suspicions and will have no confrontations."

Stella crossed her arms. "So what's with the key? Am I supposed to poke them in the eye?"

"You will not need to poke anyone in the eye," he said patiently and he picked up the large brass key, twisted the end, and poured out three pills. "The earl insisted and 'C' backed him up. These are standard in the kit."

"Why am I getting them since I can't be trusted to code or much of anything else?"

He ignored that. "This is your L."

"Yeah, yeah. I know. Lethal. Brown. Got it. Don't worry I will not be committing suicide. "

"And your E."

She nodded. E for energy. In case she had to run, which she wouldn't according to him.

"And your I pill." It was a small blue tablet that caused severe illness in whoever took it, cramps, vomiting, and diarrhea. In theory, it would let an agent escape a close encounter by taking out the suspicious.

"You won't need them, but as I said, the earl insisted." He put the pills back in the key and gave it to her. "And that's the full brief."

"What about our agents?" she asked.

Park-Welles hesitated and said, "I have given you your contact, Lester Nimitz."

"I'm talking about the two agents that have been arrested."

"You know about that." His voice was flatter than usual.

"I do. Did it ever occur to you that I might be able to get some information about them? Help locate them. Perhaps assist in a rescue operation."

To Park-Welles' credit, he didn't laugh out loud or even scoff, but she was certain both those things were going on on the inside. "That won't be necessary. We need the drop. Nimitz will do the rest."

"He's involved in a rescue operation?"

"There's no rescue operation."

"Why not? You've done it before. Successfully."

"Not this time."

"Why not?"

"That is above both our levels." Park-Welles looked at her and Stella had the impression that she was seeing him for the first time. There before her was a man who was frustrated, most likely pushed aside into training, and it wasn't sitting well.

"I don't like that," she said finally.

"No one does," he said. "Pack and I'll give you the rest."

"There's more?"

"The final touches."

Stella packed her suitcase. There wasn't much in it. Sophie wasn't a wealthy girl, but the suitcase was heavy with the large amount of money inside.

"Okay. What's next?"

He gave her two sets of travel stickers and Stella was deeply impressed with the level of detail. The first set had both French and British locations, like Paris with the Eiffel Tower and the Caledonian Hotel in Edinburgh. The second had stickers from Innsbruck and Berchtesgaden. They were all new but appeared cracked and peeling from years of use.

"Do I layer them? That won't help with the trip back."

"No," he said. "They adhere with water and remove with water. It's a new kind of plastic out of America. But you must dry them out thoroughly after use or they won't work well the next time."

"That's amazing," she said and she meant it.

He pulled out another suitcase that she hadn't noticed before and she really should have. It was a Louis Vuitton and large. "You'll use this one to transport your kit to the Savoy." He placed her work case, as she came to think of it, inside the snazzy Louis Vuitton and clicked closed the three clasps.

Stella glanced at her train tickets. She left London for Berlin bright and early the next morning. "What do I do with my things at the hotel?"

"You'll think of something," he said stone faced.

Not helpful in the least, but that was typical of Park-Welles.

"Thanks."

"You're welcome." He didn't catch the sarcasm and the man wondered why he wasn't in the field. It would be like sending a robot.

"I guess that's it," she said.

"Not quite. You've been assigned a new codename for the field."

"No more Glamour Girl?"

"You're still GG when off mission or in training. You will be known as Tarragon in the field."

"Tarragon? Isn't that an herb?" she asked.

"It is."

"What gives?"

"It is an herb with a distinct flavor. I find it unpleasant," said Park-Welles.

She sighed. "You named me after something unpleasant. Nice."

"I didn't choose it. Your codename came from 'C'."

"The old 'C' or the new 'C'?"

"I don't know."

She waited for something else to come out of him, but he just stood there so she said, "That's it?"

"It is." He put out his hand and she shook it. "Be sure to remember who your enemies are."

As if I could forget.

Park-Welles turned away from her. There would be no emotional well-wishing. Certainly no tearful goodbye for a girl he trained for a year, who, in theory, might not come back.

"I'll be seeing you then."

"I assume so."

Very reassuring.

Stella picked up the Louis Vuitton and went for the door. Park-Welles pulled out a chair behind her and she glanced back as she walked out. Her handler had retaken his spot at the desk, clicked his stopwatch, and started a new puzzle. Done. Over. Stella was on her own.

THE BELLHOP, a fifteen-year-old named Terry, dashed up to take the Louis Vuitton and happily accompanied Stella up to her room. She kept him chatting so he, hopefully, wouldn't notice how heavy the suitcase was. Terry was happy to oblige, answering all her questions and making her laugh more than once about his adventures in the blackout. Apparently, things had gotten quite wild in the dark. Terry had gotten kissed by strange women three times and counting.

"Anything goes with the war," he said, grinning from ear to ear and then the smile dropped off his face. "And I'm not going. My ma won't let me."

"You're fifteen," she said.

"But I'm big for my age. One lady thought I was twenty-five when she laid one on me by Piccadilly Circus."

"How dark *was* it?"

That got him laughing. "Dark enough."

"It's a good thing there'll be lights in the recruiter office," she said. "They'll know you're not close to eighteen."

Terry turned glum as they walked toward her room. "The war will be over before I get old enough."

Stella seriously doubted that, but she said, "I hope so."

"Oh, come on, Mrs. Lawrence. I want to do my bit."

They stopped at her door and she got out her key. "You'll do your bit. It's unavoidable."

"Carrying luggage ain't it." He started at his own words. "Sorry, ma'am."

She turned the knob, but then stopped and looked at the embarrassed boy. "It isn't. You're right. But all will be revealed in time. You'll know what to do when it comes time to do it."

"If you don't mind me saying so, you're different than they say in the papers," said Terry.

Stella put a finger to her lips. "Don't tell anyone."

He grinned. "Yes, ma'am."

She opened the door and almost started herself. Her room was filled with cigarette smoke and a man was lounging by the window. "Oh! Darling, it's you," she exclaimed.

Nicky Lawrence turned to them and forced a smile onto his chiseled cheeks. "It's me. Surprised?"

"Astonished." Stella hustled in. Terry put the big suitcase on the floor next to the bed and grinned even wider at his tip before slipping out quickly. "What are you doing here?"

Nicky didn't answer. He turned back to look out at the view over London, the bright, sunny day highlighting him in the dark room.

"Has something happened?" she asked.

"I wouldn't be here if it hadn't." He took a drag off his cigarette and the tip glowed orange. The sight sent a chill through her. Nicky rarely smoked. Only in times of great stress or pain.

She left the light off and looked him over. He wore his RAF uniform, but had draped the jacket on her desk chair along with his tie. His shirt was unbuttoned and showed off the abdominal muscles that had grown and hardened in the past year. Nicky had never carried much fat, but now he had none at all.

"You look fine so you didn't crash." Stella hoped that was true. He'd had a few close calls and had avoided being grounded although they weren't his fault.

"I didn't crash."

She took off her hat and coat before unpinning her hair. It'd grown long in the last year and when she shook it out it fell past her shoulder blades. Nicky liked it long and loose. The sight of her looking like a film star usually got a smile out of him but not this time. He gave her a glance and looked back out the window.

"How long are you here?"

"Until tomorrow morning."

"Not long then," she said.

"Long enough to see you off," he said.

Her heart grew heavy and looking at her husband's tense shoulders made it worse. "I didn't think they'd tell you."

"Neither did I."

Stella's temper flared. "Well, you don't have to stay. You can go right now."

Nicky snubbed out his cigarette and crossed his arms. "I don't want to go, Stella. I don't want anyone to *go*."

"It's too late for that."

"No, it isn't. Turn down the assignment. Don't go."

She crossed her own arms. "Like you would? If Colonel Wilson orders you to fly over and bomb Germany, you'd say no?"

"It's not the same."

"It is. You've got a rank. I've got a rank. We'll both have missions."

He ran his hands over his face. "It's not the same, Stella. It's not. I'll be flying with a squadron. You're going into enemy territory completely alone. You'll be living among them. One false move and you'll be discovered."

"And you could go down on a mission and be captured," she said.

"I'll be protected by the Geneva Convention. I'd be a prisoner of war." He lowered his voice. "They execute spies, Stella. Execute."

"I know that. Everyone knows that. Why are you acting like this is new information?"

"Because you're doing it. For real. It isn't a game, Stella. The earl and the rest of those cloak and dagger types expect you to provide intelligence against Germany."

Stella kicked off her shoes at him and they cracked him in the shins.

"Hey!"

"Hey yourself." She pointed at him. "You didn't think I'd do it. You didn't think it would really happen."

"I didn't. What of it?"

"I've been in training for almost a year, Nicky. I wasn't doing it to stay here and file my nails while Europe burns."

"I know exactly why you're doing it and you don't have to. Abel wouldn't want you to. Neither would the Sorkines or the von Bodmann sisters."

"You don't know that because they're dead and while we're at it, why are you doing it?" she asked.

"I'm not."

"You became a Canadian to fly in the RAF. Pilots and crews die every week."

"That's training," he said.

"Exactly!"

"Exactly what?"

She glared at him. "Your people are getting killed and nobody's even shooting at them yet."

That stumped him and it gave her great satisfaction. She stripped and picked out a dress to wear to lunch. Suddenly, she was starving. Pointless arguments had that effect on her.

Nicky came over and took the dress out of her hands. "I'm going to complete my training and follow my orders. Whether I survive or not is in God's hands."

"Very comforting," she said.

"You don't understand what I'm saying."

"Wanna bet?" She ripped the dress out of his hands. "You don't think I'll follow orders."

"No, I don't."

"I guess you'll have to wait and see."

He dropped onto the bed and put his head in his hands. "I can't believe this is happening."

Stella tossed aside the dress and wedged herself between his knees, pressing his head against her stomach. "I felt the same way the first time I saw you take off."

"It's di—"

"You flew around, did your maneuvers, and landed just fine. I watched and I couldn't do anything about it. Clark almost clipped your wing, remember?"

"I remember."

"The world stopped for me when I saw it. You were out there doing what you do and I couldn't help you. I hated every minute. I never wanted to see you fly again. But I did and I hated it that time, too."

Nicky looked up, his eyes shining with unshed tears. "I don't know how to let you go."

"But you will because I am."

CHAPTER 5

Two days later, Sophie Weber stepped off a train in Berlin. No one gave her a second glance and Stella knew they wouldn't. The transformation from Stella to Charlotte to Sophie had been seamless. After a night with Nicky that was somehow filled with passion and fear at the same time, they'd gotten up, packed, and left early.

At the train station, Stella took her kit out of the Louis Vuitton, put her rings and Stella clothes inside and emerged as Charlotte. Nicky took the Louis Vuitton from where she left it near a porter and walked away without a backward glance. They didn't say goodbye. It hadn't been planned that way. Goodbye just didn't happen and it made Stella feel a little relieved but also curiously empty. Nicky was gone and so was she in a strange way.

From there she crossed the channel and trained to Paris and then Amsterdam, where she took a room for the night. In the room, she took the Charlotte labels out of her clothes and neatly stitched in the Sophie ones, reorganized her kit so that all the Charlotte evidence was concealed in the false side with the money, new identification, and Kindertransport papers for Anna, and left the hotel as Sophie the next morning. She trained to Berlin using her Bavarian accent and twisted the cheap little engagement band that Sophie wore in remembrance of her lost fiancé. It was a brilliant idea. That thin little band of gold with the diamond chip on it would be useful as a man repellant if she chose it to be or it could reel them in. Big, sad eyes could soften a heart and loyalty to a lost love was catnip to some.

Werner would be useful in so many ways. Stella traced a finger across the cigarette case in her pocket with Werner's name etched on it along with 1937 and a swastika. Since she left Nicky, Mr. Bast's gift had become a talisman for her. He believed in her and wanted her to do the work she'd been trained to do. More importantly, he had given her a tool to do it.

Stella hadn't been alone since Mr. Bast dropped the cigarette case in her pocket on the bridge. She hadn't had a moment to examine it until she was in France and found herself sitting in a compartment on her own. She closed the curtains and pulled out the case. It was cheap metal made to look like silver and in a particular style, opening with a hinge at the top to reveal only the end of the cigarettes, ten in all. The case had seven real cigarettes in it and it looked completely normal. It was heavier than you'd expect but not shockingly so, which Stella thought was a minor miracle, considering that the case had a concealed camera in it. Nobody would suspect. You couldn't even tell when you looked into the case. It just looked empty. Amazing.

Mr. Bast believed she could get somewhere where a camera would be essential so he gave her one. She loved him for it. He didn't give her a weapon, but that was no bother. Stella knew that she could improvise when necessary. Her grandmother's hatpin might be stowed at Boodle's in London where Nicky had been given membership, but there were other things she could use.

Stella walked off the platform into the Anhalter Bahnhof under an enormous Nazi flag. Like Munich, those ugly flags were everywhere. No other country was like that. You didn't see the stars and stripes plastered all over Union Station in St. Louis. She could only remember one, outside. More recently she'd been all over Britain and had seen plenty of Union Jacks around, but it wasn't the same.

Inside the station, she was awed by the size and number of

surfaces Nazis found to put their flag on. It was like they wanted to pound into your head where you were, as if she could forget. The Berlin Bahnhof was unique, but even without the flags you'd know where you were from the harsh voices coming at you from every direction. This was the high German she'd been taught as a basis for the other dialects and it was different from the softer German spoken in other parts of the country and felt like an entirely different language from what Abel spoke. Every word was punctuated, rammed at you, hard and demanding. There were no lilting tones, high and sweet, like in Munich or Vienna. Tschüss sounded totally different. When her native speaker Magda Popper said it, it was a lovely generous goodbye. A sweet see you later. In the Berlin train station it came across as an accusation. But they didn't mean it that way and Stella could see that in the faces saying the words. It was simply the dialect, but she felt the people were different there. It was a bustling station like Munich, not silent with dread like Vienna had been on the eve of the Kristallnacht, but still something was changed. There was a tightness to the shoulders along with a kind of sharp-eyed pride. Was it just the way Berliners were or was it that Germany was at war and they knew they were winning?

Stella noted the attitude and filed it away for later reflection as she found her way to the S Bahn and bought a ticket. The man at the ticket counter recognized her accent and asked how things were in Munich. He was a native Bavarian and missed his home. She took her cue from him and reported things were tense with waiting to see what would happen next.

"The rationing is better there, I think," he said as he slid over her ticket.

She feigned surprise. "I believe we get the same cards. It must be fair."

"So many farms at home. My family gets extra from friends outside the city."

"Ah, yes. This is true. Very good milk and eggs."

"You won't find that here. There isn't enough to share."

She batted her eyes and became younger. "It will get better soon. Now that it's over with Poland."

"Over," he scoffed. "It is not over. Hurry now. A train will come in for you any second."

Stella thanked him and rushed away to find the right platform into the city. As the ticket man predicted, the train came a second later and she stepped on, trying not to bang her suitcase on anyone's legs. The car was tight like the ones in the tube in London. Plenty of suitcases and she was pleased to see hers fit right in with the right amount of wear and those very important stickers applied to the sides.

She tried to listen to the conversations around her, but it was too noisy and the snippets she managed to catch were of everyday things. People were tired, hungry, and ready to be home. There were no uniforms in her car, although she'd seen plenty in the station, mostly the green of the Wehrmacht. A few SS, clothed in their distinctive black, walked through with glints in their eyes. A path cleared in front of them. The regular army didn't get the same reaction.

Several men did have the Nazi Party membership pin proudly displayed on their lapels, but these men said nothing during the trip into the city center. They were a closed-mouthed group with their faces impassive and aloof.

When the train stopped at Stella's station, she stepped off with several of them. One, a younger man with close-cropped hair under his fedora, offered to carry her suitcase up the stairs. It went against every instinct she had. It was her kit, filled with a huge amount of Reichsmarks and her Charlotte cover, but she nodded gratefully as she expected any young German girl would. He was a party member and therefore due a high level of trust and respect, so she handed over her suitcase with a smile on her face and a lump in her throat.

"Are you new to Berlin?" he asked.

Her smile got bigger. "How can you tell?"

He laughed. "What a lovely voice you have. Munich?"

"Yes and you are from Berlin?"

"Ah, yes. This is obvious as well," he said with a laugh.

They came up onto a noisy street. People rushed by with their afternoon shopping, briefcases, and a general air of urgency. It might've been Stella's imagination, but people kept their heads down. The flags on the hotel across the street weren't getting the attention they deserved. Nor were the odd posters of disfigured people with price tags hung right next to pictures of sturdy mothers with passels of blond children and advertisements touting Germany's industry and strong workers. It was incongruous and off-putting grouping those things together.

"Where are you going?" the man asked.

"To the Müller boarding house."

"Irena Müller?"

"Do you know it?" Stella asked, trying to keep her eyes off the swastikas and not always succeeding.

"Of course. Some of the Valkyrie girls live there. Will you be a Valkyrie girl?"

Stella had no idea what a Valkyrie girl was. Park-Welles hadn't briefed it.

"I don't know. It is hard to get in, isn't it?"

He smiled so genially Stella could almost forget what he was and represented. He was so kind and thoughtful, nothing like Peiper or the men that left Rosa von Bodmann to die on a cold train station floor, except that he was. He was exactly and she must never forget it.

"I must admit I don't know. I've never been." He turned to the street and hailed a cab. One zipped up and jolted to a halt next to them and he said to her, "Maximillian Hoff, Berlin."

"Sophie Weber, Munich." She gave him her most charming smile. "But maybe Berlin."

"One can hope," he said. "I'm going in the direction of Frau Müller's. I will give you a lift."

"I don't want to inconvenience you," said Stella, fervently praying he'd go away and leave her to her plan.

But he was a curious man and she a pretty girl. Men like him didn't leave girls like her on the sidewalk in a strange city. He opened the cab door. "It is no trouble. I will get to ride with a future Valkyrie girl."

She couldn't refuse. It simply wasn't possible, so she got in, and he put her suitcase on the floor at her feet. That was a relief anyway. The driver gave her the once over and she found the boarding house address had dropped out of her head.

To cover it, she fumbled with her handbag, mumbling, "The address. I have it here somewhere."

"Never mind," the party member said. "I know the corner."

He gave the cross streets and then a name. "Volkischer-Beobachter."

Stella knew the name. It was a newspaper, if one considered state propaganda the news. "Is that where you work?" she asked.

He told her that he was an editor for the domestic division and worked on internal stories like rationing.

"A man at the station told me that the rationing isn't fair in Berlin," said Stella conversationally.

The party man got sharp-eyed. "Our rationing is completely fair. To be unfair would be a crime against the people."

"That's what I said."

He got out a little notebook and flipped it open with his pen poised. The driver glanced in the rearview mirror and seemed to sink down a touch. "What was this man's name?"

"I'm sorry. I don't know. We only met in the line for tickets for a moment," lied Stella easily. She wasn't about to turn in the poor man in the ticket booth.

"What did he look like?"

The driver slunk down a little more and Stella gave a vague description that could've been anyone. She didn't know where he was going or came from. He wasn't distinct, just a man who didn't like rationing.

"Probably a Jew," said the party man snapping his notebook closed. "You have to be careful."

Stella wanted to ask, "Careful with what?", but knew better. "My mother warned me."

"You have a wise mother," he said.

"I do, but she does worry so much."

"That is what good mothers do. I'm sure you will be a mother soon and will worry, too."

She shrugged. "Maybe."

He looked at her ring. "Very soon I would think."

Stella coated her face with loss and looked down. "No, not soon."

The party man practically melted and apologized for insensitivity. She forgave him and they discussed that loss for the Fatherland wasn't really loss at all. It was a gift of blood. Stella nearly corrected his assumption that Werner was lost in Poland, but the moment passed too quickly and she had to continue in that vein. This could change her cover. She might have to adapt for this little loss in concentration, but changing course didn't bother her at all. A loss in Poland was more sympathetic than pneumonia any day.

The driver announced that they were at the corner the party man had told him and the address popped back in Stella's mind. She gave it to him and they drove down a side street to park in front of an impressive brick house with three tall stories and large windows.

"Thank you, Herr Hoff," said Stella as she reached for the door, but she wasn't fast enough. Maximillian Hoff was out of the cab and around to her door in a flash.

He helped her out and said, "I will walk you in, Sophie. May I call you Sophie?"

"Please do."

"And you may call me Max as a new friend should." He took her suitcase and told the driver to wait.

"You don't have to walk me in," she said. "I've taken up too much of your time already." Stella wasn't interested in a friendship with Maximillian Hoff. If it went too far he'd lock her into his version of the fictional Werner's death. She didn't want that coming into the Müller house.

"I insist."

She internally sighed. She'd never shake him now. Stella had had enough suitors before Nicky to know that. Max was going to stick and she'd have to make what she could of it. He was with a state newspaper. He might know something useful. One never knew.

She smiled shyly at him. "That is very kind of you. I hope they have space for me. It sounds like a popular place."

"It is, but you're the right kind of girl." Max walked her across the sidewalk and up a short flight of stairs to a porch with four large pillars on the small space in front of an arched, dark wooden door. He dropped the knocker once and looked down at her. "You won't have any trouble."

There was a click and the door opened. A tall woman with stern, somewhat mannish features peered out at them. She had greying brown hair that was done in an old-fashioned style with a braid wrapped around her head and she wore a plain brown woolen dress with a heavy sweater over it. The woman quickly assessed the situation with Max's black suit and pin and a smile came over her face. She warmly said hello in a Berlin accent similar to his.

Max introduced himself and Stella as Sophie in a way that said she was important and known, which of course she wasn't. Stella didn't know if that was a good thing or not. The woman who said her name was Irena Müller certainly looked impressed, but there was a kind of wariness beneath the deference.

"Come in. Come in," she said, gesturing for them to come in a cold entry hall with a coat rack and a staircase with a heavy wooden banister. Frau Müller stood next to the newel post and eyed Stella's face in a way that gave the impression of assessment and made Stella bristle, although it shouldn't have. She wanted everything to be about the surface, a pretty face, ration cards, and the right identification saying she was an Aryan, but Stella hadn't been raised that way. How many lectures had she been given stressing beauty is as beauty does? A façade was just a façade to the Bleds, which didn't help Nicky at all when he met her parents. His façade was second to none and he kept his true worth close to the belt, making her father question if Nicky was just a pretty face. That notion had long been dispelled about her husband, but it wouldn't ever be about her. Outside the family, she was a pretty face and in that moment of judgement, she hated it, despite its obvious value in her current mission.

"I don't believe we have met, Herr Hoff," said Frau Müller.

"We have not, but I know you by reputation. You have the highest standards."

Frau Müller welcomed them to come to her sitting room, but Max said he had a cab waiting. "Do you have a room for little Sophie?" he asked. "She has just arrived from Munich and needs a safe, comfortable place to stay. Her dear mother would like her to be here." He sounded as though he knew her mother and they were close family friends.

Frau Müller and Max looked her over and Stella felt like she should take off her coat and do a spin or trot around the room like a horse at an auction.

"Why do you come to Berlin, Sophie?" she asked.

Stella went through her prepared explanation. Her mother was a widow and money was tight. She heard there were good jobs in the capital and thought she could perhaps help her mother make ends meet.

"There are no jobs in Munich?"

Max frowned. "Sophie's fiancé died for the Führer in Poland. She would like to make a fresh start. I'm sure you understand."

Frau Müller took her hand. "Your sacrifice will not be forgotten."

A quick thought of Rosa brought tears to Stella's eyes and they were noted by both Frau Müller and Max.

"I do have a small room on the third floor. One of my girls is recently married," said Frau Müller. "I was saving it for a Valkyrie girl…"

"Perhaps Sophie could be that girl," said Max, straightening his lapel and emphasizing his affiliation.

"My mother has a friend, a dear friend, Emma Klink, who knows of a position for me," Stella said hastily. "I must go to her. She is expecting me."

They nodded sagely, understanding family and connections must be respected. Stella prayed they wouldn't enquire further or God forbid want to accompany her to a non-existent woman's house.

"It must be in a factory," said Frau Müller. "The work must be done well and fast for the Führer."

"Others can do it," said Max smiling.

"I will see what Frau Klink says," said Stella. "My mother speaks very highly of her."

"I'm sure you will find the right place," said Max, pointedly, and he took Stella's hand. "Welcome to Berlin. I will see you again, Sophie."

I hope not.

"You've been very kind, Herr Hoff," she said.

"Remember," he said, tweaking her chin, "it's Max to you."

She tilted down her chin and smiled up at him. "Yes, Max. Thank you."

The annoyingly helpful Nazi shook Frau Müller's hand and quickly left. They watched him through the window next to the door as the cab pulled away and Stella took a deep breath, waiting for Frau Müller to look back at her. When she finally did, it was a relief.

"So up from the country," she said. "First time in Berlin?"

"Yes, ma'am."

She looked over Stella once more and told her to take off her coat. Stella did as instructed, bristling once more at how her body was judged and rated so blatantly.

"I think you will do for Valkyrie, but I know you must see Frau Klink and do as your mother instructs," she said.

"Yes, ma'am."

"Will the small room do for you?"

Stella nodded and was told the weekly rate that included breakfast daily and dinner if she wasn't working during the dinner hour. "You have your ration cards?"

Stella handed over her cards and Frau Müller nodded. "Very good. We can use the extra coal. It's hot water only twice a week now. I've marked a line on the tub to where you can fill it. We wash on Sundays and Thursdays. The girls are very careful about the water. We want everyone to have a chance to wash."

Stella's surprise must've shown on her face, because Frau Müller said, "Yes, I know. It must be a shock. You have so much more wood in the south. Do you use wood instead of coal?"

She had no idea and she made up a story in the moment. "Both. My mother's brother gives us wood sometimes."

"Ah, very lucky in the south." Frau Müller looked chagrined that she'd said that out loud and quickly said, "The rationing is the same everywhere. We must sacrifice for the Führer."

"Yes. We all must sacrifice," said Stella, picking up her suitcase.

Frau Müller led her up the staircase and the creaking treads were the only sound in the large house. It was four in the afternoon. The other girls must be at work.

Stella glanced around at the house as they went from floor to floor, noting everything and finding absolutely nothing remarkable, except for the incredible cold. If the house was heated at all she couldn't tell. Park-Welles had said the winter was particularly bad that year and the coal rationed. She'd been given reasonably warm clothes, a coat, and gloves, but it wasn't nearly enough. Her legs felt like they were turning blue under her stockings. She couldn't see her breath in the house but that wasn't far off.

When they got to the third floor, there was a little hall with two doors. Stella's was on the right. Frau Müller said Fräulein Hanni was on the left. She opened the door to a truly tiny room with just enough space for a single bed, a simple chair, dressing table, and a narrow wardrobe. The good news was that it was warmer than the rest of the house by virtue of being at the top, but it was only by a few degrees.

"Thank you, Frau Müller," said Stella. "It's a lovely room with a nice view, too."

"It is a nice view. If we had one more floor, you could see the Reichstag from here." She went on to say the bathrooms were on the first and second floors. The bathrooms were busy and she should use the small mirror between her windows as much as possible.

"I will be serving in an hour. I will introduce you to the girls then." Frau Müller left, closing the door behind her. Stella checked the tiny watch Park-Welles had given her. What was she serving at five o'clock?

She heaved her suitcase on the bed and clicked open the latches. Should she remove the money and hide it or leave it be? She glanced around. The options weren't endless. The top of the wardrobe? It had a small crown for concealment. She slid her hand under the clothes to find the secret compartment when the door flew open again.

"Sophie," said Frau Müller.

Stella jumped back, her hand tucked behind her back. "Oh!"

The matron laughed. "I'm sorry to startle you."

"No, no. It's fine. I was just thinking about when to go to Frau Klink's apartment."

"You should go this afternoon. A good job is not easy to find."

"Yes, of course."

"I wanted to tell you that if it is a factory job you will get new ration cards for more food. I will need those."

Stella nodded and did her best to control her hands that wanted to shake. "Yes, of course. I will give them to you immediately."

"Good girl." Frau Müller tapped her cleft chin. "See what she offers you and ask what her opinion is."

"Her opinion on what?"

"Whether you should take it or try for the Valkyrie." She waved her hands. "No matter. We'll see what the girls say. They are the best judges after all. Remember to come down in an hour." She left again and Stella went to the door, pressing her ear to the wood. Frau Müller was thin but the stairs still did a good deal of creaking as she went down.

Stella waited until the creaking faded and laid her forehead against the wood.

Stupid. So very stupid.

She carefully turned the key in the lock and turned back to her suitcase, her heart still pounding. Instead of opening the compartment, she climbed on the bed and stood on her tiptoes to see the top of the wardrobe. The space on top was empty and extremely dusty so nobody cleaned up there, which was good. Also, the crown was about four inches high. Plenty of space to conceal the money and the rest of her kit, but removing it didn't give her a chance for a quick getaway if needed.

Stella got off the bed, maneuvered herself between the bed and wardrobe door. It only opened three-fourths of the way since the room was so small and there wasn't space for her suitcase inside. She wasn't sure what to do. Park-Welles taught her concealment in her room, if at all possible, but her instinct said no. That made her wrinkle her nose. The earl said her evaluation said she'd go with her own instinct rather than her orders. Why did they have to be right? But her instinct had served her well. She was alive. Nicky was alive. Her instinct was why the SIS had been interested in her in the first place.

"Sorry, Park-Welles. Stella knows best." She unloaded her meagre belongings into the wardrobe and put her personal stuff—or rather Sophie's personal stuff—on the little table. A picture of a young man, wearing a Wehrmacht uniform, a brush and comb, stationery, stamps, and her small horde of cosmetics. Stella couldn't help but think Sophie's life was sad and she looked forward to escaping it as soon as possible.

But escape from that cold house in that cold country wouldn't happen anytime soon, so she tried to stuff her suitcase under the bed, but predictably it didn't fit so she wedged it in beside the wardrobe. It wasn't great, but she could get out fast that way. Having a party member practically adopt her out of the blue had already taught her that the unexpected could happen in Berlin, despite how well it was rumored to be controlled.

After combing her hair and exploring every inch of her tiny abode, including opening the window to look for a drainpipe to climb down if the need arose—there wasn't one—Stella headed down for whatever Frau Müller was serving at five. She got her second surprise of the day. It would not be her last.

Frau Müller's house had come alive in the hour before five. Creaking floors and muffled voices found their way through Stella's door and puzzled her exceedingly. It was like the other residents of the boarding house had all come home at the exact same time. She heard Hanni, the girl in the other room, open her door and go downstairs. Stella might've missed her going in, but she didn't think so.

When she unlocked her door and opened it to listen, laughter and a chorus of girls' voices came up the stairway to greet her. She heard Frau Müller urging girls to hurry up and fought the urge to put on a second sweater before going down into the increasing cold.

Stella followed the voices and the smell of fresh bread to the back of the house where she found the dining room packed with girls, laughing and talking a mile a minute. They spoke German, but the accents were all different. She heard the expected Berlin intonations, but also a Westphalian, and a girl from Vienna. They were all around Stella's age and very pretty, a lot taller than Stella with long legs and an elegant, showy way of moving, nothing at all like the German women on the street, who seemed to stomp in comparison. The identical black and red dresses they wore showed off their legs in the most obvious way possible. The dirndls were a Bavarian fashion and Stella knew Hitler favored the traditional look of the low cut blouse and tight laced-up bodice. A couple of the girls had long braids tied with ribbons or wrapped around their heads like Frau Müller. They could've stepped out of the eighteenth century, if it weren't for the lipstick and sheer stockings on their exposed legs.

"Oh, there you are, Sophie," exclaimed Frau Müller. "Come in. Come in."

Stella went in as a shy girl from the sticks overawed by the glamour in the room. She wasn't completely faking it. Those girls were something she hadn't expected. They reminded her of Nicky's cousin, Alma, and her description of her years at Smith in a totally different world of girly camaraderie that Stella envied, having been educated at home by crabby or disinterested governesses and tutors.

Two of the girls rushed over and took her arms.

"Don't be shy," said the one on her right, a doe-eyed girl with brown braids to her waist.

A blonde with a halo of curls said, "Oh, Irena, you are right. She's lovely."

"Do you dance?" asked another from a buffet table as she stuffed a sausage into a roll.

"Of course she dances. All Bavarian girls dance."

"I mean *real* dancing, not that knee-slapping stuff."

"Girls don't do that."

"How do you know?"

"I know."

The conversation went zinging around and Stella didn't have to say anything, which was a good thing. She was very afraid she'd drop her accent at the barrage.

"Girls. Girls," said Frau Müller, smiling indulgently. "Let her breathe. It's been a long journey."

The girl with the waist-length braids squeezed her arm. "I'm Hanni. Your neighbor."

"We're all neighbors," protested another girl with extremely pale blonde hair, blue eyes and high aristocratic forehead. "I'm Irma."

"I'm Maria," said a girl with braids wrapped around her head and lovely tilted hazel eyes that reminded Stella of Vivian Leigh. She had the Austrian accent.

Irma was from Berlin and the one that feared that Stella would be a knee-slapper. Maria had faith that she could dance but worried she was too short.

"Height isn't everything, Maria," said Frau Müller, still smiling at the chatter.

"That's right," said Hanni as she led Stella to the buffet and gave her a plate. "Louise was shorter than us and she married Hubert two weeks ago."

Inge put a roll on her plate. "Short doesn't matter if you got personality."

"You've got personality, haven't you, Sophie?" asked Hanni.

"I think so," said Stella and she gave them the smile that won over the men at the brewery when they didn't trust her to test a new batch of wort.

Hanni laughed. "There you go. You'll get in. Besides, Irena says you've got friends in high places."

"She doesn't need friends in high places with those eyes." Maria came over and looked at her. "You're not wearing mascara either?"

"No," said Stella.

"And that blue," said Inge and pouted. "Have you ever seen blue eyes with such dark lashes? She'll be engaged before me."

Frau Müller shushed her. "I told you. Sophie lost her fiancé in Poland."

Inge looked properly ashamed but almost instantly perked up. "There's still a chance for me then."

"There's no chance for you," said Irma. "You're too much of a flirt."

"Am not."

The two argued about the correct amount of flirting while the other girls loaded Stella's plate for her with slices of cheese and cold cuts along with a roll. It was a small but nice spread, especially considering the rationing. They sat at the table and asked her about Werner. She gave them her prepared biography with the unfortunate change in cause of death. She showed them her ring and they were tremendously unimpressed but hid it well. Stella suspected that they thought she was well shot of Werner and his cheap little ring and she felt sorry for her fictional fiancé.

"Well, there's a war on. You'll find a new one just like that." Inge snapped her fingers.

"Inge, please," said Hanni. "She's only just lost dear Werner. She won't want to marry for the longest time."

Inge tossed back her curls. "It won't be that long. We're not supposed to wait."

"Did you go to bride school?" asked Maria.

Stella lowered her eyes. "My mother didn't have the money, but she taught me everything I needed to know."

"I want to go, but I have to save up."

Hanni rolled her eyes. "You don't need to sit at a camp learning to darn socks and polish medals."

"I want to be a perfect wife," said Maria. "The Führer says we must prepare."

Irena touched Maria's chin. "You're perfectly beautiful. That's all you need."

That sparked a conversation about what a husband expected of a bride. Stella gathered that everything, except a brain and ambition, was on the list. They mentioned Obersturmbannführer this and Oberstleutnant that. The girls knew a lot of SS and Wehrmacht officers, not to mention politicians like Ribbentrop and Göring. They talked about Valkyrie and when, if ever, the Führer would grace their presence. Stella gathered Valkyrie was a new club and very exclusive. The girls longed for Henrich Himmler or Joseph Goebbels to make an appearance, getting them that much closer to the Führer.

The Poppers had mentioned a club called the Femina-Palast, but they made it seem like the club scene that had been wild during the Weimar Republic was practically dead now. The Valkyrie girls didn't agree with that at all and poo-pooed the Femina-Palast when Stella mentioned it. Anyone could get in there. Frau Müller had told them about Maximillian Hoff and the girls were intrigued but said that he must not be too important or close to the propaganda ministry, if he hadn't been invited to Valkyrie yet. Stella started to ask them about the ministry, but they were on to another subject, their thoughts buzzing around like bees outside a hive.

"Girls. Girls," called out Frau Müller. "Look at the time."

It was six and the girls jumped up. Stella was caught up in the crush of stacking plates and carrying them to the kitchen. They rushed into the hall, laughing and yelling, "Don't wait up!"

Frau Müller laughed back. "Don't worry."

Hanni waved at Stella. "Come with us, Sophie."

"That's right," said Inge. "You don't want to work at a factory."

Irma wrinkled her nose. "They're so dirty and what kind of men are there?"

"Old ones," said Inge.

"Or ones that can't fight," said Hanni.

They all wrinkled their noses at that. It was the ultimate in unattractive, other than poor, of course.

"I have to go to my mother's friend," said Stella. "She will be upset if I don't."

"Let her be upset," said Inge. "*We* don't need the extra rations here."

"Inge!" the girls all exclaimed together.

Inge put her hands over her mouth, but her eyes were more amused than anything else.

Hanni kissed Stella on the cheeks like they'd known each other forever. "Go see your mother's friend. We'll see you tomorrow."

The girls left in a flurry of hats, coats, and scarves. When they'd gone, Stella felt like all the air rushed out of the house with them, leaving her unbalanced and more than a little overwhelmed.

Frau Müller came into the hall drying her hands on her apron. "You'll get used to them."

"They're very…"

"Excited?"

"Yes exactly," said Stella.

"They're young and beautiful and working at Valkyrie. These are exciting times for them. The most exciting of their lives. It will be for you, too. Werner is gone. You can't bring him back."

"I know." Stella lowered her eyes demurely. "I don't know about meeting anyone else yet."

"You won't be able to help that at Club Valkyrie." She gave Stella her hat and coat. "Now go and find out if you have a job. Maybe it's at the Reichstag and then all the girls will be jealous."

They laughed together and then Stella went out into the night. She stood on the front steps for a moment to get her bearings. Berlin's blackout was in full effect and there was very little light, except for the moon and slits of yellow from windows that hadn't been totally covered.

She took a deep breath, letting herself adjust to more than just the light. Berlin was filled with people. She'd known that, of course. She studied the politics and looked at the estimations Park-Welles and the earl provided. She'd listened to Leo and Magda Popper's stories of their life in Germany before their escape. It wasn't all bad. They loved their homeland, even as they ran for their lives.

Now all those stories meant something that they couldn't possibly have meant before when Germany was Gabriele Griese holding a gun on Nicky in Paris or Peiper turning his boat toward the helpless Sorkines in the water. Germany had become more than that mindless hate and she would have to be very careful not to get comfortable and slip because those girls may laugh and tease, be beautiful and charming. They might love her in time and be the friends like she'd never really had outside of Florence and Mavis, but they could become Gabriele Griese at any moment and she must never forget it.

CHAPTER 6

Stella emerged from the Unter den Linden U Bahn station amazed to see so many people casually walking on the wide, tree-lined boulevard to and from the Pariser Platz where the American and French Embassies were along with the famous Hotel Aldon and the Brandenburg Gate. Ever the tourist, she had a moment where she considered taking a slight detour to the Platz, if nothing else but to see her embassy. It was ridiculous to go gaze at a symbol of her home like a child pressed against the glass of a candy store window, but she felt the need none the less.

Since it was dangerous as well as ridiculous, she followed her instructions with a little satisfaction that she could and would do as ordered, when it suited her anyway. Stella turned away from Pariser Platz down Wilhelmstrasse toward the now-vacant British Embassy and the Reich Chancellery. Park-Welles had made her memorize the location of Leon Klaus and had pummeled her with questions to make sure she was aware of the intricacies of finding the small bar. It wasn't a secret exactly, but it didn't bother to have a sign because in the German way of thinking if you wanted to go there, you'd know where it was.

Leon Klaus had been popularized by newspapermen and diplomats who wanted a break from the swanky Hotel Adlon, which was the place to see and be seen. The little bar was cheap, casual, and served hearty food. If she didn't spot Lester Nimitz right away, Stella was to order at the bar a Kartoffelpuffer—potato pancake—with apple sauce and a Fanta. She'd sit by the door to the men's toilet, where no one wanted to sit, and wait for him to see her when he showed up, which he was guaranteed to do every Saturday, Tuesday, and Thursday night.

If Lester Nimitz was there before Stella, she was to approach him and comment on the book he would have on the table with several others, *Mistress Devenant, The Dark Lady of Shakespeare's Sonnets*. She'd ask who he preferred as a suspect, Emilia Bassano Lanier or Marie Mountjoy. Nimitz would laugh heartily and say he favored Anne Hathaway, as a wife can often be seen as dark. He'd offer her a seat and order her Kartoffelpuffer. They'd have a lively discussion about the sonnets and when she finished eating, he'd offer to walk her to the U Bahn. On the walk, he'd give her instructions for the drop.

The way Park-Welles told it, Stella could expect this to go like clockwork, but she was ready for it to go wrong. She ran through the options as she walked down Wilhemstrasse imitating the purposeful walk of the German ladies passing her. No Italian swish of the hips or French tossing of hair desired or required. The German ladies were going somewhere and it was the shortest distance between two points. Attracting attention wasn't on the menu.

By the time she'd walked the two blocks and turned right to find the plain black door next to a lively Wursthaus, she'd gone through what she'd do if there were no seats at Nimitz's table or the seat next to the men's toilet was inexplicably taken. Satisfied that she had several plans in place, Stella opened the door to a bar, whose door didn't do it justice.

There was nothing plain about Leon Klaus. The bar was filled with a thick cloud of noxious smoke and raucous laughter. All the walls were covered in shelves that were filled with bottles, some full, some empty. The bar at the far end had every seat filled and the low trestle tables were nearly full, too. But most of the patrons, men and a few women, were standing, talking animatedly in several languages, including English and French, but mostly in German.

Stella pushed her way through a group of men arguing in a bewildering combination of English and German about when the first air strikes would hit the capital. Most said never. It wouldn't happen. A couple pessimists said it would be any day now. They ignored Stella completely and yelled over her head as she looked around for a small man in a rumpled brown suit with books. She could see why books would stand out in the bar. It would be impossible to read in the dim, smoky light and the only things most of the people were carrying were briefcases and the occasional camera. The ladies had their handbags, but that was it.

Stella skirted a pillar and decided the best course of action was to start outside and work her way in, pretending to look for a seat. Luckily, the bar wasn't all that big and there were about sixty people inside. After her trip around, she went down the right side toward the bar. She spotted her seat next to the men's toilet and it was empty and for good reason. When she got close, she caught a whiff and didn't relish eating anything in the vicinity. The need to find Nimitz already there spurred her on until she reached the pillar closest to the bar. She squeezed around it, almost knocking over a beer and calling out her apologies when she saw a brown suit behind a pillar at the other end of the bar. The man was small and bent forward like he was looking at a book.

Stella straightened her shoulders and licked her lips. Her first contact, right where he was supposed to be. What luck! The man stood up and her view was blocked by a fat German with an enormous beer stein. She darted to the left to get a view of the table from the other side of the pillar to double-check that the Shakespeare book was there. She was absolutely certain it would be and she was right. *Mistress Devenant, The Dark Lady of Shakespeare's Sonnets* sat on a stack of other studious works on various poets, like Wordsworth and Keats. She went for the table and heard to her great joy the sound of American voices.

"Look I'm going to Paris tomorrow. You can go to Poland and cover it," said a man in a New York accent.

"I just got back from Warsaw. I'll take Paris," said another man who sounded like he could be from Missouri or Kansas.

The two went back and forth about assignments when another American voice cut through the clatter. Stella stopped, every muscle in her body tensed, and she waited. It couldn't be. It simply couldn't.

"I hear you, but I promised my mother on her deathbed. I don't break a promise. Hand on heart."

That twang so distinctive in its Western roots, she'd have known it anywhere. Sweat broke out under her arms and she ducked right, but she couldn't just leave. She had to confirm. Stella took a breath and went back left, carefully ducking behind the fat German who took the opportunity to pinch her bottom, giving her a broad smile and a wink. Stella could hardly be bothered to acknowledge something that would normally have gotten him a swift kick. She leaned to the side and peeked around the German's well-padded shoulder. Two men parted and she got a good view of her contact from the side. He was a small man with a red nose in a rumpled brown suit. He was Cyril Welk.

The German pinched her again and she straightened up, calling him a naughty boy, just like Pamela Churchill would've done, and it turned him pink with pleasure. He offered to buy her a beer and she said she'd like that very much, but nothing too heavy. She was watching her figure. He said he was watching her figure, too, as if that was an original line, and made for the bar. Stella went left, doing her best not to look panicked. Cyril Welk. Her contact was Cyril Welk.

At one time she would've trusted him with her life. She *had*, in fact, trusted him with her life. His hat saved Nicky when they were escaping Vienna and then he turned up at the vineyard where she crashed after Hans' death at his brewery. Cyril was supposedly a British agent working with the resistance in Germany and Austria. He helped her get out and to Paris where she was supposed to meet Nicky. But he betrayed her, delaying her arrival at Napoleon's tomb where she was supposed to meet her husband, in order to let the SS arrest Nicky. She managed to escape Cyril when she realized he had no intention of taking her to meet Nicky and the two of them barely got away. Stella had told the earl, Mr. Bast, and Park-Welles about Cyril. He was a double agent. He was working for the Reich. They appeared to believe her, taking notes and nodding seriously. To be honest, with everything that had happened since Paris, Cyril Welk had disappeared from her mind. She assumed he'd been dealt with, eliminated somehow, and was gone for good. But now he was there, still a British agent and working in the US embassy of all places. If Stella hadn't been so intent on getting the hell out of the bar, she might've thrown up. Had he seen her? He'd recognize her, if he did. No doubt about that. Cyril had shown every sign that he'd fallen for her and he had tried to keep her back from the SS. She assumed to protect her, but who knew what he was up to.

She reached the door, but before she could grab the lever, a man flung it open, and a long plaintive wail filled the bar. He yelled about getting to the closest bunker. Stella slipped outside, heading for Wilhelmstrasse. She couldn't worry about air raids. She had to get away.

"No, no!" A man grabbed her. "This way."

She tried to wrench her arm out of his grasp, but another man came up on her other side. "You must go to safety, Fräulein."

People were yelling at each other for directions and Stella was caught up in the throng. The crowd headed for a hotel across the street. In moments she was inside and being pushed down the stairs. She heard the twang behind her. Cyril was coming, too.

WILD TALK SWIRLED around Stella as they went down a second set of stairs leading down into the musty depths below the basement of the hotel. When she reached the shelter it wasn't a rustic pit filled with cobwebs and rat droppings. The shelter had one central chamber with white-washed walls and benches around the perimeter. Off that chamber were rooms, labeled "Raum für 10 personen" ten rooms in all. Some were labeled Männer and some Frauen und Kinder. Every wall had Rauchen Verboten! painted in large letters.

The central chamber filled up quickly. Stella could hear Cyril's twang cutting through the clamor, but he was short and she couldn't see where he was. She pushed her way to the back of the room and saw with relief a sign saying "Zum Frauen Abort". That was new to her, but it was for women, so she was all for that.

She edged her way over and pushed through the door. It wasn't as she hoped, an exit, but a bathroom instead with a row of toilets and sinks. She put her back to the wall beside the door and slowed her breathing. Cyril or Lester or whoever he was wouldn't come in there unless he'd already spotted her. She could just stay there until everyone left. How long did these things take in Germany? Was it a drill or the real thing? That was when she considered for the first time where she was, the capital of Germany a couple of blocks from the Reich Chancellery, exactly where you wouldn't want to be during a bombing.

Don't panic. You're fine.

She took out her compact and powdered her nose. It gave her something to do while her mind raced around looking for solutions and finding none. She had all that money, but she'd be damned if she'd give it to Cyril Welk. It was impossible, even if she wanted to. Stella could hardly hand it over without going through the steps Park-Welles outlined. She'd be revealed and captured on her very first mission. The very idea was humiliating. She could just see Park-Welles shaking his head before going back to one of his puzzles. The new 'C' would know he was right not to put women in and Lady Churchill would be terribly let down, not to mention the earl and his personal quest for the location of little Anna Wildholz. She couldn't let him down. And Nicky. He couldn't bear it if something happened to her. There was the remote possibility that she'd get swapped in a prisoner exchange, but it was doubtful and if Peiper found out they had her, she'd be done for in the worst possible way.

No. The money would go back to where it came from. There. Decided. Of course, not accomplishing her mission meant failure and all the same things would happen, just not her death. She slid her hand in her pocket to touch Mr. Bast's cigarette case. He thought she could do something worthwhile so she'd just have to make sending her to Berlin worth it. She'd come back with something. She knew just how to do it and she'd find little Anna while she was at it. If it took more than two weeks, so be it.

There was a sharp knock and a man cracked opened the door. "Hallo?"

It wasn't the dreaded twang and she leaned over to wave. The man smiled and said the alarm was over. "A false one again," he said with a frown.

Stella sighed dramatically and he urged her to come out. She waved him off, but he insisted. Women and children first. Politeness was working against her again.

"No, no. I'm fine," she said.

"Fräulein. Now."

She gritted her teeth and tugged her hat lower on her forehead. He opened the door and she went back into the chamber, keeping her face downcast. She was herded with the few remaining women to the stairs past all the men waiting impatiently for a return to their steins.

Her heart pounded until she stepped on the stairs. Almost out. She followed a plain woman wearing glasses and a pretty blue coat who talked non-stop about "the ministry." By the time they reached the top of the rickety stairs out of the basement level Stella knew the woman was named Brunhilde and was an assistant or secretary to Goebbels, who she apparently revered. If they were all that talkative, her mission would be easy.

Stella held onto the worn handrail and thought about her path back to the U Bahn. No need to delay. She'd go straight back and get to work.

"Danke," said Brunhilde as she hurried into the main floor of the hotel. "Very kind."

A hand reached for Stella. Surprised, she took it. "Danke." She looked up and her heart stopped. Cyril looked back at her, his dark hazel eyes wide with shock and his mouth open. A woman poked her from behind. "Hurry up! I haven't got all night."

Stella let go, pushed past Cyril, and squeezed into the crowd of people coming in from all directions. There must've been other exits or other shelters. Something. She shoved her way through, knocking into the fat German, who yelped in surprise.

"Hey there!" called out Cyril, his twang holding strong.

Stella elbowed an embracing couple out of her way and stumbled onto the street.

"Somebody grab that girl!" Cyril yelled behind her. "The pretty one."

A man looked at her and made a move to take her arm. She smacked him across the face yelling, "How dare you touch me!"

He jerked back, astonished, and she ran into the slow-moving traffic, narrowly avoiding getting run down by a truck.

"Wait!"

She wasn't waiting. She was running. For her life and quite possibly Anna Wildholz's life.

CHAPTER 7

"You poor darling," exclaimed Hanni.

Stella shook her head. "I don't know what to do. My mother. I must write her."

Hanni flipped her braids back over her shoulders and hugged Stella fiercely. "Yes. Write her right away. So sad that her friend died and you missed the funeral, too"

"She might want me to come back home."

Inge whipped off her apron and tossed it on a settee before dropping exhausted onto a dining chair. "You can't go home to your mother. Where's the fun in that?"

"You know what to do," said Maria. "You'll come to work with us at Valkyrie. You'll recommend her, won't you, Irena?"

Frau Müller said that she would and offered a cup of coffee that didn't quite taste right, like someone mixed acorns in with the beans, but hit the spot regardless. "You can use the newspaperman as a reference, too."

"I wish Otto was here," said Irma. "He could get you in."

"Who's Otto?" asked Stella.

Irma beamed. "My twin brother. Otto is a Kriegsmarine and he is a comrade of the owner's son."

"That is a shame, but Sophie can use the newspaperman as a reference," said Irena.

Stella considered that. Maximillian Hoff's name might mean something, but it was best to stick to the truth as close as possible. She had enough lies to remember already. "I have to tell you the truth."

The Valkyrie girls leaned in around the dining table, a cloud of cigarette smoke and rank booze coming with them. When Stella had gotten up the next morning the girls were just coming home at six. No wonder they ate breakfast at five in the afternoon.

Inge grinned. "I knew it. He's the one who brought you to Berlin. You'll be engaged in a month." Her grin turned into a frown. "And I won't."

"Inge, please," said Frau Müller. "What is it, Sophie?"

"I don't really know Herr Hoff." She told them quickly how she met him on the platform and that he'd given her a ride. She didn't know why he acted like they were really acquainted.

Frau Müller smiled. "I suspected he didn't know you well."

Stella widened her eyes. "How did you know?"

"You didn't look happy. Like you wanted to be on your own, but he wouldn't go away."

Very true.

"I didn't want to inconvenience him or fool you into thinking I had a powerful friend. I don't. I don't know anyone," said Stella.

Hanni sat her down and said, "Yes, you do. You know us."

"We talked to Frau Bothe last night," said Irma and all the girls made a face simultaneously.

"Who's that?" asked Stella. The girls seemed to like everyone and this wasn't a good sign.

"Our matron," said Irma. "She watches over us at Valkyrie."

"She's our nanny," said Inge with her lower lip poking out.

"She's your nanny. She never says anything to me," said Hanni.

"Perfect Hanni," said Maria. "If you could just drop one glass our lives would be better."

Hanni looked scandalized. That was clearly out of the question.

"Herta Bothe is...strict," said Frau Müller.

Inge crossed her arms. "Too strict."

Frau Müller set a platter of fresh rolls on the table. "No butter today."

Irma jumped up. "Yes, there is." She dug in her handbag and came out with a square block wrapped in paper.

Hanni clapped her hands. "Oh, you genius. Who was it this time?"

"I'll never tell." Irma unwrapped the block and revealed a hefty amount of butter, probably double the weekly ration.

"Do get some chocolate next time," said Inge, taking a good smear for her roll.

"No one has chocolate."

"I bet that Wehrmacht, von Drechsel, could get it. Rudolph says he has connections to the Ritter family," said Maria.

Inge wrinkled her nose. "He won't do anything. He doesn't even talk. I don't know why he comes to the club. He only makes everyone uncomfortable."

The girls agreed but seemed vaguely guilty about it.

"So you'll work at Valkyrie with us." Hanni licked butter off her fingers. "You might get the chocolate with those eyes."

Frau Müller sat next to Stella and patted her hand. "You understand the butter is something that is not quite…what we are supposed to have."

She didn't say black market or graft, but Stella assumed the high-ranking officials that frequented Valkyrie had access to more than their fair share.

"I understand that it's good to work at Valkyrie."

She smiled. "It is."

"Can I…make enough money to help my mother?" Stella asked. "I can't send her butter."

"Don't worry about that," said Irma, smugly. "Fifty Reichsmarks a week."

"I didn't expect that." Stella bit her lip. "Do you think Frau Bothe will like me?"

"She doesn't like anyone," said Maria. "Not even Hanni, but you're very pretty and sweet. With Irena speaking for you and Herr Hoff, you won't have a problem."

"But I told you, I don't really know Herr Hoff," said Stella.

"Frau Bothe doesn't know that and besides he said he thought you'd be a Valkyrie girl. He won't mind." Irma grinned and stabbed the butter. "Men never mind helping us."

The girls finished their rolls and headed off to sleep Sunday away. It was decided. Stella would go to Valkyrie with them on Monday and request a job in the most exclusive club in Berlin. Frau Müller finished her roll and made a face when she finished her coffee. "You'll do well, Sophie. The officers need pretty girls to serve them and have a good time. Mind your manners and you won't have any problems with Frau Bothe."

"Is she really terrible?"

"She expects the girls to behave the way the Führer would want, as sweet maidens until marriage."

Stella caught a hint of sarcasm but didn't ask about it. "Will she give me the dirndl to wear?"

"Yes and I can hem it for you. Louise's will be too long."

"I can hem it. I know how," said Stella and watched with pleasure as Frau Müller warmed to the idea. "Frau Bothe will like that. Mention that you sew. It is an essential skill. Not all the girls do, but they must learn."

"I will." Stella finished her roll and coffee. The taste got worse the more she drank it.

"What will you do today?"

"I thought I would go to visit Frau Klink's grave. Mother would like that," said Stella.

"A very respectful thing to do on a Sunday." Frau Müller started to clear the dishes and shooed Stella away. "I will do it. You go pay your respects and explore our fine city."

"Thank you, Frau Müller. I will."

"You may call me Irena, like the other girls," she said kindly.

Stella thanked her and congratulated herself on being accepted into the fold completely. She got her hat, coat, and handbag and headed out, not to a cemetery but to take her first steps toward finding Anna. Now that Cyril knew she was there she would have to move fast. Two weeks in Berlin was her original timeframe so she had a little while before the earl or Park-Welles started wondering where she was. How long they would give her to return before sending out inquires wasn't something they'd briefed her on. She was expected to come back as ordered and she would, in her own sweet time.

STELLA WALKED down an avenue in the Charlottenburg district and wondered if she remembered the directions correctly. It'd taken over an hour to get to the right district. Some U Bahn lines were closed on Sundays or were closed for the construction of air raid shelters connected to the stations. As a result, Stella had to adapt and find another way that included walking fifteen blocks in the frigid cold and she needed a cup of coffee badly.

On a main avenue, she found an open bakery but realized she'd given all her ration cards to Irena. The man behind the counter nodded in understanding and then offered to sell her a cup of some kind of roasted barley concoction for half a Reichsmark. He knew the price was both ridiculous and illegal, telling Stella in a whisper she'd have to drink the cup in the back so no one would see her and question where her ration card was.

She declined because any attention was bad attention and went back out into the cold, wishing she had a map. Eventually she happened upon the right street of elegant apartment buildings that reminded Stella of Vienna with their creamy stone walls and classical pediments. The Wildholz's building was number one and their name was no longer on the label next to the buzzers. Apartment 2A had Beck next to it.

The entrance door was locked so she pushed the button and ran through her plan as she waited. The earl had no leads on Anna Wildholz's whereabouts, only addresses. He and Anna's grandfather didn't believe for a moment that the loyal nanny, Gertruda Hoppe, would abandon her to an orphanage. She'd be with the nanny somewhere in Berlin. Find the nanny. Find the girl. Stella's thoughts seesawed back and forth. In England, she felt quite confident, but it was a lot different in Berlin. The city was huge and the possibilities endless.

"Hallo?" Although it was nearly ten by this time the voice was sleepy and irritated.

"Hallo. I'm looking for Gertruda Hoppe, please," said Stella.

There was a pause and Stella got a feeling in her gut that wasn't good.

"Who is this?"

"Sophie Weber from Munich. My mother sent me to see Frau Hoppe. They are old friends and she wanted me to say hallo."

A window opened above Stella and she leaned back to see a woman in a dressing gown staring down at her. She looked her over and then closed the window. Stella waited for the woman to say something else, but nothing happened. She was about to push the buzzer again when a girl in a prim housemaids uniform showed up at the door and beckoned her inside. She was young, about fifteen, and nervous.

"Frau Beck asks you to come up." The maid fiddled with her apron and Stella couldn't decide whether she was worried that Stella would come up or that she wouldn't.

"Is she angry that I've come?" asked Stella.

The maid whispered, "Frau Hoppe worked for the Jews."

"Oh! Did she?"

"You didn't know?"

"I only know that she works here."

The maid shook her head. "Not anymore. Not since the Jews left."

Stella wanted to say that Lotti Wildholz wasn't a Jew, but it would've been revealing and unhelpful. "Do you know where she went?"

"Please come up," the maid pleaded.

"Will I get in trouble?"

She lowered her voice. "Do you have your identification?"

"Yes, of course."

She relaxed and waved her inside. They walked past a small elevator and went up an elegant but narrow staircase to the second floor. The building was very nice, but not as expensive as Stella expected. Lotti was an heiress and Joseph owned or had owned a large and successful business. The building said well-fixed but not well off and there was a difference.

"Do you know when Frau Hoppe left?" Stella asked.

"The mistress will tell you." The tone of her voice said that was the end of that and Stella decided not to press. She was a casual visitor after all. This couldn't seem too important to her.

"Thank you. I will ask her."

The maid glanced at her and the expression wasn't one that made Stella any more comfortable.

On the second floor, the door to apartment 2A was open and the woman from the window leaned on the casement smoking a cigarette in a long holder and looking at her with narrowed eyes. "You want to know about the Jews?"

"No. I came to visit Frau Hoppe. She isn't a Jew," said Stella, doing her best to appear bewildered.

"We own this apartment," said the woman, her voice raspy.

"I understand. Did Frau Hoppe work for you? My mother said she worked at this address."

A man came up behind the woman. He wore an SS uniform and a sneer. "Another one?"

"Yes," said the woman and she took a long drag while keeping her eyes on Stella.

"I'm only looking for my mother's friend."

"The Jews aren't here anymore. We own this apartment," said the officer.

"Do you know where Frau Hoppe is?"

He passed his wife and thrust out his hand at her. "Show me your identification."

"Of course." Stella got out her identification card and he snatched it out of her hand.

"Not a Jew, I see," he said, flashing the card at his wife.

"No. I'm sorry to bother you. I thought Frau Hoppe lived here."

He looked her over. His face lost all its suspicion and he smiled at her. "We bought this apartment. The Jews are gone. The servants were questioned and fined. I don't know where they went."

"Fined?"

"They worked for Jews. It is against the law."

Stella nodded sagely. "Oh, yes. I didn't know she worked for Jews. My mother didn't say so."

He sneered. "She probably lied. The Jews make people lie for them."

She pushed the anger down inside her where it couldn't possibly bubble to the surface. "May I ask when they left? I must tell my mother something."

"We bought the apartment in August. They were already gone."

Stella glanced past him into the apartment. It was quite nice, but the furniture wasn't right. Too large for the room and the artwork didn't say quality. The furniture was elegant and stylish, but the few pieces of art Stella saw were downright crappy. A print of blond children sitting next to a water lily pond. It wanted to be a Monet but was an insult to the master instead. Next to that was a bucolic landscape and the inevitable portrait of Hitler in a gilt frame, ridiculously large and pretty ugly. Stella's father would've ordered all three tossed in the trash.

"Thank you," she said. "I'm sorry to bother you."

"How long are you staying in Berlin?" the officer asked.

"I don't know. I want to get a job, but it's not easy."

He smiled at her. "A girl like you could work at the Femina-Palast. Do you dance?"

His wife frowned severely and blew smoke out the door at her. "That's enough. The Jews are gone."

Her husband stepped back inside and winked as he handed her her identification card. "Perhaps I'll see you there."

"Get in here, Greta," said the woman.

The maid scurried inside and the door slammed behind her. Stella took a breath and tucked her identification away. As she walked to the stairs she noticed the door to apartment 2B was cracked open and a faded blue eye was watching her.

"Hallo," she said cheerfully.

The door opened further and an old lady, wearing a heavy sweater and scarf, peeked out, glancing back at 2A. "They were arrested, you know," she whispered.

"Who?"

"The Jews."

"Why?"

The old lady shrugged. "Who can say? One day the Gestapo came and took the man away and then the wife. Then the SS takes the apartment. That is how it is."

Stella wanted to ask about Anna, but she didn't dare. "Do you know what happened to the servants?"

She glanced down the hall again. "They left after the wife was arrested." She looked back into her apartment. "Hilde, come here."

Another old lady, this one in a maid's uniform, appeared next to her mistress. "Yes?"

"Do you know where the Jews' servants went?"

"No, ma'am," she said. "They got in trouble for working for the Jews and they left."

"I'm looking for Frau Hoppe. Did you know her?"

The ladies nodded and the maid said, "She was a nice woman and she took very good care of the child."

"There was a child?"

They described Anna, but admitted that they'd rarely seen her. Frau Hoppe did take her for walks in her carriage and the child was quiet, clean, and well-dressed. She didn't scream and demand things like other children. Both ladies glanced down the hall at 2A.

"What happened to the child if the parents were arrested?"

"I don't know," said the mistress. "We came home one day and the SS was moving in. The child and servants were gone."

"Well, thank you," said Stella. "My mother will be disappointed that I didn't find her friend, but I don't know what else to do."

The maid tilted her head and said, "I did hear that they might have gone to the factory."

"Factory?"

They explained that the Jews had owned a fur business in the Mitte and maybe the servants had gotten work there. Stella thanked them and hurried down the stairs, out into the chill. The factory. Of course. It would still be operating in some capacity. She knew it had been confiscated as the property of a criminal, but someone might know where the family servants were. Stella only hoped it wouldn't take another hour to get there.

It DIDN'T TAKE AN HOUR, but it was hardly worth the journey. Stella stood at the entrance to a park, next to a sign saying that Jews weren't allowed to walk there. She couldn't imagine what was wrong with Jews taking a walk in the park, but apparently someone had thought of something and it was "strictly forbidden."

Across the street sat the Wildholz building. The old ladies had called it a factory and they weren't far off. It took up half the block and was six stories high. Over the door was a new name, Vogel, cheaply painted over where the name Wildholz had been carved in stone. It'd been chipped away, leaving evidence of the former owner in plain sight. They hadn't bothered to chip away the rest of the name. "& Sons" was still there.

Half the lower windows had been boarded up and the other half had new windows in place. There were the remains of red paint that someone had tried to scrub away, a hideous caricature of a face with a big nose and the word "Jüde" had been scrawled in several places. Vogel, whoever he was, had put a sign on the front door. "Under new management. No Jews."

Stella had hoped the place would be open. It was Sunday, but there was a war on. She knew from her training that businesses were being fitted to produce for the effort. Given the frigid winter, it could be reasonably expected to be producing clothing for the army or something, but the place was dark and deserted.

She'd have to come back and she dreaded it. The place had the look of a haunted house and an angry one at that. She sighed and turned around to walk back through the park, but she hadn't gotten ten feet before a Polizei stalked up and demanded her papers.

Without thinking, she retorted, "What for?" Luckily she'd done it in the correct accent and only garnered a look of irritation.

"I saw you looking at the Jews' place. Jews aren't allowed here."

Instead of giving him the good talking-to he so richly deserved, Stella pulled out her papers once again and handed them over. "I'm not a Jew." It hurt her to say it. Every time she did it felt like an indictment against Abel, the von Bodmanns, and now the Wildholzes, as if there was truly something bad in it.

He glanced at the papers and shoved them back at her, disappointed. "What were you doing?"

"I thought they might be open. I heard they were hiring," she said.

The Polizei nodded and lit a stubby cigarette. "They will be. They're closed for now."

"When will they be open again?"

He shrugged. "Politics. Who knows? A week. Maybe more."

"What has politics to do with business?" she asked.

"Everything." He turned her around and pointed through the trees at the sign. "Herman Vogel bought the business, but now someone else in the party wants it."

"If it's sold, it's sold, isn't it?"

He tweaked her chin like a kindly uncle, not a man who'd just been ready to arrest her for walking in a park. "You are young, aren't you?"

She thrust out her chin. "I'm twenty, not a child."

"All right. All right." He held up his hands as if being arrested and laughed. "It's politics and money. That is a valuable business. Vogel had a friend, who made sure he got it, and now this is being questioned. He may have to sell."

She slumped. "I hope it gets sorted out soon. I need a job."

"Factory workers get double rations, too." He finished his cigarette.

"Come back in a week. I hear they will be getting a contract for leather goods. Very lucrative."

She thanked him and hurried away through the park, hoping that she wouldn't be stopped again. Her hope was in vain. Another Polizei stopped her on the other side of the park as she exited. He wanted to know what her hurry was and demanded her papers. She went through the whole tiresome exercise again before escaping into a U Bahn station and heading back to Frau Müller's house.

THERE WAS SIMPLY no way around it. Stella had the right look. She did not have the right clothes. The Valkyrie girls had evaluated the situation on Sunday night and made a decision. She would have to go shopping and buy the right clothing to show off her assets to the dreaded Frau Bothe. There was a line of girls around the block that wanted to work at Valkyrie and Stella's cheap and "quaint" clothes wouldn't fit the bill. Stella didn't get a vote. She was hardly allowed to say anything at all.

They spent the evening playing games and counting up the points on the clothing ration cards they pooled together. Stella was too short to wear any of their clothes and Frau Bothe would recognize something borrowed anyway. Her shortness was a challenge. Frau Bothe favored long stems, so they decided shoes were in order, too. Stella's were a serviceable black and did nothing for her slim ankles.

"I wish we could go to Herzog's," said Hanni.

"They're so expensive," said Irma.

"We haven't got enough for shoes and a dress," said Marie. "One of us is bound to need something new this winter. Inge's gloves have a hole."

Inge laughed. "We don't have to have enough. We just need enough for tomorrow."

Irma wrinkled her nose. "I know what you're thinking and that isn't right."

Inge rolled her eyes. "You're so strict. It isn't hurting anyone."

"Says you."

"That's right. Says me." Inge explained her plan and she wasn't as much of a featherbrain as she seemed. They'd take Stella to Herzog's, a shoe store of the most stylish shoes, and buy something that made Stella a lot taller and would show off what the girls decided was her third best asset, her short but shapely legs.

Hanni shook her head. "That will be so expensive. Magda Goebbels gets her shoes there."

"We'll take them back on Tuesday, silly," said Inge.

"We can't do that."

"Why not?"

"Because Sophie will have worn them," said Irma with an increasing frown.

"Only for a few minutes. They won't even be scuffed." She explained that Sophie would wear her sad shoes to Valkyrie, slip on the Herzog shoes right before walking inside, Frau Bothe would see and admire Sophie's style, give her the job and the uniform to go with it. The shoes would come right off.

"That's brilliant," said Hanni. "We could do it with the dress, too."

Irma's eyes twinkled. "If I'd known you were coming, I could've gotten a dress for you."

"I don't know how you do it," said Maria. "All I've gotten is tins of sardines."

"Sardines are good for us," said Irena, looking up from her knitting. "The men know you are practical."

Maria sighed. "Obersturmbannführer Krebs is practical."

"And married," warned Inge. "Can't you find someone else?"

"He won't allow it. He says I am his sunshine."

"That's something," said Irma.

"Says you who gets dresses and butter from more officers than I can count."

The girls chattered the night away and Stella took note of the many names they mentioned. She used the memory devices that Park-Welles had taught her to lock them in her head. One of those names was going to give her what she needed, what England needed.

CHAPTER 8

Stella had her dress, a red number with a waist so tight breathing was optional, and the shoes that Inge insisted upon were in a little paper bag under her arm. They were adorable, black and red with darling little bows and heels that made her look a reasonable height. She hated to take them back, but that was the plan and she couldn't fight it.

Hanni had her by the hand as they raced up the stairs and out of the Kurfüstendamm U Bahn station for the second time that day. They'd bought Stella's dress and shoes on what the girls called the best shopping street in all of Berlin. Despite the rationing it'd been very busy and the girls' innate charm and copious use of the name Club Valkyrie had gotten them some bargains.

Nighttime wasn't any less busy. Like in London it was hard to imagine there was a war on, except for the blackout. The girls' laughter certainly didn't demonstrate any worry at all. Stella had made a few comments about the war, trying to get an impression of how they felt about it and had gotten little other than sympathy for her loss of Werner. Other than that they didn't seem to mind one way or the other about the war or why it was happening. The rationing was annoying and inconvenient. They hated the cold house and restricted hot water but seemed to accept it readily. Only Hanni and Maria had expressed any worry at all about how long it would go on. The rest of the girls and Irena didn't think it would last. Obviously the Führer knew what he was doing so why worry.

The girls garnered attention from every quarter as they pranced down the avenue. They'd left their coats open—in spite of the cold—to reveal their distinctive black dirndls with the red aprons and gold trim that were instantly recognizable as Club Valkyrie. They were extraordinarily pretty and tall and had gotten a good amount of attention shopping earlier, but it was nothing like nighttime in those dirndls. Absolutely everyone noticed them. People stopped them to say hello and made way so they could pass through the crowd unhindered. So much admiration, envy, and, yes, a little disapproval, mostly from matronly women, but a few men, too. Stella thought this must be what being a film star was like. She knew the Nazi elite were followed in the papers like stars. Where did they go? Who did they like? Who were their wives or girlfriends? Nobody felt that way about politicians or military leaders in the States. Women went wild for Hitler, which made no sense to Stella on any level, but they did, so it made sense that girls that got to mix with the elites would hold a certain kind of acclaim, but she was still surprised to see it in action. Quite a few men made sure to gently brush up against them, very discreetly, but they did it as if the glamour could rub off. Irma got four business cards with offers for dinner and so did Hanni. A young girl said that Irma should be a film star and everyone got similar compliments, except Stella. She was just another face without the black, red, and gold.

The girls left the main avenue after a few blocks and went down a more sedate street.

"It's so quiet here," said Stella.

Hanni laughed. "It won't be in a couple of hours."

"When does the club open?"

"Monday through Thursday at five. Friday and Saturday at seven."

"Why the difference?"

"So the guests won't stay out so late," said Irma. "They have work to do."

"Mondays are always short," said Maria. "Thank goodness."

"Here we are," said Hanni as she tugged on Stella's arm to cross the street toward a building on a corner. It was four stories high with pillars and pediments. The sign for Club Valkyrie was oddly understated for such a large building. Unlike every other club she'd seen, it wasn't advertising its delights. There were no posters or enticements of any kind and on the wide bank of doors there were signs saying "By Invitation Only" and three doormen keeping guard.

"Don't you have dancers and singers?" Stella asked.

Maria laughed. "It wouldn't be a club without them."

"How does anyone know who's performing?"

Irma brushed that away with her nose in the air. "Those who need to know, know. We don't want people off the streets."

Heaven forbid.

A doorman acknowledged the girls with a crisp nod and a clicking of his heels before he opened the door for them.

"Thank you, Roderick," said Hanni and she waltzed in, holding Stella's hand.

The lobby was sumptuous with thick red carpets, polished brass, and dark wood paneling. It was completely empty, but smelled amazing. Stella's mouth began to water as she smelled some of her favorite German foods, Sauerbraten and Schweinhaxe. Irena had made a very nice pork roast on Sunday using over half their meat rationing for the week, but it smelled nothing like that.

Hanni turned left and they bypassed the beautiful doors labeled main floor and went for a side door tucked away out of sight and labeled Backstage. Once through the door, Stella was instantly overwhelmed. The lobby and club may have been empty, but backstage more than made up for it. She slipped on her fancy Herzog shoes and bagged her old black ones before they headed into the fray.

The warren of hallways teemed with other girls in the club dirndls and dozens of performers in various costumes, all sparkling and ornate. Down in the depths of the club under the main stage were so many props, platforms, and set pieces, Stella had no clue what a performance might look like and couldn't see how anyone could keep it straight. They were constantly being greeted and embraced. Hanni introduced Stella to so many people, she immediately forgot their names. There wasn't any time to use one of Park-Welles techniques. They came at her too fast.

The girls squeezed past pulleys and gears, careful not to muss up their dirndls and finally got to a dressing room marked "A". Inside was a long stretch of lighted mirrors and seats. More Valkyrie girls were seated there, touching up their makeup or putting on stockings.

"Who is this?" A woman came in from another door with a clipboard and a bun in her hair so tight her eyes were stretched.

Hanni held out her arms like she was a displaying a brand new car. "This is your new girl."

The woman, who had to be the dreaded Herta Bothe, lifted her upper lip in disdain and looked over Stella with those slitted eyes. "She's too short." She made a shooing motion. "Go away."

The girls went at her like starving mosquitoes, buzzing around and darting in with demands and questions.

"We're short three girls," said Maria.

"It's been weeks," said Hanni.

"She's beautiful," said Inge.

"Some of the officers are quite short," said Irma. "They won't stand next to me."

"Hess told me I'm too tall," said Hanni, "and I'm shorter than Irma."

Frau Bothe was unmoved. "Everyone is shorter than Irma. My girls must look like a Greek statue. This girl is…not."

"But look at that face," said Maria.

"Those eyes."

"And the prettiest legs."

They wore Bothe down with her good traits, whipping off her coat to show off her figure and pulling her skirt up to admire her legs. Stella felt like a prize pig and it didn't work. What did work was Irena's recommendation and her so-called friendship with Herr Hoff.

"He hasn't been invited," said Bothe.

"Not yet, but you said yourself, we will admit the newsmen soon. It's good for the war effort," said Inge from a chair next to a redhead who looked just like Marlene Dietrich, only friendly and with even less eyebrows.

Everyone was surprised. Inge didn't remember the time of day quite literally and this came out of nowhere. She'd been admiring her ankles and feet with apparently little interest in the outcome.

"Oh, come on, Frau Bothe," said the redhead. "Just hire her. We need the help and they'll never give up."

"Look at her tiny little legs," said the sneering matron.

The redhead slapped a science journal on the makeup table, stood up, and Stella thought she was sunk. That girl was six feet tall and had legs like curvy stilts. "It's good to have variety." She bent down and looked in Stella's eyes. "My brown is nothing to her blue."

Bothe threw up her hands. "Yes, yes. Fine. Hanni, get her fitted for a dirndl. Try to find one that doesn't sweep the floor." She wrote something on her clipboard, glared at Stella, and disappeared out the door.

The redhead put out her hand. "Clara."

"Sophie. Thank you for your help."

"It was nothing. She would've hired you eventually."

"You think so?"

She sat down and extended those amazing legs. "She knows height has its limitations. I haven't gotten one proposal and I'm not likely to get any."

"You will," said Hanni. "You're lovely."

"I'm not a good candidate for a wife and you know it."

"You could learn to sew and talk about *them*."

Clara sighed. "I tried, but I can't. They just aren't as fascinating as they think they are."

Another girl shushed her and looked around nervously. Clara rolled her eyes. "Go and get your dirndl, Sophie. We'll soon know if you're easily fascinated."

The girls took Stella through to another room and got her fitted into a dirndl that was tighter than her dress.

"Don't mind Clara," said Hanni. "The men are interesting."

Maria snorted. "Not all of them."

"She's not popular," said Irma.

Hanni put a necklace around Stella's neck. It had a swastika on it and she flinched when it touched her skin. "Clara can't help herself. She makes some of the men feel stupid."

"Some of the men are stupid," said Maria.

Inge giggled. "Some of us are stupid."

"Speak for yourself," said Irma.

"Well, I'm not speaking for you."

"I hope not. Sophie, are you comfortable?" asked Maria.

Stella had never been less comfortable in her life and that was saying something, considering she'd had severe frostbite and been in a plane crash. Being in the land of the enemy was one thing, wearing the uniform was another. She couldn't have anticipated how ill it would make her feel.

"Sophie?" asked Hanni. "Are you well?"

"I'm...just worried they won't like me," she said.

"They'll like you, just don't quote Russian literature or describe how and why we failed at Cambrai. No one wants to hear about fail-ure," said Irma. "Everyone knows it's different this time. We're fated to win every battle."

The girls all nodded like this was something they truly believed.

"What about what the Führer wrote in *Mein Kampf*?" It just popped out and Stella had a split second where she pictured herself grabbing the words and stuffing them back in her mouth.

"What did he write?" asked Hanni.

"Oh, um...nothing."

"Tell us." Irma was stiff and unyielding. She'd have to say it.

"Just that one of the greatest mistakes of the Kaiser was fighting England."

The girls laughed. "The Kaiser? That foolish cripple. Why worry about what he did?" asked Hanni.

"I just worry because we are fighting England again," said Stella. "That's all."

"We're winning," said Inge. "We've sunk their ships and against us, nothing."

Hanni fluffed Stella's hair. "Don't worry. They won't really fight us."

Maria nodded. "Everyone says so."

Everyone.

"But they declared war," said Stella.

The girls waved that away and Hanni put on her apron, carefully tying the bow on the left side to show she was available. "The British will make peace. They know our strength."

"After France, it will be all over," said Maria. "And things will go back to normal."

Stella's chest tightened. "What's going to happen in France?"

"Oh, nothing. The men talk," said Irma. "We shouldn't."

The girls hustled her back out to the dressing room and showed her off, even though her skirt hung halfway down past her knees. Try as she might she couldn't get them to say another word about France and Irma was watching her with fresh eyes. She'd have to be careful with her.

CLUB VALKYRIE MIGHT NOT HAVE BEEN opulent on the outside, but it certainly was on the inside. After her appearance was approved by a clearly disapproving Bothe, Stella was taken for a quick tour of the main room and it was truly astonishing. There were exactly one hundred tables that were booked and full every night. They were arranged in an oval with several levels leading down to a center floor. The setup reminded Stella of a baseball stadium, except in this case, the field was a performance and dance space that had a series of hydraulic lifts that changed the configuration of the floor in dazzling ways. Even more interesting were the tubes built into the handrails around the tables. They were pneumatic tubes for sending messages and gift requests.

"Here's the menu," said Hanni. "It's simple really."

Stella looked through a little handbook that showed an array of gifts one could send to other tables, anything from champagne to jewelry. One just wrote down their order on the slips provided and stuck it in the tube. The request would be sucked directly to the staff in the back who sent the order out to the right table.

Inge's lower lip poked out. "We're not supposed to receive the gifts."

Maria sighed. "You're at the tables. You can flirt in person."

Inge lifted the receiver of the phone on the table. "They can flirt in person, too."

Every table had a pneumatic tube and a phone. Stella wouldn't have thought German men would need so much help with flirting, but the girls said many were shy and liked to open with a gift to see how it was received before they called or approached the table. Stella was glad that when Nicky saw her for the first time at his mother's garden party, he walked right over and said, "Don't fall over that balcony. It's a long way down. I'd hate to have to clean up your blood." His mother was horrified and harangued him about it, but he didn't take his eyes off her and they were twinkling with mirth. Stella couldn't stop smiling back. Men usually said things like, "Your eyes are like limpid pools of liquid sapphires." It was always embarrassing and didn't work, although Stella was never quite sure what they were actually going for. It would be interesting to see German men in action. Love and flirting wasn't something she'd been briefed on or anything she associated with the regime. When she thought of them she thought of hate and death. Their flags and uniforms practically demanded it. This would be a different side. One she could use.

"This will be your section tonight," said Hanni. "It's not very good, but you'll work your way up."

Stella learned about serving drinks and food in the few moments before the doors opened. Of all the things she'd studied, waitressing was not one of them and she'd never paid much attention to the skill, but even if she had it wouldn't have helped much. Waitresses in the States weren't like Valkyrie girls. She was expected to dance with the men at her tables, if requested, and sit down for a chat whenever possible. Maria described the job as mother, sister, waitress, girl-friend, and confessor all rolled into one. Irma wasn't happy with that, but the girls ignored her. Stella had four tables to care for and if she was good at it, the tips would be generous and the rationing would cease to matter. Stella was more interested in the confessions, but if mother, sister, waitress, and girlfriend got her confessor, she was all for it.

When the doors opened at five, Stella expected a trickle of patrons, but it was a surge. Getting a table at Valkyrie, even when invited, wasn't easy. The massive amount of suits and uniforms in grey, blue, and black mixed with the ladies in their finest gowns and furs.

Stella's tables were full by six when the first performance started, an under-the-sea tribute to the Nazi fleet that included octopuses and sharks wandering among the tables. After that it was a version of the Ziegfeld Follies without the Jewish housewife, of course.

Hanni thought her tables weren't any good, but they were plenty good for her. All four tables were taken up by executives from Siemens and they weren't quiet. The jolly Borland brothers, a pair of corpulent balding men, took an instant liking to Stella. They were barely taller than she was, so Frau Bothe had chosen her tables well. She brought them and their friends beers, shared stories of Munich, danced with the unmarried Heinrich, and served platters of Schwein-shaxe with potato dumplings and red cabbage while listening to their worries and woes. After beer and schnapps, they spoke freely, competing with the acts on stage that didn't interest them. They didn't like the company head who wasn't an ardent party member and they couldn't get the workers and materials they needed to meet the government demands. Something must be done and they were pushing for help from the high command to get the labor they needed.

Stella dared ask what Siemens made and they happily explained in detail how they were making essential electrical equipment for the military, like the anti-aircraft searchlights, and special components for aircraft needed for the coming movement. The movement and particular parts weren't defined. They didn't want to get technical with a woman, but she gathered these parts were important to winning the war and the factories were near Berlin. Soon they would only be engaged in war effort. She was very impressed and they were impressed with her and her big blue eyes and tiny waist.

The night was a blur, the music, the lights, the Borland brothers. Stella lost track of how many times she was on the floor whirling around and laughing. Her mouth hurt from smiling and her bottom from being pinched. By the time the last performance ended, Stella had completely lost track of time. The men at her tables never seemed to tire. They ate, talked, and danced for hours. None of them used the pneumatic tubes and had not flirted with anyone beyond her. During her short breaks, she saw Hanni who happily told her she had the Chief of the Armed Forces Field Marshal Wilhelm Keitel and his wife at her table. It was almost like having the Führer in the room to her, but Stella caught Clara rolling her eyes.

After the Siemens executives left, Stella gathered her tips, which were astonishing. She'd made nearly twenty Reichsmarks. Hanni and Maria were delighted for her. The executives usually tipped well, but not that well. They made sure that sour Frau Bothe knew how well she'd done, but she only responded with, "Have Frau Müller hem your skirt."

Stella told her that she could do it herself and that seemed more impressive than the money. Whatever worked. Hanni thought she might get to the main tables in a week if she kept it up. Several of the other girls weren't doing so well and Stella had a good chance to serve high-ranking officials. They usually came in on the weekends, commanding the tables by the dance floor where they could be seen by everyone easily.

The girls kept up a steady chatter as they put on their coats, buttoning them fully this time, and Stella couldn't keep up she was so tired.

"It's good you started on an easy night," said Irma.

"Easy?"

"No one insisted on staying late. Sometimes they do that."

The girls, including Clara, groaned in unison.

"What happens?" Stella asked.

"We stay until they're ready to leave," said Maria, a severe frown on her face. "I don't like it at all and they never tip well."

They all agreed that the demanding ones never tipped well. The tables with wives or girlfriends weren't good either. Hanni took Stella's arm and they walked out of the bowels of Club Valkyrie and into the lobby where the doormen were running little carpet sweepers and looking as tired as Stella felt.

"I'm so tired," said Stella. "I can't believe how much energy those Borland brothers had."

"I know," said Inge. "I've had them before. They're so fat you'd think they'd have to rest."

"They come ready," said Irma.

Stella didn't know what that meant and she didn't care. It was three o'clock in the morning. She had to look at the clock twice on the way out. Three o'clock. Why did the Reich allow it? Her father was so strict about work. He was in bed by ten on most nights and up at five. Even Uncle Josiah with his wild ways restricted himself to the weekends. Mostly.

"This is early?" she asked.

The girls laughed as they walked out into the cold and a cab pulled up for them. They crammed themselves into one car and Hanni said, "It's six on the weekends."

Stella sighed and closed her eyes. The earl better do something with her Siemens information or she wasn't sure this was going to be worth it.

CHAPTER 9

Stella's first week at Valkyrie went by astonishingly fast. It was Saturday and she'd done nothing to find Anna Wildholz. She'd worked and slept. Entertaining Nazis was more draining than she'd imagined and, except for the Borland brothers, she had nothing to show for it. Frau Bothe had moved her up a little, but her tables all had had wives at them. Men with wives didn't talk about the war in any kind of detail and she got nothing useful.

Having given up on her own ability to get up in the morning, Stella borrowed an alarm clock from Hanni and forced herself to set it for noon. Friday had been a night that she thought would never end. The party lasted until six thirty and they didn't leave until seven when the streets were already alive with the shops opening and the smell of morning baking wafting over the streets.

Stella dropped into bed at seven thirty and cried herself to sleep in total exhaustion. She'd started to dream in German and it felt like it was getting under her skin and she might not be able to wash it off. Park-Welles had said that when she dreamt in a language that's when she'd know she was truly fluent, but she'd rather not. All those faces and uniforms in her dreams had replaced Nicky, his smell, face, and the way he held her. She didn't dream about being in the brewery with her father testing the wort or flying with Uncle Josiah anymore. She even missed the bad dreams where Abel disappeared into the darkness of the boxcar where he would die. At least then she was thinking of someone she cared for, not some SS who pinched her leg so hard she had big purple bruises.

When the alarm went off, she very nearly went back to sleep, but a sound, like a voice, kept waking her up every time she drifted off. It couldn't be the other girls. They wouldn't get up until five at least.

"Hello?" she called out. "Irena?"

There wasn't an answer and she started to snuggle back down into the warmth of the covers, but she remembered the earl's worried face and sat up to look at the partly healed blisters on her feet. Irena had insisted on soaking them every day in some concoction that might've been Epsom salts. Irena called it bitter salt. It was helping, but dancing every night wasn't. She couldn't wait until Sunday. She'd soak her feet all day.

With a sigh, she stood up in a room so cold she could see her breath and quickly got dressed after wrapping her feet in soft bandages. Inge had let her borrow some comfy boots for going to the club and she put those on. She seemed fated to have foot trouble. If it wasn't frost bite, it was infections, and now blisters. She did smile when she thought about telling Nicky how her little feet looked like they had the pox. He'd be so worried and then he'd rub them and tell her how lovely and perfect they were. Something to look forward to.

But first she must get out to the former Wildholz factory and find Anna's nanny. The Polizei had said it might be open in a week and she had to try. It'd already been too long. Dashing as fast as she could dash, Stella went downstairs, surprising Irena as she sat at the dining table counting the tins of sardines Maria had gotten from the lovelorn Obersturmbannführer Krebs who, to her dismay, showed up on Wednesday and Thursday with tinned fish and pitiful compliments. Stella didn't think it was possible to feel sorry for an SS, but Obersturmbannführer Krebs was coming close to managing it until she heard him talking about expelling the Polish Jews from Karlsruhe, personally rounding them up and putting them on boxcars to the

Polish border. She considered nabbing some of Irena's bitter salz and giving him a good dose. He deserved to die of diarrhea.

"Where can you be going?" asked Irena. "You barely got any sleep."

"An officer told me about a pharmacy that has a special tea for foot pain. I thought I'd go get some."

Horrified, Irena asked, "You complained to an officer? Sophie, that will get back to Bothe."

"I didn't. He noticed my bandages. I couldn't hide them completely and Bothe doesn't want me bleeding in my shoes."

Irena looked like she thought bleeding was the better option. "Oh, Sophie. You must be careful."

"Bothe knows about it."

Her eyes widened. "What did she say? Are you fired?"

Stella laughed. "She can't say anything. The officer spoke to her about taking good care of me and he said he expects to see me again."

"Ah, I see. And who is this officer?"

"Obersturmbannführer von Drechsel."

She thought it over. "His name is not familiar."

"I think he's newly arrived from Poland."

"You better go. If he does come back, you want to say that you got the tea." She made Stella a quick sandwich of sardines and butter, wrapped it in waxed paper and put it in a paper sack. "Please eat this. You're getting thinner by the day."

Stella promised she would and left with high hopes and her ration cards so she could go to a shop for some coffee. Irena had heard a certain grocer had a stash in the back of real beans for special customers, not the ersatz stuff he sold to regular people off the street. Valkyrie girls were not regular and Irena looped Hanni's swastika necklace around her neck. She'd just finished repairing the clasp for her and said the grocer would recognize it. Stella suppressed a grimace at both the necklace itself and the reason for wearing it. Special treatment went against everything her family, particularly Uncle Josiah, taught her about fairness. The States didn't do rationing during the Great War, but her grandmother had instituted all the government's recommendations anyway. The family still talked about the meatless meals and loss of butter. The Bleds could afford to eat as much beef as they wanted and they didn't have to plant a war garden, but Eulalie Bled sent her sons to war and they didn't have beef for a year and a half. Having Irena flout the Reich's rules surprised Stella. No one in the house had said much about the war. They certainly hadn't criticized it or Hitler. Stella bit back her questions and merely said she'd love some real coffee. She didn't say that if it took it out of a German soldier's hands so much the better. Irena gave her a wad of Reichsmarks to bribe the grocer and gave her directions to the shop, but Stella put that off.

She went to the Wildholz factory instead, choosing to walk around the park instead of through it that time. The wad of Reichsmarks made her handbag fat and, if she had to get out her identification, a Polizei might notice and that wouldn't be good for anyone so she walked down a long side street past a large house with large stone columns in front but no iron fence connecting them. They looked weird and forlorn in front of the elegant address like soldiers that had been abandoned after a retreat.

All the houses on the block were the same with their fences gone. It must have something to do with the war effort. Nicky had said that Germany's greatest deficit was lack of natural resources, like iron. That was one way to get iron, but it wasn't exactly an unlimited supply and the war hadn't really begun.

She turned around the last corner, her feet burning, and was rewarded with the sight of the factory wide awake and buzzing with activity. More than buzzing. Yelling was a more accurate description. A huge clamor of bangs and grinding metal sounds came from the unboarded windows. Men were installing new glass. Two women scrubbed off the hideous slurs that had been scrawled across the front and a fat, well-dressed man was leaning on a long, black Mercedes looking over an architect's plan.

Stella marched right up to him with her collar open so he could see her Valkyrie necklace and wished him a good morning.

He didn't look up and said brusquely, "We're not hiring yet."

She went stiff and touched the necklace. "I'm not looking for a job."

"Don't bother me. Can't you see I'm busy."

"Are you the original buyer or the other one?"

He looked up sharply and his eyes fell right where she wanted them to. Her necklace. "Oh! I didn't see *you* there."

Stella gave him the big eyes and a saucy smile. "As you can see, I don't need a job."

"I would assume not." He stood up and allowed his plans to coil into a long tube.

"Do I have the pleasure of speaking to Herr Vogel?"

He grinned at her and straightened his tie. "You do not. I am Herr König. Claus König."

Appropriate.

"And you won the day against the unfortunate Herr Vogel," she said.

"The buying process must be fair. Don't you agree?"

"I do, naturally." That was what Stella said, but on the inside she was thinking about the Wildholz family. Fair was not something that applied to them and a new flame of anger sparked inside of her.

"What can I do for you, Fräulein…"

She almost gave a fake name she had in her back pocket but decided against it. This was a man with power. He might very well end up in Valkyrie. "I'm Sophie Weber and I'd like a little information, if you can spare it."

He was utterly charmed, the fat fool. Maybe if she could talk the earl into recommending a bombing run to wipe out the Siemens factory, they could spare a bomb for that despicable thief, too. "I will do anything I can." He kissed her hand and she resisted the urge to wipe off his spittle.

"I'm looking for a woman. Frau Hoppe. Gertruda Hoppe."

Herr König wrinkled his brow. "The name isn't familiar to me. Who is she?"

"A nanny and a friend of my mother's friend Frau Klink. I came to Berlin looking for her, but Frau Klink had passed away. A neighbor told me to find Frau Hoppe. She would know what happened to Frau Klink. My mother will want to know if she suffered."

He nodded sagely. "You're a good girl and a good daughter."

"I try my best as I was taught." She twisted the Werner ring to draw attention to it.

"You are engaged. Congratulations. He is a lucky man."

"My beloved Werner was lost in Poland." Her eyes got moist and she could feel him twisting around her finger. She needed that because he was about to be unhappy with her.

"A loss for the Führer is a gift to the greater Germany."

She wanted to roll her eyes, but said instead, "Yes. I believe that and so does his family. You don't know Frau Hoppe at all?"

"I don't. I'm sorry. Did she work here?"

"I think she worked for the family that owned it before."

Herr König's face hardened. "The Jews."

"I don't know. No one said that. She was a nanny."

"A Jew."

"Not if she was Frau Klink's friend," said Stella harshly while touching the swastika.

"No, no, of course not. I didn't mean to imply…" he trailed off.

"I understand completely. It's hard to know if someone is on the right side," she said. "In your new factory, did you keep any of the workers?"

"Not the Jews."

She laughed. "Of course not. I meant someone who might know the nanny, a good Aryan worker."

"Ah, yes. It would be foolish to let them all go. Many were duped into working for the Jews," he said. "Franz! Franz!"

One of the men working on the windows looked back at them.

"Come here!" yelled Herr König.

Fritz dashed over. "Yes, sir."

"Fräulein Weber is asking about a nanny." He looked at Stella.

"Frau Gertruda Hoppe," she said quickly. "Do you know her?"

Fritz shook his head. "No, ma'am."

"She worked for the Jews," said Herr König.

"Oh, then I wouldn't know her. I came after the Jews left. Herr Vogel hired me."

"Is there anyone here today from before?" asked Stella. "Frau Hoppe isn't a Jew and I'd like to find her for my mother."

Fritz nodded. "Yes, there is. Ralf and Paul. They did the maintenance for the Jews. Very good workers though," he said hastily.

"Are they here today?" asked Herr König.

"They are installing the new looms."

"Take Fräulein Weber to see them."

Fritz nodded and beckoned Stella to come inside with him.

"Thank you, Herr König," she said. "You've been very kind."

He nodded and went back to his plans. She followed Fritz inside and they went through a maze of wooden crates and walked around a pile of rabbit furs tossed aside on the floor.

"What is all this?" she asked. "Aren't you making fur coats anymore?"

Fritz chuckled. "The Reich doesn't need fur coats for ladies. It needs warm uniforms for our warriors."

"And fur is *too* warm? I thought Poland is cold."

"Don't worry. We're keeping the fur for later. Herr König's orders."

Later?

She twisted her ring and Fritz noticed. "My Werner said we would go to France, but France is warm."

He frowned. "This man is an officer?"

"No and he died for the Führer in Poland."

"Then he did not know." Fritz smiled. "France is warm. We don't need fur for France." He pointed to a pair of men next to an enormous piece of equipment. It could've been a loom or a piece of farm equipment for all Stella knew. "There they are. Ralf and Paul. Tell them that Herr König said to help you."

She thanked him and then walked over, passing more fur on the floor and boxes labeled "König Textilien". The men had their back to her as one held a bolt in place with a heavy screwdriver and the other cranked on a nut on the end of it. She hesitated a moment and heard one say, "It is unbelievable. They were only boys."

"This is what happens now."

"But death for stealing a handbag?"

"It is the law."

Stella couldn't move. She could barely breathe. They were going to execute children for stealing? No. It wasn't possible. That was insane.

"These new decrees, they go too far."

"Shush. Someone will—" The man with the screwdriver looked up and froze when he saw her. They stood there looking at each other, both in horror. Stella knew very well that as a supposedly good German she should report any talk like that and he knew it, too. If you could get executed for petty theft, what would they do to Ralf and Paul?

"Hey, Ralf! I'm spinning here," said Paul and he looked up. His weathered face went pale under the remains of a summer tan.

She had to say something. The men looked like they might pass out and she felt scarcely any better.

"It's so loud in here!" Stella yelled. "I can't hear anything!"

Both men let go of their held breath and they bent over in a kind of spasm of relief.

"I wanted to ask for your help," she said.

They nodded and wiped their brows, looking around nervously, but no one was remotely close to them.

"Yes," said Paul. "What can we do for you?"

She told them about Frau Hoppe, including her cover story about the dead friend.

"She worked for the Jews," said Ralf, his face now closed and his eyes furtively looking behind her.

"I know. Herr König told me, but he said you could help me."

"Herr König said that?"

"Yes. Frau Hoppe isn't a Jew, so it's all right that I find her for my mother."

They considered this, but she could tell they were nervous to admit that they knew anyone that worked for the Wildholzes.

"I thought she might get a job here now that the Jews are gone," said Stella.

With a quick glance around, Paul and Ralf came closer and she could see the sweat on their temples betraying their fear in the unheated factory.

"I'm glad you're closer," she said. "I couldn't hear anything before. Nothing at all."

They nodded and Paul took a breath. "Frau Hoppe wouldn't work here now."

"No?" she asked.

"No. She…was a nanny, like you said. She worked in the apartment."

"And the factory isn't to her taste?"

They nodded. Frau Hoppe was loyal. Their eyes said it all. She wouldn't work for the men that stole the Wildholzes' business and they felt a little guilty that they obviously were.

"All must make their own choices," she said.

They nodded.

"Do you know where she lives?"

Paul gave her the address of the apartment.

"She's not there. The Jews are gone."

"Of course," said Ralf, shrugging. "She always lived with them, even in the big villa."

"Villa?"

The men glanced around and Paul said quietly, "Before they lived in a big villa on Torhausstraße. It had blue doors and shutters. Very large and beautiful."

Wide-eyed, Stella asked, "What happened?"

"What do you think? They're Jews."

"Oh, right. I forget that."

Paul gave her an intense look. "You shouldn't. Not ever."

"I won't, not ever again. Do you know anyone else that might know where Frau Hoppe's family is?"

Ralf slapped his hefty wrench in his dirty palm. "She had a sister. I don't know her name."

"They don't speak. Gertruda was angry with her about the villa," said Paul.

"Yes, yes. When the family had to leave the villa, the sister didn't go."

"Lisa. It was Lisa. She was a maid and she stayed at the villa."

Relief flooded over Stella. It wasn't a lot but it was a lead. "Perhaps they couldn't employ her at the new place."

"That's what she said. Gertruda didn't care. She said, 'Easier to get a new job than a new soul.' That was Gertruda."

A good person in other words.

"She sounds stubborn," said Stella.

The men laughed and agreed. Gertruda was a fierce and unyielding woman.

"Does this help you?" asked Paul.

"Maybe. I will go to the villa and ask for Lisa. Then I can tell my mother I tried."

"This is important. We must keep faith with our mothers," said Ralf. "But be careful about Gertruda. I think she will come to a bad end."

Paul nodded. "She is too strong for her own good. I heard when the Gestapo came with the papers to put the Jews out of the villa, she cursed them. She wouldn't be quiet." He lowered his voice. "She was questioned."

"I see," said Stella, holding out Irena's paper sack. "I'll be careful and please take this. I know it isn't much."

Paul cautiously took the bag and looked inside. Then he smiled but shook his head no. "Sardines? It must be a whole tin. We can't take your sandwich. It's most of your meat for a week."

She refused to take it back. "No, I want you to have it for helping me." She touched the swastika. "I work at Valkyrie and sometimes we get a little extra. You should have it. You work hard for the Führer."

Ralf swallowed hard, hunger plainly etched on his face. "Fräulein… you are—"

"A little spoiled, I know. Please take it for the Fatherland," said Stella appealing to their patriotism. She needed them to take it. A little food was good for keeping conversations quiet. Her interest in Frau

Hoppe didn't need to get around and Stella was heartily tired of sardines anyway.

"We will take it with many thanks," said Paul as he took out the sandwich. The men tore it in half, grinning at her, and Stella hurried out with a quick check of the time. It had taken too long. She had to get to that wretched shop and buy illegal coffee and that stupid tea. There wasn't time to go to the outskirts of Berlin to the Wildholz's stolen villa.

"Fräulein Weber," called out Herr König.

She hid a grimace and went over to the new owner. She told him the men knew little about the Jews or their servants, but thought she might find something out at the villa.

"I'm glad they were helpful to you," he said.

"They tried their best," she said. "Very good workers, I think." She looked up at the stone above the door were Wildholz had been chiseled off and still had the name Vogel painted on. "And a good factory. I'm sure you will serve the Fatherland well."

He clicked his heels. "All is for the Führer."

She beamed at him. "Perhaps I will see you at Valkyrie some time."

"I expect to be asked soon and I look forward to you serving me."

Her skin crawled, but she said, "That is my wish also," before hurrying away and feeling his eyes on her until she turned the corner.

IRENA MET Stella at the front door, her face flushed. "Where have you been? I've been so worried."

She held out a small but heavy sack. "I got everything and went to do an errand for my mother. Why? What's wrong?"

The housemother patted her chest. "Thank the Führer."

"I don't understand."

Hanni walked in, smiling. "I told you she's fine."

"We heard there were arrests," said Irena.

Marie came in while running a comb through her hair. "In the Spandauer Vorstadt. Sophie wouldn't go there."

"Of course not," said Hanni.

"Is it a bad area?" asked Stella.

Maria wrinkled her nose. "It's for the Jews. There's nothing *good* there."

I imagine not.

"I don't think I was anywhere near there, but I did get lost a couple of times. The streets are so confusing." This was all true. Finding the Apotheke with the SS's recommended tea was easy. The grocer wasn't and she got turned around several times.

Hanni snatched up the sack and sniffed the contents. "Oh, you darling girl, you got it. Real coffee before the club."

"Give me that, greedy girl," said Irena, taking the sack. "I will make the coffee. Sophie must change and soak her feet."

"How long?" pouted Maria.

Irena shooed them toward the stairs. "Go on. Hurry up."

Hanni took Stella's arm. "Come on. I'll help you braid your hair."

"What's the hurry? It's not late," said Stella as she gingerly walked up the stairs. She had taken her sweet time walking around because her feet were getting worse by the minute.

"Oh, that's right. You don't know. Bothe sent a message. We have to be in early."

It was everything Stella could do not to groan out loud.

"I know," said Hanni. "I wanted to cry when I heard, but wait until you hear what happened."

Inge came out of her room on the second floor. "Did you tell her?"

"Not yet."

"I'm wearing my perfume. I've been saving it." Inge spritzed her neck and the liquid ran down into her bodice. "Oh, no!" She ran back in the room, trying to dab at her neck with her wrists.

Hanni and Stella burst out laughing and dashed up the remaining flight of stairs. Stella ignored the burning in her feet. She'd gotten quite good at that. Pain was temporary. Victory forever.

"So what's this big news?" she asked as they turned right to her door. Stella jolted to a halt. It was open and she knew she'd closed it.

Hanni charged in front of her and whipped open the door. "Hey! What are you doing in here?"

Irma sat on Stella's bed with her copy of *Vom Winde Verweht* in her hand and Werner's framed photo lying next to her. "Oh, you're back. That's good."

"What are you doing in here?" Stella asked.

"You were gone so long we got worried. I wanted to see if you left anything that told us where you went," said Irma with a very focused look at Stella. "You might have been arrested."

"We knew where she went," said Hanni.

"She might have gone somewhere else."

Stella crossed her arms. "I did." She couldn't hide anything. That was very clear. Irma was going to be a problem. "I went to the König factory to look for Frau Klink's friend. I heard she might work there."

"What did you want her for?"

Hanni took Stella's book out of Irma's hands. "None of your business."

"You shouldn't be reading that book. It's American trash."

"My mother gave it to me after Werner died. It's about war," said Stella.

"I heard it was a romance."

Stella shrugged. "It is, but the Americans had a war and that's when it happens."

"It doesn't matter," said Hanni. "Frau Bothe read it, so it must be all right."

Irma was suitably astonished. "Old Bothe read that?"

"She did. I had to go down for a fresh apron and I saw her. She hid it when she saw me because she was supposed to be working, but she was reading it."

"Oh. That's different. Is it good?"

Was Gone with the Wind any good? What a question.

"I like it," said Stella.

"I saw copies at the bookshops, but I have to send my money home now that my father's in the Luftwaffe," said Hanni. "His rank isn't very high."

"You shouldn't complain," said Irma.

"I'm explaining. Not complaining."

The two girls eyed each other and then Hanni said, "Sophie got the coffee. Irena's making some now."

Irma stood up. "We shouldn't have that. It's for the Fatherland."

Hanni rolled her eyes. "You bring home butter and sausage sometimes. Aren't those for the Fatherland?"

Irma clenched her jaw and then said, "Gifts from the officers are different."

"Oh, really?"

"They want us to have it. We're taking the coffee from them."

Hanni sighed. "Why do you have to be so serious?"

"It is serious." Irma walked toward the door and bumped into Stella's suitcase, knocking it flat.

Stella's heart instantly started racing and she rushed to pick the suitcase up. "I have no room in here."

"Why don't you put it on the wardrobe?" asked Irma.

Stella decided to take another tack and tilted her head, harrumphing obviously. "I wonder why."

To her surprise and relief, both girls burst out laughing.

"Why are you so short?" asked Irma.

"I'm tall for my family."

"I can put it up there," offered Hanni, holding out her hand.

Stella sighed dramatically. "I'd never be able to get it down."

"That's true," said Irma as she put Werner's photo back on the side table. "He's very handsome."

"Yes, he was," said Stella, still not giving up the suitcase and feeling as though she might throw up.

"I'll take it," said Hanni, "and put it downstairs."

"Um...but..."

It was Irma's turn to roll her eyes. "No one wants your old suitcase, Sophie. Hanni will just put it in the cellar. Mine's down there."

"And mine," said Hanni. "We don't have a lot of space."

"At least you don't have to share with Inge," said Irma.

"She just sprayed perfume."

"You let her?" Irma charged out of Stella's room and thundered down the stairs.

Hanni yelled after her. "I didn't let her. I'm not in charge of her."

"Irma doesn't like perfume?" asked Stella.

"She doesn't like a lot of things, but Inge gets carried away and stinks up the whole room."

Stella sidestepped and put the suitcase behind her legs saying, "You never told me why we have to go in early tonight."

Hanni threw up her hands. "They're coming. Finally."

"Who?" She couldn't think who the Valkyrie girls would get so worked up over, unless… "Is the Führer coming?"

She laughed. "You know he's not in Berlin right now."

Stella didn't, but she took it on faith. "Oh, right."

"He doesn't like the clubs anyway." Hanni looked guilty. "All the drinking and meat isn't good. He keeps his body pure."

Stella's eyes wanted to roll so badly, but she knew Hitler supposedly didn't drink or eat meat. She found such things impossible for an odious man like him. He'd order attacks on Jews and steal their property, but he won't eat meat? Ridiculous. "I should try to do better myself," she said as seriously as she could muster.

"We all should try to live up to his example." Then Hanni grinned. "I'm still having coffee though."

Stella grinned back. "Me, too. A little coffee can't hurt."

"Especially tonight."

"Are you ever going to tell me what it is?"

She laughed. "It's him. He's finally coming. Reichsminister Goebbels and he's bringing his wife. I've never seen her, but I've heard she's very elegant."

"Oh…that's exciting." Stella couldn't have been less excited. She'd never get near the table, being as low-ranked as she was, and she'd seen the minister's work, hideous posters comparing Jews to rats or ticks and those strange new posters with people portrayed as monkeys or some sort of degenerates. There was every chance she might "accidentally" kick him in the shin.

"It is. Bothe is going crazy though. We have to decorate and put on special lipstick." Without warning she reached down and grabbed the suitcase. "I'll take this down and you get those boots off. I'll be right back."

Stella wasn't fast enough, not even close, and Hanni was out the door and going downstairs with the suitcase and the Reichsmarks concealed inside. She stood frozen with her mouth open. Her thoughts pinged around, trying to find a way to reasonably get the suitcase back up in her room, but she found nothing that wouldn't be seen as odd. Irma was already getting nosy and critical. She couldn't light a flare and expect her not to see it.

Please help me. Please don't let her notice anything odd about it and look inside. Please.

Praying helped her calm her heart rate and she sat on the bed. There was nothing to be done. Either Hanni would open the suitcase or she wouldn't. Stella had to get ready to go see the propaganda minister like it was the only thing that mattered so she did. Forward was the only direction she could choose.

CHAPTER 10

*I*rma stood on the second floor landing, waiting with her pale blond hair still loose around her shoulders. Her face was turned up and from Stella's vantage point she looked angelic, but Stella feared she was anything but.

Stella took a breath and kept walking down, her feet bare and tingling from the cold in the house. If she could've dashed by Irma and avoided what was coming, she would've, but there wasn't anywhere to run and it would only increase her suspicions. And Hanni was downstairs. Anything could've happened and she had nowhere that was safe. If she opened that suitcase… If she noticed how heavy it was…

Stella opened her mouth to ask what Irma wanted when the other girl blurted out, "I'm sorry, Sophie. I shouldn't have gone in your room and looked at your things."

"Oh!" Stella couldn't contain her surprise. "I…I thought you were angry with me."

"I wasn't angry. Well, not with you, I wanted to know more about you."

"You could've asked."

Irma looked down, flushing with embarrassment. "I know, but you didn't come back and I was worried you'd been caught buying on the black market. It's very serious now." She took Stella's hand and their nearly identical blue eyes met. "And I know you agree with me."

Stella couldn't think what to say. "Well…I…"

"I saw your face when Irena told you to go buy the coffee."

"Where were you?" she asked.

"In the dining room. I could see you through the door and I know you didn't like it," said Irma.

"I was taught to obey," said Stella without committing to who she was supposed to obey, the rules or Irena.

Irma took her other hand, her eyes shining with fervor. "I knew you'd understand me. Hanni doesn't. She thinks we are special. That we should have special rules. But all is for the Fatherland."

Apparently, all the gifts Irma received didn't count, but all Stella could think was how much she needed that coffee. Real coffee, not toasted barley or, even worse, acorns. "I do believe in the Fatherland. We must sacrifice and we do, don't we?"

Irma stepped back. "You are thinner. Irena is right." Then she pulled Stella in and gave her a hug. "It will all be over soon."

"What?"

"The war. The papers say the Poles are under control. They won't attack again."

They never attacked in the first place.

"I hope you're right."

"And then we can eat like before," said Irma.

"And have hot baths."

"As many as we want." She grinned at Stella. "I'm so glad I have you here."

"I'm glad, too."

Then Irma said shyly, "May I borrow your book? I shouldn't have criticized you."

"Of course, you can."

"And you can borrow one of my books."

"What do you have?" asked Stella, wondering what in the world Irma would deem important to read and she wasn't disappointed.

"Have you read *Der Totale Krieg*? It's all the rage now."

The Total War. Sounds like a laugh riot.

"I've heard of it, but I don't know what it's about."

Irma lowered her voice. "The Kaiser's war and the men's suffering. You must read it."

"Thank you. I'd like to." Stella surprised herself at how genuine she sounded as if reading about German men suffering in a war they started was of real interest. She'd become an accomplished liar and it was a little disturbing.

Irma hooked her arm through Stella's and they went down the stairs arm in arm. Park-Welles would be pleased, if he could've seen it. She'd been completely accepted, but these girls were not what she expected. They knew very little about what was going on with the war and believed the propaganda because there wasn't anything else competing for their attention.

"What are you two doing up there?" asked Hanni from the bottom of the stairs, her lovely face stern, causing Stella's heart to pound.

"Nothing, Fräulein Nosy," said Irma.

"Hurry up."

"We are. Sophie's feet are bad."

Stella stepped down too hard and winced at the pain in her feet.

"Oh, you poor thing. What can I do?" asked Irma.

Impulsively, Stella said, "Forgive me."

Her companion sucked in a breath. "What do you mean?"

"I want some coffee. I really do." Stella gave her the big eyes and Irma laughed.

"Of course, you should have it."

"Really?"

"Yes. You went all that way on those feet."

"And we already have it," said Stella, taking a prolonged sniff of the coffee-scented air. "We can't take it back."

"That is true." Irma squeezed her arm. "I think it's all right this one time."

Hanni came running up the stairs. "Why are you delaying? Her feet are so white. She's freezing, Irma."

"I know. I know. Is the water ready?" asked Irma.

"Yes, but it's getting cold."

The girls practically carried Stella down the stairs and into the dining room where everyone else was assembled. Stella kept sneaking peeks at Hanni's face, trying to judge what had happened, but nothing showed. She was simply Hanni.

Irena gestured to a chair and Stella sat down, dipping her feet in the now lukewarm water. It still felt amazing since the house was so cold. Hanni mock wiped her brow. "You're almost as heavy as your suitcase."

A zing went through Stella's body and her lungs stopped functioning.

"Those old suitcases are heavy," said Maria. "I weighed mine before I came here. It weighed more than my little cousin."

"It's so huge she could fit inside," said Inge.

"She did. We tried it."

They all laughed and began digging into the usual spread of rolls, but the rolls were different, not wheat but some kind of dense potato and rye.

Inge made a face. "No wurst?"

"We've used all our rations for the week. Have some of Maria's sardines," said Irena. "And be sure not to complain tonight. Reichsminister Goebbels will not like it."

"I wouldn't complain to Reichsminister Goebbels," said Inge.

"Wouldn't you?" asked Hanni. "You told that officer how you saw the fences taken from your home for smelting."

"Well, they were."

"But you don't say it," said Irena. "It's indiscreet."

"It's a fact and how was I supposed to know that he'd tell Bothe. He was so nice." Inge's face was open and not understanding at all. No one said anything. There wasn't anything to say. The men were all nice until they weren't, but no one wanted to say that out loud.

Stella accepted a cup of coffee and took a heavenly sip. It wasn't good coffee, not like what they had in Italy, but, for the first time in a week, she felt awake and had some modicum of energy.

Irma caught her eye and they smiled together. Irma about the coffee and Stella about her suitcase somewhere in the cellar, unopened and safe.

T HE GIRLS LEFT the U Bahn two hours before the normal schedule. The coffee had helped but it had worn off quickly and Stella found herself yawning constantly. She was flanked by Irma and Hanni and had her coat open to show off her dirndl to the passersby. This wasn't new anymore and she'd become used to the reaction their uniforms got. The only ones not paying them any mind were the workmen hanging new flags on the clubs' street and putting up some posters proclaiming Germany's perfect people's right to rule or something nasty and bizarre. Where they got the idea that Jews looked like what they thought they looked like was a mystery to Stella.

When they reached the club, the doormen were tacking up posters outside. They'd never had any kind of poster before, so Stella assumed it was all about Goebbels and he had something against swing and jazz. Two of the posters had a hideous caricature of what she presumed was a black man playing a saxophone.

"Oh, no," whispered Hanni. "They'll have to change the show."

"Of course they should," said Irma. "They know the rules."

Hanni sighed and they went into a lobby that for once wasn't empty. Performers were practicing steps and Julius, who was in charge of choreography, was shouting that they were getting it all wrong. Swastikas were being hung on every available surface and someone was yelling about the flowers.

"We're having flowers?" asked Stella.

"It only happens when someone really important comes," said Hanni.

Irma sniffed. "They're all important."

Hanni rolled her eyes and they went into the back, which was more crowded than ever. Sets were being pulled out of storage and racks of costumes shoved every which way.

"There you are!" Bothe stood in the dressing room, sweating and panting. "You're late."

"We're two hours early," protested Maria.

"Today that's late. Change your aprons. Your hair must be up. He likes it up. Traditional. Get the flowers. Where are those vases?"

The questions and orders kept coming and the two hours went by in a flash. Stella found herself doing flower arrangements for the main tables, even though she said she didn't know how. She did know how. Francesqua Bled was the queen of flower arrangers and she insisted Stella learn how to properly strip thorns off a rose and which flowers said what and went where, but this wasn't part of Sophie's knowledge. She was basically a shop girl from Munich. It was doubtful she'd have ever handled roses at all.

"Just do it," Bothe had bellowed and she had with as many annoying questions and concerns about her inadequacy as she could muster. The florists were rushing around and, in an effort to impress, kept making arrangements that blocked the all-important view of the stage. Stella had finally complained to Bothe and gotten them thrown out with only a half hour to go.

Irma and Maria helped and they got the arrangements done just in the nick of time and Bothe staggered up to look at them. "They are acceptable. We are opening the doors in five minutes. Go powder your noses and do not be sweaty."

Stella was sweaty and she'd never been sweaty in her life. She didn't just powder her nose. She powdered her underarms and back as well with the help of Irma, who looked so cool and collected you'd have thought she'd been standing out in the cold, not running around and yelling at florists and busboys.

Someone yelled, "Opening now. Get up top."

The girls ran up the stairs, smoothed their aprons, and plastered on smiles that were really more like grimaces. Bothe was still sweaty and even more red-faced than usual. "You!" she yelled at Irma.

Irma froze and Stella could feel her quake. Instinctively, she put her arm around the girl's waist to steady her.

"Yes, Frau Bothe?" asked Irma in a voice that completely hid her fear.

"You look very well. You'll do for the Reichsminister."

She looked stunned, but Inge jumped up and down. Hanni clapped and hugged her. "You can do it."

"I thought you would get it, Hanni," said Irma.

"No, I haven't got your hair. He will like you best."

The girls got their assignments and Stella's was mediocre. Bothe glared at her and insisted on examining her feet. "You've not healed yet."

It was so ridiculous. How could she heal doing the same thing night after night?

"No, ma'am," she said.

"Did you get that tea?"

"Yes, ma'am."

"Did you drink it?"

Stella bit her lip. There'd been a choice. Coffee or the questionable tea. She'd gone with the coffee. No one doubted that she would.

Bothe groaned. "He's coming tonight with the Reichsminister and you didn't drink it?"

"I didn't know he was coming. Why's he with the Reichsminister?"

Bothe gave her a stinging slap on the arm. "Don't ask questions. Did you bring it?"

"It's in my handbag."

She checked her watch. "You will drink it on your break in three hours. Until then you are to avoid being seen by Obersturmbann-führer von Drechsel."

How could she possibly do that? The club was wide open. The point was to be seen.

"He probably won't even remember me," she said. "I only spoke to him for a few minutes. I don't know why he came to you."

"Because you are young, beautiful, and clearly an empty-headed ninny. He will remember. They always remember their orders."

Orders.

Stella had considered the tea a suggestion, a moment of kindness from an SS who wasn't naturally inclined toward the emotion. But from the look on Bothe's face, it was an order and must be obeyed.

"Yes, ma'am."

"Go to your tables and wait." She eyed Stella in cold appraisal. "Finally, your shortness will come in handy."

"Yes, ma'am." Stella hurried away as the guests arrived. She'd been told Saturday nights were an experience, but the other girls didn't elaborate on it. They thought she shouldn't be warned and Stella could see why. Usually, the guests were calm as they came in. That night they were harried and ordered drinks before they even got to their tables, all tight smiles and forced laughter.

Stella's guests were a relief and a disappointment. She had four tables of Wehrmacht officers, Luftwaffe, and some executives from Temmler, a pharmaceutical company. They all had wives and girl-friends and were careful not to look too long at Stella as she brought drinks and failed to answer questions about when Reichsminister Goebbels would appear. Nobody knew that and it was nearly two hours into the night before he showed.

The entire club hushed when a slight man, not much taller than Stella, walked in the doors. He looked around with an expression of extreme arrogance and then spoke to the woman with him. Judging by the look on her face, she was his wife, Magda Goebbels, and she wasn't happy. Her face was pinched and miserable, but her husband didn't notice as they were taken to their table. He limped slightly and looked around as if daring anyone to notice.

The crowd began talking again but in hushed tones. More people came in behind the Reichsminister and filled the remaining tables around the stage. Stella's table raised their glasses to Goebbels and soon the whole club did the same. Everyone toasted him and then there was thunderous applause, although Stella couldn't have said why. She understood that he was third in the power lineup, but why escaped her. He did propaganda. When Keitel had come, nobody had much cared and he was head of the army. Nazis made no sense to Stella.

The maître d' took the stage and announced the next performance, a salute to the Luftwaffe. Stella spotted Obersturmbannführer von Drechsel coming in in his black uniform that everyone got so excited about. The SS were the most revered, but the worst tippers. She much preferred the Wehrmacht, who were simply the army and seemed to put Germany ahead of the party or, at least, that was the way it appeared to Stella. They didn't pinch as much and didn't have the cold authority that the SS reeked of. Even if Peiper hadn't tried to kill her, Stella would've known the SS weren't men you wanted to know, but she was definitely the only one that felt that way. The other girls vied for their tables. It was an honor to serve them and it was all Stella could do not to show how much she hated it when she was given their tables.

The performance began and Stella turned her back on the Obersturmbannführer, heading for the bar to load up with more beer. Her tables could definitely drink, but they weren't talking about anything interesting. She'd even gone so far as to mention winter uniforms and France to the officers, but they thought she was an idiot, so she dropped it. Ralf and Paul seemed to know something that the military didn't. At least not at their level, which wasn't very high. They were thrilled to be in the same room as Goebbels whom none of them had ever seen in person.

Stella spun around and almost knocked into Irma who was rushing to the bar beaming and breathless.

"Watch out," she said.

"Sorry," said Stella. "It's been a long night already."

"Not for me. He's very polite, Sophie. So elegant and cultured."

Stella had noticed when making the rounds with Nicky's mother that "elegant and cultured" were often synonymous with "cold and disinterested", but people chose to see it in the best light given the person's stature.

"Is he?"

"He must get manicures. His nails are perfectly buffed. And his wife, she's so stylish. She said she liked my hair."

"Your hair is lovely," said Stella, wishing they'd say something with a point.

"You've got interesting tables tonight, too," said Irma.

Stella snorted. "Do I?"

"Yes. You must. Reichsminister Goebbels said he wanted to talk to some of them and he isn't at all happy with where they're sitting."

She looked across the room at her tables at the lower part of medium importance. Honestly, she'd been surprised they'd been put that high. "Well, they're not interesting. I can tell you that."

Irma laughed. "As long as you don't tell *them* that."

"I'm absolutely fascinated and impressed. Which ones are important? It can't be the Wehrmacht. They keep talking about socks."

She gathered up her beers. "I'll find out. Maybe you can make something of it."

Maybe.

"We'll see. I just want them to have a good night," said Stella and she returned to her tables. The Wehrmacht were still talking about socks and the Luftwaffe about the Metropol.

"The girls there aren't nearly so pretty," said one of the men with an exaggerated wink.

His wife laughed and gave him a gentle slap. "Don't mind him, Fräulein. He's always been trouble, especially during wartime."

Stella laughed, too, and said she didn't believe it. That got the whole table talking about various amounts of trouble they'd been in during the Kaiser's war. France, to hear them tell it, was a good time. Uncle Josiah certainly had fun. At least when he wasn't on the edge of being killed or captured, which was frequent.

The last table were no longer happy. They'd gotten edgy and snapped about how long it took to bring the beer, but they immediately apologized.

"My husband was hoping to be in a different position tonight," said the older of the two wives, a woman who really was elegant and cultured, having spent a great deal of time in Paris, and, for good measure, she'd studied art in Vienna. Stella could've talked to her all night, but it wasn't going to help with the war.

"You aren't pleased with your table, ma'am?"

"The tables are fine. It's just…business."

Her husband glanced in the direction of Goebbels' tables. Interesting. She could make something of it. Stella bent over and looked around. "I did hear something at the bar."

The entire table leaned in.

"Perhaps I shouldn't say."

"Please do," said the elegant wife.

The other wife groaned. "Don't make us have a night of crabby husbands and no dancing for nothing."

The husbands chuckled but gave Stella stares of intense interest.

"Fräulein, if you have something you can share," said the older man.

"Well, first I heard I had an important section tonight, but they didn't tell me why," said Stella.

That made them very happy. The men puffed up and the ladies preened.

"What else?" asked the elegant wife.

"It's not very secret so I think I can say. Reichsminister Goebbels isn't pleased about where your table is."

They took deep breaths and relaxed.

"I told you, Magnus," said the elegant wife.

"You did indeed, Sonja. You did."

The other wife leaned forward. "Is there anything you can do to get us closer?"

There wasn't. The tables were filled.

"Were you supposed to have a meeting with the Reichsminister?"

"Informally. He has the Führer's ear and we believe we can help insure our success in the coming months. We have made contact through our staffs."

"Many meetings happen here in Valkyrie," said Stella.

They nodded.

"Should we send a message through the tubes?" asked Magnus.

"No, no. My friend is their girl. I will ask her what to do."

Magnus pushed twenty Reichsmarks across the table. "We appreciate it."

Stella pushed it back. "That is not necessary. It is my duty to help you help the Führer."

They glowed with pleasure and Stella spun around nearly bumping into a broad black chest. She yelped and jolted back, bumping into the table with visions of Peiper in her head.

"Fräulein Weber," said Obersturmbannführer von Drechsel, "be careful."

Stella put her hands on her chest, willing her heart to stop pounding. "I didn't see you there, sir."

"Obviously."

She turned to her table. "I'm very sorry. Did I spill anything?"

"No, Fräulein," said Sonja. "Don't worry yourself."

They were looking at her so intently she knew they just wanted to hurry up and get going.

"I will put in your order directly," she said and turned back to the SS. "Excuse me. I must tend to my guests."

The SS watched her for a moment and didn't move. He had that entitlement thing that she found repulsive, as if he had some prior claim on her time and her personally, but she'd barely spoken to him on Wednesday. His companions were all more talkative and more handsome. They were the typical SS, tall, well-groomed, hair parted severely on the left and slicked down. Any of them could've been pictured on one of Goebbels' posters about fighting men. Stella found them hard to tell apart, except for von Drechsel. His nose had been broken at some point and badly set. It gave his face some character that the others lacked, but it wasn't a good thing.

"Did you take the tea?" he demanded.

She didn't have time to think it through, so she just answered truthfully and with irritation, "No, I didn't."

The ladies behind her gasped. One didn't say "no" to an SS and certainly not like that.

"Why not?"

"I only got it today and I didn't have time to make it before coming to the club. I will make some on my break. You're welcome to share it with me."

He eyed her for a moment and then said, "Are you having much pain?"

She thrust her chin out. "I'm fine."

"You're not. I saw you limping."

"I will have my tea soon. You said it would be better."

Von Drechsel's face softened just the smallest amount. "You should have it now."

"I have things to attend to."

He snapped his fingers and then, like magic, Maria appeared at his elbow. "Yes, sir."

"Please attend these tables while Fräulein Weber takes a break." He didn't wait for an answer. He took Stella's arm and guided her away. She glanced back at Maria, who was gaping at her.

"Please sir, my guests."

"I want you to meet someone." He guided her out of the club and into the lobby past Frau Bothe. She, too, gaped at Stella, but didn't make a move to stop them.

"Who?" she asked.

He stopped in the lobby, pulled a flask out of his breast pocket to take a large swig. "You're used to pain."

"What?"

"Your feet."

"They're just blisters," she said.

"It's more than that," he said, turning to look at her with dark brown eyes that held a noteworthy intelligence. "You understand pain."

"I…" She didn't know what to say. It was true. Pain was her constant companion, sometimes physical, sometimes not. She'd come to accept it would always be there.

"Werner, your lost fiancé."

"Yes. What about him?"

"He wrote to you?"

"Yes."

"You understood his pain."

She was bewildered, but she nodded. "I did."

"And you bear that pain still."

"Yes."

"But you are here in the club smiling, even with bloody feet," said the SS and Stella looked down. There was a tinge of blood on the bandage she'd tried so hard to hide.

Looking at his face she saw, much to her dismay, something of her father in it. Aleksej Bled had a way of questioning her without asking a question and she had better have the right answer, so she decided to answer the SS the way she'd have answered her father, with strength and an eye to the future.

"It helps to keep going. Every day gets better that way."

"I hoped you'd say that." He pointed out the glass of the door. "That is my younger brother."

A man wearing a Wehrmacht uniform stood by a streetlamp. He leaned on the pole with his back to them and smoked a cigarette sending thick streams of smoke out into the night. There was something vaguely familiar about the distant figure, but Stella couldn't say what since she couldn't see his face.

"*Your* brother isn't allowed in?" That didn't make sense, but she had to ask. The Nazis were all about nepotism among other things.

He took another swig. "He won't come in."

Stella tried to judge what to say next. His face gave away nothing. Was he angry? Frustrated? Sad? It was impossible to tell. "It's very cold out."

He stared at his brother's back. "He must come in."

Clearly, she was supposed to solve this problem, but she hadn't a clue how. "I assume his presence is important."

"It is required." He drained his flask. "He must be in his place."

There was something in that. His place. The Nazis had a place for everyone and everything. His place would be important not only to him but to his ambitious brother. If she could make this happen, she could get somewhere with him.

"I can persuade him to come in." It came out more certain than she meant it to.

He looked at her. "I know. That's why I picked you. He noticed you on Wednesday."

"Here?"

"Walking by coming here."

She laughed. "It's the dirndl."

"It's not." He made a shooing gesture. "Now go and hurry up about it."

"What's his name?"

He gave her a harsh glance. "That is unimportant. Go."

I will never understand these people.

"I'll do my best," she said.

"I know you will." There was a threat in his voice, but Stella shook it off easily as the doorman rushed over to let her out. The fool just asked a British agent to be involved with his situation and family. She intended to make the most of it.

CHAPTER 11

$\mathcal{H}$auptmann von Drechsel didn't speak for a full two minutes and Stella could barely control her shivering. It did give her a chance to find her footing and scrutinize her target. She usually didn't get much time to think. Things just happened and she had to react, hoping for the best. But the Wehrmacht officer was in no hurry to acknowledge her or do anything other than smoke and glower at the dark.

He had a good reason to glower in her opinion. That von Drechsel looked more like his brother's SS companions than he did, a poster perfect Aryan with a narrow nose, high cheekbones, and close-cropped blond hair under his cap. But that was his right side. His left was a completely different story. Stella wasn't within ten feet before she spotted the injuries. No wonder he didn't want to come into the opulent club. She'd seen a few injuries inside, but they'd been minor, a bandage here, a scar there. The higher ranks weren't exactly down in the trenches, so to speak. Hauptmann von Drechsel had been down. He'd been way down and she knew who he reminded her of. Albert. They weren't similar in any obvious way, their height, hair color and bone structures were all as different as different could be, but there was a sadness in the way they held themselves. Sorrow radiated off the Nazi and it touched her the way Albert's pain did despite who and what he was.

Hauptmann von Drechsel's left arm was heavily bandaged and he was missing at least two fingers, possibly his thumb. His ear looked like someone had gone at it with a spiky meat mallet and was missing more than half. Deep scarring marked his head around the ear so that thick red scar tissue covered a fourth of the area where he should've had hair. The scarring extended down his jawline in twisted lumps to his lips that were dramatically pulled down on the left side in a forced frown.

Stella had approached him on the left where he leaned on the lamppost, considered going to the right, in case he'd be more comfortable with her there, but then decided that would look like *she* was more comfortable on his right. If his brother picked her for the pain, she couldn't avoid it like she was afraid.

So when he looked at her as she walked up, showing off the two sides of his visage, she didn't look away and chose the left, standing there and waiting for him to do something. Just when she was about to give up, he said in a gravelly voice that might have had something to do with the damage to his throat, "Go inside. You're freezing."

"Not unless you're coming with me," she said pleasantly.

"Then you'll freeze."

"Everyone says blue's a good color on me."

He glanced at her and she made sure to look him in the eyes without flinching or reacting to his disfigurement at all. "Why did he send you? Are you the prettiest?"

Stella laughed and found it easy. Her life was ridiculous. She was out there with teeth chattering trying to soothe a Nazi, whom she'd much rather have died of his injuries. "No. That's Hanni."

He frowned and it pulled on his scars in a way that looked painful. "Why you then?"

"Your brother said you noticed me."

"It wasn't a compliment."

"Then what was it?" she asked.

He tossed the stub of his cigarette out into the street and lit another one. "Doesn't matter. Go inside."

"I told you. I can't. Your brother thinks I'm the girl to bring you in so I'm going to."

"Maybe he should've sent Hanni instead," he said.

"He thinks I have something she doesn't."

Hauptmann von Drechsel scrutinized her and asked, "What?"

"He thinks I'm in pain," she said.

"Are you?"

Stella sighed and made a good show of thinking it over. "Oh, I don't know."

"How is it that you don't know?" He reached up and put the cigarette to his lips off to the right side where he could still reasonably pucker. "I know."

"It's just there. I don't think about it anymore."

He looked down at her feet. "You limped on Wednesday."

"Did I?" Stella was very disappointed. "I thought I covered it well."

"You did. Oscar didn't see it, but I see more than most. At least I do now."

"Oscar is your brother's name?"

That got the smallest sign of amusement out of him. "He didn't tell you his name?"

"His last name. Not his first." She paused. "Actually, he didn't. He spoke to the matron and she told me."

"Did you get in trouble?"

"He wanted me to drink some tea for my feet, for the pain."

"Did you?"

"No."

He looked at her sharply. "Don't tell him that."

"Too late. I already did," she said. "You sound like that's dangerous."

His expression said that it was, but he didn't actually say it. "The tea would probably help you."

"Has it helped you?" she asked.

"I'm beyond tea."

Stella looked out into the dark. Beyond tea. That was an apt thing to say. How much tea had she drank after they'd arrived at Bickford House from Italy? Agatha and the earl believed in tea like it went to medical school. She and Albert had had buckets of the stuff and it made no difference to how they felt, but the loving parents seemed to think it did. Tea didn't change the urn that sat in the library among the books on history and architecture. It didn't change anything.

"You're beyond it, too," he said. It wasn't a question.

"Tea doesn't heal," said Stella. "It just makes you feel better for a second and then it's gone and everything's just the way it was."

He spewed smoke in a hard stream in front of them. "Yes."

"Have they given you tea and thought something was different?"

"Among other things, but I'm still here in Berlin and this is where I'll stay."

"Where should you be?"

"Poland with my men."

Thinking practically, she asked, "Are you left-handed?"

He looked at her, surprise on his face, mostly the right. "No."

"So you can shoot."

"Do you think that's all there is to leadership?" he asked, his voice growing deeper and more gravelly.

Stella hadn't ever given much thought to leadership, but her father's face appeared in her mind. Aleksej Bled was the undisputed leader of Bled Brewery and his ability to hammer a bung into a barrel had little or nothing to do with it. "I think that's the least of it, but it seems like something the Wehrmacht would deem vital."

He smiled and a thrill of triumph went through Stella's frigid limbs.

"They do." He reached out with his bandaged limb and gestured across the street. "I was on a poster, you know. It hung over there."

"I didn't know," she said, but it made sense since he had the kind of face Goebbels would put on a poster. "Where did it go?"

"It's gone. They put my name on it, but now I'm like this, so I can't be on posters anymore."

"Or in Poland, apparently." Stella pointedly twisted Werner's ring, hoping to catch his eye.

"Exactly." He finished his cigarette and tossed it into the street. He'd made quite a pile. "You're engaged."

"I was."

"Poland?"

"Yes."

"Where?"

"Warsaw." She took a breath and decided to chance revealing Sophie a little. "I don't understand what happened. Nobody would say."

"A lot of people died. That's what happened," he said.

People.

That was oddly nonspecific. Not men. Not troops. People. The numbers had been staggering on the Polish side and she wondered if he thought so, too.

"You're not like your brother," she said.

He looked at her sharply. "I'm a von Drechsel."

"Of course." She smiled. "But I think *you* might tell me your name."

It took a second, but he relaxed. "Call me Ulrich."

"And I'm Sophie." She glanced back at the door and saw Bothe scowling at her through the door. "Oh, no."

Ulrich looked back. "Is that your matron?"

"Unfortunately. I hope she doesn't fire me. I need this job."

He stared across the street at where his poster had been. "She won't. Oscar won't allow it."

"His patronage comes with a price," she said.

He chuckled. "How well you understand him."

"I think so."

"But you didn't drink the tea."

"There aren't enough hours in the day to follow all the orders I get," she said, thinking of the missing Anna Wildholz and her nanny.

"You brought the tea with you?" he asked.

"Yes, I'm supposed to have it on my break."

"And avoid my brother until you'd had it."

She laughed. "That didn't work."

"Because of me."

"Yes. It's *all* your fault," she said sarcastically.

He stuck out his bandaged arm. "I can't have that."

"You'll go in?" she asked.

"It's necessary, isn't it?"

"For me, not so much you," she said.

"Goebbels is expecting me. I was only hoping a truck would hit me before I couldn't avoid it anymore."

"The Reichsminister?"

"I work for him now. I get the honor of censoring the news out of Poland instead of making the news myself."

"There are worse jobs," she said.

"Are there?"

"Plenty of bedpans at Charité."

He laughed again, this time fully and from deep in the chest. "My brother might actually be the genius he believes himself to be."

"Yes?"

"Oscar picked you to get me in to do my duty. I doubt Hanni could've done that, beautiful or not."

Ulrich turned her around and they walked toward the doors. Bothe instantly vanished and a doorman stood at the ready to admit them.

"Your duty is very important to your brother," she said.

"My brother's career is very important to him. Second only to the Reich. Sometimes he thinks they are the same thing."

"His career and the Reich?"

"Oscar has plans and I'm to help him get them done."

They walked in and Bothe rushed over with a cup of tea. "With Oberstrumbannführer von Drechsel's compliments, Sophie."

She took the cup and sipped the dark liquid. Not exactly unpleasant, but it wasn't going to cure what ailed her. "Thank you."

Bothe nodded and hurried away. Stella's hands started shaking so hard, Ulrich had to take the cup from her. "Give it a moment. I shouldn't have made you stand out there. It was unkind of me."

"Don't forget it was Oscar who sent me. Let's lay it on his doorstep."

He smiled broadly and then winced at the jerk on his left side. "Yes, Oscar and his ideas."

Stella calculated the risks of inquiring too much, but decided to go ahead anyway. "You must think well of his plans if you're helping."

"I haven't got much choice and he's my brother. He got me in with Goebbels for a reason."

"He is very important to the Führer," said Stella.

"And I don't have to be whole to work for him."

"Will you be able to do what Oscar wants?"

Ulrich looked past her at the door. "Goebbels wants it, too. He just doesn't know it yet." He gave her back the tea and encouraged her to down it quickly.

She drank the stuff that got spicier with every gulp and handed the cup to the doorman, who whisked it away.

"How big are these plans?"

"Big."

"Do you agree with them?"

"Nobody cares what I think."

The doorman returned and raised a questioning eyebrow. Ulrich nodded and the man opened the door for them. Stella took his wounded arm and they walked in. Reichsminister Goebbels was looking right at them.

STELLA ESCORTED Ulrich to his table, two over from Goebbels. She was very aware how the room was staring and from the tension in Ulrich's arm he was, too.

"Does it have to be permanent?" she asked.

He tried to jerk away from her and hissed, "You think this is going to change?"

She wouldn't release his arm. Now that she had him she wouldn't be letting him go. "Not that. Your banishment to Berlin."

"Oh. Yes, it probably is," he said with a harshness that she thought was there to cover the sadness that hung on his heart.

"If your brother is successful, your choices might not be so…limited."

"He'll probably want me to run it, not return to the field."

Run it. An operation.

"But if it's a military operation, then surely—"

"It's not."

They reached the table and Irma came over looking both welcoming and slightly repulsed. "What may I serve you, Hauptmann von Drechsel?"

"Nothing."

Oscar cleared his throat harshly from the next table over and Ulrich tensed. "It's difficult for me to drink," he said quietly. "The glasses…"

Stella looked at the beers on the tables. There was a certain glass for each beer, but they were all pretty big. Ulrich needed something small, but not weak.

"May I suggest Göring-schnapps?" she asked.

"Jägermeister?" Irma frowned. One didn't usually start the evening with the liquor.

Stella gave Ulrich's arm a gentle squeeze. "Master of the hunt."

He gave out a little snort. "Used to be."

"And can be again."

"I'll have a Jägermeister."

Irma nodded and dashed off.

"You should be at my table," he said.

"I have my own tables and a problem to solve," said Stella, intentionally cryptic and it worked.

Ulrich stopped in the process of sitting and stood back up to ask, "What do you need? To sit? Your feet?"

"I told you I don't think about pain anymore. It gets me nowhere. One of my tables was seated incorrectly." She quickly told him about the Temmler couples and how she believed they should be near the Reichsminister. Oscar was listening and he was interested in what he heard. This could be a good test for her and Stella wouldn't disappoint.

"Don't worry I will ask the matron," she said. "Do you dance, Hauptmann von Drechsel?"

Ulrich swallowed hard and looked down at her just in time to see her widen her eyes meaningfully. "I…I used to dance."

"But not since you became a hero to the Fatherland in Poland, yes?" Stella asked a little more loudly than necessary.

"I have not."

"Perhaps it's time to show the Fatherland and our company how well you are." Stella threw her arm wide to the center dance floor, where the first show had just cleared. The band would begin playing momentarily, so the timing couldn't have been better.

"Perhaps."

Irma arrived with her tray, five enormous beers and one small shot of Jägermeister.

"Perfect." Stella took the shot off the tray and neatly turned Ulrich so that his good side was facing Goebbels, who was watching with cold, lifeless eyes. This was the first time Stella got a good look at Hitler's most loyal follower and he was even less pleasing than she had imagined. His dark hair was slicked back from his thin, pinched face, reminding Stella of Bela Lugosi when he played Dracula, except Lugosi could reasonably be considered handsome. How Goebbels managed to be a ladies' man was a mystery to Stella.

Ulrich took the shot glass, raised it to Stella, and threw back the liquid with complete confidence that she was sure he didn't feel, but the glass was small enough that it could fit on the right without a problem.

She took the glass and asked, "Good?"

"Yes." His eyes said no, but she wasn't deterred. An unhappy man never had that effect on her and she rather enjoyed that they were always surprised.

Irma finished serving the beers and turned back to them. She leaned over to Stella and whispered, "What are you doing?"

"Clearing your table for the Temmler men."

"How?"

Stella beamed up at Ulrich. "I'd love to." Then she looked at the rest of the table, two high-ranking Wehrmacht officers and their dates. "Let's all dance. It's a night for celebration with all the good news."

"What have you heard, Fräulein?" one asked.

"We've sunk the HMS Rawalpindi, have we not? Another triumph for the Führer."

The whole table clinked glasses. "To the crew being entirely lost."

"Death to the British."

Stella squeezed Ulrich's arm gently. "And we should dance on their graves."

The women yanked on their men's arms to pull them out of their chairs. "We *have* to now."

"For the Führer."

"And the Fatherland."

The men didn't look best pleased, but they complied and allowed themselves to be whisked onto the dance floor as the band director sprinted in front of his players, plunked down his drink, and picked up his baton. Stella and Ulrich followed more slowly and Stella gave Irma a wink behind the Wehrmacht's shoulder. Irma returned a sparkling smile and got busy.

On the dance floor, Ulrich's scars were increasingly red and he glared at her. "Why did you do this to me?"

"Because they're looking at you anyway and you're not ashamed." She rested his damaged hand on her hip and took his right one, poised for dancing.

"I'm not good at dancing. Not even before."

"How are you at pretending? Pretty good, I think." She smiled up at him with all the charm she possessed. This was going to work. She willed it to work.

The band's singer ran up on stage a second before he was to start the lyrics of "You're Driving Me Crazy."

"I won't forgive you for this," said Ulrich.

"Yes, you will. I'm very forgivable. Besides, the Reichsminister and your brother want you to succeed, so I suggest you give them what they want."

He took a breath and they danced, not well and not fast, but they did dance. It was a slower and boring version of swing dancing since actual swing was outlawed for reasons Stella couldn't fathom. Ulrich loosened up halfway through and, although it would be a stretch to say he enjoyed himself, he did warm up to Stella a little.

"Why are you looking at me that way?" he asked.

"It's not you. The song's different."

"Ah, yes. In honor of the Reichsminister, they're doing his lyrics."

Stella said, "Oh," because there wasn't any possibility of saying anything else. The lyrics were an abomination and it was everything she could do to keep a neutral expression on her face.

"You don't like dancing to a song about the Lügenlord?" Ulrich asked.

"Who?"

"Lügenlord. Churchill."

Lying Lord. I'll have to tell Lady Churchill.

"Oh, I just never heard it before. It doesn't flow quite as well."

Ulrich spun her out and then back in again, growing more confident. "The change to from *You* to *Jews* is good though."

Stella forced herself to nod and say, "Yes, very natural."

"Don't look now, but my brother is smiling."

They took a turn around to that side of the floor and Oscar was indeed smiling. Stella wasn't sure if it was because his brother was inside and doing so well or because of the rancid lyrics about Jews controlling Churchill, but she supposed it didn't matter. She wanted him smiling. A smiling man was a talkative man.

The song ended and another started, this time "You Can't Stop Me From Dreaming." Stella didn't want to know how Goebbels ruined it. Luckily, Ulrich was fading and had developed a slight limp.

"Have we proved the point?" he asked, his voice strained.

"I think so," said Stella and they worked their way off the now crowded dance floor.

"What in the world?" Ulrich stopped short at his table. Looking up at him were the Temmler executives and their wives. They were outright beaming at Stella.

Magnus jumped up and pulled out an empty chair. "Hauptmann von Drechsel, please join us. We are honored to have a hero of the Reich sit with us."

"Thank you, Herr..."

"Riedel, Magnus Riedel."

Ulrich sat down and said, "Thank you, Sophie."

"My pleasure, Hauptmann von Drechsel." Stella started back to her tables when Sonja waved to her.

"Sophie, please, one moment," said Sonja. "Can you direct me to the ladies' room?"

"Yes, ma'am."

Stella walked Sonja out of the high-ranking section and the lady grabbed her arm, squeezing it almost painfully. "You are a treasure, my dear. We'd almost lost hope of connecting with Reichsminister Goebbels. How did you do it?"

"Just a well-placed dance and a wink."

Sonja laughed. "I don't know what that means, but I don't care. I know we'll get the orders now. Reichsminister Goebbels was pleased. He allowed us to come over to his table to talk."

How big of him.

"I'm pleased I could help," she said.

"You did. You most certainly did. Magnus has a meeting tomorrow. We're sure to ship thirty thousand units." Sonja gave Stella a lightning fast hug and was off to the ladies' room before Stella could ask units of what. She returned to her tables to find the high-ranking Wehrmacht officers sitting there and they weren't happy at all. They berated her and questioned how she dare remove them from their rightful table. Stella played dumb and it was effective since she hadn't actually removed them. That unpleasant task had fallen to Irma, who was well-protected over at Goebbels' table.

Stella said she'd do what she could and did manage to get them free drinks for the night. Within an hour they didn't remember where they were and wouldn't have cared if they did. The wives had great affection for Jägermeister and it was a bad thing. Stella had to clean them up in the bathroom more than once, but they didn't stop. No one stopped. The club got louder and louder. She thought that once the second performance ended people would be tired and go out to crawl back under their respective rocks, but they didn't. They got more wild. The dancing left the main floor and the whole place became a dance floor. Trying to get from the bar to her tables was like crossing a mine field of thrown elbows and thrusting hips. She thought jazz was out, but it wasn't that night. The later it got the wilder it got. Fifty-year-old Wehrmacht officers were singing "Heil Hitler Dir" in competition with some of the SS. They were all terrible singers. Several fights broke out after three and by five Stella wondered if this was actually hell and she just didn't know she was dead. Her tables were still going strong and they were old. She was young and she wanted to curl up in a corner and pull her apron over her head.

At some point Goebbels had left and Stella had hoped that would cool off the party. It didn't. Her feet were hurting badly and had formed new blisters on top of those that had already popped. Ulrich, the quietest guest, was sitting at his table nursing a shot that he'd had for four hours and picking at a plate of cabbage and pork that he struggled to chew. His older brother worked the crowd like a master politician and had surprised Stella by thanking her with a gift from the catalog on his table. Hanni delivered the simple necklace with a small diamond and a gold swastika with nothing short of joy. The tips had been high, but Oscar's gift was the best of the night so far. Goebbels hadn't tipped Irma at all. That she was allowed to serve him was the tip, apparently, and no one questioned it, at least not out loud. Clara, the gorgeous redhead, had caught Goebbels' eye and she'd been given a note inviting her to lunch. She rolled her eyes at Stella and dropped the note in a bowl of cold potato soup.

Stella was so tired at seven she staggered over to a chair in an out of the way corner and sat down. That was a huge no-no. She was only allowed to sit in the back or at a table when invited. She'd leaned against a wall and closed her eyes when someone shook her shoulder. She could barely force her eyelids up, only the thought of Bothe firing her made her do it. It wasn't Bothe and she should've known that with her eyes closed. The matron wasn't a gentle shaker. She was more likely to attack Stella with a broom.

"Sophie?" Magnus and his wife, Sonja, bent over Stella with concern. "Are you well?"

She sat up and stifled a yawn. "Oh, yes. The party is quite something."

He offered his hand and helped her to her feet. "Perhaps you need a little help."

Sonja put something in Stella's hand, but, before she could see what it was, Frau Bothe came charging over. "Fräulein Weber, how dare you sit in the presence of our esteemed guests."

Stella slipped Sonja's gift in her pocket and hung her head.

Magnus held up his hands. "It is our fault. We urged her to sit."

Bothe gritted her teeth. She knew that wasn't true, but she couldn't call a guest a liar. "I see."

"I'm glad you do," said Magnus with a glint in his eye. "We have very much enjoyed Sophie's service tonight. She has helped our company and Reichsminister Goebbels come to an understanding. We will want her service the next time we come, which will be soon as the Reichsminister has invited us for next Saturday."

He made a show of giving Stella a huge tip of thirty Reichsmarks and another thirty to Bothe, who was so astonished she could barely thank him before they left.

"What did you do?" she asked suspiciously.

"The Temmler table was too far from the Reichsminister. He was expecting to be near them, so Irma and I made a switch."

"Is that how that happened?"

"Yes." Stella made herself as wide-eyed as possible. "That was the right thing, wasn't it?"

Bothe wanted to say no, since it hadn't been her doing, but the Reichsmarks in her hand said yes. She gave Stella a curt nod and directed her back to her tables who were wide awake and shouting for strudel. The Wehrmachts didn't seem capable of getting tired and Stella went off in search of pastry.

She was right about the tired. The party didn't end until noon and even then half the guests seemed like they could've gone on for another hour or two. Only the band's exhaustion had put a halt to the dancing and management began to suggest it was time to have their Sunday rest. Stella's Wehrmachts had insisted on one more beer for the road and she had a hard time carrying them to the table. Happily, they wasted no time in drinking them since two of the wives had finally fallen asleep. Then the entire group got up, failed to tip Stella for serving them for over twelve hours of non-stop partying and left, belching and squinting at the lights that had been turned up to encourage their exit.

The girls cleared their tables and staggered out into the bright noonday sun. Someone called a cab and a second later, Hanni was shaking Stella and saying they were home.

Irena met them at the door, wreathed in smiles. "A successful night, girls?"

They agreed that it was as they tromped in and hung up their coats.

"Would you like something to eat? I have some fresh rolls."

No one wanted anything but sleep. They went for the stairs, but Irena held Stella back. "Your feet. You must soak them."

She looked down at her feet that were still in her Valkyrie shoes. She'd forgotten to change into the boots and the stained bandages were clearly visible. "Oh. Not now. I can't."

"You must for your health." Irena steered her into the sitting room where there was, for once, a small fire burning in the grate, giving the area a hint of warmth and a small radio with only a few approved stations marked on its dial played a song that could've been written by Sousa but not as good. "Sit here."

Stella sat in an armchair with embroidered cushions and bathed in warm sunlight. It was so comfortable she nearly went to sleep right then, but she did the unpleasant instead. She kicked off her shoes. The bandages were disgusting and not all that effective. The inside of her shoes would have to be cleaned. She peeled off the cotton strips and sighed.

"Oh!" Irena gasped. "It is worse than I thought."

Stella couldn't tell her that, for her, it wasn't so bad. Blisters were nothing to what her feet had endured before. "They'll heal."

"You are an unusual girl. Inge was panicked when her feet blistered. You should've heard the complaining."

"Yes, well, I'm not Inge," said Stella. "I'm much shorter for one."

Irena laughed. "You still have humor. That's good. You'll do well." She put a pan of hot water, cloudy with bitter salz, on the floor and gently put Stella's feet in. "Tell me. Did you meet Reichsminister Goebbels?"

"No. Irma got his tables, but I saw him."

"Was he as…" Irena was at a loss for words. Stella assumed she was trying to think of something complimentary but found it impossible.

"Yes. He made an impression," she said, not noting what kind of impression the Nazi gave, but Irena was pleased.

"I heard that about him. Very impressive."

"He liked Clara a lot."

"Really? She's so tall. I thought perhaps you'd catch his eye," said Irena.

Heaven forbid.

"I'm not that lucky." She yawned and untied her apron.

Irena took it and examined it for stains. There were plenty.

"I'm sorry. I tried to keep it clean."

"No matter. You girls worked a long, long time. It was bound to be messy. I will give it a good scrubbing today." She smiled and felt the box in the hidden pocket of the apron. "Were the tips good?"

"See for yourself."

Irena took out the box and oohed and ahhed over the necklace. "From an Obersturmbannführer no less. He must be someone of importance."

"He's working on something to do with Reichsminister Goebbels so I think so."

The matron was suitably impressed, placed the necklace on the table next to Stella, and said, "Try to sleep a little here and when the water is cold you can go up to bed."

Stella nodded and yawned again, her hands falling limp on her lap.

Her right hand nudged something hard in her skirt pocket. Sonja's gift. She pulled it out expecting a small wad of Reichsmarks, but it wasn't that. Sonja had given her a small cylinder. It was brown with the word *Pervitin* emblazoned on a white label. She unscrewed the top and found it full of little white tablets. For her feet maybe. The label didn't say much, just the amount, twelve tabletten, 0.003g, and mysteriously the words *Wachhaltemittel* and *Vorsicht!*

She was so tired she couldn't think what in the world *Wachhaltemittel* meant, but *Vorsicht* was attention. Attention to what? She fell asleep wondering with the little tube in her hand.

CHAPTER 12

When Stella woke up hours later, the water wasn't just cold, it was freezing. She gingerly lifted her feet out of the icy tub and put them on the towel Irena had left on the floor next to it. Oddly, while rubbery and shriveled, they actually did look and feel better.

The clock said it was already five in the afternoon so she'd slept with her feet in cold water for a good long time. The fire had died in the grate and the sun was down taking what little warmth it provided with it. Stella thought that was what had woken her up until she heard voices behind her.

"Shush," whispered Irena. "One of them might have woken up."

"Not this early," Maria whispered back.

"You never know. I should've gotten you up before."

"I'm glad you let me sleep."

"You'll have to hurry," said Irena. "You can't be gone when they do get up, especially Sophie."

Stella froze and then shrank down into the chair, lifting her legs onto the seat. Her back was to the door. Maybe they wouldn't see her.

"Why Sophie? She's very nice."

"They're all nice, but Sophie, I don't know, she's done very well very fast."

"That's good," said Maria.

"It might be too good," said Irena.

Too good?

"What do you suspect her of?"

"I don't know, but she's a smart one. She seems so innocent, just a country girl, but I can see her thinking. She's always thinking."

"Not about me," said Maria. "I've done nothing."

"Ruth, you must be careful. You can't trust her."

Ruth?

"I don't. I promise," said Maria or whoever she was.

"Now take this and go as fast as you can."

"It's too much. We can't spare it. They'll notice."

"They won't notice a couple of cans of sardines here and there," said Irena. "And here's some money."

"Whose is it?"

"Mine," said Irena. "We can do with a little less soap."

"But—"

"Go now and for God's sake hurry."

The front door opened and closed. Irena said quietly, "Grüß Gott," and the hall floor creaked as she walked back to the kitchen. Stella quickly stood up and grabbed Oscar's gift. She hated to do it but could see no way around putting the hated thing on, so she swapped it out with Hanni's swastika and then looked around for the Pervitin bottle, but it wasn't there. Someone must've taken it, she thought with irritation. Those pills would've been good to take back to Park-Welles and the earl.

Giving up, she tiptoed to the door, peeking down the hall and then going up the stairs praying fervently that they wouldn't creak.

They did, but not until the second floor and Stella made it to her room without anyone looking up the stairs or out of their rooms. When she finally closed her door behind her, she took a deep breath and collapsed on the narrow bed. This wasn't good. It wasn't good at all. Irena and Maria/Ruth were up to something. Stella couldn't afford to get caught up in it.

She stripped off her dirndl and hung it in the wardrobe. Should she move to another location? It was tempting to disappear into Berlin, but she had made so many good connections at Valkyrie, it might be worth the risk to stay. The von Drechsels were doing something with Goebbels; if she could find out what it was, it might prove her worth. And the Temmler company. Thirty thousand units? What was that about?

No. She wasn't leaving. Not yet. Yawning, she got a dress out of her wardrobe, swallowing down her concern. It was nothing. Whatever Irena and Maria/Ruth were up to, they'd gotten away with it so far, why not a little longer. Stella had another week minimum before she was due to leave. She assumed SIS wouldn't start wondering where she was for another week after that. Two more weeks. She could find Anna Wildholz in that amount of time surely. The rest would be more difficult. If it took more than two weeks, so be it.

She wrapped her feet up and forced them into the sturdy black shoes she'd arrived in. They might've been ugly, but they were comfortable, even fat with bandages. Then she crept downstairs to wash her face and comb out the snarls she created by sleeping in the chair. No one came out to ask where she was going and she allowed herself to think she could get out the front door without garnering any notice, but while going down the last flight of stairs there was a sharp rap on the door. The floorboards creaked and Stella saw Irena through the bannister going to answer the door. She sat down on the steps and waited, her heart pounding as she told herself it was nothing. People came to the door. Irena's friends mostly. The girls worked too much to have friendships outside the group and Irena discouraged dating, unless it was an invitation from a club member. Those were considered orders that must be obeyed.

The door opened and Irena said, "Good afternoon."

Stella could hear the concern in the matron's voice and her heart beat even faster.

"Good morning, ma'am. I wonder if you can help me," said a man in German but with a French accent.

Stella's hands shot to her mouth, clamping over it tightly.

"Yes?" asked Irena.

"I'm looking for a young lady I think might be living here." Despite the German and the accent, Stella would've recognized that voice anywhere. It was Cyril Welk. The bastard. How did he come to end up on her doorstep?

"Who are you?" Irena asked.

"Herr Caron," lied Cyril.

"What is this girl's name?"

"I don't know, but she's very pretty."

"All my girls are very pretty," said Irena, now relaxed but irritated.

"Yes, but this one is new to Berlin and short. Long brown hair and pale blue eyes. Very pretty."

Irena laughed. "Short? My girls are Valkyrie girls. Do you know Valkyrie?"

"I've not been, but I've heard of it."

"They only like tall girls. Ones with the long, beautiful legs."

"But this girl is—"

"Very pretty, I'm sure, but I don't have anyone new." Now Irena started sounding angry. "Why are you asking after a girl you don't know? Who is she? What kind of girls do you think I have living here?"

Cyril hastily said that he'd met the girl in a bar and hadn't gotten her name so he was looking for her in the better boarding houses.

"My girls don't go to bars with strange Frenchmen. They're good girls and work hard. What are you doing here? We are at war."

"I'm Belgian," he said. "And a reporter."

Irena snorted and Cyril apologized for bothering her. She said that he ought to find a Belgian lady not some young beautiful German girl he didn't know. He agreed and the door closed.

Stella waited on the steps, not knowing what to do or what to think. Irena must've known he was looking for her, but she lied and she was damn good at it. If Cyril doubted her denials, Stella couldn't detect it in his voice. But she couldn't be sure he wouldn't be back. And what about Irena? What did she think? Should Stella ignore the situation or talk to her about it? This definitely wasn't in her training. No one bothered to cover rogue contacts. Even risk versus reward wasn't talked about much. It was expected she would go, find a place, and observe quietly with no fuss until she was to exit. The risks were getting in and out successfully. But now she was in more successfully than she'd ever imagined. Now what?

Cyril Welk. Why did he have to ruin things? If she'd known what a little devil he'd turn out to be she'd have thrown him off the train to Paris instead of trading Shakespearean quotes and trusting him completely. It made her furious just thinking about it and she jolted to her feet. Decision made. She wasn't going to let him ruin it. She had something on Irena. If she had to use it, she would.

Marching down the stairs, Stella made sure the steps creaked like crazy. She would be heard and she would handle the situation. When she reached the bottom, she found Irena rushing down the hall, looking startled with her hat in her hands. "Sophie, what are you doing up?"

"I've been up for a while," she said.

"Have…have you?"

"Yes. Are you going out?"

"I was going to visit my mother for an hour or two," said Irena, twisting her hat. "I didn't think any of you would be up."

"Do you mind if I walk with you?" Stella asked.

"Where are you going?"

"I have an idea where Frau Klink's friend is and today is my only day off. I have to write my mother or she's going to worry and I don't have the full story of what happened yet."

Irena's lips were pressed into a firm, thin line, but she nodded and pinned a plain brown hat over her braids. Stella followed suit and they left the house after Irena wrote a short note in case someone else got up.

A few snowflakes drifted down out of the dark sky and they walked for a block in silence. Stella thought the older woman might start, but she was much more shaken than Stella had expected so she knew she'd have to do it.

"I wanted to get you away from everyone else so I could thank you in private," said Stella.

Irena's shoulders that had been pulled up around her ears lowered slightly. "Thank me for what?"

"That man. I heard you lie to him about me and I have to thank you."

"You heard that."

"I have excellent hearing."

She nodded, her shoulders creeping back up. "I thought you might."

"Your kindness means very much to me and I want you to know I will always be grateful."

"Will you?" The shoulders went down a smidgen.

Stella stopped and put her hand on Irena's shoulder. "I will, both to you and the other girls, especially Maria."

"Maria's a special girl."

"Very sweet and I enjoy her company," said Stella.

Irena nodded, but her eyes were darting around, looking for a way out.

"Don't you want to ask me who he is?"

"Oh, yes. I…"

"He's one of the reasons I came to Berlin. My mother thought if I left Munich he would leave me alone. We never thought he would follow me here." It was a lie with enough truth in it to come easily and Stella felt her own sincerity as she spoke to the kindly matron.

"He's bothering you then?" she asked.

"And he won't take no for an answer. It got worse after Werner died and he's always there. I just…I can't get away from him. Do you think he'll come back?"

Irena put Stella's arm through hers and they began walking again. "I don't think so, but we should tell the other girls about Herr Caron."

"Do you think they'll understand?"

"Certainly. They've all had unwanted attention," said Irena.

They walked silently for a few minutes and then Stella decided to ask, "Why did you do it? Lie for me."

The matron smiled at her for the first time. "He was French. We owe him nothing."

Stella laughed on the inside. It was a huge mistake for Cyril to use a French accent. Of course, it was. Irena wasn't fooled by that Belgian nonsense. Germans had no love for the French and to use that accent to get to a supposedly German girl, a tactical error of the first order. "I wish he could understand that."

"We might have to make him understand."

"How?"

"You've made friends at the club. They are not men who stand for our girls being bothered by the likes of him," she said.

"I just want him to go away."

Irena squeezed her arm. "And he will."

Stella squeezed back and they walked in silence to the U Bahn station. Down beside the tracks, Stella impulsively hugged Irena, making the lady laugh in surprise.

"What was that for?"

"For making a safe place for me." Stella glanced around for a second time, just in case Cyril came out of the stairs to accost her. "I'm always worried. I'm always thinking that he'll show up."

Irena's shoulders were all the way down, the tension gone. "I have seen that in you and I won't let anything happen. If we need to, we'll tell Frau Bothe."

"Her?"

"She's very protective." She patted Stella's cheek. "And she knows a good one when she sees her."

"I hope so."

"I know so. You've done well."

Irena's train pulled up and she got on. "You'll be home for dinner?"

"Oh, yes," said Stella. "This won't take long."

The doors closed and Irena was gone, safely away so she couldn't see where Stella was going.

It wasn't hard to find the Wildholzes' former villa. Stella had been prepared to walk the entire avenue in search of it, but the first people she asked in the U Bahn station knew the address. She was surprised her minimal description was enough until she saw the place. The avenue had plenty of mansions on it, all displaying swastikas, but the Wildholzes' villa was one of a kind. On an avenue filled with traditional mansions, very symmetrical with conservative lines and little embellishment beyond arched windows and columns, the Wildholzes' villa looked like joy and brought an instant smile to Stella's face. It was white stucco with multiple levels and balconies. The blue that Ralf and Paul had mentioned was actually incredible tile work in deep Cerulean blue and was around every door and window. It was so pretty, so absolutely perfect, Stella could understand why the Nazis took it first. Living in that villa would be like living in art. Now the over-sized furniture in the Wildholz apartment made sense. It wasn't supposed to be in an apartment at all.

Stella didn't go to the front door, although she longed to see what the entrance hall would look like, and went to the service entrance around back. There were so many Mercedes parked out front the new "owners" must be having a party and the last thing she wanted was to be seen by anyone from the club. It was definitely a possibility on that street.

She knocked on a door that was as decorative as the rest of the villa and waited. It took a few minutes, but a man in a stiff uniform finally answered and he was none too happy to see her, despite the glowing smile she gave him.

"Yes?"

"I'm sorry to bother you."

His face said he doubted that as he gazed at her with steely dark eyes. "Yes, yes. Go on."

"I'm looking for Frau Hoppe."

He started to slam the door. "She left."

Stella stuck her foot in the door and was rewarded with intense pain when the heavy wooden door hit it. She screeched in pain and he looked horrified.

"Why did you do that, girl?" He grabbed her and pulled her inside. Staff came from everywhere, exclaiming, "What happened?"

"My foot," wailed Stella for maximum affect. She may as well go with it.

"Herr Lange!" A rotund woman rushed up and saw the bandages. "She's injured. How could you, Herr Lange?"

Herr Lange was aghast and panicking. "Someone get a chair. A chair. A chair!"

A chair was produced from somewhere and Stella got pushed down into it unceremoniously. Herr Lange wiped his brow and asked, "Did anyone upstairs hear?"

The woman snorted. "Over that racket? I don't think so."

Everyone stopped for a second and listened to the strains of jazz coming down from the ceiling. Someone wasn't concerned with Goebbels' rules on music because there was a saxophone and they were really going to town.

"Who are you?" asked Herr Lange. "Why did you do that?"

Stella dabbed at her eyes and said, "I only wanted to ask you where she was. You didn't need to slam the door on me."

That got Herr Lange some vicious looks and he had to wipe his forehead again. "She's gone. That's all we know."

"Who?" asked the large woman, who was sitting next to Stella and patting her hand.

Stella bit her lip and looked at Herr Lange.

He patted his stiff vest and pulled out an old-fashioned pocket watch. "We need to serve the ices soon, Frau Brandt."

Frau Brandt continued to pat Stella's hand and said, "Yes, yes. We will. Now what happened to your feet, my little cabbage?"

Stella had never thought of cabbage being associated with affection, but like Dorothy she wasn't in Kansas anymore. "They're fine. I bought some shoes that hurt my feet. I shouldn't have worn them, but—"

"The rationing? Yes, of course," she said. "We have to make do."

Herr Lange held out a hand. "Now if you'll kindly go and come back tomorrow, we can get back to work."

"Can't you just tell me now?" Stella asked. "Where is—"

He raised his finger to his lips. "Shush."

Frau Brandt leaned in close. "Frau Hoppe?"

Stella nodded. "My mother sent me. She had a friend that knew her and I was supposed to say hello."

"Lisa, I hope. Not…the other one," said Frau Brandt rather harshly.

"Yes," said Stella automatically. Obviously, it couldn't be Gertruda. The brittle look in the woman's eyes told her that, not to mention the patting of her hand that got ever so slightly harder.

"Good."

Stella looked around, hoping to see some hint at what she should say next and finding nothing. The fences were up and they only wanted her out.

"Doesn't she work here?" she asked finally.

"No. Not anymore." Frau Brandt heaved herself to her feet and pulled Stella up with her. "I know you mean no harm, but the less said about her the better."

"Lange!" A man wearing the SS uniform of an Oberführer marched in and bellowed, "What are you doing?"

The entire staff went to attention, but no one answered. The SS was older, about sixty, with grey hair and a turkey neck. He snapped his fingers in Lange's face and the servant blinked once before saying, "Yes, sir. We will come right up."

"You're late."

Frau Brandt stiffened at that but said nothing. Herr Lange immediately gave orders to serve ices and champagne, but the SS didn't leave. He'd spotted Stella and was looking her over carefully.

"Who is this?" he demanded.

Lange did an about face and said, "Just a girl looking for work."

"Work?"

"Yes, sir. As a maid."

He looked at her so hard, Stella began to feel his intense scrutiny on her skin, hot and tingly, but she looked back innocently.

"You're a maid?"

"I hope to be, sir," she said.

"You have references?"

"Yes."

He thrust out a hand. "Give them to me."

"I...I only came to ask if there was a position. I didn't bring them."

"Give me your papers."

Stella handed over her identification and he scrutinized it closely, especially the part where she was marked as an Aryan. "Why did you come here?"

Her mind darted around and came up with a guess. "Someone mentioned that you'd fired a maid and might need a new one."

"Yes, I fired that Jew-lover Hoppe. Do you think you can take her place?"

Stella couldn't think of anything that would induce her to work in that house, but she said, "Yes, sir."

"Well, you're too pretty for a maid. My wife won't like it, but I could be induced to give you a try," he said without what she would've expected, a look of lust or even interest. He simply stared coldly and then said, "Come back with your references tomorrow."

"Yes, sir," she said.

The SS gazed around the room with a look of a tyrant surveying his domain, which Stella realized he was, and then he abruptly left as quickly as he had come.

Frau Brandt whipped Stella around and pushed her toward the door. "Do not come back. He likes you."

"He does?"

"Yes," she hissed. "And it is not good."

"Can you tell me about Frau Hoppe? My mother—"

"Don't ask me about that Jew-loving bitch. She's caused enough trouble already." She flung open the door and a gust of chilly air almost blew off Stella's hat. "Go and don't come back."

"What Jews? I don't understand."

Frau Brandt gave her a push. "We had to work for the Jew parasites for years in this house until the party finally got rid of them. Vermin every one of them."

It was their house.

"But what has that got to do with Frau Hoppe?"

"I should've fired her when her slut of a sister chose the Jews, but, oh, no, Herr Lange said we should be fair."

Herr Lange marched up, pushed Stella out the door, and turned on Frau Brandt. "Enough. We need more strawberry or perhaps you would like to go the way of the sisters?"

Frau Brandt's jaw twitched and then she turned to Stella. "Don't look for them. They're gone and good riddance." Then she turned around yelling and the other servants scattered like terrified chickens.

"Herr Lange, please," said Stella. "I told my mother I'd try to find her."

He closed the door until only his beaky nose was visible above his narrow mouth. "Lisa had a friend in the Mitte. I don't know her name, but she lived above the Maier Backerei. I think she went there."

"Why was she fired?" Stella asked.

"She wrote to her sister at the Jews' apartment." He closed the door and she heard a click as he locked it. That was the end of that.

Stella walked away from the house feeling unsteady on her feet. Lisa Hoppe was fired for writing to her own sister? Nothing made any sense. Why did they care? What harm could it possibly do? Of course, in a world where the saxophone was deemed akin to the devil, one couldn't expect sense. She walked toward the U Bahn, squinting in the dark. It was too late to go to Maier Backerei on a Sunday, so she concocted her story for Irena and the girls. It was all perfectly rehearsed in her head, but it turned out that she didn't need it.

THE LIGHTS WERE BLAZING in Irena's house. Tiny slivers of yellow showed on the sides of the blackout curtains and through pinholes in the thick fabric. Stella had taken the long way around, approaching from the left instead of the right in case Cyril hadn't believed Irena after all, but she saw no one.

The light gave her pause and she stood on the street knowing she had to go in and having a powerful desire not to at the same time. It was true that nothing made sense in the Third Reich, but she'd gotten her feet under her now. The visit to the former Wildholz mansion had done that for her. She understood what the earl, Park-Welles, and the Poppers had tried to tell her. Trust no one, they said. Of course, she had replied, not knowing really what that meant. Now she did. No one could be trusted because no one was free to be trusted. Absolutely no one.

And now she had to go in and see what that light was about. The possibilities ran through her mind as she went to the door. So many possibilities. Caught up in her own thoughts and fears, she didn't hear it until she touched the doorknob. Wailing. A high keening wail that came from the soul and it sent a shock through her. She was back in Venice, seeing Rosa von Bodmann on the floor and her beloved sister-in-law, Karolina, wailing. The crowd was around her. The smell of the oily tracks, strong coffee, and the sea. Rosa's mouth slack. Her head hitting the floor. Mr. Bast's arms around her. She couldn't breathe.

The doorknob slipped away from her fingers and light flooded the doorstep. "Sophie?"

Stella heard the voice, but she couldn't focus. She couldn't make it stop.

Someone grabbed her and pulled her inside, shutting the door firmly behind her. They were speaking German and Stella couldn't understand them. Her mind was in Venice. But there weren't any trains. She wasn't in a station. But she could smell the oil and the exhaust. Feel the damp and the severe burning in her feet.

"Sophie." Irena shook her.

"Ah…"

The matron put cold hands on Stella's cheeks and they sent a jolt through her. She blinked rapidly and focused on the woman's face speaking rapidly to her in German. For a few minutes, Stella understood not a single word, but then slowly she got every other word and then she was back. Back in Berlin. Back to Sophie. Sophie, not Stella.

She spoke haltingly in German, "What happened?"

The wailing was still going and other crying, too, of the low, sympathetic kind. "Did you hear me?" asked Irena.

"I…"

"He's dead. The notice came right after we left." Irena took off Stella's coat and hung it up.

Stella couldn't quite focus and Irena took off her hat for her. "Did something happen to you?" She drew her close. "Did that man do something to you?"

She shook her head. "The wailing…I…"

"Oh, my poor, poor girl." The matron hugged her fiercely. "Is it like when you heard about Werner."

Stella nodded woodenly, but for the moment she wasn't quite sure who Werner was.

"Of course, it is. Irma is shattered. It's not the same thing but very nearly. Otto was so young and a good brother. She loved him very much."

Otto?

Irena steered Stella into the sitting room where the girls were gathered around the chair that she'd been asleep in hours earlier. Irma was there now, clutching a pillow and wailing with her eyes squeezed shut. Other people were there, too. Neighbors Stella had been introduced to in passing and a couple that she didn't recognize. They were tall and slim with the same willowy paleness that Irma possessed. The couple was crying together on the settee and didn't notice Stella or anything else.

"Sophie!" Hanni rushed over and threw her arms around Stella's neck. "I can't believe it. Otto. How can it be Otto?"

Then she remembered. Otto, Irma's beloved twin, who'd volunteered for the navy.

"What happened?" Stella managed to say.

"The British sank his ship and reports say all hands were lost." Hanni began crying and Stella held her, crying herself, not for Otto, whom she'd never met, but for the picture of Rosa that she couldn't get out of her head.

The night passed like that in a swirl of tears and visitors expressing their sympathies. Irma pulled Stella into the chair with her where they sat with their foreheads pressed together as they looked through a photo album full of a blond boy with a wide, open smile. Irma twisted Werner's ring on Stella's finger. "I know you understand how much this hurts," she whispered with tears dripping off her chin and soaking the thick black pages of the album. And Stella did. She felt their grief deep in her own chest, weighing heavy on her own heart, even as she knew this was only the beginning and she would be the cause of so much more of it, if successful, and she must be a success. But what did it mean? This sorrow. It was all so much harder now.

CHAPTER 13

*H*anni lay stretched out on Stella's bed, her long supple limbs gracefully arranged in a way that was alluring but also completely unconscious. Stella had studied her movements and could now move the way Hanni moved but it took thought and would never be quite so effortless.

"Do you think he'll come back?" Hanni's eyes were gleaming with the intrigue of having a man travel all the way from Munich out of love for her. She could not be dissuaded from the notion that it was all so very romantic, even when Irena described Cyril as old, lumpy and entirely unappealing.

"I hope not," said Stella. "This isn't fun."

"His love is unrequited. So sad."

She groaned. "Hanni, please, he's trying to requite it and that's the problem."

"That's the romantic part."

"You have an odd idea of romance."

"And you have none at all," Hanni said as she twisted her long braid around her fingers. "Are you telling your mother about it?"

Stella looked up from the letter she was writing and brought her fountain pen up to tap it on her lips. "I don't want to upset her."

"She'd want to know."

"Maybe." Stella had been trying to compose a letter to her "mother" for three days and found it practically impossible. Being Sophie in practice was easier than on paper. This letter would be read by someone in Munich and then forwarded to London. She was to send it to an address that Park-Welles had her memorize, where it would be retrieved by someone who was either an agent or a friendly. Stella had to hide who she was but also give pertinent information on what was going on and the letter was already late.

This current letter was her fourth try and she'd finally settled on writing it to her real mother, telling Francesqua—while calling her Mutti—all her news in the way she would normally do. Giving her mother enough to satisfy curiosity but not incite more worry was a balance she'd worked hard on in the last year. Francesqua hated Stella being so far away in a country at war and Stella decided Sophie's mother would feel the same.

"You should mention Otto and the memorial next Sunday, too." Hanni wrote her mother every day and they were very close, something Stella both envied and feared. Close with Francesqua felt like stifling control along with the love, but Hanni didn't seem to feel like that at all. Her Mutti was lovely and perfect. She wrote about her garden and the neighbors, sometimes sending a carefully packed box of eggs or a jar of red sauerkraut along with her letters. Francesqua usually sent her worries with the news and Stella found that she could happily do without both. Uncle Josiah's letters were the ones she wanted, being full of bawdy tales of debauchery and overindulgence. He gave her the brewery news and the gossip. Tom O'Malley left his wife. Again. Mary Stonestreet had another baby and it had the family ears. Uncle Josiah never asked when Stella was coming home or if she was pregnant. He expressed no worries about invasion or vitamin deficiency. Her uncle didn't care what she ate or how much. Stella hoped there would be a letter or two from him when she got back to England. She'd curl up and read them first. Then Florence's letters, full of the girls and their antics. Poor Francesqua would be pushed aside until much later.

"It will just remind her of the war," said Stella, going back to writing.

Hanni rolled her eyes. "I don't think she forgot. You could put a clipping in."

"Of what?"

"You're hopeless. Otto's notice." She tapped the newspaper lying next to her on the bed. Stella was going to say no, but then she rethought it. A death notice said a lot and did it very quietly. Otto's said he died for the Führer, not the Fatherland, which was an important distinction. Some families put in "for the Fatherland" and it was one of the few things that hinted at your feelings on the Führer and you wouldn't be arrested for doing it.

The notice also gave parents' names and, in Otto's case, his sisters'. Whoever saw the notice would know who Stella was with and what their allegiance was. Very nice touch and completely normal.

"I think I will," she said.

"Do you want me to get my scissors?"

"Yes, please."

Hanni went for the scissors and Stella, suddenly inspired, finished her letter in a flurry of words. She signed it with a large "S" and blew on the ink to dry it.

"Girls!" Irena called up the stairs. "Are you coming?"

"We're coming!" Hanni rushed in, clipped the notice, and Stella tucked it in the envelope with her letter.

Hanni pasted it closed while Stella put on the ugly boots and tied the elaborate bow on her apron. "It seems like we were just at work."

"We were." Hanni handed her the envelope. "Address it and Irena can post it with mine tonight."

"There's no hurry."

"I bet your mother doesn't think that."

Stella sighed, thinking of Francesqua at one of her garden parties, frowning and counting the days since her last letter. "You're right. She's waiting." She wrote the address and waved the envelope in the air to dry the ink.

"It's fine," said Hanni. "Come on. We should say goodbye to Irma on the way down."

The girls dashed out and down the stairs, stopping on the second floor where they met Inge who said, "Don't bother. She won't let you in. I had to sleep in Maria's room."

Irma had been crying on and off since Sunday. She'd been given a few days off from the club, but Frau Bothe was growing impatient. Grief for one's twin was all well and good, but it ought not go on too long. In the stern club matron's mind, two days was certainly enough.

"I'm going to say goodbye anyway." Hanni went to the door and knocked on the wood so softly it could barely be heard. "We're going now, Irma. We'll miss you."

There wasn't any answer, as predicted, other than muffled weeping.

Hanni pointed at the door and Stella stepped up. It was accepted that she understood Irma's pain more than anyone else and she was at the front lines of comforting. She did the best she could and it was easier to sit with the grieving German girl than she would've thought, but it wasn't enough and would never be enough. Irma had told her in a quiet moment that she'd lost her other half and she'd never be whole again. What could she say to that? There was no comparison to anything in Stella's life.

"Irma, it's Sophie," she said. "Irena says your parents are coming to dinner tonight. Try to eat something. You need to eat."

More weeping.

"We'll see you when we get back." Stella joined Inge and Hanni on the stairs. "I hope she eats something."

"I hope she stops crying," said Inge.

"She'll cry for a long time," said Hanni.

"But she's always talking about sacrificing for the Führer. Otto died for the Führer. She ought to be proud."

"Inge!"

"What?"

Hanni took Stella's hand and pushed past Inge on the stairs.

"Are you mad?" Inge called after them. "Why are you mad?"

Irena met them at the bottom of the stairs. "Go in and get some rolls. I'll explain it to her."

"Good luck," Stella said without thinking and she meant that sincerely. Inge was silly, but she wasn't wrong. Everything was about the Führer for Irma and although no one would say it, except Inge, they were all surprised at the bitter grief that spewed out of Irma. They had expected tearful pride at the sacrifice, but there was none of that, only loss.

What in the world did Irma think happened in war? Ships sank. Men died and, if you were Polish, women and children, too. Stella knew exactly what was going on with the civilian population, but she had to admit the average German didn't. Their newspapers weren't exactly reporting the news as it happened, more like the news as Hitler wanted it to be seen.

They quickly wrapped up some rolls smeared with Quark, a thick spreadable cheese that Stella had gotten from an auto manufacturer up from Stuttgart. He seemed to think a pot of cheese would get him more than a polite thank you, but Frau Bothe set him straight when she caught him trying to follow her down into the dressing rooms.

"Are you excited?" asked Maria after she licked the side of her roll.

Stella smiled. "The cheese isn't that good."

"No, silly. About tonight."

"Oh, that." Stella wasn't exactly excited. She was nervous. Because Irma wasn't coming to the club and the von Drechsel brothers were, she'd been assigned their table. Some of the other girls weren't happy that she'd already moved to the main floor, but beyond a few sharp words and elbows, nothing had happened so far, but she expected that night to be different.

Stella knew this was good thing as far as being close to the action, but she couldn't help but think she was moving too fast and becoming too noticeable as Irena had said. She was supposed to move about in German society, quietly observing, and now people were talking about her. Somehow her tables last night had known and congratulated her. They told the tables next to them. Apparently, Obersturmbannführer von Drechsel was thought to be on the rise and might soon be working directly for Reinhard Heydrich. One of the Wehrmachts at Stella's table had said jokingly, "You'll want to stay on the good side of him if he gets Heydrich's ear. All things are possible." The men raised their glasses to possibilities and a chill went down Stella's spine. Never had that word sounded so ominous.

"The Obersturmbannführer likes you," said Inge, flouncing in after stern words from Irena. "Frau Bothe says that you are to give him the best of everything."

"I don't think he likes me." *Or anyone.*

Inge rolled her eyes at the other girls. "She's just being modest. He probably loves her after she got that brother of his inside *and* dancing. It was practically a miracle."

They agreed and thought Ulrich a tragic figure, but somehow none of them thought he was in any way romantic, not even Hanni, who saw romance around every corner. Mostly, they were just happy they hadn't had to dance with him. War and its costs seemed beyond their grasp most of the time.

"Maybe you can get him to bring in his new boss," said Maria.

"Who's that?" asked Inge.

"The Blond Beast."

A thrill of excitement went through the girls at the moniker. Heydrich was the director of security, including the Gestapo, and he had a few nicknames, none of them pleasant.

"Oh, he's handsome," said Inge. "I'd like to serve him."

"He's married," said Hanni.

"Why are the good ones always married?" She pouted and snatched up a roll.

"Ulrich isn't married," said Stella, surprising herself.

The other girls looked at her puzzled.

"Obersturmbannführer von Drechsel's brother."

Inge wrinkled her nose. "He doesn't count. Who would marry him?"

Who would marry Reinhard Heydrich was the better question to Stella. He ran the infamous House Prison, according to the whispers at the club. The Wehrmacht went out of their way to avoid the building because they didn't want to hear the screaming or so she'd heard.

No one bothered to answer Inge's query about Ulrich. No one needed to. The damage to his face and body took him out of the running for more reasons than simply looks. In the last couple of days, Stella had come to understand that the high command preferred perfection. Ulrich wouldn't go far. He was a reminder that war wasn't all winning. His brother got him on Goebbels' staff and he was lucky not to be stuck somewhere in a basement filing out of sight.

"Let's go," said Hanni. "We don't want to be late for Sophie's big night."

The girls got their coats and hats, bundling up against the increasing cold for another night at the club that wouldn't be just another night to Stella.

"Do you want me to come with you?" asked Hanni as they left the U Bahn.

"No," said Stella. "It's fine. I know the way now."

Hanni nodded gratefully and dashed off with everyone else, leaving Stella to take the long way around to the back of the club. It'd been decided that it was best if she wasn't seen going in the front for a while in case Cyril—who was now known as the dirty frog—was watching.

Stella was tempted to say never mind and follow them. It was so cold that night that she'd lost the feeling in her feet before they'd even made it to the U Bahn and now they were burning. But Hanni and the rest were so fast, she'd have had to run and the pain would've been bad, not to mention the effect that would have on her healing blisters, so she did as Irena insisted and left to go down two blocks before taking a right to the back alley where she could head for the club without anyone of note watching.

The alley was pretty dark with the minimum of light from cracks around the blackout curtains and she had to run her hand along the bricks to find her way when there wasn't any. The plan probably wasn't the best idea: one girl walking alone, but why should anyone else have to freeze?

When she got close enough, Stella could make out the club with its many curtains drawn. It had many windows with their tiny hints of light, the alley easy to make out behind it. She hurried up, running through the steam of her own breath and ignoring the stinging in her feet.

She was concentrating so hard on the back entrance, not thirty feet away, she didn't see him. He reached out from the dark of the side alley and yanked her off her feet, pinning her to his chest with a heavy gloved hand over her mouth.

Stella clawed at his hand, biting and screaming into the fabric, while kicking back, trying to connect her heels with his shins.

"Stop it, for God's sake, it's me," said the man.

She recognized Cyril's voice, but it didn't have the effect he was hoping for. She fought harder and connected. He yelped and almost dropped her.

"Stella, stop," he hissed in her ear. "I'm your contact dammit." He turned her around and pressed her against the wall in the dim alley.

She panted and tried to see something around to use as a weapon, a brick or something. All she had was her handbag and unless she could get one of her pills out of the key and shove it in his mouth, it was useless.

"Stop looking for a weapon, my darling girl." Cyril pulled down the rabbit fur fedora he wore. Was it the same one from before? She couldn't tell.

"You're working for them," she said.

He chuckled. "That's what they think."

"That's what I think." She slammed her fists against his chest and he staggered back. She darted sideways, but he snagged her and they tussled in the dark. Stella had done well in her combat classes, but he had the advantage of her, first surprise and now experience. Cyril wasn't an impressive man, but he was good and able to control her in three moves.

"Listen to me." His face was close to hers and she felt his breath on her lips. A vision of him kissing her bloomed in her mind. He was thinking about it. She could tell.

"Let go."

He pushed her back harder, his body pressed against her and his lips, just for a moment, brushed hers. "Listen. I need that drop. Why haven't you made contact?"

"How did you find me?" she asked.

"Elementary, my dear Stella," said Cyril. "I'm hardly an amateur."

"A professional that pretends to be French to get information out of a German. I'm so impressed."

"You think that was a mistake?"

She squirmed and said, "It was."

"I found you," he said.

"Only because you knew who I was."

"I didn't know. When you didn't turn up, I sent a message out through the embassy."

She set her teeth. "And then they told you how to find me? So much for security."

"No, they didn't," he said. "They used 'she' when they answered. It was either a mistake—which I doubt— or an order."

"How is that an order?"

"She?" He chuckled. "SIS isn't full of idiots for the most part. They don't make those kind of errors. I gathered that they were worried. That made you a new asset and a woman. Very smart in my opinion, sending a female."

"That wouldn't help you find me?"

Her eyes had adjusted and she could see him smile.

"'Knowledge is the wing wherewith we fly to heaven.'"

"Shut up," said Stella. "That doesn't answer the question."

"But it does," said Cyril. "A woman, new and alone, in Berlin. You'd be sent to a boarding house exclusively for women. I admit I went to ones for older women first, an incorrect assumption obviously."

"But my matron lied to you about me."

"She did and quite well I must say, but word gets around. A beautiful, *short* girl at Valkyrie, making her way up quickly. I knew your matron was lying to me. I just don't know why."

"She doesn't want creepy, old men hanging about the house."

"You wound me."

"Good."

"Very smart sending a girl. I wouldn't have thought the new 'C' would've been so creative," he said.

He wasn't.

"Get off me," she said.

He reached up and ran a finger along her jawline. "Especially a girl like you. So young. So innocent."

"I hate you," she hissed.

"Where's the money?"

"Are you kidding? I'm not giving it to you."

"You have to," he said. "That's what you're here for."

"Too bad."

"What's your plan?" he asked. "You leave on Saturday."

"As if I'd tell you," she whispered.

Cyril's body pressed hard against her. "Have you got a connection? Information?"

"I wouldn't tell you if I did. You'd just warn them or turn me in."

His lips brushed hers. "I would never."

"You turned in Nicky."

He pulled back and said, "To save you."

She got an arm free and smacked him across the mouth. The sound was muffled by her glove, but her hand hurt. "You're a double-crossing bastard."

"Didn't you read the inscription in your book?"

Stella had read what he wrote in *The Hobbit* a million times. It was a message. He wasn't what he seemed, but it didn't make him any less treacherous. "How could they send me to you? I told them what you are."

"Like I said, SIS isn't full of idiots," he said. "They know what they're doing, even if you don't."

"They're idiots if they trust you."

"It's my greatest skill. People trust me. You trusted me. *They* trust me."

"I bet they do. They're your real masters. So why don't you go back and tell them who I am. I know you want to," she said.

He shoved himself against her, pushing the air out of her lungs. "Never. I'm on the side of angels."

"That's rich," she whispered

"I'm doing what I can while I can and I need that money," said Cyril.

"Let go or I'll scream," said Stella.

"You wouldn't."

"'Doubt thou the stars are fire; Doubt that the sun doth move; Doubt truth to be a liar.'"

Cyril pressed his hand against her face. "'But never doubt I love.'"

"You love nothing if you don't love your country," she said.

"Countries are nothing compared to people."

Stella looked in his eyes, searching for what he would do next and finding nothing but sorrow. "I don't know what that means."

He stepped back. "I know."

Stella darted away into the alley and ran to the back door of the club without looking back.

CHAPTER 14

Stella leaned forward and smeared the Valkyrie-approved lipstick on her lips. Her hands were still shaking, but she got it on without incident.

"Are you sure you're all right?" Clara sat on the chair next to her. The redhead's brown eyes were filled with concern despite the way she was draped across her chair and the dressing table.

"I'm fine," she said.

"You've had a scare."

More than that. So much more. Stella had rushed inside and ran right into Frau Bothe. She was out of breath and shaking. The matron went on alert and Stella didn't know what to do. She couldn't say she got lost. She wasn't a nitwit and it would be very suspicious. So she'd stuck to her training and stayed as close to the truth as possible. She told Frau Bothe that the hideous Herr Caron had accosted her in the alley and she'd barely gotten away. It turned out she was an idiot. Frau Bothe had immediately called the Polizei and sent men out to search the area. If they found Cyril, she was sunk.

Stella set down the lipstick and pressed her palms against the table to make them be still. "I'm fine."

Clara raised an eyebrow. "The more you say that the less I believe you."

"I'm fine."

Hanni came in and wrapped her long arms around Stella's shoulders, her eyes moist. "I should've gone with you. I'm so sorry."

"It's not your fault," said Stella.

"I think it is."

Inge retied her apron bow so that it was larger than allowed and farther to the left, in yet another attempt to show how very single she was. "I can take your tables if you're too upset."

Clara rolled her eyes. "I just bet you would."

"I'm trying to be nice."

The girls laughed in unison and Inge stamped her foot. "You don't listen to me. I'm trying to be nice."

They laughed again and the sound echoed around Stella's heart. If they found out about her, they would hate her and curse her. That was the least of her worries, but it really bothered her and it shouldn't have.

"Remember," said Stella, her voice more steady, "you'd have to serve Ulrich, too, not just the Obersturmbannführer."

Inge made a face, eliciting more laughter.

"That's what I thought."

Clara stretched out and plucked the lipstick off Stella's table. She unscrewed the top and touched up her pouty lower lip. "I can't believe he lets you call him Ulrich."

"I don't know why he does," said Stella.

"Don't you?" Clara gave her a look that she didn't quite understand. "You're not Inge."

"Hey," protested Inge. "What does that mean?"

Frau Bothe came in and said, "It means get on the floor and be fascinated by whoever you serve, Inge."

Inge batted her eyes. "I do that every night."

She flounced out and Frau Bothe sighed, "What a ninny."

"She means well," said Hanni.

"I don't know what she means and I doubt she does either." Frau Bothe eyed Stella and started her heart racing.

"Did…did you find him?" she asked.

"No. I'm sorry to say. The Polizei will put out an alert. He'll turn up, the dirty frog."

"I hope so." Stella clenched her jaw while internally sighing with relief. If Cyril got away, he wouldn't be found unless he wanted to be. Now she just had to hope that when he said "never" he meant it or she'd be in the House Prison screaming.

Frau Bothe put a shot glass in front of her and said, "For your nerves."

The shot had flecks of gold in it and when Stella took a sniff it reminded her of Christmas with cloves and cinnamon among other spices. "What is it?"

"Danzig Goldwasser. Drink now. The guests will be arriving and Obersturmbannführer von Drechsel expects the best."

Stella took a breath and downed the stuff in one swift drink. It burned its way down and she couldn't stop coughing. Clara and Hanni laughed while pounding on her back.

"You should've given her a shot of champagne," said Clara.

Frau Bothe scoffed. "Champagne doesn't give strength. It lightens the head. I don't want her to be Inge."

"I heard that!" yelled Inge from the hall.

"Good, you ninny. Go to your tables." Frau Bothe marched out while Stella was still bent over hacking.

Once she stopped, the girls had to hoist her to her feet. The room swam a little. She wasn't sure if it was the fear or the alcohol that made her woozy.

"Can you go out?" asked Hanni.

"I'm fine," she croaked and Clara laughed.

"You are going to have a time being fascinated by the von Drechsel brothers," she said. "Unless they are actually fascinating."

"Of course, they're fascinating," said Hanni. "They all are."

"You will make one of those *fascinating* men an excellent wife," said Clara and she straightened her apron.

"I never know if you're insulting me or them."

"Them, my dear, always them."

"Shush, you shouldn't."

Clara gave her a hug. "Don't worry about me. Goebbels likes me remember."

"Are you going to lunch with him after all?" Hanni was wide-eyed with something like astonishment or it could've been envy.

"Not on your life, but I'll string him along for a while and see what I can make of it." Clara sashayed out, leaving a hint of her musky perfume behind.

Hanni frowned. "That's an odd thing to say."

It was. It really was. Stella shook it off and went upstairs with Hanni, clutching the handrail and wishing to God she hadn't drunk that herb stuff. Her head was swimming and if Cyril went to his German handlers she needed her wits. What had she been thinking? She could've found a way to say no. Maybe. Somehow. But the Germans did love their alcohol and, in particular, schnapps. It might've been suspicious.

It was too late in any case and Hanni had her by the waist as they entered the dining room that looked sedate compared to Saturday night's party for Goebbels. The swastikas and hideous posters were all down, making the club look like it could be anywhere in the world.

Frau Bothe assigned Stella her tables, very good ones near where Goebbels had sat. Then she took Stella's hands and checked them for steadiness.

"Good. You will not shame us." The matron eyed Stella, making her get a little shaky. "I've decided."

"Um…what? Did I do something wrong?"

Frau Bothe made a phlegmy sound in her throat that was distinctly German and Hanni gave her a hug. "Good luck."

"With what?" asked Stella.

"You will have two tables tonight," said Frau Bothe.

Hanni's smile went from ear to ear. "It will be so good for you."

"I've been demoted?"

Both women made the noise and Stella made a note to herself that she'd have to work on perfecting the disagreeable back of the throat sound for later.

"You've been promoted," said Hanni.

Frau Bothe put a finger in Stella's face. "Just for tonight. You go back to four tomorrow." Then she marched off to yell at Inge for flirting with the band's drummer.

"How is this a promotion?" Stella asked Hanni.

"I heard that Obersturmbannführer von Drechsel requested that you give them special attention tonight." Hanni's eyes gleamed. "You're doing so well, but you will have to dance with that other one."

"Ulrich?"

"Yes, but it won't be too bad. If the Obersturmbannführer is pleased, you might get to serve Heydrich when he comes in."

Stella took a breath and concentrated on the tabletop. "What does special attention mean?"

"You'll have only two tables so you'll spend more time with them. Sit. Talk. Plenty of time for dancing."

"I'm the entertainment," said Stella. "Like a geisha."

"A what?"

Stella's heart pounded so hard she heard it in her ears. A mistake. A dreadful, drunken mistake. "I…oh, nothing. Do I ask them questions? How much do I talk?"

Hanni hugged her again. "Don't worry. Just be yourself."

That's what I'm worried about.

"I hope I'm interesting," she said.

"You are." Hanni bent over Stella and whispered. "Really you just have to be interested in them and they'll think you're fabulous."

"Good to know."

Hanni rushed off to her tables one tier below Stella's, fluffed out her skirt, and flipped her braids over her shoulders before giving Stella a wink. The doors opened exactly on time and guests began to come in. Every time the door opened, Stella's heart would jump, but the Polizei never came in. After an hour, she left her post at her two empty tables and began helping out the other girls.

Clara had four tables of Kriegsmarines. Stella knew the ranks and the uniforms of dull blue suits and gold braid, but she'd never actually seen them in real life. Berlin was a long way from a port and the men themselves were anything but dull. They downed beer at a record pace interspersed with shots of schnapps.

Stella ran to refill their beers for a fourth time while Clara went for more Schweinhaxe. The sailors ate pork like pigs.

"Thank you. Thank you," said Clara. "I owe you."

"Happy to help." Stella *was* happy to help. It was a sight better than staring at the door waiting for catastrophe so she went on serving other tables until Frau Bothe grabbed her at the bar.

"What do you think you're doing?" she hissed.

"Helping. My tables are empty."

She spun Stella around and her eyes landed on Ulrich sitting alone at one of her tables. "When did he come in?"

"I don't know, but you better fix this immediately." Frau Bothe shoved her into the club, but Stella wheeled around and ordered a Kölsch and a shot of Jägermeister. The bartender gave her a silver tray. "Good luck," he said with a smile that said that she would definitely need it.

"Thank you." She turned and almost ran right into Obersturmbannführer von Drechsel and he was not pleased.

"Why is my brother alone?" he demanded. "Did you not understand your orders?"

Stella stammered and he sniffed. "You've had a drink. You've been drinking instead of serving a Wehrmacht officer who has served the Führer with distinction."

Stella drew up to her full, insubstantial height and decided there was nothing for it, but to go at him. He was SS. He only understood strength. "I certainly have not been drinking."

His cold eyes flashed for a second and she thought he might strike her. "I can smell it on you."

"My matron insisted I have one small shot of Goldwasser and I did as I was told. Would you have me do otherwise?"

"Your matron?"

"Yes, and these are for Ulrich," she said. "I don't usually serve Kölsch, but the narrow rim will be good for him."

"Do not use his name."

"He told me to."

"He told you to?"

"Yes." Stella's heart was pounding harder than ever and she was having a hard time hearing him over her intense fear, but somehow the SS didn't see it. He defrosted a tiny bit, but said in a tone as harsh as ever, "You're wearing my necklace."

"Yes," she said without trying to sound like she was happy about it, but he either didn't care or didn't notice.

"Good," he said. "Why did she make you drink Goldwasser?"

"I had an unpleasant incident and I was shaky."

The frost came back full force. "What incident?"

She hadn't planned on mentioning the Frog situation as it was now known, but something in those cold eyes told her it might prove to be useful and if he heard about it somewhere else, like from the chatty Inge, she would be in trouble. So she told him what she told everyone else and she detected a slight bit of concern, but she doubted it was about her welfare.

"You will be here on Saturday?" he asked.

"Yes."

"My brother really told you his name is Ulrich?"

Stella paused and frowned. "Are you saying it isn't?"

"No."

"Can I go now?"

"Yes."

Stella sidestepped the SS and hurried down to her tables. One was still empty while Ulrich sat alone at his. She put the tray on the table and decided to take Hanni's advice. She would be herself.

"Your brother leaves a lot to be desired." She sat down and slid over to serve the beer and shot to his bad side.

"Where have you been?" Ulrich was so tense he looked about to pop.

"I was going to ask you that."

"I'm the guest," he said. "And why are you wearing that necklace?"

"You think I have a choice in the matter?"

Ulrich's scars reddened, but he didn't respond. Stella pushed the shot in front of him. "I should've been here when you arrived, but I don't like to stand around doing nothing when I could be working. Didn't you see me working?"

Ulrich fingered the shot with his good hand but didn't drink it. "I saw you."

"Then you know I wasn't reading or at a movie." Stella nudged him with her shoulder and smiled up at him.

"You were enjoying yourself."

"With the Kriegsmarines? No. I'm not fond of pinching. Do you like to be pinched?"

He looked back at the Kriegsmarines and scowled. "They pinched you?"

She leaned over to him. "Everyone pinches me, except you and your brother."

"He's late." Ulrich drank the Jägermeister carefully from his good side and relaxed back into his chair.

"Your brother is here," she said.

"You saw him?"

"He saw me and he's not happy."

He turned the little glass around and around with his long delicate fingers. "It didn't go well then."

"I don't know what you're talking about, but mostly he was angry with me." Stella turned to see if she could see the Obersturmbann-führer at the bar, but he was gone.

"Because I was alone?"

"Yes and I..." Stella widened her eyes and looked away, "had a drink."

"Goldwasser?"

"Yes."

"Oscar didn't like that?"

"He didn't." She told him the story and watched as the scars on his face grew fiery red, so red that she thought this play for sympathy and protection had gone awry.

"What is being done to find him?" Ulrich asked when he regained his composure.

She shrugged. "The Polizei is looking and I won't go anywhere alone anymore."

His hand tightened around the glass and she feared he might break it so she peeled his fingers off and put the Kölsch in it instead. "Everyone knows about him now. I'm not as scared as I was when I got here." She shivered for effect and asked, "So what do you think didn't go well? I hear your brother is on the way up."

"Who told you that?"

"Everyone. I'm supposed to make the two of you happy, but I'm not very good at it," she said. "He doesn't like me. Maybe Hanni would've been better or Clara."

He reached for her with his bad hand, but then stopped himself and looked away. "No. He chose well. Oscar is always right."

"Maybe not. He was late. Later than you by the way."

"I didn't want to come," he said.

"I'm flattered."

He reached for her again, pulled back, and then slammed his good hand into his wounded one, muttering an obscenity under his breath. She reached for him, it was instinct, kindness for one suffering.

"Don't," he said and she stopped but said, "So why didn't you want to come? We're pretty high on most people's lists."

"They come here to be seen."

"And talk and make deals, I think."

"To make rank," he said.

"You don't want to do any of that?" she asked although she knew the answer.

He squeezed his bad hand so hard it had to be terribly painful. "No."

"But Oscar wants you to?"

Ulrich looked at her and released his arm. "He does and he won't stop. He never stops."

"You work for Reichsminister Goebbels. That's very good," she said.

"But it won't change the war."

Stella wanted so badly to ask what would change the war, but she mustn't look too curious. "Don't tell Reichsminister Goebbels that."

He smiled his lopsided smile. "If Oscar has his way, I won't be there long and he always gets his way."

"No? Where do you want to go?"

He took a careful drink of his beer. "Koblenz, but I don't think he'll allow it."

"What's in Koblenz?"

"Who. A genius."

A sea of black uniforms surrounded them and Stella felt the usual jolt of fear at the sight. "Are you entertained, Ulrich?" asked his brother.

"Yes."

Obersturmbannführer von Drechsel waved a pair of thin black leather gloves in Stella's face. "Get us the same."

She slid out of the chair and nodded curtly, but the SS grabbed her arm. "I have spoken to your matron."

"Yes?"

"The Goldwasser will not happen again."

She nodded again and slipped away as the men sat down at her tables. At the bar, Frau Bothe was waiting, her face red and wisps of hair floating around her face. For a moment Stella thought he'd knocked her around, but then the matron smiled. "He's very pleased with you and the club. I think we will get Heydrich again and perhaps even Reichsführer Himmler." She snapped her fingers and a barman rushed over, looking at them expectantly. "What do you need?"

"Kölsch and Jägermeister for all of them," said Stella.

"Kölsch? But that is Cologne beer. No matter." She snapped her fingers twice more. "Hurry up there."

Stella took the first tray down to find the men in deep discussions with a couple of Wehrmachts that had joined them. Ulrich sat silent and watched her serve.

Koblenz. Who's in Koblenz?

TRY AS STELLA MIGHT, the night did not go as planned. Obersturmbannführer von Drechsel wasn't interested in being entertained. She wasn't invited to sit down and chat, although several of the men looked like she would've been a welcome relief from the onslaught of whatever Oscar was going on about. He'd situated himself between the two tables so he could hold court with both of them, barely pausing to take bites of the food she brought. He did drink, but not much in comparison to the others. Occasionally he would take a sip from his flask and offer it to the others, but they always refused.

Around midnight, Stella caught several of the men checking the time. One even yawned and Ulrich looked as though he would gladly slit his throat to get out of there, but then again he always looked like that, at least a little. She brought another round of beer and marveled at Oscar's focus. He never stopped talking. Sometimes he would get up and work the room, passing from table to table to be greeted with what Stella saw as wary resignation. Oscar wasn't exactly popular, but he was someone that couldn't be ignored or affronted. If she had any doubts that he would end up on Heydrich's staff they were dispelled by the way he compelled generals to listen to him. Ulrich said that Oscar never stopped. If Stella had to guess, he simply didn't know how.

She tried to hear what he was talking about, but the club was so loud and since she wasn't allowed to join the table, she only caught snippets of what was being said. Names of towns, for instance, that sounded Polish and numbers that she wasn't sure corresponded to people or equipment or something else entirely. The whole night was an exercise in frustration until two when one of the older officers stood up and excused himself without ceremony.

"I will speak to you tomorrow," said Oscar.

The other man outranked him, but he nodded and quickly left.

Others followed suit as soon as politely possible, but Oscar didn't stop talking, moving, and working. Finally, Ulrich stood up and announced, "I have to work in the morning."

"We must discuss that."

Ulrich turned away and Oscar said, "Sit. We're not done."

"Everyone is leaving."

Oscar looked up and was surprised to see that it was true. He snorted in irritation and turned to Stella. "Get our coats."

That wasn't Stella's job, but she scurried off anyway without thinking about it. He had that effect on people. She'd watched it all night. Oscar had something and it was intense. No one pushed back at him, not even the highest ranking in the room. She doubted that Goebbels or Heydrich would resist him such was the power and persistence he displayed and it caused a seed of fear to form in Stella's chest. All the men in that room were her enemies, but none—not even the other SS officers—were like Oscar. She couldn't compare him to any other Nazi she'd met, not Peiper or Gabriele Griese or that boy in Venice who hated her beyond reason. What had Ulrich said? Oscar had a plan. She feared that plan.

Stella's hands hit the coat check counter and she leaned over, peering down into the half empty racks. "Hello?"

No one answered.

Frau Bothe ran up, panting. "Wilma's gone to the toilet. She's sick. Is it the Obersturmbannführer?"

"He sent me to get their coats."

She fluttered a hand on her chest. "Thank the Führer that he didn't come himself." She flipped up the counter and waved Stella in. "Go. Go."

"But I don't know the system," she protested.

"I'm sure you'll figure it out." Frau Bothe hurried off to Hanni who waved frantically at her and Stella took a look at the board behind the counter. Wilma's system was written in incomprehensible jibberish in a kind of grid in chalk. Why in the world they didn't have a regular chit system or tickets was beyond Stella. Frau Bothe had merely said that wasn't personal enough for their esteemed guests. Maybe that was a nice way of saying the drunks couldn't be trusted to keep ahold of a chit or ticket. But most of the guests had a stunningly high tolerance. Any one of them could've drank Uncle Josiah under the table and that took some doing.

Since Wilma's board was pointless, Stella started going through the coats one by one. The middle row had only civilian coats so a least that was easy. She glanced back to see where the men were and saw Oscar haranguing Ulrich as they made their way toward the coat check. She ran to the next row and searched for Oscar's rank on the row of black overcoats and found it just as she heard voices at the counter.

"Where is my coat?" yelled Oscar.

"I'm just brushing it," called out Stella, although his coat was as immaculate as he was and she started searching for Ulrich's coat. She'd gotten through half a rack when she heard Ulrich say, "Leave me alone."

"You can ensure success," said Oscar.

"You're a fool if you think that. They barely talked him out of the twelfth."

"We weren't ready. He saw that, but we have taken stock. Replacements will be ready."

"Not for months," said Ulrich.

"He sees the way forward. I'm assured of that," said Oscar.

"Then let me go to Koblenz. You can convince Reichsführer Himmler to help you."

"I couldn't get the meeting. I need Himmler *and* Goebbels."

"Oscar, only you can talk of this to Goebbels," said Ulrich. "I'm useless in that capacity. Send me to Koblenz. There I can do something."

"That will not happen. Stop talking about it. That plan is too radical. *He* will not even hear anything that comes out of Koblenz."

"He should hear. He should know everything."

Oscar scoffed. "Everything? What is everything?"

"All the information, Oscar," said Ulrich. "If I go to—"

"You'll go where I decide. When the time is right, I want you there. In front."

Ulrich's voice deepened. "So I can help you with your plan."

"So you can help me protect and preserve the Fatherland."

"The resources you're talking about, Oscar. The sheer amount of planning and manpower to do this thing."

"This thing? This thing?" Oscar's voice went icy and Stella could hardly breathe. "None of your precious plans in Koblenz will do any good, if the Jews are still sucking the life's blood out of our veins."

"But that other plan, the one from the ambassador. What about that?"

"I will stop that foolishness. If he was important, he wouldn't be in Uruguay."

"I'm telling you that we should focus on rearming. The losses in Poland—"

"Enough." Oscar raised his voice. "Where are our coats?"

Stella grabbed Ulrich's overcoat off his hanger, breathed hard for a moment, and then rushed out. "I'm so sorry. The girl, she was sick, and I had to—never mind." She handed the coats over the counter and slowed her breathing.

Oscar eyed his coat with a sneer.

"Oh, it's fine. Completely. She wasn't…it's fine."

He examined his coat and then said, "You will serve us on Saturday."

"Yes, of course."

"You will be at the table when we arrive."

"Yes."

"I will accept no excuses and I want that man caught." Oscar said it like Stella had some control over the situation, so she nodded like she did.

Ulrich looked at her and she tried to read his expression, but she wasn't sure what he was thinking, but he was definitely thinking. The seed grew in her chest and she said, "I will see you both on Saturday."

Oscar didn't reply but turned his back on her. Ulrich moved to follow his brother automatically, but then stopped and met her eyes. "Goodbye, Sophie."

"Goodbye, Ulrich."

The men left and several others came up for their coats. Stella had to search through the racks again and again, her hands moving over the fabric without any real brain power being applied to it. The brothers were talking about an invasion. That had to be it and some plan to do with the Jews. Koblenz. Uruguay. Her mind was spinning and she had to find out what in the world they were up to. The most obvious country to invade would be France, but the Maginot Line was in place and the French were well armed, according to the papers in England. If Ulrich was right, the Germans weren't strong enough to take it.

"Stella," said Clara. "Are you in there?"

"Huh?" Stella stuck her head out.

"I've been calling you."

"Oh, I'm sorry. I was…" She saw a coat she recognized "Trying to find Herr Koblenz's coat for Hanni."

"Who?"

A zing went through her. "I mean, Herr Köhler. My head. I'm such a *Dummkopf*."

Clara frowned and held out her arms. "You're anything but stupid. Give it to me and I'll take it. He'll get very testy if it's delayed and he likes me."

Stella ran the coat out and handed over the musty thing that smelled of fried cabbage and mold. It was a good thing it hadn't been hung next to Oscar's coat. She'd never have heard the end of it. Clara ran off to Herr Köhler and Stella leaned out to look around the club. There were coats left and no guests.

Hanni staggered up and dropped her head on the counter. "I have blisters."

"I thought you didn't get them anymore," said Stella.

"Didn't you see me with Herr Köhler?"

She couldn't help but laugh. The heavyset publisher danced every dance with Hanni and loved to dip and spin.

"It's not funny. He stepped on my feet while he was trying to spin me."

"I bet you got a nice tip though," said Stella.

Hanni smiled at her with mischievous green eyes. "I did. He was very generous. I'm lucky his wife didn't come. She's a real pill. Did Obersturmbannführer von Drechsel appreciate you?"

She sighed. "What do you think? Two tables full of SS."

"Not even the Wehrmacht? They're usually good tippers."

"Nothing. And just my luck, they're coming back on Saturday," said Stella dramatically. She wanted them back, but it was best not to look that way.

Frau Bothe stomped up and said, "Was that a complaint I heard?"

"Von Drechsel brothers are coming back."

"I know and they want you again, although I don't know what you've done to deserve their patronage."

Stella pouted. "If I knew, I'd stop doing it."

The matron cracked a rare smile. "I wouldn't allow it. The Obersturmbannführer hinted he might be bringing a guest. Any idea who that might be?"

"No. They don't talk to me. I never even sat with him."

Clara walked up, stifling a big yawn. "Stop complaining. This could lead to big things for you."

"Like what?" Stella asked.

"A new job, like Gisela Bauer. She served Herr Kissel and now she's got a good job at Daimler."

"We've got good jobs," said Hanni.

Clara nodded without meaning it and Stella pushed Hanni off the counter, flipped it up, and came out to see the rest of the girls heading down to get their coats. Hanni took off her shoes and wrinkled her pretty little nose at the bulging bags of watery goo on her big toes.

Inge walked up and said, "That is disgusting."

"I know and I'm to serve Herr Porsche tomorrow."

Inge stomped her foot and tossed back her blond curls. "I never get anyone good. Why can't I have Ferdinand?"

"Because you'd call him Ferdinand," said Frau Bothe. "Go on home and, Hanni, soak those feet."

Inge took Hanni's arm and said, "I'll make sure she does even if she takes all the good customers."

"I do not."

"You do, too, you and those big weepy eyes."

"I don't have weepy eyes."

"You do. You have big cow eyes and everyone falls for them. It's not my fault my eyes are squinty."

The girls went back and forth as they disappeared through the back of the club door. Frau Bothe eyed Stella's feet. "Best soak yours, too."

"I will."

"And do something different with your hair."

"What's wrong with it?" Stella asked as she touched the braids winding around her head.

"I think Obersturmbannführer von Drechsel would like some variety."

Clara evaluated Stella. "I think so, too. Maybe bring curls down to frame the eyes."

"And that's going to lead to *big things*, is it?" Stella asked.

Clara took her arm. "It could."

"It's not going to lead to better tips. I know that much."

"I don't mean tips." She took Stella's arm and they walked away from Frau Bothe who was already yelling at the busboys who were being unreasonably slow while moving as fast as humanly possible.

"Well, I'm not marrying anybody. I don't care what anyone says," said Stella, twisting her Werner ring.

"You don't want to stay here forever, do you?" asked Clara.

"I only just got here."

"You know what I mean."

Stella didn't actually. As far as she could tell the goal was marriage and children and it was the only goal for women. Hitler even had a law encouraging it. Inge wanted that Motherhood Cross with all her heart, gold, if possible. Stella had wanted to marry Nicky and she presumed children would happen at some point, but her goals lie with the brewery. Nicky still struggled with the fact that she was going to work, but she never considered it work. Not really. She was a Bled. Bleds brewed. What else would she do?

"So," Stella said as they walked down the stairs past a couple of crying dancers. Dancers were always crying about something and if you asked what was wrong they'd tell you and you'd regret it. They all had multiple boyfriends, some they shared, and there was forever a tragedy in the making. In Stella's opinion, the dancers made Inge look like a college professor, "You aren't getting married. What are you going to do?"

"I can't get married." Clara looked down from her towering height. "It's not an option."

"Your mother must be tall."

"She's barely taller than you."

"That's…surprising," said Stella.

"You're not the first to say so," said Clara. "I have my father's height and hair. My brother is a tiny brunette. You look a lot like him actually."

She smiled up at the statuesque Clara. "Then he's adorable."

Clara's face lightened up. "He is and despite what it may sound like, I love him very much. I'd die if anything happened to him."

"Is he in Poland?"

"Not yet."

They were quiet walking through to the dressing rooms.

"Wehrmacht?" Stella asked finally.

"Yes. Why did you say that?"

She laughed. "Well, you said he's adorable. The SS is anything but adorable."

"I wouldn't have him in the SS," whispered Clara. "Don't tell anyone I said that."

"Your secret's safe with me. So what are your plans?"

"I'm going to get into the Reichsministry. I've taken typing and shorthand. No one will care how tall I am if I'm sitting at a desk."

"You could do more than that, I'm sure. You don't seem like a secretary."

"I wanted to study physics, but that's not possible," said Clara with a bitter tinge to her voice.

Stella almost asked why not, but she remembered in time that women were strongly discouraged from going to university. It got in the way of breeding. "You should have my tables," she said impulsively.

Clara made the dissatisfied snort that Stella needed to master. "I'm too tall to please them. Obersturmbannführer von Drechsel is very taken with you and your tiny self. I'm a statue, good for looking at at a distance."

"But he's on the way up. You said so yourself," said Stella.

"And he'll take you. He's never done more than look across the room at me. You're the first girl he's talked to or requested." Clara got their coats and rolled her eyes at Inge and Hanni giggling over a note a Kriegsmarine had passed Hanni. "You've managed to convince him that he's fascinating."

"No, I haven't." An idea popped into Stella's head as she looked up at Clara's highly intelligent face. She wasn't like any of the other girls. She didn't talk like them or think like them. She didn't want her brother in the prestigious SS and she thought pretty much every official that walked through the door was a joke, even though she was desperate to get somewhere. Perhaps this was someone who could be turned to their way of thinking.

"What makes you say that?" Clara asked.

Stella decided to go ahead and ask. It might be a risk, but the whole reason she was in Berlin was to find things out. "They talk about things I don't understand."

Intrigued, Clara asked, "Like what?"

"Apparently, there's a genius in Koblenz and Ulrich assumes I know who it is and I don't. I pretended today, but he's going to catch on that I don't know anything." Stella put on her coat and sighed.

"Koblenz?" Clara's stunning face creased into a frown as she began working the puzzle. "The Wehrmacht is there. Group A."

"Are there geniuses in the Wehrmacht?" asked Stella with doubt, although it was highly dangerous to imply they weren't. All Nazis were geniuses, according to themselves.

"I wouldn't say so," whispered Clara. "But I'm just a woman who can't go to university."

"I don't know what I'm going to do."

"Who said it? The genius thing."

"Ulrich."

"The brother? The scarred one?"

"Yes."

Clara began plucking at her lower lip with a long perfectly polished nail. "He was in Poland."

"He was," Stella said eagerly.

"I heard something about that."

"What? Something about him getting injured?"

"Something about Bzura," said Clara.

Hanni interrupted. "What are you two talking about? I want to go home. I have to soak these feet."

Maria came up and sighed. "Yes, let's go home. I've got more sardines."

The girls laughed and headed for the stairs. Maria and Hanni had taken Stella's arms so she had to go, but when she glanced back at Clara, the girl mouthed, "I'll figure it out."

I know you will.

CHAPTER 15

The sound woke Stella up, but it took a long time for her to realize she was awake and hearing something real. It was so faint it was like a dream or a memory, a sort of squeal and then something else.

Stella forced her eyes open and pulled down the blankets to reluctantly expose her head to the frigid air. Irena thought that now that Poland was completely controlled the restrictions on coal might be let up, but so far her hopes were in vain and Stella had begun to think she'd never be truly warm in Germany. The club got comfortable when it was full, but somehow the chill stayed deep in her bones.

Another weird squeal and then a crackle came into Stella's room and she sat bolt upright. She definitely heard that, but, looking around, she couldn't figure out what the source was. Stella slid out of bed and looked out of her little window. There was nothing to be seen and no traffic on an early Thursday afternoon so she trotted around to go out her door. It creaked loudly and she stood shivering on the landing, listening to nothing, except a couple of voices on the floor below, Inge and Maria bickering about something or other.

She knocked on Hanni's door. "Hanni, did you hear something? Hanni?"

Footsteps made the floorboards creak and Hanni opened the door, her long hair stuffed under a stocking cap for warmth. She rubbed her eyes and asked, "What?"

"I heard something."

"What?"

"I don't know. Something…it could be a radio," said Stella.

Hanni laughed. "You heard Irena's radio way up here. You must have ears like a bat."

"No, not Irena's radio," said Stella, yawning. "Oh, I don't know."

"Maybe you were dreaming."

She shrugged. "I don't think so. It woke me up."

"What time is it?" asked Hanni.

"Two."

Hanni pushed her back gently. "Are you crazy? Go back to bed."

"I can't sleep now."

"Well, I can," she said. "Wake me up at five."

"We could go shopping," said Stella, trying to think of something to say that would get a negative response and give her a reason to leave the house. It was getting harder to find excuses when all the girls did was work.

"For what? We've used all our ration cards for clothing, even after returning your shoes."

"Oh, right."

Hanni rolled her eyes. "Go to sleep. It's the best entertainment."

"I just feel like shopping."

"Go buy some bitter salz. I used them up last night."

Stella grinned at her. "We *can* shop."

"Oh, yes. The Apotheke is so exciting."

"We do need them for your feet and mine."

"Have fun shopping for foot salz." Hanni closed her door and Stella smiled. Success.

She went back in her room and threw on her warmest dress and a pair of itchy woolen tights that had been darned no less than seven times. Then she gathered up the money she'd gotten from tips when she wasn't serving the SS and put it all in her handbag. She'd gotten by so far without bribing anybody, but that couldn't last forever.

It was Inge and Maria bickering about the bathroom and who used the little hot water to be had. Stella hurried past them, not wanting to get hauled into an endless round of who did what when.

On the ground floor, she smelled the heavenly scent of fresh bread. A few extremely generous people had given Irena their flour ration so she could bake for Otto's memorial.

"Irena!" she called out.

The matron appeared from the kitchen, wiping her hands on her apron. "What are you doing up?"

"Something woke me and I couldn't go back to sleep," said Stella.

"What woke you?"

"Oh, I don't know. Hanni said I was dreaming, but now I'm anxious. I want to shop."

Irena burst out laughing and unexpectedly hugged her. "I love your optimism."

Stella found herself laughing, too. It felt odd and slightly uncomfortable knowing that poor Irma was upstairs with tears crusted to her face. "I don't know that I am. I just want to get out and do something that isn't serving beer."

"I know. It's been all work since you got here and dear Irma…we can't do anything for her."

"Is there any news?" Stella lowered her voice. "Will they get Otto's body back?"

"I shouldn't think so. That poor family," she said. "You know Otto was the only boy. There's no one to carry on the family name. No cousins at all."

"I didn't know and that makes it worse, doesn't it?"

Irena nodded and blinked back tears.

To change the subject, Stella said, "Hanni said the bitter salz are gone. I can shop for that."

Irena wiped her eyes with her apron. "You don't mind? It's bitter cold out there today."

Stella stuck out a leg. "I've got your stockings on."

"Those old things? I just gave them to you for around the house, not for being seen out in public."

"I don't mind and they are so warm."

Irena laughed again and patted Stella's cheek. "You are the funniest girl. Inge would rather die."

"I'm not Inge."

"You are not, but what about that dirty frog?"

"It's daylight and I'll be careful. No alleys."

Irena frowned. "I don't know."

"I do. I can't hide in here forever and I promise to stay where people can see me all the time."

"If you're sure, let me get you some money. Salz aren't rationed yet, thank goodness."

Stella waved that away. "I've got my tips. They won't cost much anyway."

"Are you sure?"

"Of course."

"Hold on." Irena went into the dining room and came back with a roll with a thick layer of jam that Stella could see through the well-used waxed paper. "Take this with you." Then she gave Stella a small cup of good coffee, which she downed in one gulp.

"Thanks, but where did you get the jam?"

"My mother gave it to us. She still has a few jars from the summer."

"That's very kind of her."

"She likes to help where she can and it's only her at home now," said Irena, giving Stella another hug before opening the front door. "Be careful."

Stella assured her that she would and hurried out before the matron could have second thoughts.

MAIER BÄCKEREI SAT on a corner in a quiet section of the Berlin Mitte and it was busy, despite being rundown with peeling paint and a sign that looked like it had been bolted on the front long before the last war.

Stella flirted with the idea of bypassing the line since she wasn't going to buy anything but thought better of it. She might have a riot on her hands. Hungry people were testy people and everyone was hungry in Berlin. So she took her place in the back of the line and queued for an hour. By the time she got to the front her stomach was rumbling and the smells coming from the hot ovens in the back weren't helping matters.

The exhausted woman at the counter turned to her after the last woman in front of Stella had finished haranguing her about everything from the size of their loaves to the amount of wheat in them. She looked at Stella with hangdog eyes and said, "Can I help you?"

"I'm just looking for someone who lives above your shop," said Stella.

"Do you want any bread?"

"No. I need to find—"

"Next!" the woman yelled.

Stella put her pocketbook on the counter with twenty Reichsmarks sticking out. "Please help me. I'd be very grateful."

The woman eyed her and called out, "Hans!"

"Yeah?" a man yelled from the back.

"I'm taking my break!"

The line erupted in protests and Stella didn't blame them. An hour was a long time to wait for Kriegsbrot, especially when theirs appeared to have peas in it, but the woman didn't care. She whipped off her apron and threw it on a crumb-covered table. A man ran out with his hands up. "What's happening? What's happening?"

"I'm taking my break. That's what." The woman looked at Stella, jerked a thumb at a side door, marched over, and left.

The man stared at Stella with red spreading up from his neck to his face.

"Sorry." She grabbed her pocketbook and ran after the woman through the door and up a flight of creaking, dusty stairs to a landing that had a tall window with dirty glass and an ashtray on the sill.

The woman stopped on the landing and took a red and white pastilles box out of her pocket. She popped the top open and, instead of lozenges for cough and congestion, it was filled with cigarette papers and a little sack of tobacco. She held the tin out to Stella.

"No, thank you," Stella said.

"You don't smoke?"

"No."

"I can tell." She put the tin on the windowsill and opened the sack.

Stella didn't say so, but she could tell the woman did smoke and quite a lot. She had a fine network of lines around her mouth and eyes that she was too young to have. She couldn't have been much older than Florence, but the lines and frizzy grey hairs at her temples belied her age.

"Who are you?" she asked.

"I'm Sophie Weber and may I ask who you are?" asked Stella.

"Berta Meier. Very nice manners," Berta looked over Stella's coat and darned stockings. "We're all coming down in the world, aren't we?"

Stella had no idea what to say to that, so she just said, "Does Lisa Hoppe live here?"

Berta selected a paper and sprinkled some tobacco in a line down the crease. "You don't know her."

"How do you know?"

"Because I know everyone Lisa knows," She worked the cigarette into a tube, "and she doesn't know you."

"I'm actually looking for her sister, Gertruda."

She sighed and licked the edge of the paper. "Of course, you are."

"What do you mean?"

"You aren't the first one to ask about Lisa to find Gertruda," she looked Stella over critically, "but you aren't Polizei or Gestapo."

"No. My mother sent me."

She laughed harshly and it gave Stella the funniest feeling of déjà vu, but she'd never seen Berta before.

"Your mother sent you. You look like your mother sent you. How old are you?"

"Twenty. Why does that matter?"

"It doesn't. Who's your mother?"

"Ursula Weber. We live in Munich," said Stella.

"Never heard of her either."

Stella quickly explained that she was looking for Gertruda because she might know something about Frau Klink, who had died. "They were very close friends and my mother just wants to know what happened."

"Where was this?"

She gave her the address of the old lady who lived next to the Wildholz's former apartment and Berta's never very friendly face got less so.

"I don't know anything about that," she said.

"Of course not, but Gertruda might. I heard she attended her when she died."

"Sounds like Gertruda. Every lost dog. Always a fool. Always."

"Is Lisa here?"

Berta lit her cigarette and looked at Stella's pocketbook.

Stella crossed her arms. "Do you know where she is?"

"I do, but I don't know if I want to tell you."

"Why not?"

"Because I don't want the Gestapo coming around here anymore."

Stella gave Berta the big eyes that made her seem years younger and said, "I'm not going to tell the Gestapo. Why would they care about Lisa anyway?"

"Because Gertruda was arrested," said Berta bitterly.

Stella had heard of the ground shifting under people's feet when they got a shock, but she always thought that was a bit dramatic. It turned out to be something that did happen. The stairs tilted and she bumped up against the windowsill.

"Are you all right?"

She nodded. "I…just haven't eaten very much today."

"Imagine what it's like to smell bread all day that you can't eat," said Berta.

"I can't imagine it. I really can't."

She nodded and her eyes softened. "It'll get worse before it gets better."

"I hope not."

"Hope all you want. That's not rationed. Yet."

Stella took a breath and asked, "Why did Gertruda get arrested?"

"Traveling on false papers." Berta took a deep puff and burned her little cigarette down to a third.

"What about her child?"

Berta frowned. "Gertruda doesn't have a child."

"I thought my mother said she did, a little girl. Mother said she adored her."

"Oh, that girl. She's not Gertruda's."

"She's got someone else's child?" asked Stella, feeling rather proud of how it sounded, honestly curious and natural.

Berta grew wary again. "Why do you care?"

"It's just odd, isn't it?" Stella thought fast. Lisa must have Anna and Berta was protecting her. "Is Lisa here? She might know how to write to Gertruda."

"How do I know you won't tell the Gestapo to come back?"

"Why would they come back?" Stella asked.

"They want to know where she got the papers. They think Lisa knows, but she doesn't. She would've told me if she did."

"It's not her fault that Gertruda got arrested."

"I know. She tried to stay out of it. She didn't go to the Jews' apartment with Gertruda and she still got fired," said Berta. "Nothing makes sense anymore."

"Why did Gertruda go? Money?"

Berta finished the cigarette and said, "She loved that girl. Foolish, like I said." She shook her head. "The Jews got arrested and now Gertruda."

"What happened to the child?" asked Stella.

She shrugged. "Just another Jew." She picked a piece of paper off her tongue and flicked it away.

Breathe. You're Sophie. You don't care.

"If you could just tell me where—"

A man yelled up the stairs. "Berta! Hurry up!"

"In a minute!" she yelled back.

"About Lisa," said Stella.

Berta held out her hand and Stella considered her options. They were limited, so she gave Berta the twenty Reichsmarks. "I don't have any more for you or I won't eat. Is Lisa here?"

She shook her head sadly. "No. I wish she was. I truly do. But Gertruda got arrested and she brought that kid here. *Here.* Can you imagine? Hans saw her and he…never mind about that."

"Why was he so angry?" asked Stella with a feeling in the pit of her stomach that grew larger with every word Berta said. Where was Anna? That poor child.

"She was sick. Lisa brought *a sick Jew* here." Berta sounded like there were diseases specific to the Jews. Of course, if she believed Goebbels' posters, she would think that, just the way she was supposed to.

Stella clutched her handbag to her chest. "Oh, Berta. What did you do? A sick child and Lisa's your friend."

Berta made another cigarette and her hands shook a little. "I don't mind telling you it was a very bad day. That girl, she was crying for Gertruda and Lisa was hysterical." She wiped a tear off her cheek with the palm of her hand so hard it left a red mark. "I didn't know what to do and the Gestapo said they'd be back. They don't forget things. They have records. Files on people."

"Berta!" yelled Hans. "You stupid cow, hurry up!"

"Just a minute!" Berta yelled back and turned to stare out the window.

"Is Hans your husband?" Stella asked.

She continued looking out at nothing and said, "Yes, he's mine." She said it like Hans was a faulty appliance that the store wouldn't take back and she was forced to have burnt toast for the rest of her life.

"Did he decide what to do?" Stella asked.

"What do you think?" Berta's expression was one of total exhaustion and sorrow. Stella hesitated to say anything and when Berta sighed, the sense of déjà vu hit again, but this time Stella knew that she had been there before, in a manner of speaking. She'd seen that look on another woman, Joan Berry, a friend of Florence's. She was a widow of five years with a son and little money when she agreed to marry John "the badger" Berry, a man twenty-five years her senior, obese, and obnoxious. But he had piles of money and Joan was tired of being the poor relation that everyone pitied. At the wedding, the ladies of Stella's mother's garden club laid bets on how long "the badger" would live. Since he was sixty, sweated profusely in the winter, and was permanently red in the face they gave him five years at the outside. But he was still alive and Joan had had the burnt toast look since he turned sixty-six, four years ago. Now the ladies were taking bets on whether Joan would "accidentally" put drain cleaner in his lime Rickey and they still pitied her.

"My mother has a friend that married a man who isn't very nice," said Stella.

Berta raised an eyebrow and took a drag. "Does she?"

Stella lowered her voice. "He's gone into the Wehrmacht and they think that's the one good thing about the war."

She looked blank for a moment and Stella thought she'd made the wrong gamble, but a big smile spread over Berta's face and she chuckled quietly. "One can hope."

"I hear it's still free." Stella beamed at her. "Is Hans fit for the Wehrmacht?"

She smiled with the cigarette poised in front of her lips. "Conscriptions will go up."

"Soon, I think."

"I do, too." Berta glanced down the stairs and said, "Hans hit Lisa. He smacked her right in the mouth. I should've…"

"What did she do?"

"Nothing. She packed her things and left. I caught up with her and gave her some money, all I had."

"And you never saw her again?" Stella asked.

She finished the cigarette and ground it to dust in the ashtray. "I did. She sent me a note to meet her at the train station three weeks ago."

Stella's heart began to pound. "Where was she going?"

"Karlsruhe. She has a maiden aunt there."

"She took the Jew with her?" asked Stella with wide eyes.

Berta scoffed. "To Karlsruhe? She may as well have thrown her in the sewer. Gertruda would never forgive her. No, she took her to a doctor and he said the girl had to go to the hospital."

"She must've had something very bad."

She shrugged. "Jews carry all kinds of diseases. Lisa was happy to be rid of her."

"I'm surprised the doctor would see her."

"Dr. Ehlich didn't know she was a Jew. Lisa lied and said she lost her identification. But you didn't hear that from me."

Stella nodded. "She could get in trouble, even all the way in Karlsruhe."

"You can write to Lisa and ask about…who was it?"

"Frau Klink."

"Frau Klink. Maybe Gertruda told her something about the woman's death or maybe she knows where Gertruda is now, so you can write her," said Berta.

"That would satisfy my mother," said Stella. "Can you tell me the address?"

Berta rattled off a Karlsruhe address and Stella earnestly repeated it. She might need it, if the doctor wouldn't tell her anything.

"Berta!" yelled Hans. "I will come up there and drag you down by your hair."

Berta's face hardened once again. "And he means it."

"I know," said Stella.

The women went down the stairs, the creaking echoing all around them and walked out the door to a bakery full of irate customers. Berta went behind the counter and Hans shoved her into the table where her apron was. She kept her eyes down, but there was a certain set to her shoulders and Stella thought that Berta, like Joan, might not wait for nature to take its course. The war or a lime Rickey, where there was a will, there was a way.

Stella walked out and was immediately grabbed by a woman with three skinny children in tow. "Are they out? I need something for the children."

"No, no. They're not out," Stella said. "I didn't have enough rations to get a loaf."

The woman frowned and picked up her youngest, a little boy no older than Anna Wildholz. "I hope he isn't too strict about the rations. The children must eat."

Stella wasn't optimistic, but she nodded and smiled. "I don't know. I have to wait until next week."

The child began to whine and suck on his fingers as if he might get milk from them. His mother tugged on his threadbare coat and said, "I have waited a long time out here."

"I know and it is so cold. The children might get sick."

"They are sick. This little one, he coughs and coughs at night."

Stella made sure she looked very sympathetic, all the while her mind was racing. "Do you have a good doctor?"

"A doctor? Who can afford a doctor?"

"I heard a Dr. Ehlich was good with children."

The woman tilted her head and thought about it. "Yes, he is. But one must still pay."

"My sister is looking for a doctor for her little girl. Is Dr. Ehlich nearby?"

"Does she have money?"

"A little," said Stella. "She's getting worried. I will help if I have to."

"You will have to," she said. "Dr. Ehlich is very good with the children. Very kind and so very busy. Be ready with your Reichsmarks."

"I will tell her. Where is his office?"

The woman gave her directions to the doctor's house several blocks away and Stella thanked her before glancing back at the bakery. Berta was watching her through the open door. She nodded at Stella with a new understanding in her eye, but somehow Stella wasn't worried. Berta wouldn't say anything. They had an understanding and it would hold. Besides what did Berta care if she was really looking for a sick little Jew anyway? The trail led away from Lisa and that was all that mattered to her friend.

Dr. Ehlich lived on a quiet street with large but ordinary houses and old trees that spread their skeletal branches over the street to touch, making the area seem colder and more desolate than other streets.

There was a brass plaque on the brick pillars that gave the doctor's name and specialties, obstetrics and pediatrics, but there was no longer a gate or fencing. More iron gone to the war effort.

Stella followed the arrow on the plaque and went around the right side of the house to a side door where there was another plaque with hours and days of the week. She would've made it under the wire at four thirty, but another sign hung above the plaque and it said the doctor was closed. No explanation and the sign was hastily written on a piece of cardboard.

She cupped her hands and peered through the glass at the dark office. Then she tried the door. Stella wasn't above going in and rummaging through the files, but the door was locked and breaking the glass was a bad idea so she rang the bell and pounded on the door, fully expecting for someone, a servant at the very least, to come down to tell her off in annoyance, but no one did.

She rattled the handle in frustration. This was ridiculous. She only had until Sunday before her time was officially up and she'd never imagined that Anna Wildholz would be in a hospital or that Gertruda was out of the picture. It wasn't simply a matter of location and handing over new paperwork and money for another Kindertransport anymore. Stella had to get the child out herself, but how and where was she? Anna could still be in the hospital, but if she were that sick, what were the chances of Stella being able to get her out of there? Low. Lower than low, being that she wasn't a relation. Lying was all well and good, but a hospital would want paperwork. Come to think of it, so would an orphanage.

An icy wind kicked up and clouds came over to block out most of the remaining sun. Stella shivered in her thin coat and rushed around the house to the front. She poked the bell a half dozen times until a young maid, no older than fourteen, opened the door. The girl's eyes were swollen and her nose red.

"Yes?" she asked in a voice raw from crying.

"I need to see the doctor. I'm looking for a ch—"

"He's gone. They're all gone." She wiped away a tear and went to close the door.

"I saw the sign. When will the doctor be home? I need to see him or his nurse," said Stella.

"I don't know."

"Well, where are they?"

A sob rippled through her slim body and she squeaked out, "Neuburg an der Donau."

The name wasn't familiar to Stella and she asked, "Why are they there?"

The girl could hardly speak for crying and it came out slowly that the doctor's sons were in Neuburg an der Donau for flight training. One of the sons was flying at night using his instruments, lost his bearings, and crashed into the base, killing several men including the other son. The doctor and his wife were retrieving the bodies and their remaining children were with relatives.

Stella listened to the story with a feeling of heavy dread coming over her, the way it always did when she heard about a training crash and there were so many in England. Hardly a day went by without something awful being reported. One good thing about being in Germany was that she wasn't allowed to follow the news in England and the state propaganda didn't like to cover accidents where men died for no reason other than a mistake. Now the dread was back and she found it hard to speak.

"I didn't know," she said, picturing Nicky dead and mutilated in some field somewhere.

The girl blew her nose on a soggy handkerchief. "Did you know them?"

"No, I didn't."

"They were lovely. Always nice to everyone, even me," she said with a fresh sob.

"I'm sure they were." Stella took a breath and tucked the image of Nicky away in a little worry box somewhere deep inside where she could think about it later when it wouldn't scare her quite so much. "When did the doctor leave?"

"Three days ago."

"And you haven't heard from him?" she asked.

The little maid shook her head.

Three days. Three days.

"Do you think he'll be back soon?"

"I don't know."

Stella wanted to scream. How long did it take to get bodies and transport them back home? She had no idea. That wasn't part of any training. Thinking of all the time she spent learning the different ranks and medals, Stella wanted to throw something. Utterly useless. Hanni didn't know medals and the rank structure. Ridiculous waste of time.

"You see," Stella was careful to speak respectfully and softly, "I'm looking for a child that came to the doctor a few weeks ago. She was very sick and was sent to the hospital."

The girl went blank. "I'm only a maid. I don't have anything to do with the surgery."

"Do you know where the doctor sends children when they have to go to the hospital?"

She sucked in her lips and then shrugged. "What was wrong with her?"

"I don't know," said Stella.

"There are a few hospitals for the children. Go to them."

"You see, I'm from Munich. I don't know the hospitals."

"Oh, Munich. I hear that it is very beautiful. The Führer loves Munich. Have you seen the Führer there?"

Stella swallowed hard and said, "I haven't. Can you tell me the hospitals where the doctor sends children?"

"Charité is a big hospital, but it is not close." She blew her nose. "There's Weißensee and St. Joseph's."

The girl went on to name several other hospitals, but Stella knew after the first three it was over. She couldn't go to every hospital and ask about a patient she had no right to be asking about. It would take forever and getting out of the house was difficult at best. If she could get the girl to let her in… No. One good look at the girl's thin face told her that wasn't possible. The sons had been nice, she said, even to her. She didn't have any status and it would be a huge risk for her.

"Thank you," said Stella. "I think I'll come back."

The girl nodded and closed the door. Stella stood there for a moment, wondering what to do. It was unlikely that the doctor would be back the next day and Saturday was Otto's memorial. And Valkyrie. There was always Valkyrie. She'd have to wait until Sunday to come back.

Stella spun around and hurried down the walk to the street, putting Anna out of her mind. She couldn't do anything. No one knew Anna was Jewish and if she was so sick that she was still in the hospital, that was the best place for her. An orphanage wasn't ideal, but she hadn't been abandoned on the streets. That, at least, was a comfort.

CHAPTER 16

"Sophie! Hurry!" yelled Irena. "You'll be late!"

Stella ran a comb through her hair and tied her apron as she ran out of her room. "I'm coming."

The girls were all waiting at the foot of the stairs and they were a somber group. Irma stood by the door with Maria and Hanni supporting her. Frau Bothe had called and said Irma was expected back at work, no excuses and no crying.

"Your apron," said Inge.

Stella looked down and it was all askew. "I'll fix it later."

"Let me. You represent Valkyrie and Frau Bothe is already mad at us. We can't make her any madder." Inge fussed over Stella's apron, but it was such a trivial thing with Irma standing there, colorless and glassy-eyed, that Stella was annoyed. Irma wasn't crying, but every so often a quake went through her gaunt body and Stella couldn't see how she could get through a night at Valkyrie as devastated as she was.

"Why is she mad?" Stella asked, although it was practically irrele-vant. Frau Bothe was always mad about something.

"It's my fault," said Maria.

"No, it's mine," said Irma.

Irena shook her head. "I should never have given you the phone."

"I said it," said Maria.

"It was about me," said Irma.

Irena took one of Irma's hands. "You can't be held responsible."

Stella threw up her hands and asked, "Someone tell me what happened."

Maria blushed furiously. "I told Frau Bothe that she was being mean for making Irma come back when she wasn't ready and she should have until Monday after the memorial."

"What did she say?"

"That if we didn't like how she ran Valkyrie, we could look for other jobs. She heard that Siemens was hiring."

A shudder went through the girls. They didn't see themselves as factory girls in the slightest and neither did Stella. If they got fired, she would find Anna and leave Germany immediately. There wasn't a whole lot of information to be had on a factory floor.

"I guess we'll just have to be extra charming then," said Stella.

"You don't have to be anything," pouted Inge. "You've got Obersturmbannführer von Drechsel twisted around your tiny little fingers."

Stella rolled her eyes. "He has no interest in me. He's only interested in the war."

"He keeps requesting you."

"The Führer only knows why."

"Just keep him happy," said Irena. "We all need your work at Valkyrie to keep things going."

She opened the door and the girls filed out. Irma was walking, but Stella wasn't entirely sure it was on her own.

"I'm sorry it took so long," Stella said as she grabbed her coat and hat off the rack. "I'll be extra sweet to the Obersturmbannführer on Saturday."

"See that you do."

Stella went for the door, but Irena called out to the others, "Sophie will be right there," and she closed the door. "I need to talk to you."

Stella's chest got tight and she ran through what she could've done to give herself away. Someone saw her at the bakery and reported back to Irena. Or the doctor's house. Or the pharmacy called and said there wasn't any line to delay her.

"Don't look so scared," said Irena. "You aren't in trouble. At least, I hope not."

"What do you mean?"

Irena held out her hand and in the palm was the little tube Sonja, the Temmler executive's wife, gave her. "Is this yours?"

"Yes. Where did you find it?" Stella asked.

"In the sitting room on the floor." Irena exuded disapproval, but Stella couldn't imagine why. She went to take the Pervitin, but the matron closed her hand into a fist. "Why do you have this? Is this why you wanted to go to the pharmacy?"

"No. I don't even know what it is."

Irena crossed her arms.

"I don't. A guest gave it to me as a kind of thank you," said Stella.

"A guest? Which guest?"

"Magnus Riedel's wife. They were at my tables one night."

"Who is he?"

"A Temmler executive. Why?"

Irena took a breath and relaxed. "Now I understand."

Maria opened the door and peeked in. "We have to go."

"Yes, yes. Start walking. Sophie will catch up."

"All right." Maria was puzzled but she obeyed.

Stella put on her coat and buttoned it. "Well, I don't understand. Is there something wrong?"

"No, dear girl, not as long as you're not taking them."

"What are they?"

"Pills for energy, but they're very bad for you."

"But don't they sell them at the pharmacy?" Stella asked.

"They do, but they shouldn't. My brother is a doctor in Mannheim. He says they are addictive and you must not take them. None of my girls take them. I should've talked to you before, but I forgot."

Stella put on her hat and tried to seem worried when she really wanted to smile. "I understand and I won't take them. I promise."

Irena hugged her. "I'm glad you trust me and will not."

"But can I have the tube?"

She went stiff. "Why would you want them?"

"Herr Riedel will probably come back. He might ask me about them. Shouldn't I have them with me?"

Irena thought about it and then nodded. "Yes, you should. Other girls at the club take them to keep up and he will think it odd if you don't have his gift."

Stella took the tube and put it in her handbag. "Thank you for the warning. My mother wouldn't want me to take a pill like that."

"That's what I'm here for," said Irena. "Have a good night."

A good night was guaranteed. Stella allowed herself to smile as she went out into the darkness. So the military had ordered 30,000 units of energy pills. It was a very good night indeed.

STELLA's good cheer didn't last long. Valkyrie was packed as always and Irma wasn't able to do her bit. The girls raced around covering for her while Frau Bothe scowled from the wings. The woman had absolutely no sympathy for a girl in mourning and had declared that Otto was only a brother, not a husband. Such grief was only required for husbands and, in a nod to Stella's grief, possibly fiancés. She said it like Irma had bought grief pills and decided to take too many. It was ridiculous and insulting. Stella could only imagine what she would feel if one of her brothers died. They were loud and smelly at the best of times, but she loved them dearly.

The best thing to do was keep quiet. Frau Bothe was angry at Maria for accurately calling her mean and had moved her off her good tables to a spot way out by the kitchens where the least desirable guests sat. Stella got moved up next to Irma's tables, where she and Hanni did their best to help, but Irma hadn't been eating and she was weak. Sometimes she seemed disoriented.

A hand reached out and snagged Stella's skirt, almost pulling her off her feet since she'd been nearly running to cover the extra tables.

"Can I help you, sir?" she asked the SS who glared up at her.

"What is she doing?" He pointed up two levels to where Irma was standing on the stairs, holding a large tray and staring blankly at the band, where the musicians were ripping off Glen Miller. Some Reich songwriter wrote "Moonlight Serenade". Right.

"I'll take care of it, sir," she said. "Right away."

"You better or I'm talking to your matron."

"Yes, sir." Stella dashed up the stairs and gently took the tray, laden with shots and beer, away from Irma.

"Otto would've loved that song," she said, a tear slipping down her cheek.

"I know." Stella managed to balance the tray on one hand—a feat she wouldn't have thought possible a month ago—and turned Irma around with the other. "Go take a break."

"I can't."

Stella pushed her up the stairs and then rushed back down to serve the grouchy SS. She talked them out of complaining by batting her eyes and saying that Irma had lost a beloved brother for the Führer. Frau Bothe said not to mention that to any guest because the war didn't belong inside Valkyrie as if the massive amount of uniforms wasn't a dead giveaway.

The plea for sympathy worked barely, but the men thought Irma ought to shape up for the Führer. Whatever that meant. She took some food orders and went to her tables to check on them. While she was discussing the merits of adding Leberkäse to the menu with a couple of intoxicated Luftwaffe pilots from Augsburg—drunk Bavarians always wanted Leberkäse—Stella saw Frau Bothe go after Irma with Clara intervening. The redhead sent Irma to the bar and had a tense discussion with Bothe, who gave her something and then marched away.

"I will ask the kitchen if they can find you Leberkäse," said Stella, backing away.

"God, you're beautiful," slurred the younger of the duo.

"She's married," said the other.

"I heard he died."

"Did he die?" The pilot grabbed her wrist and trained an unfocused eye on her Werner ring.

"Yes, he did." She peeled his fingers off and straightened his tie. "I will be right back."

"I think I love…" He fell over and took his fellow Bavarian with him.

For crying out loud.

Stella checked on the men, both of whom looked perfectly happy lying on the floor. "I'm going to get…something."

She ran up the stairs and caught sight of Clara tucking something in her pocket. "Clara!"

Clara turned around, looking like she ought to be on stage, and raised an eyebrow, perfectly penciled. "Oh, Sophie. Thank goodness."

"What did Bothe say?" Stella panted and leaned on the bar.

"Are you sure you want to know?"

"I think I have to. Is she firing Irma?"

"Not yet, the wretched witch," said Clara. "I talked her out of it."

"Did she give you something?" asked Stella.

Clara leaned on the bar, too, but not like she was exhausted, which they all were. Clara never looked exhausted or anything less than perfect. "Have you been watching me?"

At times like that it was best to be completely honest. "Yes. You got in the way of something with Irma. What happened?"

Clara gave out a surprisingly undignified snort. "Bothe knows about your matron."

"Irena? What about her?"

"You know, how she won't let her girls have a little bump. She wanted to talk Irma into it anyway. I told her I'd do it."

"What are you talking about?" asked Stella.

Clara eyed her and asked, "Where are you from?"

"Munich."

"Don't they have Pervitin there?"

"Oh, that," said Stella. "Irena doesn't want us to take that. She told me today."

"You didn't know about it before?"

"The Temmler executive gave me some, but I didn't know what it was. Why does Bothe want Irma to take it?"

"To wake her up, of course," said Clara. "It would work, but in her state, it might kill her."

"Kill her?"

The state ordered 30,000 pills of something that could kill their men?

The barman offered Clara a shot of cherry schnapps and she downed the fiery liquid in one go, despite drinking being forbidden. "Don't look so worried. She'd probably be fine. I use it all the time."

"You do?"

"Sure. How do you think I get through Saturday nights?" She swept a long arm across the club. "How do you think they do?"

"I did wonder how in the world they could be here for twelve hours and never get tired," said Stella.

"Twelve hours? That's nothing. After Warsaw fell, try twenty-four. I thought we'd never get out of here."

"That's amazing."

"It is. You should try it sometime. Just half a pill though, if you want to sleep in the near future."

"You aren't going to give it to Irma, are you?" Stella couldn't allow that.

"No. Of course not. Irma's never taken it before and she looks like she might throw herself out a window already."

"Good. Thank you for intervening."

"I'm happy to help and I got a pill for free so it all works out."

Bothe marched back over. "What are you two talking about?"

"We are taking a break," said Clara, haughtily as possible.

"No breaks. Look at this place. And where is Irma?"

"Adjusting to her bump." Clara steered Bothe to the backstage door. "You should take a break. We've got the club. Don't worry."

"Irma's back?"

"Absolutely." Clara rolled her eyes over Bothe's head at Stella. "You go put your feet up. I think they're swelling."

Frau Bothe looked down at her fat ankles and exclaimed. "I really must sit down."

"See. You have to take care of yourself." Clara gently pushed Bothe through the door to the office and closed it firmly behind. "If only we could bolt it shut."

"I wish," said Stella, turning to put in her drink orders. "I have to ask the kitchen about Leberkäse again."

"Don't ask. Say you asked."

"I hate to lie," said Stella, innocently.

Clara laughed. "You are too good for this club. Just do it, Sophie. You can't bother the kitchen every time you have drunk Bavarians because that's every night."

"Not *every* night."

The girls laughed and the barman gave them their trays.

"Oh," said Clara. "Catch up with me later. I have news for you."

"News?"

She leaned over to whisper in Stella's ear. "There *is* a genius in Koblenz." Then Clara was off, working her way above the crowd in more ways than one, leaving Stella exhilarated and antsy to get the night over with.

But the night wasn't anxious to end. It went on and on into the wee hours, straining Stella's patience and ability to keep Frau Bothe away from Irma. All the girls helped, including ones that didn't live at Irena's. Maybe Frau Bothe didn't understand loss and grief, but Valkyrie did. Practically everyone from the barmen to the band had lost someone at some time and they helped. A drummer cornered the matron on a break to discuss what songs she thought might be the most appropriate when attacks on Britain began in earnest. A barman insisted they didn't have enough Elderflower liquor and took her down to storage to count the bottles. Stella had never had anyone order Elderflower liquor so she doubted there was a pressing short-age. People came up with all kinds of ploys. Girls broke glasses, faked proposals, and Inge went so far as to slip in a non-existent puddle in a showy fall that got her quite a bit of attention from a handsome Kriegsmarine. Stella wasn't sure if it was entirely for Irma's benefit, but it kept Bothe away from their grieving housemate and that was good enough.

When the last guests heaved themselves out of their seats and staggered to the coat check, Stella went in search of Clara and found Irma instead, sitting in a dark corner on the floor with her legs in a pool of spilled beer.

"Irma, what are you doing?" exclaimed Stella.

She pushed her long blond hair out of her face, revealing swollen eyes and blotchy red cheeks. "I don't care."

Stella got a towel, dried her legs, and wiped up the beer. "Don't care about what?"

"This."

"The club?"

She shrugged and began to cry again.

"It will get better," said Stella because that's what people said about such things.

"Otto's always going to be dead. I'll always be alone."

She wasn't wrong and there was nothing to be said that could make it different. Stella wished she could tell her that things did change, that they'd changed for her, but she couldn't because they hadn't. Not really. There were still moments when she felt exactly the same way she did when Uncle Josiah told her that Abel was dead, like no time had passed, not a minute, not an hour. Agatha swore time would heal, but Stella was fairly sure that only action would heal, but she could hardly tell Irma any of that.

"All I know is someday it will get better. It has to get better," said Stella.

"Do you feel better?"

Stick to the truth.

"Not really, but I don't cry all the time anymore, so I guess that's something."

Irma surprised her by saying, "You aren't very good at comforting."

"That's why I serve beer and get my bottom pinched."

"How bad was it tonight?"

"Average." Stella showed the marks on her thighs, a testament to how she'd gotten Irma's SS officers to forget about her.

"I'm sorry," said Irma.

"I'm not. What's another pinch here or there? You've still got a job and now we're getting out of here."

Maria and Inge came up and asked if everything was all right. They said that because that's what you say and Irma got up. The other girls put their arms around her waist, saying that Bothe was in the kitchens so they'd better hurry up.

Stella scanned the club, looking for Clara, until Inge called back, "Coming, Sophie?"

"I am." She went after them, waving to Wilma in coat check and the barmen who were wiping the many counters at the enormous bar before she went downstairs into the chaos of the dressing rooms. Everyone was exhausted and trying to get home as quickly as possible. Coats and hats were tossed across the room and a shoe went zinging past Stella's ear.

"What is happening?" she asked a girl next to her, who was pulling on a pair of rubber boots.

"There's a storm coming in. Sleet and lots of snow."

Stella groaned.

"If we don't hurry, we won't get a cab. They'll go home," said the girl.

"Sophie!" Hanni waved from the coat room and then threw Stella's handbag over. Stella caught it and three more. One went too high for her, but Clara came through the door and nabbed it with no difficulty.

"Sometimes I hate being short," said Stella.

"You'll get no sympathy from me." Clara took her coat and hat from one of her housemates. "I have to get out of here. This is insane."

"I'll take the handbags up to get out of the way," she called over to Hanni.

"Good. We'll be right up. I can't find my hat," said Hanni.

Stella squeezed through the door between two male dancers who were trying to cut through to their dressing room and ran up the stairs, keeping her eyes trained on Clara's red hair. It wasn't easy. The cleaning staff had been released without finishing their work and Stella could barely fit up the stairs past the rotund ladies, whom she suspected feasted on guest's leftovers while they scrubbed the kitchen and the rest of the club.

She weaved through the barmen who were heading for the stairs and spotted Clara at the door to the lobby. "Clara! Wait!"

Clara tugged on a particularly ugly wool hat and turned around. "Oh, Sophie. What's wrong?"

"Nothing. You were going to tell me about that thing in Koblenz."

"Right. I forgot." She pushed open the door and they went into the lobby to peer out into the storm. It was no joke. Ice pinged against the windows and several girls piled into a cab that had spun up onto the sidewalk when it pulled up.

"I hope my girls hurry," said Clara. "I don't want to sleep here again."

"Again?"

"It happened twice last year, but at least it's Thursday and we're getting out at a reasonable time."

Stella noted that reasonable in Clara's book was three o'clock in the morning. When she thought about it, it was a wonder that there were any cabs at all. "So what's this about the genius in Koblenz? I really want to sound like I'm not a ninny."

"If you were a ninny, Obersturmbannführer von Drechsel wouldn't have bothered with you. He has little patience with stupidity or anything else, for that matter."

"So you know him well?" asked Stella.

Clara's face creased into an expression of extreme distaste. Stella wouldn't have thought it possible for her to have so many folds in her frown. "I know about him. He isn't quiet or subtle."

"Subtle about what?"

"Anything. He's a man of passionate dislikes."

"And this genius that Ulrich wants to work with? Oscar dislikes him?"

"If he does, it's because he thinks there's no advantage in him. By advantage, I mean advantage to the Obersturmbannführer." Clara's nose touched the glass. "I don't see any more cabs. This is not good."

"Who is it?"

"Huh?"

Stella could barely contain the desire to shake Clara. "The genius."

Clara turned her attention back where Stella wanted it. "I forget you're not exactly an operator."

Stella frowned. "What do you mean?"

"You've not been here long and aren't exactly interested in the government."

Her heart leapt a little in her nervous chest. That was perfect, exactly what she wanted. "I never thought about it."

"That's what I mean," said Clara. "So the genius is Erich von Manstein, Chief of Staff of Group A in Koblenz."

Stella made a face. "I thought a genius would mean science."

Clara smiled down at her. "I do find you funny. Military science. That's the science that matters now and Manstein is the best at it, according to some."

Stella was frantic for information. This could be just what she needed. "Then why is he just a Chief of Staff?"

"Why do you think? He's not a favorite. I heard he went against General Halder. That's not a good idea."

"So Halder's the favorite then," said Stella. "But if Ulrich likes von Manstein, I should talk about him and not Halder. I wonder if that's who Oscar wants Ulrich with. Halder, I mean."

"Oscar. Ulrich. You do sound chummy," said Clara.

"I'd rather sound smart."

"You will. You don't have to say much."

What to say? How much to say?

"Oscar wants him to be at the front of something. He said so. But maybe Ulrich would be safer with von Manstein."

Clara smiled at her, knowingly. "You like him."

Stella thought about it and found she did or, at least, she had some compassion for his injuries. Ulrich was still the enemy, compassion or no. "I do. He's interesting."

"Interesting. Right." She glanced back and said, "Thank goodness. Here they come."

"Maybe he should just stay with Goebbels. He's injured."

"Darling, he's just there to get on his feet and help his brother. When that's done he'll be gone."

"Help him with what?"

Clara's housemates crowded around them, complaining about the weather and then yelling that a cab was coming down the street.

"See you tomorrow!" called out Clara. "Get a cab as soon as you can."

Stella nodded and waved as Hanni and the rest of the girls came into the lobby. She could barely talk she was so full of information. Halder. Manstein. Plans. Oscar's plan and something that was coming out of Koblenz, probably from the genius. It didn't seem like the same thing. Oscar didn't want Ulrich in Koblenz, so the plans were different.

The whole thing made Stella's tired head hurt and she let the girls sweep her out the door and through a truly miserable shower of freezing rain into a crowded cab. The girls chattered endlessly on the long and very slow drive home, all except Irma who stared out into the storm, unseeing, and Stella who wanted to see everything.

It was close to five in the morning when Stella fell into bed wearing Irena's woolen stockings under her nightgown, two sweaters, and a knitted cap that Inge let her borrow that smelled like fish and onions, but Stella was too tired and cold to mind. The freezing rain was so intense that the girls got partially soaked on their way into the cab and thoroughly soaked on their way out.

When Irena met them at the door, she had a pile of towels and blankets, but it wasn't enough in a house where you could see your breath. They crowded around a tiny coal fire in the sitting room and rubbed their wet skin raw, trying to warm up. Irma didn't even try to dry herself. Hanni caught her climbing into bed still wet and forced her back downstairs to the fire. They all worked on her, drying her long hair with their towels and wrapping her up in blankets so that she could barely raise a foot to climb the stairs. Irena poured hot tea down their throats and generally fussed about catching the flu, but Stella could tell her chatter was covering her real worries about Irma. She hardly seemed to notice the cold and worse she almost welcomed the suffering it brought. When Stella thought of her feet in Venice, she often wondered how she'd kept going on them and the pain, she remembered it in the strangest way.

She felt she deserved it, even though she knew she didn't. Irma's face made her wonder if Irma felt like that. If Otto couldn't be alive, she should suffer.

When they'd finally gotten themselves not completely miserable, they stumbled up to bed and crawled under covers that felt like sheets of ice. Stella thought she'd sleep like the dead once the bed got lukewarm, but something kept coming into her sleep and disturbing her. That sound. That annoying sound. It woke her up just enough to know it was there, but not enough to force her to investigate.

Hanni's alarm clock went off at two the next day and she turned it off. She couldn't do it. She couldn't get out of bed and she went back to sleep for another three hours until Irena banged on her door, yelling that she ought to get up. The streets were a mess and it would take them a long time to get to the club.

Stella rolled out of bed and flinched as her stockinged feet hit the floor. It was that cold. Her window had ice on both sides and there was no way she was getting dressed without standing next to the fire or the kitchen stove so she grabbed her clothes and carried them with her.

Hanni was coming out of her room, fully dressed and looking quite miserable.

"Are you all right?" Stella asked.

"Just cold."

"Did you sleep? That noise kept waking me up."

She looked away and started down the stairs. "What noise?"

"I don't know. A noise." She caught up to Hanni and they walked down together, but Hanni wouldn't look at her. She answered questions with yes or no.

Irena met them at the bottom of the stairs with huge bags under her eyes and wearing her coat. "This is impossible. They must give us more coal. The people will freeze."

"They don't care," said Hanni and she went into the sitting room with her head down.

"What's wrong with her?" asked Irena.

"I don't know. The cold maybe," said Stella.

Irena pursed her lips. "Hanni never complains. She's the sweetest thing. Now Inge, the griping never ends."

"I heard that!" yelled Inge from the sitting room.

"If only your discretion was as strong as your hearing!" Irena yelled back, inciting laughter from the sitting room.

"Unfair," complained Inge as they walked in. "I'm cold."

"We're all cold," said Maria. "How's Irma? Has anyone seen her?"

"She was crying all night again," said Inge. "I wish she'd stop."

"It'll get better," said Irena.

"That's what I told her," said Stella. "I don't think she believes me."

Inge shivered and held out her hand to the small flame in the fireplace. "You don't cry all the time."

"It has been a while and losing a twin must be something different."

They all nodded and Irena passed out rolls with some kind of patty made of rice with onions inside. If Stella hadn't been so hungry, she'd have thrown it out. The taste was unspeakable, gamey and sour.

Once they'd finished, Stella got dressed, despite the shaking it caused. "I forgot my apron," she groaned.

Irena checked the time. "Well, hurry up and get it. I'll find you some rubber boots. You'll get frost bite if you wear Hanni's boots."

Hanni hadn't said a word the whole time. She'd eaten her weird sandwich and stared out the window until Stella was leaving. "You think she'll be all right, don't you?" Hanni asked.

"Sophie?" Inge licked her fingers and made a face.

"Irma."

Irena went to Hanni and put an arm around her shoulders. "Yes, of course. Time heals. She will learn to live without Otto."

They kept talking about grief and Stella left, grateful to get away from the discussion. Irma was doing a lot worse than she would've expected. But, even as she thought it, she knew these things couldn't be *expected*. Grief was entirely unique, like people.

She got to the third floor and stopped on the landing. Her door was open and a jolt went through her chest. Stella took a breath.

There was nothing revealing in there. It was fine and she walked in to find Irma fruitlessly rustling around in her wardrobe.

"What are you doing?" asked Stella.

Irma jerked back and looked at Stella guiltily. "Oh, I was just looking for...that book you said I could borrow."

Sure you were.

"Hanni has it."

"Oh. All right. I'll ask her if I can have it." Irma squeezed past her and Stella heard her run down the stairs creaking the whole way down.

What in the world? Who was Irma? Did she suspect Stella of something? If she did, why? Stella had been so careful and she was one of them without question. She went through the meagre amount of clothes in the wardrobe and Irma had clearly gone through every pocket. If she thought Stella was a spy, she must think she was an idiot that would keep evidence in her pockets.

Stella grabbed her apron and closed the door behind her to go downstairs. The girls and Irena were still in the sitting room, trying to figure out when they had to leave. No one was anxious to go out into the cold. The storm had calmed down, but everything was coated in ice and there was an ice fog that made the outdoors particularly unappealing.

"I think we should just go," said Stella. "They'll have heat at the club."

"Don't get me started on that," said Irena, practically growling. "Did you see Irma upstairs?"

Stella decided to keep mum about her room and said, "I did and I thought she came down."

"Go see, will you, Inge?"

Inge wrinkled her nose. "Are you kidding? I'm not leaving this fire."

"I'll go," said Stella and she went into the hall to find Irma rifling through the coats, sticking her hands in the pockets, all the pockets. Stella watched for a moment and then silently turned around.

Back in the sitting room, she said, "She's come down."

"How does she look?" asked Maria.

"I really couldn't say. Not crying."

"Thank goodness," said Inge.

"You're all heart," said Irena.

Inge stuck her tongue out. "I am."

Irma walked in, looking wan and weak, but not crying and everyone exclaimed over that. Hanni was quiet and said nothing and neither did Stella until they put on their coats and went out into a cold that Stella had never experienced before. Then it was all complaints from all of them. The inside of Stella's nose got crunchy and they all fell on the ice at least three times on their way to the U Bahn.

There was some fear that the U Bahn wouldn't be running, but it was and they made it to the club bruised but on time. Frau Bothe gave Irma the once over and noted the swollen but dry eyes and said nothing about them. Stella had assumed people would want to stay home in that weather, but she was very wrong. The club filled up surprisingly fast, just like always. Her largest group was all women, something she'd never seen before. There were always women at the club, but they were invariably accompanied by men. These were ten women alone, elegantly dressed and older. They had requested Stella and she had no idea why, but they definitely knew her, using her first name without asking it and teasing her about her tiny stature.

They kept her busy with unusual drinks that were French. French anything wasn't in style, but the ladies reveled in ordering champagne with a dash of Crème de Framboise among other things while they toasted to success. Stella's other tables were glum by comparison. One table of Wehrmacht officers seemed intent on drinking themselves to death and her table of Luftwaffe had just lost some friends in a crash. They weren't demanding and she was able to help Irma without much of a struggle, although she didn't need much help and as the night wore on, she needed less and less.

Maria caught up to Stella at the bar and said, "She seems a lot better."

Stella nodded, but she didn't feel good about it. Irma was moving, serving, but not talking. Forget about smiling.

When Maria walked off with her serving platter of beer, Hanni came up. "I don't think Irma is doing well, do you?"

"She's not crying," said Stella.

"That's what worries me."

They turned and watched Irma walking mechanically to the kitchens. She looked straight ahead, no more seeing than the night before.

"I'm closest," said Stella. "I'll watch her."

"Thank you. Frau Bothe has me out by the bathrooms tonight. She hates me."

"Just serve well and she'll get over it."

Hanni bit her lip and then picked up her order. Stella's ladies were looking around and she rushed back with her tray of champagne flutes.

"There you are, Sophie," said one lady. "We thought we'd lost you."

"I'm short but hard to lose, ma'am," said Stella, handing out their champagne flutes this time with Chambord. They were quite beautiful with pools of raspberry pink at the bottom and she made a note to try the combination when the mission was over.

"Ma'am? That's so formal. You should call me Sonja," said the lady.

Stella controlled her surprise and happily came up with the right name. "I'm honored. May I ask if Herr Riedel is well? I look forward to seeing him again."

"Magnus is very busy as are all our husbands, which is why we have this night out and they don't. We were supposed to come tomorrow, but the company is too busy."

The ladies raised their glasses and clinked.

"Please sit, Sophie," said Sonja. "I believe that is allowed or is that only for entertaining the men?"

Stella laughed. "It's allowed and encouraged." She raised a hand to a busboy, he nodded and ran for a chair. "I just have to be invited."

"You are invited," said a lady whose silver hair had a blueish tint to it that was surprisingly becoming.

The busboy set down the chair, dusted the seat with a napkin, and blushed furiously when Stella thanked him.

"Winning hearts everywhere, I see," said Sonja.

"You'll have to watch Magnus, dear. He's quite smitten with the tiny Valkyrie girl."

The ladies all laughed and Stella joined them, but she was a little nervous. Things like husbands and younger women weren't usually funny to older ladies.

"I don't know what I did, but I'm happy to have served you well."

The blue-haired lady put a hand over a delicate little burp and said, "You didn't serve. You arranged. That's what my Johannes said. They've been trying and trying to get a meeting and oops there Magnus was, right next to Goebbels."

"That's where the table always should have been," said Stella.

"This is how women help," said another lady.

"It won't be like last time," said another.

Another lady raised her flute. "To 30,000 units of success."

They clinked their flutes and practically shouted, "Prost!"

Pervitin. Stella stayed quiet, hoping they'd let her in on something new, but they didn't get specific.

"Do you really think I helped the Reich?" she asked when it became clear that they wouldn't say anything useful without a nudge.

"Oh, yes," said Sonja.

Stella frowned and gave them the look that never worked on her grandmother, she knew her too well to buy it, but it always worked on the garden party crowd. Stella could look quite young, innocent, and sweet when she wanted something. But her grandmother would look down her nose and say, "Put those limpid pools of blue away. What kind of fool do you think I am? I'm a Bled. We invented persuasion." The garden party crowd would say, "Aren't you just the sweetest thing."

"I don't see how," said Stella, the limpid pools working overtime. "What difference did I make?"

Sonja took her by the arm. "You moved things along. Our contract with the Reich is being worked out as we speak. It won't be long now."

"The contract is for our men?"

"For Pervitin. I thought Magnus gave you some."

"Oh, he did and the girls were jealous that I got some for free, but they said it was only for Saturday nights."

The ladies laughed uproariously and drained their champagne.

"For Saturdays. For Wednesday. For every day," they said.

"I think we should contract with Daimler-Benz," said the blue-haired lady. "How many tanks would they build then?"

"You are right, Jutta," said Sonja. "I'll mention it to Magnus."

"But I thought it was for having a good time?" asked Stella.

"Pervitin is for everything," said Jutta. "Workers can work harder and longer."

"Then it will help our men to fight."

The ladies smiled at her.

"It will help our men to win," said Sonja.

30,000 units of winning.

"Maybe we won't need it. My matron thinks it might be over," said Stella.

"Dear girl, it won't be over until General Foch's wagon is here in Berlin," said Sonja.

France.

"I hope it will happen easily."

"With the help of Temmler, it will," said Jutta. "Be a dear and get us more champagne so we can toast to owning the valley where it is grown."

With her heart pounding, Stella gathered their flutes and took the orders for champagne, some with Framboise, some with Chambord. It was all the same to Stella, toasting to victory, and if Pervitin worked the way they thought it did, her side was in trouble.

She hurried up to the bar and put her order in. The barman was astonished. "Again. We don't like the French."

"But we want to own the French. They make champagne."

He grinned at her. "I hear good things."

"About France?"

He sneered. "The dirty, unkempt dogs? No. About how weak they are."

"Yes?"

"Very weak and we aren't anymore. They can't grind us under their heels ever again." He started pouring champagne.

"The ladies are from Temmler. They are certain of victory."

"Ah. I wondered who they were. If our men are well-supplied, we cannot lose."

"Supplied with Pervitin?"

He leaned over. "The army has ordered Pervitin?"

"I think so."

"Then we cannot fail."

"I've never taken it. What's it like?" Stella asked.

The barman measured out the Chambord and whispered. "My brother took it in Poland. He said it was like being a god. He could do anything and never got tired."

Stella knew about the *anythings* that had been done in Poland and she suppressed a shudder. "That is good news for our men and bad news for our enemies."

"They will be part of the Reich soon enough." He loaded the tray and pushed it over to her. "Be careful. It's a heavy burden."

"Yes, it is." She picked up the tray and turned around to go down the stairs. Maria came up, carrying a huge tray of Dampfnudel and little pitchers of custard. "Have you seen Irma?"

"No." Stella scanned the club. Irma's white blond hair stood out and was usually easy to spot, but she didn't appear to be on the floor.

"Her tables are getting mad," said Maria.

"Well, she was fine and moving pretty fast."

"Their glasses are empty and I think they're about to complain. Where were you?"

"Sitting with the Temmler ladies, at their request."

"Is that who they are? Everyone has been wondering," she said. "Can you get Irma's tables? My officers want me to have dessert with them."

"I'll take care of them. Don't worry." Stella skirted the traffic heading to the dance floor as the sets were cleared and the band warmed up before bursting into a rousing rendition of "Happy Days Are Here Again", another American hit adulterated by Goebbels into something vile.

The crowd started clapping along as she passed out the champagne and excused herself to rush over to Irma's tables. They weren't happy with her vague excuses but gave her their drink orders. They would've been better described as demands, but she smiled and apologized, even as an SS slid his hand up her leg and snapped her garter. It was everything she could do not to slap him upside the head. Instead, she politely backed away and hurried back up to the bar.

"Those ladies must be lushes," said the barman with a toothy grin.

"Different tables," said Stella.

"You all right?"

"I'm fine. This just feels like a long night."

He filled the tall beer glasses and said, "Don't they all."

"Hey, have you seen Irma?" Stella asked. "I have a message for her from a certain interested party."

The barman sneered. "Are you sure about that? Irma's been a pill this last week."

"Her brother died."

"That's no excuse."

Isn't it? Who are these people?

"She's coming out of it," said Stella. "The memorial is tomorrow."

"Good. Nobody wants a pretty girl frowning at them all night." He slid the tray over.

"So have you seen her?"

He jerked a thumb to the backstage door. "I think she's on a break."

Stella slapped her forehead. "Of course, I forgot."

That got her an eye roll and it was irksome. Men were always so willing to believe she was a dizzy broad, despite all of the evidence to the contrary. It was a good thing for her current situation, but it still stung. They wouldn't think that about a man.

She pasted on a smile and turned to walk down to Irma's tables when Hanni grabbed her arm. "Irma's gone."

Stella grinned back at the barman, who was listening. "She's on a break, silly."

Hanni's eyes went wide for a split second and then she casually said, "I forgot. I am silly."

"Do you have a moment? You have an admirer at my Wehrmacht table and they're so glum, I could use some help. My smiles aren't doing anything."

"Of course."

They walked down a couple of levels before Hanni asked, "Where's Irma?"

"Well, he thinks she's on a break, but she didn't tell me."

"We have to find her."

"I know. Let me take care of her tables first and then I'll go down after her."

"No, no," she said. "I'll go through the kitchens. You keep on her tables. They look mad."

Stella agreed under the glare of multiple SS officers. They weren't used to anything but instant satisfaction and it showed in their tight jaws and narrowed eyes. She hurried over, making more vague apologies, and taking some food orders. One demanded to dance with her and she quickly agreed, but said she had to check on her Wehrmacht tables.

"The Wehrmacht can wait," he growled.

"They do," she said with a meaningful tilt to her head. "They don't like it."

That got a mean-spirited laugh out of the SS and she rushed to take orders from her own tables. The Temmler ladies were seriously tipsy and were listing to the left, but they wanted more champagne and, for some reason Stella couldn't divine, sweet red sauerkraut. The kitchens always had sauerkraut, but whether it was sweet or not, she couldn't say. The glum tables wanted shots and requested that the band play the depressing "Ich hatt' einen Kameraden". That was not going to happen, but Stella said she'd try.

She raced over to the kitchens, put in her order, and then slipped out the backstage door when the barman wasn't looking. As usual, downstairs was complete anarchy with performers jostling for mirror space and stripping in front of God and everyone. Stella had gotten used to it. Almost. Naked women were one thing, but the men still made her blush and the dancers thought it was adorable.

One of the chorus boys, wearing tiny panties oddly trimmed in lace, grabbed her around the waist. "She's come over to our side, ladies."

A cheer went up from the men and the women laughed. He spun her around and passed her through a gauntlet of sweaty, heavily perfumed bodies. She struggled to get away, but they kept twirling her and trying to put ornate headdresses for the underwater sequence on her head. As frustrating as it was, they didn't pinch her and it was all in fun.

"Why so serious, tiny waitress?" asked a chorus boy dressed in a tuxedo, from the top up anyway.

"I'm looking for Irma."

"Oh, Irma." Heavily kohled eyes rolled. "She's no fun."

Stella slapped his hands away when he tried for twirling again. "Her brother's dead. Of course, she isn't fun."

His hands went to his mouth and the dressing room went silent.

"No one told us," said a female dancer.

"We didn't know," said the chorus boy.

"Did she come through here?" Stella asked. "I need to find her."

All the performers agreed that they hadn't seen her.

"What about Hanni?"

A dancer asked, "Which one is Hanni?"

"The sweet one," said the chorus boy.

"Oh, I love her. Was she here? I wasn't paying attention."

"No."

Another shrugged. "I don't think so."

"I haven't seen Hanni either, but a few of the others. I can't keep track," said the lead performer, a man with silver at his temples and an air of Fred Astaire. "They keep marrying you girls off and that uniform."

They all wrinkled their noses.

"I know. We all look alike," said Stella.

"Not Clara," he said.

"You can't miss Clara," said one of the women.

"Horst wouldn't miss her," said another chorus boy.

They started reciting poetry and Horst blushed under his makeup to the roots of his silver hair.

"Has she been down?" Stella asked.

Clara hadn't been down. None of the girls had, but Stella wasn't sure they'd really know. Costume changes were crazy at the best of times.

"Try the alley," said a girl in a mermaid costume. "Maybe they're smoking."

"They don't smoke."

She shrugged and looked around. "Well, they're not in here."

"Can I get to the alley through here?" Stella asked.

The performer in panties took her through and showed her a doorway in the back past the rows of mirrors and racks of costumes. "Darling, tell Irma I'm sorry." He kissed her cheeks and exclaimed over her curls before rushing off, yelling about where his tux was.

Stella tried the door half-expecting it to be locked, but it opened easily and as soon as it cracked open she heard crying. "Irma, please, Irma."

Hanni was on the ground, cradling a limp Irma in her arms. Stella slammed the door open so hard it bounced off the wall and rammed into her as she ran out. She dropped to her knees. "What happened? What happened?"

"I don't know. I don't know," cried Hanni.

Drool dripped off Irma's lip onto the cracked pavement, but she was warm and her eyes were fluttering. Stella slapped her gently to no avail and then the chorus boys were around her, ignoring the frigid cold in their half-dressed state. Horst came out and took charge. "Bring her in immediately. Dieter, make sure no one from the floor comes down. Rolf, towels."

The boys carried Irma in and laid her on the floor. Horst lifted her eyelids and muttered, "Poor child." Then he checked her arms. Stella had no idea what for, but he didn't appear to find it.

"What are you doing?" asked Hanni.

"She took something."

"She's sick."

Horst glanced at Hanni's innocent and tearful face. "Yes, but she took something."

"What?"

"I don't know."

Rolf, the one in panties, put towels under Irma's head. She was muttering something, but all Stella could make out was, "Otto."

"She's so upset and they made her come to work," wailed Hanni.

"They would," said Horst.

The mermaid girl came in and held out her hand. "I found this. She must've taken them all."

Stella held out her hand and the girl dropped a Pervitin bottle in it. "Oh, no."

"Maybe it wasn't full," said Rolf.

"It was," said Stella. "A Temmler executive gave it to me and I didn't take any."

"Why do you think it's yours?" asked Hanni.

Stella took a breath and told her about Irma being in her room and looking through the coats. "I guess she knew Irena had given them to me."

"Quiet," said Horst. "Help me roll her."

Rolf carefully rolled her toward him and Horst opened Irma's mouth and stuck his long fingers down her throat. She fought him and then spasmed, spewing forth a flood of beer and the remains of the Pervitin pills.

Hanni gasped and slapped her hands over her mouth. "She tried to."

"Yes," said Horst and he stuck his fingers down her throat again. A little more came up, but no more pills. "How many have we got?"

Stella counted, but it was hard to say. The pills were sort of melted and she wasn't sure if some were one or two. "Ten, I think."

"There were twelve in the bottle," said the mermaid with a sigh. "Thank goodness. I wish we had some coffee."

"No, no. She can't have another stimulant," said Horst. "Get some juice. Does anyone have some juice?"

One of the chorus boys grinned and produced a bottle filled with a kind of syrup. "I swiped this when nobody was watching."

Horst frowned. "Sugar syrup? Why?"

"How else am I going to get sugar for my sister's birthday cake?" He handed it over and, between Rolf and Horst, they poured half the bottle down Irma's throat. She threw up a little, but most stayed down. After a minute or so, she responded to them but was still pretty incoherent.

Horst took a spare towel and wiped his hands on it. "She'll be fine, but you'll have to cover for her somehow."

"She's got to go back to the club," said Hanni.

He shook his head. "Maybe tomorrow. Not tonight. And you'll have to watch her."

"Watch her?" Stella asked. "We have to take her to the hospital."

The performers and Hanni went silent. Stella's skin tingled and she knew this was a mistake. They knew something that she should've known. A normal German would've known it.

"My mother always says go to the doctor if you're sick. Don't wait until you get sicker," she said. That was true. Francesqua said that. She didn't hesitate to call the doctor and it annoyed Stella to no end, but her mother wanted an expert at illness, not guesses by just anyone.

Rolf gently wiped Irma's face and made a pillow out of the towels. "Not this kind of sick. You don't want anyone to know she's this kind of sick."

"But...but someone has to help her." The idea of ignoring what Irma had done was inconceivable. Her grief wasn't going away. She'd do it again. The Bleds weren't strangers to that kind of illness. Uncle Josiah wasn't the most stable man the world had ever seen, but he was just the latest in a long line of eccentrics. Grandmother said they got to be eccentrics because they were rich. If they were poor, they'd be garden variety loonies. She ought to know. Grandfather's brother, Elias the Odd, had leapt off a bridge in Paris, not to mention Cousin Selena, who was on what the family called a long vacation, and there were others. It never went away, that sadness, it just didn't. "I'm not going to abandon her," said Stella.

Horst pulled Stella to her feet. "You're not. You're going to help her."

"I can't do that. I'm not a doctor."

"The last thing you want is a doctor."

"That doesn't make any sense." Stella moved toward the door and he grabbed her by the shoulders asking, "Do you want them to send her to Charité or worse Brandenburg?"

"No, no!" exclaimed Hanni. "We won't say anything. Will we, Sophie?"

Stella nodded, wondering why a sick person couldn't go to a hospital. Germany had good hospitals. Leo and Magda had told her. They were proud of their homeland's hospitals, if nothing else, at the moment.

Horst tossed away his towel and said, "This girl went outside to have a cigarette. She slipped on the ice and hit her head. Do we all understand?"

Everyone nodded, including Stella. Then he ordered everyone to hurry up and finish all their costume changes. He would go up and tell Frau Bothe what happened. Stella and Hanni would confirm it and then everyone would go back to work.

"But won't she come down here to see for herself?" Stella asked.

The chorus laughed.

"What?"

Rolf put an arm around Stella's shoulders. "That old hag won't go against Horst. He's a star. If he says this girl fell, she fell. Coming down would insult him." He made eyes at Stella and she wrinkled her nose. He tweaked it and said, "You are adorable. If I had that face, I'd be in Hollywood right now."

"Bothe…is interested in Horst?"

This time Hanni laughed. "Haven't you noticed how she touches her hair when he's around?"

She hadn't and it was an embarrassment. She was trained to notice things like that and she'd completely missed it. "I didn't. She's so…"

"Old?" asked Horst, although he was clearly about the same age. "They all love me, especially when they're over forty."

"It's your bread and butter," said Rolf sadly. "I'll never have that kind of following."

Horst pointed at his panties. "Not wearing that, you won't. They can tell." Then he guided the girls back through the dressing room and out to the stairs.

"What about Irma?" Stella asked. "She shouldn't be left alone."

"She's fine and she certainly isn't going anywhere," said Horst.

"But what if something happens?"

He smiled and Stella had to admit it was electric. He had that kind of face and charm, like Uncle Josiah, except elegant and all grown up. Uncle Josiah was perennially a little boy. Horst looked like he was born in a tuxedo.

"Let me do all the talking," said Horst. "You two just look worried. Yes. That's it. Perfect."

Horst did do all the talking and he did it so well, Frau Bothe never even looked at Stella and Hanni. She casually waved them back onto the floor and they went to the kitchens to pick up their orders.

Stella hefted her tray loaded with dishes of sauerkraut and waited for Hanni, who had the bigger load of Schweinhaxe. When she turned around her big eyes were clear and determined, surprising Stella. Given how frightened she'd been, it was quite a turn around.

"It's all right," said Hanni.

"How?" Stella moved closer. "This is very serious."

"Don't worry. I know what to do."

"What can you do?"

"It will be fine," she said with a determined smile.

"Hanni, she might do it again," said Stella. "My pills are gone, but she can get more or try something else."

She shook her head. "No, she won't. It's fine." And she headed off to her dreadful tables way off by the bathrooms and Stella was forced to go the other way down to the premier spots. She gave the ladies their sauerkraut and explained where she'd been with Irma's fall. The poor girl hit her head, but she'd be fine. The ladies were too drunk and happy to mind sharing Stella. Her other tables were singing "Ich hatt' einen Kameraden" together and starting to get the other tables to join in, much to the annoyance of the band. The officers were drunk enough that it almost sounded cheerful and before she got to Irma's tables, the SS officers were up and raising their beers, belting it out.

Stella stood back, barraged by incredible noise as they competed with the band and endured it with a smile she hoped appeared genuine. The song ended and she contained a sigh of relief with effort, but then her tables spontaneously began singing the Nazi Anthem "Die Fahne hoch" to great effect. Those who hadn't been singing before joined and the clamor was deafening. She thought it would never end and grabbed her tray, heading up to the bar to get out of the center when the song ended and chants of "Sieg heil" began.

Stella tucked herself away by a pillar, half hidden next to the bar as the whole club raised their arms stiff in salute to the lone swastika in the room high above the band. The chants got louder until they were screaming it in some kind of collective madness. Stella wondered if that kind of devotion could happen anywhere else in the world. Outside of soccer in England and baseball in America, she doubted it. The Bleds were ardent Cardinals fans and Stella had seen her father and uncles scream themselves hoarse more than once at Sportsman's Park, but that was different. They were happy, thrilled actually, to have an afternoon with the family watching baseball. The family's love of baseball seemed at odds with their devotion to art and artists, although her father liked to lecture her on the art of baseball.

The Germans in the club didn't appear to be happy, angry more like, intensely so. Stella watched them with fear gripping her so tight she could hardly breathe. Seeing that kind of thing in a news reel was one thing, being in it was another. She shrank back against the wall and looked around, hoping to God no one saw her with her arm down, but someone did. Maria stood in a similar position, her arm down and her face both incredulous and terrified. The curve of the upper deck allowed them to see each other while everyone else was facing the swastika. The girls stared at each other, alone but together in a world full of strangers.

CHAPTER 18

*H*orst's plan worked. Frau Bothe left Irma alone, transfixed by his attention, and by the time the club closed at five in the morning, Irma was on her feet. The fall on the ice story was readily accepted by everyone, although Irma looked terrible and had smelly beer vomit on her dirndl.

They bundled her up and got her into a cab before anyone important asked any questions. Rolf was particularly good at spinning the lie. He dramatically told the story to the upstairs staff and made himself the hero with a wink at Stella. She couldn't help grinning at him and wondered what he would've done if he'd been upstairs when the chanting happened. None of the performers looked very easy in their skins when they retook the stage afterwards. She'd seen them perform the arrangement enough times to know the difference, but no one else commented on the change in their demeanor, so restrained and wary.

"We'll get you right to bed," said Inge in the cab.

"I think we have some milk," said Maria. "That will settle your stomach."

Hanni said nothing. She just stroked Irma's arm while her friend nodded to all the suggestions. They'd have to tell the others the truth when they got back home. How else could they hope to keep Irma from hurting herself?

When they got to the house, Irma walked in and was immediately taken under Irena's wing. She made a toddy of milk, using some of their precious sugar and a touch of cinnamon. Irma drank it to be polite, Stella suspected, but no matter what Hanni said she wasn't going to be suddenly all right and all the milk toddies in the world wouldn't change that.

"Can I have a milk toddy if I hit my head?" asked Inge.

"Don't. We can't take the chance of knocking you any more silly," said Irena.

"Well, I've had a hard night, too. Herr Dönitz kissed me. It was horrible."

Maria pulled Inge away as Irena shooed them off to bed. "It couldn't be that bad."

"He has an enormous tongue," said Inge. "How would you like it if a man kissed you without asking?"

"It happens all the time," said Maria. "Let's go to bed."

"There's leftover toddy. Somebody should drink it."

Irena flicked a towel at her. "That someone is Irma."

Complaining, Inge went up to bed and Irena waited until the stairs stopped creaking before she looked out the door to check. Since the coast was clear, she came back and said, "What really happened?"

"I hit my head," said Irma dully.

Hanni nodded and then Irena looked at Stella.

"Irma found my Per—"

"Sophie, don't!" exclaimed Hanni.

"She has to know," said Stella and she told the real story. Irena wiped her cheeks and tried to comfort Irma, but the girl was blank. She said the right things, but Stella wouldn't have been surprised if she walked to the top of the stairs and threw herself down headfirst.

"Darling, it's fine," said Hanni. "Let's go up and talk."

"I don't want to talk," said Irma. "I just want to sleep."

The word *sleep* had a dark tone to it.

"We'll get you to bed then," said Irena. "I'll stay with you tonight."

"No. I can sleep here."

They couldn't persuade her to go and Stella became convinced that if they left her in the sitting room, she wouldn't be there when they woke up. She wasn't the only one.

"Well, I'll just stay here with you until the memorial. It's still at noon," said Irena.

"I'm not going," said Irma.

"You have to go, dear."

"I'm not going."

They exchanged looks of surprise, unable to fathom what was going through her mind. Goodbyes were important. It was the done thing.

"If we can just talk," said Hanni, "I know you'll change your mind."

"I won't."

"Let's go upstairs, please. I need to talk to you."

Irma shook her head and pushed Hanni away from her. "Please just go away. There's nothing you can say to bring Otto back."

"There is," Hanni burst out and they all jerked to attention.

Irena stood up. "That's enough. Go up to bed now."

"No," said Hanni. "I can make it better. Just come with me."

"This is cruel. Go to bed."

"It's not cruel. It's true."

Hanni's face was so open and honest Stella believed her. If Hanni could lie, she'd seen no evidence of it. "Then what is it, Hanni? Tell her."

"Sophie, do not encourage this." Irena pulled Hanni away and tried to push her to the door.

"Let go," said Hanni. "Come upstairs, Irma. Please."

"Leave me alone," said Irma with such finality that it touched Stella's heart and broke Irena's. The matron began to cry as she pushed Hanni.

"He's not dead!" shouted Hanni and they froze.

"Hanni, for God's sake, how could you?" hissed Irena. "I've never heard anything so heartless in my life."

Hanni went around the matron to kneel before Irma. "It's true. He's not dead. None of them are."

"How…" Irma trailed off stunned.

"I…I have a radio and I heard it on the BBC. It's not true. The ship went down, but the British picked up the crew. There wasn't a battle or anything like that. It was an accident and they were all rescued."

"You have a real radio and you didn't tell me?" Inge was standing in the door, hands on hips.

Hanni drew back in horror and clapped her hands over her mouth and Irena stammered, "Nothing. Nothing happened."

"I heard Hanni say she had a radio," said Inge.

"For goodness sake, shush."

Irma got to her feet, shakily, and asked Hanni, "When did you find out?"

Hanni balled her hands into fists on her chin. "This morning, but I was afraid to say."

"You knew Otto wasn't dead and you didn't tell her?" asked Stella. "Why? You knew she was in tatters."

Maria appeared in the door behind Inge and asked, "What's happened?"

"Otto's alive," said Inge.

Irena stalked over and yanked her into the room by her arm hard. "Tell everyone why don't you?"

"Ouch. Why can't we tell Maria?" she asked with a protracted whine.

"Because we aren't supposed to know," said Irena and she pulled Maria in, closing the door firmly behind her. Just who she was guarding against was a mystery since everyone was already there.

"It's true?" asked Maria. "Really and truly?"

They all looked at Hanni, who managed a weak smile above her fists. "He is. I suspected yesterday when they reported bringing survivors in, but I wasn't sure if it was all the men. This morning they reported that the entire crew was rescued."

"You're sure?" asked Irma.

Hanni nodded and Irma threw her arms around her friend, sobbing in relief.

"I want to know why she didn't tell us she had a real radio before," said Inge. "It's stingy and mean."

"It's nothing like that, you silly sausage," said Irena.

"Yes, it is. We've been listening to that thing." She pointed at the Volksempfänger. "They don't broadcast anything good. I want to hear Vera Lynn."

Maria looked up and wiped her eyes. "You could always hear Vera Lynn. We just can't listen."

Inge pointed at Irena's little radio again. "You mean it works?"

"Of course, it works," said Irena. "We just can't—"

"Well, then, let's listen to something good." Inge marched over to twist the tuner. "How did you find the BBC, Hanni?"

Irma snatched her hand away and the radio squealed. "Don't."

"Why not? Otto's alive. Let's celebrate."

"It's illegal," said Irena, going over to tune the radio back to the approved station marked on the dial.

Stella did her best to look like she knew that foreign stations were illegal and was incredibly grateful that she'd never thought to change the station to anything but Goebbels' propaganda.

Inge rolled her eyes. "Oh that. Nobody cares about that."

"They do care."

"It's silly."

Irena took Inge by the shoulders. "Listen to me. You can't tell anyone about Hanni's radio or Otto."

"But that's ridiculous. We can't have a memorial for someone who isn't dead."

Irena looked around the room at them. "We're going on like nothing's changed. After the memorial, we'll tell the people that should know. Irma, do you agree?"

Irma nodded, her smile so wide it looked like it hurt. "He's alive. That's all that matters. We'll tell Mutti and Papa later when it's safe."

"Then it's agreed," said Irena. "Inge, do you understand?"

"I'm not stupid. I understand, but I still want to hear the BBC."

Maria took her arm and guided her out of the room. "Maybe later. We have to go to bed now."

Inge reluctantly agreed and went upstairs. The creaking gradually disappeared and Irma blew her nose on a handkerchief.

"Do you forgive me?" asked Hanni, twisting her apron in her hands.

"Forgive you? There's nothing to forgive. I'm grateful to you," said Irma. "I can't imagine what I would've…"

"I wanted to tell you this morning, but I thought for certain our news would broadcast the truth."

Irena pursed her lips and then said, "Never mind that. We know now and you can finally rest, Irma."

Irma nodded and yawned. "I was miserable and now I'm so happy. I don't know what to do or where to go."

Hanni laughed. "Go to bed. You'll have to use all your acting skills at the memorial in a few hours."

"It won't be hard. I'll just think about how I felt in the alley." Irma drew Hanni and Stella close. "And you saved me. What would I do without you?"

They put their heads together and Hanni said, "You'll never have to find out."

Listening to her words, Stella felt a queer kind of sadness form in her chest, a longing like homesickness for those girls, for that house. She'd never had girlfriends like other girls her age did, except Mavis, and that was entirely different. They weren't the same, doing a job and living together. These people, her enemies, that she'd won over in order to betray them and their country, were likely the only friends like that she'd ever have. In a few days, she'd be gone and they'd hate her. She'd deserve their hate, but she'd regret it, too. Park-Welles briefed her on an endless list of things she had to know, but he never briefed feelings. Maybe he didn't know about them or maybe it was something she had to find out on her own. They would be first on a list of things she wished she'd never learned.

THE MEMORIAL WENT off without a hitch. Neighbors, friends, family all gathered at Irena's house. It was packed to the rafters with grief and, oddly, included plenty of talk about glorious Germany and Otto's heroic sacrifice for the Fatherland. Irma did an excellent job portraying a grieving twin. Stella thought she should be in pictures her performance was so convincing and all the girls did well. All except Inge, who only gave a passing attempt of wiping her eyes. No one was paying her much mind and she might not have garnered any attention if it weren't for the yawning and checking the time. Irena had several quiet words with her, but it did no good. Every chance she got, she tried to sneak up to Hanni's room to hear the radio. Never mind that someone might've heard it, Inge was intent on hearing something "good" as she put it.

Maria and Stella had to keep an eye on her, but she'd manage to slip out the second they looked away and they'd be dragging her down the stairs much to the puzzlement of the mourners.

Once it was over, all the carefully prepared dishes eaten and the mourners sent home, Irma sat her parents and grandparents, aunts and uncles down in the sitting room, surrounded by condolence cards and pictures of Otto. She told them he was alive. They listened in stunned silence and then cried in relief before hugging Hanni and thanking her. Irma didn't mention her suicide attempt, but her mother, an older version of Irma, said that she had feared she'd lose both of them and thanked Hanni again.

Irena brought out a precious bottle of Mosel Riesling and they toasted to second chances and to Otto, a young man who would spend his war safe in a prisoner of war camp in England. Stella marveled that no one spoke of the lies their government told them. They weren't bitter or wanting to know why. The lie was accepted as necessary, she supposed, but what of the other families grieving in agony? Not a word was spoken about them.

When the family left, it was time to dress and get to the club. The girls had gotten almost no sleep but were lighter in spirit and ready to face a Saturday with its endless party.

"Irma, dear," said Irena, "you must stop smiling. They'll know."

Irma forced her face into a frown.

"The eyes," said Maria. "They're still smiling."

That made them laugh and Irma tried to frown with her eyes, but she was only successful when she thought of the alley.

"What alley?" asked Inge.

"Nothing," said Irma, Hanni, and Stella in chorus.

"You always say 'nothing' when it's something."

Hanni steered her toward the door. "Yes, we do, but I have a feeling this is going to be a good night for you."

"Me?" asked Inge. "Why?"

"I just feel good. Maybe you'll meet your officer tonight."

"I'll say the wrong thing. I always say the wrong thing and they think I'm silly and noodle-brained."

Maria bit her lip and Irma's frown turned upside-down behind Inge's back.

"Not tonight," said Hanni, sweetly. "Tonight you'll do better. We're all going to do better."

With that, they went out into the dark, frigid streets and headed for the U Bahn. Everything was running normally again after the big snowfall and they got to the club early. Downstairs the performers gathered around Irma under the guise of giving condolences about Otto's memorial, but they were really checking to see how she was faring. She gave another marvelous performance, complete with tears and nose-blowing.

"I'm just happy to be here with you all," she said. "My parents need me."

Horst patted her back and said, "You must stay strong for them."

"I am. I will." She wiped her eyes and glanced at Frau Bothe who was watching closely from the wings. She didn't dare complain since her beloved Horst was at the center and, genius that he was, the head-liner turned to her and said, "We all have your best interests at heart, don't we, Herta?"

Frau Bothe blushed and nodded. "Yes, of course, Horst. Now girls, we must go up. The guests will be arriving any minute."

In truth, the doors had been open a full two minutes, but she'd been unable to order the grieving to end. They all nodded, did a quick check in the mirrors and hurried up to greet the crowd that was already filling the club.

Saturday was *the* night to be seen at Valkyrie and requests for tables had doubled since Goebbels had deigned to sit at their tables. Not to be outdone, Heinrich Himmler had a table that night with his loyal deputies. Stella feared Oscar and Ulrich to be at his table and she'd lose the chance to get information from them, but they were at her tables, nearly on the other side of the stage, and Oscar wasn't pleased at all.

"Why are we here?" he demanded.

"I wasn't told the reason," Stella said as she seated them.

"This is fine, Oscar," said Ulrich.

"Obersturmbannführer," barked Oscar and the men got shifty-eyed. Stella wouldn't have thought the SS could get nervous, but it appeared they could. They sat down and immediately ordered two beers apiece, which was usually a good sign for tips but not so with the SS. The more they drank the cheaper they got. Her other tables were filled with Wehrmacht and businessmen. Ulrich glanced over at them with something like longing, but it was hard to tell since she was on his bad side. Ulrich was the only one to order something different.

"Killepitsch," he said, avoiding Stella's eyes by looking at the empty stage.

She noticed the SS officers raising an eyebrow, but Oscar didn't seem to notice. He was too busy keeping an eye on the door, watching for Reichsführer Himmler to arrive.

The other tables wanted beer and she went to the bar to find the usual man there waiting for her. "Good tables."

"You think?"

"That Obersturmbannführer von Drechsel is on his way up."

"Not to Reichsführer Himmler's table and Irma has him."

He raised a brow. "Really?"

"Horst convinced Bothe that she's better," said Stella.

He filled another beer glass and nodded. "It will be a night of frustration for you both then."

"I suppose so," she said.

"Unless you move him like the Temmler men," said the barman with a wink.

"You heard about that?"

"Everyone heard about that. Very good."

"That was different. Reichsminister Goebbels wanted to sit near them."

"Himmler doesn't?"

"I don't know." Stella didn't know, but she did know that if she could keep Oscar from Himmler it was likely a good thing. Whatever Oscar wanted didn't sound like something she would want to have happen. Her arranging the Temmler move helped get Pervitin to the German army so they could use it to attack France. It probably would've happened anyway, but it made her spitting mad—as Aunt Florence would say—and she wasn't making anything Oscar wanted easier.

"You're a bright little thing. You'll figure out something," he said. "That it? Only beer?"

"Oh, and some kind of drink. I've never heard of it. Killepitsch."

The barman groaned and arched his back with his hands raised to the ceiling. "It is over. You may as well go home."

"What? Is it bad?" she asked.

"No. It's very good, if you have a sour stomach or have had a large meal. This early means someone is in a bad mood. You won't be able to please the Obersturmbannführer tonight."

"He didn't order it."

"No? Who was it?"

"His brother. The Wehrmacht."

He tapped his cheek. "The one with the face?"

"Yes," she said.

"Then it doesn't matter. If I were him, I would drink this all day every day." He leaned over the bar. "It helps with the pain."

She glanced back and caught a glimpse of Ulrich von Drechsel, the one who didn't matter. His head was slightly bowed as his brother talked at him incessantly.

"Here it is." The barman produced a dusty bottle. "It is not very popular as you see."

"What's it like?" Stella asked.

He tilted the half-full bottle filled with an incredibly dark liquor toward her. "Have a sniff."

She did and got a snout full of heavily alcoholic herby scent. It wasn't unpleasant but reminded her of the cough syrup her nanny used to concoct to put her to sleep when she was sick. "I like it."

"Not for you. Too strong. It will make him feel better though." He poured the liquor in a fluted Killepitsch glass that had the same design as the bottle and put in on her tray. "I think he will have an early night."

Stella returned to her tables to see Oscar taking a glug out of his flask. He scowled at her and said, "I don't pay you to look at me."

He didn't pay her at all, but it wasn't good to point that out. "I won't look at you anymore ever, sir," she said with a saucy grin that she'd learned from Pamela Churchill.

Oscar started to say something else, but the other officers started laughing.

"You can look at me all you want," said one.

"No, no. Look at me."

The requests spread to other tables and then everyone was laughing. Stella, true to her word, didn't look at Oscar, but Ulrich had a slight smile on his good side when she put his glass in front of him. He drank it quickly, despite the thickness of the nearly black liquid and asked for another as soon as she checked back with the table. The other men were cheering at the performers who had worked out scenes from *The Wizard of Oz* and ignored her. Oscar and Ulrich didn't join in. Oscar was grinding his teeth in frustration and Ulrich just drank.

The show was a refreshing diversion and Stella didn't get pinched once while the players sang their hearts out. Horst had been excited to debut it for Himmler. They had found costumes and made sets. Horst claimed the songs were sent to him by a friend in Hollywood and they were very good, obviously not yet touched by Goebbels' misery-making machine, but was a little confusing since Horst sang most of the songs and Dorothy was played by Eva who had to be twenty-five. She did little but simper and show off her fabulous legs.

The only person not paying attention was Reichsführer Himmler. He had no interest in the show or Oscar and only had eyes for the young woman with him, a frizzy-haired blond who gazed at him as if he weren't a chinless little toad with the worst haircut Stella had ever seen. She considered herself to be an authority since her brothers had decided to cut each other's hair when they were little and her mother had screamed when she saw the results. Their heads had to be shaved bald. They were that bad.

The performers announced a break after the chorus sang a song Stella couldn't stop humming. *"Du bust aus dem Wald. Du bust aus der Dunkelheit."* It was just lovely and she was ever so glad Goebbels hadn't gotten to it yet.

She floated around the club, checking on Irma and making sure she kept frowning. She did. Mostly. Luckily, her tables were drunk, except for Himmler, and not paying much attention. Frau Bothe was watching though, her eyes narrowed. She knew something had happened and Stella just hoped that word would come officially that Otto was alive soon. Irma wasn't going to be able to pretend for months. That much was obvious. Everyone was smiling and it was hard not to join in, not that Stella had much to smile about.

The new show went well, but Stella's plan was not going at all. She tried to entice Ulrich into talking to her, but he was more glum than even the first night they'd met. Oscar was angry and annoyed with her. The other officers didn't respond to her gentle prodding about what they did or if they were leaving soon. The night was a bust and it was her last official night in Berlin. At least it was supposed to be. She wasn't leaving until she found out where Anna Wildholz was and she wanted to give the earl more than the Pervitin and an unspecified attack on France. They needed more and she was there with the plans living in the brains right below her nose, but she couldn't get at them.

Once the stage cleared, the singer, Maxine, took her place in front of the band and began singing bastardized versions of The Andrews

Sisters' songs by herself. Maxine was good, but one couldn't compete with three. People got up to take the floor to dance, careful not to actually swing or look too happy in front of Reichsführer Himmler, whose eyes were half-closed as the frizzy-blond tried to pull him out of his chair. Stella passed them on the way to the bar and put in an order when a hand flipped her around.

Oscar pinned her to the bar and got in her face. "Move my table."

Panic washed over her and she could barely stop herself from shoving him away and running. His uniform. The look in his eye. He wanted to hurt her. He was like the boy in Venice, focused and vicious. "I can't. Reichsführer Himmler has not requested it and the generals at the table would not be pleased."

"You're doing nothing. My brother...nothing." His lips brushed hers, but she didn't flinch. Something grew steely inside her and she gazed at him levelly.

"Your brother wants to go to Koblenz," she hissed. "Perhaps you should let him."

Oscar drew back and then he squeezed her arms tighter. "What do you know about it?"

"I know he's unhappy."

"Happy doesn't matter. It is all for the good of the Reich."

"Perhaps a happy Ulrich is good for the Reich," she said. "Have you considered that?"

"Manstein is not favored. Ulrich will go to Halder's staff. It's arranged."

"Can't he stay here? Goebbels can use him, can't he?"

"My brother has been useless there."

Useless at what?

"Perhaps if he had more time," Stella said.

Oscar pushed himself against her and she felt his arousal on her stomach. "I'm not waiting. I finally have a meeting set for Wednesday with the Reichsminister."

"What's one meeting going to do?"

"I'm very persuasive and he already wants what I have." He pushed his hips forward, painfully ramming her back into the rail of the bar. "Like you."

"I doubt Goebbels and I want the same thing," she said, trying not to gasp in pain.

"Do you believe in the supremacy of our race?" he asked, his lips now against her ear.

"I do."

"Then you do."

"I don't understand," she said.

"There's a solution to the Jewish problem and I will be the man to implement it. Soon I will be at that table where you put Reichsführer Himmler. Me. Not him."

Breathe, Stella. Don't think. Just ask.

She pulled her head back so far her neck popped and asked, "What is the solution? They're everywhere, like rats."

"And we'll exterminate them." Oscar kissed her. His tongue pushed its way into her mouth and she knew she should react in a good way, but she couldn't. It simply wasn't possible. He finally stopped just when she thought her stomach might not obey and she would heave right into his mouth. "I knew you liked me."

That's when she knew he was insane, but the kind of insane that got things done, like murder.

"I thought you wanted me to like Ulrich," she said.

"No one can help Ulrich. He won't have it," he said. "I want you here with me or maybe we'll have to go somewhere else, if you won't move my table."

"I can't." Stella struggled, realizing he could make her leave with him. Bothe wouldn't like it, but she couldn't stop it. "Please let go."

"I don't think I will. My brother likes you, did you know that?"

She twisted, but his hips pressed so hard against her it didn't help.

"He was the handsome one, that tall one, *the one*. Now who's the one?"

Oscar stumbled backward, nearly yanked off his feet. Ulrich spun him round with his one good hand and grabbed him by the throat. "I'm still the one." Then he shoved his brother away and grabbed

Stella, dragging her stumbling away from the bar. He marched down the levels to his table, not looking back and not noticing everyone watching them, including the Reichsführer.

Ulrich didn't sit down. He grabbed his glass and drained his fifth Killepitsch before asking, "He thinks I'm done, doesn't he? Because of my face and my hand."

Stella couldn't think. The world was looking at her. She wasn't supposed to be seen. Heinrich Himmler was seeing her. A room full of Nazis was seeing her and not as just a Valkyrie girl but as someone interesting and, even worse, memorable. "I...I think so. I'm sorry."

"I'm not." He turned her around and said, "Let's dance."

"Oh...okay."

He took her onto the floor and they danced cheek to damaged cheek. The room went back to drinking and talking, but the Reichs-führer was still watching and Stella was shaking. She couldn't control it.

"You're all right now," whispered Ulrich. "He won't do it again."

"Promise?"

"Yes." Ulrich had a look in his eye that she hoped to see in Albert's one day. He was back from the sorrow.

"He said you have to leave," she said.

"I do. I'm on General Halder's staff now," he said.

"Who's that?" she asked.

"A man who thinks plans that failed in 1914 can succeed in 1940," said Ulrich. "Tell me what happened with Oscar."

"I made him mad. I told him that you should go to Koblenz."

Ulrich held her back and frowned but in a quizzical way. "You did?"

"I did. You should be with that genius you talked about," said Stella.

"You astonish me. No one talks to Oscar like that. No wonder he... never mind."

The night was turning out better than Stella thought as well as worse. She would have to go and soon. This might be her last chance with Ulrich. "I was trying to help. You should go there, if you want to. I'm sure you could help that Manstein you talked about with his plan."

"How do you know about him?"

"I asked. People know who the genius in Koblenz is," she said.

"He is a genius, if only he could get the Führer to listen." He twirled her out and she imagined what Ulrich was like before his injuries. The one, Oscar called him, and she could see that. Even drunk he could command the floor well, now that he was trying.

"Why is he a genius?" she asked.

"His ability to see the coming battles, the logistics, everything."

"Could it make a difference to the Reich, if the Führer would listen to his plan?"

"It could make the greatest difference. It won't be like last time, if he has his way. That old fool Halder would have us take the same path and end in disaster. We must change with the times." Ulrich's eyes were shining with an intensity she hadn't seen before and it worried her. If this Manstein had a quarter of his fire, that plan of his might get adopted. She needed more.

"That's what Herr Riedel said," she said because she couldn't think of anything else.

Ulrich dipped her over his bad arm and said, "Who?"

"Herr Riedel from the Temmler company. He says their Pervitin will change things and ensure success."

"So the man has a big head as well as a big mouth," said Ulrich with a hard look coming into his eyes.

"Oh, no," she said. "He was just happy that our future is bright."

"With their help."

"Well, yes. Isn't it?"

They turned around the dance floor and Stella got a little dizzy, even though she hadn't been drinking. Ulrich was slurring the slightest bit, but he was steady on his feet. Stella wondered if he'd taken Pervitin. Was this part of the effect?

"It is," he said. "If we choose the right course, Temmler will be important. If we don't, it won't make any difference."

Stella squeezed his shoulder and looked pleadingly up into his eyes. "Do you really think Manstein can make such a difference?"

"He will make all the difference. We will have Blitzkrieg and the French will fall before our fire," he said with fervor.

Blitzkrieg. Lightning war.

"That will be incredible," she said.

"Do you doubt me?"

"No. I just fear…my mother told me about the last time. She lost her brothers in France. She still grieves for them to this day."

Ulrich pulled her tight to him, much the same way as Oscar had. "There will be no Somme this time."

She kept her body tense and her eyes locked with his. "But they have a wall."

He bent over her and she had a flash of Nicky doing the same, holding her, touching her, protecting her, and a flush came into her cheeks.

"Can we get over it?" she asked.

Their noses touched and he said, "We can get around it."

She frowned and then laughed. "Those fools built a short wall?"

Ulrich dipped her in front of the Reichsführer and Stella could see him watching with something akin to admiration but whether it was for her or Ulrich, she couldn't say.

"It isn't a wall exactly, but yes, they did in a manner of speaking."

"So they are stupid," she said, smiling her flirtiest smile. "If you build a wall or whatever they built, you should build the whole thing. I could've told them that."

He pulled her tight to him again. "They thought they did."

"So they're confused as well."

"A forest is not a wall."

A forest?

"So it will be easy then?" she asked.

Ulrich got a funny look in his eyes, like he'd just realized he'd been talking of things he shouldn't, so she quickly whispered, "Can I tell my mother?"

He looked puzzled. "Tell her what?"

"That my cousins will be safe when they join the Wehrmacht. She is afraid they will end up like their fathers."

Ulrich laughed. "You can tell her they won't end up like that but not why."

She relaxed in his arms. "She will be so happy."

"Are you happy?" he asked and she could tell he really wanted to know.

"I'm perfectly happy. Except…"

He frowned and got that look again. She had to put him at ease and make him forget his lapse in judgement.

"Except that, when do you think we'll get more coal?" she asked.

"Coal?" The change in topic befuddled his liquor-soaked mind.

"It's freezing. I love my boarding house, but it's so cold. My fingers feel like they're permanently numb."

The look vanished and Ulrich said, "Not this winter. You will have to endure."

Stella pouted in the way that always made Uncle Josiah laugh and give in to a ridiculous request, like taking his precious Sopwith Camel up on her own well before she was ready or drive his Pierce-Arrow coupe roadster with soap boxes tied to the peddles so she could reach them. It worked with Uncle Josiah and it worked with Ulrich von Drechsel.

"All winter? Can't we get this over?"

She could practically see him melting and she held her breath.

"Spring will have to be soon enough," he said and put his damaged cheek to hers tenderly.

Stella sighed. "I suppose if I must wait for the good of the Reich, I will."

He pulled back to check if she was serious and Stella grinned in response. "As long as you promise next winter I'll be toasty warm and not eating bread with peas in it."

"Or what will you do?" Ulrich showed a teasing spark she didn't know he had.

"I won't dance with you anymore," she said. "How's that?"

"You think you can resist me?"

"I think I might have to." Stella felt a bubble of genuine laughter form inside her. She'd done it. She had it.

"You are so beautiful right now," he said.

"I'm very happy. Everything is perfect."

"It's going to stay that way."

"Promise?" she asked.

"Promise," he said and the band leader announced that their set was finished. The performance of *The Wizard of Oz* would continue in five minutes.

Ulrich dipped her one last time and they headed off the floor with the Reichsführer watching. Stella could see his little brain was interested, very interested, but it wasn't in her. He was looking at Ulrich and she hoped that interest wouldn't come back to haunt her.

They went to Ulrich's table and no one was there. The SS officers were off flirting in the wings. Stella, to her amazement, saw Inge chatting with the handsomest of the group. She was glowing and flipping her hair. How she ended up entrancing him of all people she couldn't imagine. Inge usually had the crummy tables of old grumpy men and their even grumpier wives. Her getting in with the better guests wasn't something that normally happened.

Ulrich sat down and patted the chair next to him. "Sit with me."

She glanced at her other tables and they were on empty. "I would love to, but I have to look after my guests first."

"I'm your guest," he said.

"My number one guest, but they have empty glasses. You don't want me to get fired, do you?"

"Maybe you won't be working here that long anyway."

She knew what he meant. Nicky had much the same look shortly before he proposed, but she played dumb and went to take orders of beer and pork before going up the stairs.

Maria passed her on the second level and leaned over to whisper, "Watch out." Then she was gone and Stella didn't get a chance to ask why, but she knew before she'd gone up to the fourth level. Oscar was still at the bar. He glared at her and drained his flask. The barman behind him looked at her and jerked his head to the left toward the kitchens. In other words, go away, and she did, turning left to put orders in at the kitchen first instead of the bar.

When she'd given her order to the kitchen staff, she reluctantly turned around to go to the bar, calculating which area was best to avoid Oscar, but she needn't have bothered. Clara was with him. The leggy redhead had strategically draped herself on the bar counter, making herself a tad less than Oscar's height. The anger had left Oscar's face and he was looking at Clara with a calculating interest that made the happiness in Stella's chest vanish on sight.

Oscar thrust his flask back across the bar without looking and the barman filled it with clear alcohol. Then he swirled it, smiled a creepy little smile, and nodded to Clara before he took a big glug.

Stella took a breath and started for the bar as the performers took the stage. The band tuned their instruments and Clara walked away from Oscar down toward her tables on the second tier. She had a radiant smile on her face as if Oscar made her happy, but Oscar wasn't in the business of making people happy, especially not Clara. She said he'd barely ever looked at her.

Oscar screwed the cap on his flask and tucked it away in his breast pocket. To Stella's horror, he turned toward her, walking with that stiff gait of his. They had to cross paths and her heart started pounding. She glanced down and Ulrich wasn't looking. There was nowhere else to go unless she outright turned on her heels and went the other way. She would've done it, just to avoid whatever he would do to her, but there was Frau Bothe next to the backstage door watching her, much as she'd been watching Irma all night. More suspicion was the last thing they needed so she made herself walk straight.

She was sure he'd grab her, hit her, something, but he didn't. Obersturmbannführer von Drechsel just smiled a smile full of vile satisfaction and a chill raced up Stella's back. Clara didn't know about her, did she? What could she have said?

When she reached the bar, she had to hold onto the edge for a minute before speaking.

"That was a narrow miss," said the barman as he wiped a tray clean.

"What was that all about?" Stella asked.

"I don't know, but if I were you, I'd avoid him."

Stella took a deep breath and asked, "Do you think I can?"

He picked up a tall glass and thought about it. "After the way he touched you, no, probably not."

"I don't know what to do."

"Nothing to do. See what happens. The brother likes you. Maybe he'll help."

She nodded and told him her order. All she could think was how she had to leave Berlin, immediately. But there was still little Anna Wildholz. She couldn't leave without knowing, at the very least, if she was alive and where she was. There was absolutely no way she could return to the earl without that information. But she had so little time.

The barman pushed her tray across the bar and she took it.

"Good luck," he said.

"Thanks. I'm going to need it."

But she didn't need it, not for the rest of the night. Oscar sat at the table in silence. Stella danced with Ulrich again after Dorothy tossed a bucket of silver tinsel at the Wicked Witch and he was just as light on his feet but not willing to talk about anything at all. To Stella he seemed wary under the beady eyes of his older brother, who drained his flask two more times. Ulrich only relaxed after Oscar got up and left without saying anything to his brother or anyone else. Then Ulrich showed his own skills by talking to people he'd ignored before, including Himmler, which made Stella nervous, but there was nothing she could do about it.

It was a typical Saturday, but the party broke up early. Five o'clock in the morning was plenty late for Stella, but it put some kind of bug in Frau Bothe's ear that the girls hadn't been entertaining enough. She certainly wasn't going to blame Horst, who was still taking the precaution of chatting her up, enabling Stella to escape her questions and run down the stairs to the dressing rooms to try and catch up with Clara, who'd gone down early.

She searched the dressing room, but Clara was gone.

"Did anyone see Clara leave?" Stella called out and everyone shook their heads.

"I didn't see her go," said Rolf, who was applying cold cream to the heavy makeup he wore for his part as the scarecrow. "But she was happy."

"Happy?" asked Maria. "That doesn't sound like Clara."

"She's never happy," said Hanni.

Irma walked in smiling, got a look from Maria, and then quickly regained her tragic face. "Who's happy?"

"Clara," said Stella. "Do you know why?"

"I couldn't say. It's never happened before."

That made everyone laugh and Irma managed to only let a flicker of a smile cross her lips.

"I wish I knew what was going on," said Stella.

Hanni took her arm. "Don't worry. Clara isn't our problem. She enjoys hating it here."

"That's what I'm worried about."

She frowned. "Why?"

"I don't know. I just…have a feeling," said Stella.

Irma came out of the bathroom holding up a wrinkled dirndl. "Whose is this?"

"Where'd you find it?" asked Maria as she put her coat on. "We all have ours on."

"In the bathroom thrown in a corner."

"Hold it up to you," said Stella.

Irma held the dirndl against her chest and the skirt hung well past the hem of hers.

"It has to be Clara's," said Maria. "Why in the Fatherland would she do that? Frau Bothe will be so angry."

"I hope she doesn't get fired," said Hanni.

Stella didn't say anything. She couldn't. The bad feeling had gotten a whole lot worse.

CHAPTER 19

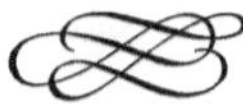

Stella woke up screaming. The covers were ripped off her bed and two men in the Gestapo green-grey uniform flipped the bed up, tumbling her to the floor. She hit cold wood full-force without a moment to catch herself and searing pain burned through her shoulder and hip. The mattress was over her and she scrambled backward, hitting the wall and the cold radiator with her head.

"Please, stop!" yelled Irena. "What are you doing? What is happening?"

"Get up!" one of the men screamed. "Get up, treacherous whore!"

They know. They know. What do I do? What do I do?

"Stop!" yelled Irena. "She's just a girl! Sophie! Sophie!"

"Sophie?" bellowed a man. "Where is she?"

Stella struggled to push off the mattress and the man yelled, "Get that off of her!"

It was Oscar. Stella didn't know if she was relieved or more terrified. The mattress was lifted off of her and there were a full four men and Irena in her room. Oscar stood in the doorway, glaring down at her. He reached in his pocket and she flinched. He noticed and it pleased him, but he pulled out a white starched handkerchief. "Stand up." He tossed the handkerchief at her and she looked down to see bright red blood droplets splashing onto the front of her nightgown. She couldn't think what to do about it and it hardly mattered. A bloody nose was nothing compared to what would come next. Park-Welles had drilled her in what to do, but it didn't amount to much. Evade capture at all costs and the ways to do that were the pills in her key that was in her handbag across the room. Useless. And if you're captured, essentially don't tell them anything about anything or anyone, no matter what.

"Clean yourself," he said, pointing at the handkerchief, an odd beginning to an interrogation, nothing like what Park-Welles had taught her to expect.

She picked up the handkerchief with a shaking hand and pinched her nose with it. "What's happening?" she asked, sounding like she had a bad cold.

Oscar stepped into her room and ordered the other men out. "Find her."

"We have orders to search all the rooms," said one.

"Yes, I know." He pointed at one man. "You search this room and then proceed to the others."

That man began going through Stella's wardrobe after checking the top and Irena started to go around the bed to Stella, but Oscar grabbed her arm. "Out. We will question you when we're through."

Irena looked at Stella with red, frightened eyes. Stella wanted to say something. That she was sorry because she was sorry. She couldn't imagine Oscar or the Gestapo would go easy on them for harboring her. They'd think they were spies, too, or collaborators. Her hands shook harder when she thought of what would happen to them.

A man yelled from the hall, "The door is locked!"

"Break it down!" Oscar yelled back.

"No," said Irena. "I have a key. Please. What are you looking for?"

"We'll tell you when we find it. Unlock that door before we kick it down."

Irena hurried out, her shoulders visibly shaking. Stella heard the lock clink and a violent ramming of the door before Hanni screamed.

Stella dropped the handkerchief, anger swelling inside her. "Don't do that to her! Leave her alone! What's she got to do with anything?"

"Have you got it then?" Oscar asked.

Got it? They're looking for something. Not me. The money? My suitcase?

"What?" she asked. "You can see what I have."

Oscar looked around the room where nothing could reasonably be hidden and his eyes landed on her Werner photo. He picked it up and looked at the young man's face with a sneer before tossing it on the bed. "What is her name?"

"Who?"

He jerked his head back, indicating the crying from across the hall. "Her."

"Why do you—"

"Her name, Sophie!"

She couldn't think of a reason not to give it, but it felt like a betrayal for some reason. Oscar took a step toward her and she said, "Hanni Räfle, but why—"

"That's her!" Oscar yelled and there was the sound of a stinging slap, followed by Hanni's screaming and cries of outrage from Irena.

Oh, my God. The radio.

"Please, tell me what is happening," said Stella, her voice quavering despite her attempts to control it.

The Gestapo straightened up from looking under her bed and examining her mattress. "Nothing here, sir."

"Very good. Help across the hall. Find that radio."

The man snuck a quick look at Stella and then left. The room seemed to get even colder without him there. She knew he wouldn't protect her, but the presence of another person made it better somehow. Now she was alone with Oscar. He watched her shivering for a minute and then grabbed a sweater out of the wardrobe and tossed it to her. She put it on and wrapped her arms around herself, causing her shoulder to burn again. All she could think about was her suitcase somewhere in the cellar. Would they search down there? Would they be observant enough to notice the weight and find the money and her fake identities?

"You knew about the radio," he stated.

What should I say? Yes? No?

Stella decided to error on the side of loyalty. "What radio?"

Oscar snorted in derision, but a genuine smile came onto his face. "Of course, you did, but I admire your loyalty, however misplaced."

"I don't know what you're talking about."

A man shouted, "We have it!"

"I didn't do anything wrong!" protested Hanni. "Please. It's just a radio."

"Tuned to the BBC!" yelled one of them. "Look at this! See this place on the dial?"

"I don't know. I only listen to approved stations. I'm loyal to the Führer!"

"Arrest her!" ordered Oscar and it surprised Stella. He was SS, not secret police, but the men obeyed him. Hanni was crying and Irena was begging.

"Please don't arrest her," said Stella. "She didn't do anything."

"Yes, she did and you know it," said Oscar. "Perhaps you did, too. Should I arrest you, too?"

"For what?"

"Listening to the BBC, which is against the law."

"But, if she did, it's such a small thing. Take the radio. Destroy it."

Hanni was in the hall, sobbing with her face in her hands. Stella dashed around the bed past Oscar to throw her arms around the girl, sobbing herself. "Hanni, it will be all right."

"I'm sorry. I'm sorry."

"It's all right. It's all right."

Irena hugged them both before the men separated them.

"Please have some decency and let her dress," said Irena.

The men looked like they thought they should but were afraid to say so. Stella turned to Oscar. "Please."

He came into the hall and eyed the sobbing and shivering Hanni. "Get dressed."

She went back in the room and was forced to dress in front of the men, although they did avert their eyes from what Stella could tell.

When Hanni came out she was more composed. She took Stella's hands and they exchanged cheek kisses.

"Your nose," she said. "I'm sorry."

"It's nothing," said Stella. "You'll be all right. It's just a little thing. A mistake. A nothing."

Hanni nodded, tears streaming down her face, and she pulled her knit cap down tight. "I hope I will come back."

"You will come back. Of course, you will."

One of the men gave her a push. It was more gentle than Stella would've expected. Now that the excitement was over they looked rather guilty and embarrassed. They kept glancing at the Valkyrie dirndls that had been neatly hung up on the sides of their wardrobes and they knew they were arresting someone that they'd rather not.

"Let's go," said one and Hanni started down the stairs, wobbly, and Irena pushed one of the men out of the way to walk with her, supporting her by the waist and whispering comfort in her ear.

The man who'd searched Stella's room came up the stairs and told Oscar, "We've searched all the other bedrooms and found nothing. Should we continue with the rest of the house?"

Stella held her breath.

"No. We have it," said Oscar.

The man nodded curtly and followed the others down the stairs. Now they were truly alone and Stella stepped back to press her back against the wall. She had no protection. None at all. Oscar turned back to her and smiled before he picked up the Werner picture, unclipped the cardboard backing, and slipped the photo out of the frame. "You won't be needing this anymore." He folded the photo in fourths and put it in his pocket.

Stella was so astonished her mouth dropped open and his smile grew wider. "You'll want to move soon, I think."

"Why would I move?" she asked.

"There are better lodgings, warmer with more privacy."

No. No. No.

"I like it here."

Oscar ignored that and said, "I believe Frau Durchdenwald will have an empty space soon."

Durchdenwald. Sounds familiar.

"I don't want to move."

He smiled again. "You will come around I'm sure. Is your identification up here?"

"Yes."

"Get it and we will go down to talk about the situation here with your housemates."

Stella's handbag was on the other side of the bed and she was forced to squeeze past Oscar to get it. He took the liberty of touching her rear as she passed and she had to ball up her hands to keep from slapping his away.

"Hurry up."

"I am." She turned her back on him and popped open her handbag. Her papers were in a pocket on the side, but the key was at the bottom under her wallet. She made a show of digging and pulled out the key and her papers at the same time. The key went in her left hand and the papers her right. She turned to the right, extending the papers toward Oscar while slipping the key into her nightgown pocket.

He waved the papers away and said, "Go downstairs."

"Does Ulrich know you're here?"

"You mean, does he know you live with a traitor to the Reich?"

"Hanni isn't a traitor."

"She listens to foreigners and lets her mind be infected with their lies. She spread those lies to you."

"I don't know what you're talking about. Does Ulrich know?" Stella asked.

Oscar considered things for a moment and then said, "He doesn't and nor will he."

"Why not?"

"He's on his way to Koblenz as we speak. It turns out my little brother can be useful."

Stella wrapped her sweater tightly around herself, careful to cover the pocket with the key. "What do you mean? I thought he didn't help with Goebbels."

"He didn't, but he spoke to Reichsführer Himmler last night and wisely got me a meeting tomorrow. I will outline my plan. I'm sure he will be persuaded to act immediately. I've thought of every detail and contingency."

Stella did her best to look puzzled and interested when she was really horrified. "Are you talking about your solution for the Jews?"

"Yes, and I have you to thank," he said.

Oh, my God.

"I didn't do anything," she said modestly.

He took her arm firmly and directed her out the door. "You made my pathetic brother appear attractive and interesting."

"He always was," she said.

His grip tightened and his eyes flashed as they started down the stairs. "You are very free with your opinions. Perhaps you'd like to talk about Otto Koch."

They reached the second floor and the other girls were huddled next to Irma's door, their faces tear-stained and shocked. Stella gave them an intense look and said, "Otto is dead. Everyone knows that."

"Do they?" he asked and they rounded the corner to start down the stairs to the ground floor.

"Yes. The family was sent the official notice. It was in the paper and we had the memorial yesterday." Stella caught Maria's eye a second before they were out of sight and she nodded. "The family is devastated."

"Are they?"

"Yes, of course."

"No one has any cause to think any differently?" he asked.

"Why would they?" Stella asked.

He squeezed her arm. "No one heard something to the contrary and told the family?"

They reached the bottom of the stairs. The front door was wide open and a strong wind was blowing icy snow particles into the hall.

Two of the Gestapo men were standing there just looking at them, not caring about the cold or anything else it seemed.

Outside, Hanni was heaved into the back of a truck and Irena was clinging to a fence post, shaking. Stella went to shut the door, but Oscar grabbed her, turning her around to face him. "Has anyone heard anything about this Otto Koch?"

She would've thought he'd want her to confess, but his eyes said no, and she said, "Otto's dead. His ship was attacked by the British. It went down with all hands. Anyone who said otherwise would be lying and that's just cruel to give hope where there is none."

His back was to the Gestapo and he gave her a slight smile. "You would swear to that?"

"Of course. I'm very sorry Otto is dead, but we are at war. Men die."

He nodded and said, "Close the door. It's freezing in here."

Stella closed the door, but then opened it again as Irena stumbled up the stairs to the door. She took Stella's hand with hers and said, "She'll be all right."

"I'm sure she will," said Stella.

"Where are they taking her?" Irena asked Oscar.

"Prinz-Albrecht-Straße 8," he said and she recoiled in horror.

"But she's just a girl."

"We'll see. Get the others down here and turn on the furnace immediately." Oscar directed Stella into the sitting room and the others came in slowly, creeping like if they were very quiet Oscar and the Gestapo wouldn't notice them, which was ridiculous as they were the main attraction.

Oscar went on to ask them about Hanni, the radio, and the BBC. The girls were easily able to answer truthfully that they didn't know anything about it. The questions about Otto were more difficult, but they stuck to Stella's script that they knew he was dead and nothing else was possible. They denied being told anything different by Hanni and they did it well. The Gestapo were looking quite bored and glanced at the clock several times. It was Sunday after all. They probably had things they'd rather be doing like being home with their families or at least interrogating suspects that weren't terrified Valkyrie girls, who knew and served the Nazi elite.

Oscar saw this and changed his tact. "You have offered us nothing."

Irena started and said, "I didn't…what would you like?"

He just eyed her and she quickly said, "I will get you what I have. Tea and rolls." She stood up. "I have a nice jam. I have been saving it."

"Send a girl," he said. "I have questions for you."

Maria stood up and said, "I'll get it."

Irena nodded and she left. Irma and Inge looked desperate to go, too, but they couldn't come up with a reason to leave. Oscar walked over to the radiator and touched it. "Finally." He took off his heavy black leather coat and thrust it in Stella's direction. She got up and took it, folding it gently over her arm.

"Hang it up," he ordered. "On a hanger."

She nodded and went out into the hall, wishing she could run upstairs, get dressed, and jump out a window. But the suitcase was in the cellar. She wouldn't get far without the money and papers.

Stella found Irena's good coat on the back of the coat rack. It had a wooden hanger, so she hung Irena's coat on a hook and put the SS's coat on the hanger before putting it on a wall hook. One side wasn't hanging flat and she pressed it down to find a lump on the breast pocket. She glanced back. She was out of view from everyone in the sitting room so she quickly felt in the pocket. Oscar's flask.

Stella stood there for a moment and that's how long it took to know what she was going to do. The key was in her pocket. The flask in her hand. He had meetings set with Goebbels and Himmler. A solution to the Jewish problem. Exterminate them. Oscar's big plan and Ulrich said he always gets his way.

She got out the key and unscrewed the end. The pills slid into her hand and she chose the L pill, putting the others back and the key in her pocket. The rubber coating was meant to be bit through, but she obviously couldn't do that. Instead, she took the top off of Oscar's flask and pressed the pill between the two edges of metal. There was a tiny pop as the ampule broke. She heard a creak and looked up. Maria stood in the hall, holding a tray with the tea and rolls. The girls stared at each other and then Stella lifted the flask lid. The broken ampule fell in the flask with a little plop.

Maria didn't blink. She walked into the sitting room and said, "I brought the best jam from your mother, Irena."

"Thank you, dear," said Irena.

Stella screwed the cap back on the flask, swirled the alcohol, and tucked it back in Oscar's coat pocket. It was done and she straightened up, taking a breath. With any luck there would be no meetings and no plan. No extermination. She walked back in and sat on the settee next to Maria, taking her cold hands in hers. Maria didn't look at her, but she squeezed Stella's hands and they sat like that while Oscar drank all the tea and ate the rolls. He asked them over and over about Otto and the radio until he'd eaten everything. Then he stood up and said, "I think that's all we need for now."

The Gestapo men went out into the hall and Oscar ordered Stella to get his coat. She went to get it under the gaze of the men, who were starting to look angry, not at her exactly but she'd do to take it out on.

She grabbed the coat and one of the men reached for her. She darted out of his reach and rushed into the sitting room. Oscar noticed and raised an eyebrow. She cocked her head back toward the hall where the men were and his eyes narrowed.

He tossed their papers on a side table and took his coat from her. "I will speak to Frau Durchdenwald. Prepare." Then he looked at Irena. "Expect another visit in a few days. We're not done here yet."

Oscar gave Stella a sharp nod and stalked out. The front door opened and slammed, but no one moved for a minute or two.

"Are they gone?" Inge whispered.

Stella looked out the window and saw Oscar getting into a long black sedan. "They are getting in their auto." She took a breath and held it.

The sound of a car struggling to start in the bitter cold came through the windows and then it fired up. Stella breathed and said, "They've gone."

The girls collapsed in their seats and Irena fell into her chair. Stella thought she might start sobbing, but the matron looked at them with fiery eyes. "Who told?"

They all protested and said they didn't. Of course, they didn't.

"I would never call the Gestapo on Hanni," said Irma. "She saved me. If she hadn't said the truth…"

"I wouldn't either," said Maria.

"Or me," said Stella. "I wouldn't know how to call them. What is Prinz-Albrecht-Straße 8 anyway?"

The girls gasped and Irma said, "No. They wouldn't take Hanni there. That is for the enemies of the State."

"What is it?" Stella asked again.

Irena took a breath and gripped the arms of her chair. "It is where the Gestapo interrogate their prisoners. Who told them about Hanni's radio? Who did it?"

"Who said anything about Prinz-Albrecht-Straße 8?" asked Maria. "They wouldn't take her there. Surely she will go to a little station nearby."

"The Obersturmbannführer said it," said Irena, looking at Stella.

She nodded. "He did."

"No," said Maria. "That is…not good."

Irena jolted to her feet. "Who told? Somebody told!"

"Well, your family, Irma…" said Inge.

Irma pointed at her. "Don't you dare accuse them. They only found out yesterday afternoon and the Gestapo is here in the morning. My family went home. Nowhere else. They would tell no one. It happened at the club. One of you told." She turned on Stella. "You were dancing with his crippled brother all night. Was it you?"

"No! Ulrich has no interest in you or Otto. I doubt he even knows your name," said Stella.

"Then you told the Obersturmbannführer. He clearly likes you. What was that about you moving? Are you to be his mistress?"

"Never. I'm not moving. I won't go."

Maria said in a shaky voice, "Sophie wouldn't tell him. She doesn't like him."

"How do you know?" demanded Irma.

"Because he was…forcing himself on her last night," said Maria. "She didn't like it. She was afraid and Ulrich came. He got her away from him."

"That's right," said Stella. "I'm not going to that woman's house. He can't make me."

Irena angrily brushed a lock of hair out of her face. "He probably can and, you heard him, they're coming back."

Maria looked at Stella with something like relief on her face. "But they won't come back, if he…forgets."

"They're not going to forget," said Irena. "The Gestapo doesn't forget."

"Where does he want you to go?" asked Irma.

"Frau Durchenwald's," said Stella. "I don't know who that is."

Irma crossed her arms. "I do."

"Who is it?"

"That's where Clara lives and she left her dirndl in the bathroom last night."

"She left her dirndl?" asked Irena. "But she needs it."

"That's what I'm saying. She's not coming back to the club."

Clara. Of course. She'd talked to Oscar. She'd been very happy and so had he. Stella hated herself for breathing a bit of a sigh of relief. It could've been worse. For her anyway.

"I saw her talking to Oscar last night," said Stella. "I thought it was odd because she said he had no interest in her and they both looked very happy afterward."

"But how would she know?" asked Maria. "I didn't tell her. Sophie?"

"I didn't talk to her at all last night."

Irma twisted in her seat and said to Inge, "You did."

The color drained from Inge's face. "I…I didn't. I wouldn't."

Irma shot to her feet. "You did, you little twit."

The accusations came at Inge until she'd sunk to the floor with her hands over her head. Irma was screaming at her and Irena was in a rage yelling that she had to get out of the house that day and she didn't care where she went as long as she left.

"Stop!" yelled Stella. "You can't kick her out."

"I already have," spat Irena.

"How's that going to look to the Gestapo? We told them we don't know anything about it and you kick Inge out of the house right after they leave? Clara told Oscar about Hanni so she probably told him who told her. Why wouldn't she? She doesn't care about us."

"Why did you do it?" asked Maria in a small pleading voice. "Hanni loves you. Why?"

"It was Clara. She asked me about Irma being so much better. She kept asking." Inge wiped her nose on her sleeve.

"So you just told her?" asked Irena. "How could you be so foolish?"

"I don't know. She…I didn't know she'd tell. I trusted her."

"Like we trusted you!" yelled Irma. "They're probably going to my parents' house right now. I don't know if I should call them or go there or do nothing. What do I do? Tell me that?"

"Do nothing," said Stella. "If you warn them, they'll know and they'll look guilty. Will they say anything?"

Irma shook her head. "No. Never."

"Then leave it," said Irena. "Sophie is right. We know nothing and we must act like we know nothing."

"What about Hanni?" asked Maria. "What will happen to her?"

Through shuddering sobs, Inge said, "They have to let her come home. It was just a radio."

The other three and Stella exchanged looks of understanding. Nothing was "just a radio" anymore.

"Who do we know that can help?" asked Irma, looking at Stella. "What about the Obersturmbannführer's brother?"

"He sent him to Koblenz," said Stella. "What about you? You've got the important tables."

Irma sneered. "Important, not friendly. I doubt they know my name. Maria?"

"I can ask Obersturmbannführer Krebs, but he isn't powerful or persuasive."

"Would he help?"

"I don't know."

Stella racked her brain. She had to get out of the house to find out where Anna was and she ran through a series of ideas. Maybe she could say she needed to go to the bakery. Oscar probably ate everything. But that would be fast. The trip to the doctor's house would take longer than that.

Inge sniffed. "Sophie knows that editor. Editors know people."

They turned to her and their faces lit up. Hers did, too. She should've thought of it herself. "I don't know him well, but it's worth a try."

"Do you know where he lives?" asked Irena.

"No. I'll go to the paper. They can tell me." Stella left the sitting room and ran up the stairs. She almost wanted to drag Maria with her, keep her close and quiet, but she couldn't do that. Maria couldn't see where she was really going, so she'd have to trust that Maria wasn't Inge and especially not Clara.

CHAPTER 20

*D*r. Ehlich's house was lit up on that dark cloudy Sunday afternoon and Stella slipped around on the icy, unsalted walk up to the front door along with several other people wearing grim faces and black. Stella briefly considered turning back. Her mother would say it was the height of ill-bred to intrude, but it couldn't be helped. She could hardly wait until their mourning was over. Oscar was going to die, if he hadn't already, and she had to go. The sooner the better.

A different maid opened the door for an elderly couple in front of Stella and she slipped in the house behind them unnoticed. She avoided the male servant taking people's coats and headed inside, trying to think of a gracious way to ask the doctor about a patient while his house was draped in black and his sons were being embalmed.

She did her best to blend in, not saying specifically that she knew the dead, just nodding and looking tragic when required. No one paid her much mind and she was able to listen to the muffled conversations about "the boys" and gathered they were the only boys in the family. The doctor had two daughters, but they were considered a consolation prize at best. "The boys" were what mattered and they were lost. No one was talking about glorious Germany in that house and she heard several people whisper about keeping their sons out of "it". Stella tried to locate the doctor, but she didn't know who she was looking for. She imagined a portly older man with wire-rimmed glasses and sparse hair, but she was very wrong on that. When she wandered into the dining room, a woman pressed a plate into her hands and practically ordered her to eat. Without a place to escape or put the plate down, Stella did as she was told and it was a good thing. The woman, a friend of the mother's, was a talker. She asked a lot of questions that Stella was able to avoid with her mouth full. Luckily, the woman liked answering her own questions and assumed that Stella was a certain girl named Dagmar that Gerhardt had known at school.

"I'd recognize that face anywhere," she said. "Gerhardt carried his photo with you everywhere. I'm very glad you could come all the way from Hamburg."

Stella nodded and took another bite of cake. She'd hadn't seen that much food in one place outside the club the entire time she'd been in Germany. Irena had barely been able to pool her resources to make two cakes and some breads. Dr. Ehlich had no less than fifteen cakes, wurst salads galore, and piles of rolls. The wurst salads were cold and vinegary, but she ate them, stuffing herself as directed, until she found herself quite lightheaded. She hadn't been full for over two weeks and she'd grown accustomed to a vague hunger that never left. Even at the club, the staff was given little. It wasn't unusual to see girls eating off the guests' plates once they were finished. Stella hadn't done that. She couldn't eat Oscar's dredges. The thought repulsed her, and she wasn't happy to eat Nazi funeral food either, but it couldn't be helped.

She swallowed her last piece of Kugelhopf, a molded cake filled with raisins and nuts and asked, "Is there a recent picture of Gerhardt? It has been a long time since school."

The lady cupped her cheeks with icy hands. "He would be so..." She choked on her words and a man rushed over. "What is it, my dearest one?"

"Gerhardt," she managed to whisper.

"Oh, yes." He tucked her under his arm and looked at Stella, his face puzzled as he tried to recognize her.

Stella took a huge gamble and quietly said, "Dagmar. I'm sorry I asked to see a recent picture. I hadn't…seen him in his uniform."

He shook her hand. "I understand. There are pictures in the sitting room. You haven't seen the display?"

"I must've missed it. There were a lot of people," she said. "Excuse me."

"Of course and don't forget to speak to Karl and Marta. They will want to see you."

"Do you know where they are?"

He shook his head and turned back to comforting the woman. Stella worked her way through the crowd. More and more people were coming in, but she got into what she presumed was the sitting room—it was hard to tell—and found a piano with photos arranged on top. She had to admit it was a lovely family with handsome parents who'd given birth to even more attractive children. Dr. Ehlich wasn't bald and paunchy. He was thin, fit, with what could've been either blond or silver hair. His wife was similar and seemed to favor the Ginger Rodgers look of sculpted waves and curls in her hair.

From the sitting room, Stella started searching for the grieving parents, but came up empty. Eventually someone said that Frau Ehlich had been overcome and had to go lie down. She didn't want to ask about Dr. Ehlich, the less talking the better, but found she had to. In the front was a male servant who looked less upset and a lot more irritated than the weeping maids, so he seemed a safe choice.

"I was looking for Dr. Ehlich," she said. "I'd like to give him my condolences."

"Do not bother the doctor. He has had enough condolences."

Stella couldn't risk saying she was Dagmar. He worked in the house. He might actually know the girl. "Please," she said. "My mother would say I was rude if I don't speak to Gerhardt's family. Frau Ehlich is lying down. I won't bother him. It'll only take a small moment."

The servant sighed. "I suppose your mother is right. But please be quick about it. The doctor…he is not well."

"I understand. Loss is a burden we are all carrying now." She raised her blue eyes and willed them to fill with tears. They obeyed and the servant's stiffness melted.

"The doctor is in his office. Don't tell anyone else."

"I won't. I promise."

"You know where it is?"

Oh, no.

"I only visited from the outside. Is there another way?"

He cracked a smile and pointed to a door tucked under the staircase. "Use that way." Then he touched her arm. "Are you Dagmar?"

She smiled but didn't nod before ducking away to the door under the stairs. With the crush of the crowd it wasn't easy to open, but she finally managed to squeeze herself through onto a narrow staircase with a single lit lightbulb swinging from a cord.

She tiptoed down the stairs away from the increasing noise of the mourners into the quiet of the cellar office. Cellar didn't seem quite right since there weren't any cobwebs, mold, or damp. At the foot of the stairs was a small reception area with a little desk and filing cabinets. The appointment book was open with pencil slashes through the last week's appointments.

Stella glanced at the two closed doors on either side of the desk, neither labeled, and went around to flip through the appointments. Lisa Hoppe had gotten on a train to Karlsruhe three weeks ago without Anna. So the appointment with the doctor was before that but after Lisa got fired. Stella was looking for a child's appointment, assuming that Lisa would've used a fake name, but she didn't, and Stella found an appointment for Lisa Hoppe and an unnamed child on November third. Nothing else was written down, no symptoms, address, or phone number.

She turned the pages back to the current week and looked at the doors. Neither had any signs of life. The doctor wasn't wailing, that much was certain and a relief. Stella knocked softly on the closest door, got no answer, and opened it. The exam room was painted a brilliant white and was scrupulously clean as well as empty.

The other door had to be the office. She knocked and received silence. He had to be in there, unless he'd left by the outside door and had run off into the waning shadows of the late afternoon.

A harder knock got a curt, "Come in," and she opened the door slowly, suddenly hesitant to face the father of two dead young men. If her brothers died, she imagined her father to be angry and hostile. Aleksej Bled didn't like things to happen that were out of his control, forcing him to deal with it whether he liked it or not. He preferred out of sight out of mind as his philosophy and that had served Stella well. If he didn't see her flying a plane, he didn't have to worry about it. Her father knew England was at war, but he assumed her well and safe unless something intruded on him to prove otherwise.

But there wasn't any way to ignore the noise coming down from the memorial. Even through the floor boards the crying was easy to make out. There was a certain tenor to grief that forced the ear to hear it.

And the doctor heard it. He was listening, sitting behind his plain wooden desk in a padded chair with his head cocked to the side. A woman was wailing about why the Lord would let such a tragedy happen to two good boys. The answer was nonsensical and he fixed his eyes on Stella, slowly as if he could hardly bear to move them.

"I'm very sorry, doctor," she said as another burst of crying erupted over their heads.

"Do I know you?" he asked without the slightest interest.

Stella came in, uninvited, and closed the door. "No and I'm very sorry to bother you."

"Bother me," he whispered and she wasn't sure what to say. It wasn't a question, more of a musing like he had no idea what the words meant and she wondered if he could focus at all. The man before her wasn't the man from the pictures on the piano. He had deep purple shadows under his eyes and his nose was red, swollen with painful-looking cracks around the nostrils, even his hair looked thinner.

"I'm leaving Berlin tomorrow or I wouldn't have bothered you at all."

He didn't answer, his eyes drifting off to the right, so she continued, "You saw a patient a month ago, a little girl. She was sick and you sent her to the hospital. She was with a woman named Lisa Hoppe. Do you remember her?"

Nothing. He was listening again to the grief that was growing louder.

"Doctor?"

She approached the desk and sat down in a hard wooden chair. "Can you please tell me what was wrong with her? What hospital did you send her to?"

Dr. Ehlich straightened up and asked, "What?"

"Lisa Hoppe brought a little girl to you over a month ago on November third. It was a Friday."

"Yes."

Thank goodness.

"What was wrong with her?" Stella asked.

"I sent her to the hospital," he said, tilting his head once again.

"Doctor," she said loudly. "Please. I know this is hard, terrible in fact, but my mother sent me. I have to find out where the child is."

That got his attention. "Your mother?"

"Yes. Where is she?"

"Is the child your sister?"

Stella hesitated. What was the right answer? Truth or close to it was best.

"No. She's the child of a friend's friend."

"Who was this child?"

Lisa used her own name, so Stella ventured a guess that she wasn't terribly creative. "Anna. She's only two. A cute little thing."

"You know the child."

"No. I've seen a picture though."

He nodded. "Yes, yes. I remember. She looks fine."

"I thought she was sick."

"I filed the paperwork and I believe she was seen immediately."

"At the hospital?" Stella asked.

"Wherever she was living," he said. "I have nothing to do with it after that."

What in the world?

"Well, the family wants to know where she's gone."

Dr. Ehlich waved that away. "No, no. Leave her be. This is best."

"What is?"

"I followed the law."

What are we talking about?

"What law? What hospital is she in?"

"The girl will be well-cared for. She's in a special children's ward where they will care for her," he said. "Please go."

"I will," said Stella. "What hospital is she in? Charité?"

"No, no. I told you to let her be."

"Her parents will want her back."

He frowned and said, "That is not possible. She is a ward of the State now." He stood up and Stella followed suit.

"Because she's sick?" she asked.

"Yes." He looked at the ceiling. "I should go back."

Stella blocked his exit from around the desk. "When will she be well enough to come home?"

"The child will stay at the hospital. They are best suited to care for her. The parents will know and understand this."

"Well, they don't. They're going to want their daughter back."

"This is not possible."

The door behind Stella opened and a matronly lady walked in saying, "Doctor, your parents have arrived and I—" She stopped short and stared at Stella. "Excuse me."

"This girl was leaving," said Dr. Ehlich. "Please take her away."

"Doctor, please. The hospital?"

"No. It is done for the best. Go now. I am going to…" His voice faded away and he went back to his chair to cock his head at the ceiling again.

The woman stepped in and pointed out the door. "Young lady."

Stella gritted her teeth, but she had to go.

"Who are you to bother the doctor today?" she demanded as she closed the door behind them.

Stella explained and the woman shook her head. "As Dr. Ehlich said it is done and is for the best."

"The child is not an orphan."

"The parents have agreed to the hospital."

"They haven't."

The woman turned the key in the outside door. "Now you will go."

"Please tell me the hospital she's in," said Stella, cooking up the tears again. "My mother sent me to find out and I always try to be obedient."

She turned around and pursed her lips. "Who is this child to you?"

"No one actually. As I said, my mother's friend had a connection. She died and…my mother was so upset. They were friends always."

The lady's eyes filled. "There has been so much grief for so many."

"I know and I'm only trying to help my mother. I think if she knows the child is cared for, she can rest easy," said Stella.

She took Stella's hand and said, "Tell your mother she is well and cared for."

Stella wanted to scream, "Tell me!" But she said sweetly, "If I could tell her the place, she would know it is nice with a good staff."

"Ah, yes. These things are important. The child is in Brandenburg in a special ward," she said.

"Is that here in Berlin?"

The lady frowned. "Are you thinking of going there?"

Stella widened her eyes dramatically. "Do you think I should?"

"There is no need. She will be happy there."

"And they will keep her?"

"Yes, of course."

Her mind was flailing about, trying to understand. "Forever, until she is grown up?"

"Yes." She patted Stella's arm. "They are specially trained."

For what?

She sighed. "This will be such a relief for my mother and I can tell her tomorrow. I'm going home to Munich in the morning. So Brandenburg is not in Berlin then?"

"You really don't know the North, do you?"

"I don't." Stella held her breath.

"The hospital is in Brandenburg an Der Havel, a lovely small city. The child will love it there."

There was a click and the sound of the memorial got louder as the door at the top of the stairs opened.

"Thank you," said Stella. "I will go now."

"You're welcome and tell your mother to be at ease," she said.

"Hilda," called out a woman.

"Yes, Frau Ehlich," answer the lady.

They looked up and the grieving mother looked down. Then a wan smile came over her face. "It *is* you." She started down the stairs and Stella grabbed the door lever.

"Dagmar, where are you going?" asked Frau Ehlich.

"Dagmar?" asked Hilda.

Stella whipped open the door and the woman grabbed her arm, spinning her around. "Who are you?"

Frau Ehlich made a beeline for them and then stopped suddenly. "You aren't Dagmar."

The office door opened and the doctor came out. "Dagmar is here?"

"Walther said Dagmar came down here."

He squinted at her. "She does look like her, but she's not Dagmar."

Stella shook her head. "That's right. I only came to ask a question."

"Elsa said you said you were Dagmar," said Frau Ehlich.

Hilda's hand got tighter.

"I didn't."

"You did."

Dr. Ehlich yelled up the stairs, "Walther!"

"Yes, doctor?"

"Is this the girl that—"

Stella shoved Hilda. The lady stumbled backward and fell. The doctor grabbed for her, but she rammed the door in his face.

"Walther!" yelled Frau Ehlich. "Get her!"

Stella ran out the door with Frau Ehlich on her heels. The snow hadn't been shoveled and she crunched through it up to her calves.

Frau Ehlich didn't follow, but people were yelling and flooding out of the house. Stella heard yelps as they slipped and fell on the ice. The snow was slowing but not slippery and she made it to the street well ahead of them to run on the packed snow toward the U Bahn.

"Get a car!"

A man yelped in pain, but then a car roared to life. She'd never beat a car so she darted off the road to run through the houses. The snow slowed her down considerably and she lost a boot, but she got away in the maze of houses and trees.

She hid by a dark house until she heard nothing in the distance and then walked double the distance to the next U Bahn station, fearing that they'd be waiting for her at their stop. Her foot was freezing and a bit battered from the ice and snow, but she'd had worse so she walked into the station with barely a limp.

There were only two other people in the station and they eyed her with suspicion, which she ignored, having so many other things to worry about. Brandenburg. Could that be the Brandenburg the girls were scared of sending Irma to? They'd implied it was a mental institution, but Anna Wildholz was two years old. Nobody sent little children to mental institutions, did they? Even if they did, Anna looked perfectly fine in her picture and the doctor had said she looked fine. "Looked" being the important thing, she supposed.

Stella looked at the train schedule. There was a train coming that went to the Halensee, where the Völkische Beobachter office was and where she was supposed to be going in search of Herr Hoff, the helpful editor. But there was another train going to the Unter den Linden U Bahn station and the Berlin Mitte. There was a kind of help there, if she dared ask for it.

A train rushed toward the station and Stella watched it, biting her lip. Hanni was in jail for a ridiculous crime and Anna Wildholz was in Brandenburg, essentially forever. One would have to wait. Stella got on the train.

CHAPTER 21

By the time Stella was walking on the boulevard toward Pariser Platz, she began to think she'd made a mistake. There were a surprising number of people out for a stroll for a late Sunday afternoon and they all noticed a shivering girl missing a boot. There wasn't any way to hide it, no shops open to buy shoes, and no ration card to do it, even if they were open. Park-Welles had drilled her on the German love of rules and while he never mentioned lack of shoes being an issue, from the looks she was getting, she was pretty sure there was a law that covered it. If someone called the Polizei, she could very well be in jail alongside Hanni. Being shoeless wasn't any less ridiculous a crime than listening to a radio in her opinion and could ruin her plan.

Up ahead, a group of SS turned onto the boulevard, laughing and slapping themselves on the back, and Stella darted into an alley. If Leon Klaus wasn't open, she'd feel like a prize idiot. It wasn't something she'd considered when she stepped on the train. She'd simply pictured a little girl alone and sick in an asylum and the choice was made. But it was Sunday and she wasn't even sure they were allowed to be open. Park-Welles hadn't covered that either. Him and his stupid medals. She needed practical things, real life things. She'd give him a piece of her mind if she got back to England.

When. Not if. When.

She walked out of the alley and back on the main street with her teeth chattering so hard they hurt.

Please let it be open. Please. Please.

There it was. Leon Klaus with its lights blazing. Stella almost cried in relief. She didn't even care if Cyril was there or not. She had to get out of the cold and have something hot to drink. Thank God for her tips.

A man opened the door for her and raised a brow at her legs.

"I slipped and my boot fell off," she said, sweet and helpless.

"Why didn't you pick it up?" he asked incredulous.

"It slid into the grate. I couldn't get at it."

He hustled her over to a table and bullied several men into making room for her by the big ceramic stove. "You should've gone home. Why did you come here?"

"My friend said she would meet me, but I don't see her. Maybe it was too cold," said Stella, glancing around for Cyril.

"Very inconsiderate," he said and it dawned on her that he was not German, although his accent was practically perfect.

"You are…Dutch?" she asked and was rewarded with laughter by all the men.

"You can't fool her, Lars."

"A German girl always knows a clog-wearing cheese eater."

Lars slapped one of the men on the back of the head. "You didn't know for a month, Wilhelm."

"That doesn't matter," said another. "He's half Swiss."

"And you are all idiots," said Lars, leaning over her. "You have a good ear."

"I don't know what made me think you were Dutch," she said, smiling.

"How about how tall and skinny he is?" asked Wilhelm.

"He is quite tall."

"I am happy to always reach the top shelf, unlike Alwin." He thumbed his nose at a man so short the table wasn't far under his chin. "And your name is…"

"Sophie," she said.

"Can I get you something warm to distract you from this company?"

"Thank you. I would like that very much."

"Glühwein?"

"Oh, yes. That would be lovely," she said.

Lars went to the bar and she answered questions from every man at the table while looking around in vain. Cyril wasn't there. She wasn't sure what she was going to do if he had been. He had promised not to turn her over to the Nazis and he hadn't. That was a good sign and she still had his money. He wanted it and a little help for Anna wouldn't be too much to ask.

Lars returned with her glühwein and she sipped the hot spiced wine with pleasure. "I have my ration card." She opened her handbag, but he pushed it down onto her lap as she hoped he would.

"My pleasure. The barman always keeps a little extra for a lady in distress."

"That's very kind."

"Would you like something to eat?"

"I just came from a memorial, but thank you."

The Ehlich memorial gave her something to talk about. They were all newspapermen from various countries and had heard the story. They got into a rousing discussion of which planes were the easiest to train on. To Stella's surprise and pleasure, several men rated the Spitfire as one of the best. The Germans nearby weren't nearly so pleased and another argument ensued.

Stella just sipped her wine and flexed her feet to get the blood flowing. It had a shot of schnapps in it, which probably wasn't the best idea for her alertness, but it couldn't be helped. She glanced at a clock above the bar and decided to wait another half hour. If Cyril was coming, he'd be there by then.

Lars tired of the plane evaluations and turned back to Stella with a smile, "How did you get so good at recognizing accents? You sound like you are from Munich."

"You're right, I am," she said with a great deal of satisfaction as she counted another person as successfully fooled. "But I work at Club Valkyrie and it is a skill that is prized."

That got the men's attention. None had been able to wrangle an invitation, but as journalists, they were desperate to get in.

"Perhaps you could put in a good word for us," said Alwin.

"I have no say at all and our tables are booked in advance."

"Surely there's something you can do," said Lars, "for the men who bought you a glühwein."

She tilted her chin down and gave them her most charming smile. "The glühwein is good, but if you had a pair shoes in your pocket, that might get you somewhere."

The men laughed uproariously and Wilhelm said, "That is the first time I've ever heard of a request for shoes from a man instead of flowers or jewelry."

"It won't be the last," said Alwin.

The door opened and a blast of air came in. Lars leaned to the side and yelled, "Close that door!"

The man stamped his feet and yelled back in heavily-accented German, "It is."

Stella was glad she was taking a sip of glühwein when she heard Cyril's voice or else she might've reacted. Instead, she simply sipped and glanced over without interest as the double agent unwound a double layer of scarves and slapped his fedora on a wall hook.

"Come over and speak German to us," said Lars with mirth in his voice.

"My German is perfect," Cyril groused and turned back to the table. Stella caught him seeing her in her peripheral vision, but he didn't react as she knew he wouldn't. He came to the table, continuing to grouse about the weather and yelling for a glühwein.

"Thank God for glühwein," he said. "It almost makes the rest of the year worth it."

Lars turned to Stella and asked, "Where is he from?"

"Who is this?" Cyril asked with sudden interest. He smiled and smoothed his greying hair, which got smug expressions from the other men. Stella wondered if he'd styled himself as a letch. Pretty easy characterization for his cover since he was naturally.

"Sophie," she said.

"From Valkyrie," said Wilhelm.

"The Valkyrie? What are you doing here?" Cyril asked.

"I was supposed to meet someone, but she hasn't come," said Stella

"Go on," said Alwin, "tell us where he's from."

Stella sucked in her lips and then said sweetly as if she was hesitant to insult him, "Not German obviously."

The men slapped the table and laughed. Some started laying bets on whether she would get it right.

"How did you know?" Cyril asked.

She shrugged and wrinkled her little nose. "I just know."

"Where am I from then?"

"America, I think."

The men toasted and drank heartily.

"Wait, wait," said Wilhelm. "Where in America?"

She sucked in her lips. "Oh, that's so very hard. No Americans come in the club."

"Try."

"The West? You sound like a cowboy from the movies."

Wilhelm stuck out his hand and another man unhappily slapped a bill in it. "I knew she would get it."

"You see American movies?" Cyril asked.

"When I was a child. My mother loves the cinema."

"What was your favorite?"

"*Captain Blood*."

Cyril smiled. "That is Flynn's best."

Lars elbowed him. "No! *The Adventures of Robin Hood* is better."

"I haven't seen it."

"You have to go to France or Italy," said Alwin. "It's worth the trip."

Cyril laughed. "I would, but there's a war on in case you forgot."

Wilhelm threw up his hands. "What is that to you? You've got a diplomatic passport, haven't you?"

"And orders to stay put. What's so great about *Robin Hood*? You can't beat that sword fight with Basil Rathbone."

"He's in the new one, too." Wilhelm stood up and pointed at Alwin saying in heavily-accented English, "'Do you know any prayers, my friend?'"

Alwin jumped up on the bench, making him almost as tall as Lars. "'I'll say one for you!'"

Before Stella knew what was happening the two journalists were beating the hell out of each other with canes yelling, "On guard, you scurvy rogue!"

She leaned over to Cyril and said, "What are they saying?"

He moved to the bench beside her and translated. When no one was looking he slid a card under her thigh. She retrieved it and slipped it in her pocket during a particularly vicious matchup of Errol Flynn and John Wayne, which made no sense at all but made her laugh out loud.

When the men had worn themselves out and had come back to the table for a restorative drink, Stella stood up and excused herself. "I must go now."

"No, no," said Lars. "I haven't convinced you to get me into Valkyrie."

She smiled and put on her coat. "And you haven't found me any shoes."

Lars looked at Cyril and asked, "How do you say it? She drives a hard bargain."

He laughed and said, "That's right. She's a tough little broad." He said *broad* in English.

Stella gave him a sideways stare. "What is this 'broad'?"

The men laughed and Lars quickly escorted her out. "Don't worry. It is a compliment," he said when they were outside.

"It did not sound like a compliment."

"That's because he is an American. They are gauche and unrefined."

"He certainly is," she said with a bit of a pout.

"Don't let him stop you from coming back," said Lars as he signaled for a cab. "I still have to persuade you to get me in Valkyrie."

Stella got in the back seat and said, "You can try."

He tweaked the brim of her hat. "Count on it."

"I will see you soon then."

"You will." Lars closed her door and slapped the roof.

Stella told the driver to start driving to Irena's house and pulled out the card Cyril had given her. It had a nearby address, but she wasn't sure what he expected until she glanced back and saw him leaving the bar.

"I changed my mind. I should see if my friend is well," she told the driver and then gave him the address. The driver shrugged and drove around the block to go in the opposite direction.

He stopped at a large apartment block that was totally different from the surrounding buildings with their staid traditional lines. Cyril's building was Bauhaus, modern and clean, and it stood out like his crappy American accent.

Stella paid the driver and stepped out to fumble with her handbag to give herself a minute so he'd drive away and not see where she was really going, the alley on the left where she would wait for an intolerable ten minutes until Cyril ambled down the alley with a smug smile on his face.

"I knew you'd come," he said.

"You couldn't because I didn't."

"My dearest girl, I've been in this game for a good while now and I have instincts."

"I think you just stink," she said.

He chuckled and unlocked a side service door to usher her out of the cold into what appeared to be a janitor's storeroom. It was barely warmer than the outside, but a relief all the same.

"Shall we?" he asked.

"Forget it," she said. "Here is fine."

"My apartment is warm."

"I'm fine."

Cyril sighed and leaned on a set of shelves containing a large bottle of vinegar for cleaning. "How'd you lose your boot?"

"Don't worry about it."

"I worry about everything to do with you."

"Get over it," she said.

"What happened?" he asked.

Stella found a bucket and turned it over to sit on. She watched him take off his fedora and shape the brim while he waited, reminding herself that she had no choice if she was going to help Anna. "I need some papers."

"You have papers."

"Different papers. For someone else."

He put the fedora on a vinegar bottle and asked, "Are you in danger?"

She lifted a shoulder and said nothing.

"Get out now. I have money and some paperwork that should get you over the border without a problem." He went for the door, but she said, "I'm not leaving until I get what I need."

"Who is this person? A Jew?"

"It doesn't matter. I need papers. Can you get them?"

"Then it is a Jew. You can't do this, Stella. You weren't sent here to rescue anyone."

She stood up. "You don't know why I was sent here."

That took him aback. "I suppose I don't, but I'm an old hand at this. 'C' didn't send a baby agent on a rescue operation. That does *not* happen."

She crossed her arms. "Fine. Are you going to help me or not?"

"Is it him?" he asked.

"Who?"

"Your friend, the tour guide, the one they arrested in Vienna."

Stella got a flash of Abel disappearing into the boxcar, but she managed to push it away. "No. He's dead. Your people murdered him on the way to Dachau."

Cyril approached her slowly like he was a lion tamer wishing he had a whip and chair. "I didn't know that."

"Clearly."

"They're not my people. What can I do to convince you?"

She sidestepped him and said, "Get me the papers and I'll consider it."

He ran his fingers through his hair and started pacing. "What do you need?"

"Two sets of papers for a two-year-old girl."

Whatever Cyril expected her to say it definitely wasn't that. "You can't be serious."

"Can you do it?" she asked.

"I can, but I won't. You are not risking yourself and this operation for some kid."

"It's my risk."

He turned on his heels and was on her so fast she didn't have a second to react. He grabbed her shoulders and said in her face, "It's not your risk. It's mine. Your handlers. It's the entire networks' risk. How long did they spend training you? Money. Resources. Not to mention your future successes."

Stella felt that old Bled stubbornness. The more he said no, the more she had to do it. "I'm not leaving without her."

"She's just one child," he said.

"What if she was yours? Would you say 'just' then?"

Cyril dropped his hands and turned away. He'd talked about a daughter, but Stella never knew if she was a real person or another trick to lure her in. "Well?" she asked.

"I can't be…swayed by this emotion," he said quietly and she wasn't sure if he was saying it to himself or her.

"Can you do it?" she asked.

He turned around, his face normal and uncaring. "Your handler didn't send you for this girl, so I won't."

Stella took a breath. She didn't want to do it, but she thought about the earl's face, Agatha's, but mostly Anna's, a tiny child abandoned to the wolves and it was worth the price. "I'll give you the money."

Cyril raised a brow. "You will? Even knowing what you think you know about me?"

"Yes. Can you do it?"

He started pacing again. "This is extraordinary. Maybe this is why we don't use women."

She marched over and slammed him against the wall. "I've done my duty and this is part of it. Being a girl helped. It didn't hurt."

"You've got something then," he said.

"And I'm not telling you what it is."

"All the more reason to get you out immediately."

She got in his face. "Yes. Fine. Get me the papers."

"Tell me who she is. You may as well. You've come this far."

That was true, but she hated giving him anything. He could use it to hurt so many people from Anna to Berta at the bakery.

"I won't betray you," he said. "I swear on my daughter's life."

"If she exists," said Stella.

"She exists."

She looked for a sign that he was lying and found none, but that would be the mark of a good spy and Cyril was good, very good.

"On your daughter's life," she said and then she told him about Anna Wildholz and he started pacing again, muttering, "Unbelievable."

"The hospital is in Brandenburg an Der Havel," said Stella. "The doctor said she's in a special ward, but I have to get her out."

"It's a prison," he said.

Her mouth dropped.

"And a mental institution and God knows what else," he said.

"I don't...understand what they're doing," she said. "Why on Earth..."

"What's wrong with her?"

"Nothing. She was sick and that woman, Lisa Hoppe, took her to the doctor."

He shook his head. "That wouldn't do it. There must be something else."

"Wouldn't do what?"

"You saw a picture of this child?"

"Yes."

"Describe her."

Stella described Anna, but she was a typical child. In Stella's opinion, little girls were much the same.

"You have no idea what she has?" he asked.

"Well, I assumed a cold or the flu. What are you getting at?"

He struggled with the words, but finally asked, "She wasn't deformed or obviously defective?"

She recoiled. "Defective? She's not a car part."

"I didn't mean that way."

"What other way can you possibly mean it?"

He ran his fingers through his hair again. "She looked good then. Normal."

"Yes. She was perfect."

"And you weren't told there was a problem?"

"No."

"Well, she could be blind. Deaf maybe," he said.

"She could be, I suppose, but no one said that," said Stella.

He nodded. "She would look perfect as you said."

"Would they send her to a mental institution if she were deaf? Why? It makes no sense."

"It does if you're a Nazi." Cyril told her about a new law, signed in October, but then backdated to the beginning of the war. A little trick by Hitler to make it seem like it was all part of the war effort when it was really about purifying the German race. A notice had been sent to doctors and health administration offices that they were to report any child under three with congenital problems like mongolism, mental defects, blindness, deafness, or any physical deformity. The report would go to a committee and they would decide whether or not to remove the child from the family for care in a special children's ward.

"Why?" Stella asked. "What for?"

"It's supposed to free the family from the burden of raising a child with these kind of…problems. They can work and be able to create a stronger Germany."

She rolled her eyes. "People aren't going to just let them take their children."

"Stella, they've been sterilizing people for years and nobody cares." Cyril's voice got tighter. "If you're depressed, an alcoholic, a habitual criminal, or defective in some way they find to be a blight on their perfect race, then they make sure you won't spread your disease."

"You can't spread deafness."

"But you could, in theory, make more deaf people and that's not perfect, is it?"

She wrapped her arms around herself. "At the doctor's office, the woman said they were going to keep her. Forever."

"I'd say that's a fair assessment," said Cyril. "The Nazis aren't fond of live and let live."

"I have to get her out."

"You can't. It *is* a prison, Stella."

"I'm not going back to England and tell them that I left that child to rot in *prison*."

"Well, how do you expect to break her out?" he asked.

"I'm not going to break her out. It isn't Alcatraz," she said.

"It may as well be. Anna has papers saying she's there for a reason and you can't go in and say it's not true. It probably is true."

She smiled at him. "Let's get some different papers then."

"Saying what, for instance?"

"Are they doing this…this thing all over the Reich?"

He nodded. "They don't do anything by halves."

Stella thought about Oscar and his desire to annihilate the Jews. He definitely wasn't into halves. "Then there must be other places for these children. There'd be a lot of them."

A smile came over Cyril's face. "I like the way you think."

"I'll reserve my judgement on your thinking until you tell me you have a plan," she said.

"I have a plan and it's a pretty good one, if I do say so myself."

Stella crossed her arms. "Let me have it."

"We're going to transfer her to another institution."

"Exactly what I was thinking."

"Great minds think alike," he said.

"Let's talk great deeds," she said. "Can you get that paperwork?"

He eyed her and she could see the wheels turning. "You'll give me the money?" Cyril asked.

"I will."

"Then I can."

Irena's house was lit up and people were going up the walk with somber faces much like Dr. Ehlich's house, but there weren't any black sedans or trucks parked out front. Stella decided to take that as a good sign and limped up the front walk on her one boot.

Inside was a quiet affair. No sobbing thankfully, but the smell of the ersatz coffee hung heavy in the air, reminding Stella of how the Bled gardeners burnt the leaves every fall, leaving the house inside and out smelling of earthy decay.

"Sophie!" exclaimed Irena. "Where have you—what happened to your boot?"

She told Irena and the audience around her the story about falling and the sewer. It sounded mildly ridiculous to her, but they bought it completely as Cyril had assured her they would. She'd crossed the Rubicon as he put it. She couldn't replace the boot with an identical one so there was no going back. He wasn't worried at all. They'd bought her cover and he was envious. He'd never been able to quite fit the way she did and they'd worked out everything she should say going forward. Stella had to admit it was nice not to be alone in Berlin, even if Cyril was her company.

"I don't know what I'm going to do," she said. "I haven't got enough stamps to replace the boots."

To her surprise, offers of extra boots came from many quarters. The neighbors had heard what had happened and came to commiserate about Hanni's arrest. Stella very nearly said how very upset she was, but a warning from Cyril sounded in her head. Her situation outside the house wasn't certain and the neighbors were outsiders.

"Were you able to find out how bad it is?" asked a man with two days of red beard.

"No, I couldn't," she said. "My friend wasn't there."

"That girl," said his wife. "You must make him understand she has nothing to do with you or this house."

Irena gave Stella a worried look and quietly said, "We are praying it was a mistake."

"Mistake or not," said another woman. "You can't have her here."

"The Gestapo," said a man. "They know you now."

Hanni had gone from a Valkyrie girl to a dangerous commodity and it didn't matter whether she'd done it or not. They didn't want her in the neighborhood. It seemed the gathering was more of a warning of how things should go than a commiseration.

Irma and Maria came out of the sitting room and took her away from the so-called guests.

"We have to get you out of those stockings," said Maria.

"You can't get sick," said Irma. "We're going to be short-handed at the club as it is."

That set off a whole new list of recriminations against Hanni for not doing her part for Germany as if serving at a club was vital to the war effort. Maria and Irma stayed silent on the way upstairs to Stella's room. Irma checked to see if anyone followed before they closed the door behind them.

"You really didn't see him?" asked Maria when it seemed safe.

"No. I'm sorry. There wasn't anyone there. Just a few low level staff. It took forever, and they wouldn't even give me his address," said Stella.

Irma set about making her bed that was still a jumble from Oscar's raid. "Don't worry. My parents are going to ask some friends for help."

"I hope they're not friends like those downstairs."

"No. They will understand why Hanni did it and they'll help if they can. One is on Göring's staff. He helped get me my job at the club."

Stella stripped off the stockings and flung them over the lukewarm radiator with a wet slap. Maria gave her a small rough towel to dry her legs and asked, "How did you get so wet?" Her eyes said it wasn't exactly an innocent question. She knew Stella was up to something.

"Isn't everything shoveled?" asked Irma. "It should be. It's the law."

"Nobody told the newspaper and it's all a mess around there. So icy." She showed them the spot on her hip that she'd rubbed raw to look like she'd fallen.

"That's very ugly," said Maria, losing the edge in her eyes.

"A compress with the bitter salz," said Irma.

Stella made a face. "I've had enough of wet. I just want to go to bed."

"Hold on. I'll be right back." Irma dashed out and they heard her pounding down the stairs. Stella put on her nightgown, the front stiff from her bloody nose, and crawled under the covers. Maria watched her silently, looking as though she wanted to ask something but was terrified to open her mouth to do it.

Irma pounded back up the stairs with a book in her hand. "Here. I borrowed your American book from Hanni. I needed a distraction after this morning."

"She's been reading it out to us," said Maria. "I don't think Ashley cares for Scarlett at all."

"Oh, he cares for her," said Irma. "Not in the marrying way though."

"Irma!"

"It's true, isn't it, Sophie?"

Stella laughed and relaxed back onto the wall and her thin pillow. "Irma's right. Ashley wouldn't ever *marry* Scarlett."

Maria sat on the edge of the bed. "She isn't a nice girl."

"That's not why," said Irma. "He's a weakling."

"So is Charles and he married her," Stella pointed out.

"Charles is a fool."

"And she had to have his baby," said Maria, wrinkling her nose.

"That was the worst," proclaimed Irma. "I'd rather die than have Charles' baby."

Stella tucked her hands under the covers and said, "So you haven't gotten very far yet?"

"Why?" asked Maria.

"There are worse things than having Charles' baby."

She clasped her hands under her chin. "What happens?"

"I can't tell you," said Stella.

"Does Rhett Butler kidnap her? He seems the type."

Irma draped herself across the end of the bed. "He could kidnap me anytime he wanted."

"Irma!"

The girls read lines out of the book and started talking about the merits of Ashley vs Rhett, Scarlett's mother's lifelong grief, for which Irma had a newfound compassion, and the slavery system that the German girls found both bizarre and abhorrent.

Stella allowed herself to be one of them, talking about books and boys with a strange sadness in her heart. In forty-eight hours she'd be gone and with any luck they'd never know why.

CHAPTER 22

$\mathcal{M}$onday came in colder than ever and making it colder still was Hanni's absence. They'd hoped she'd be interviewed and let go, but she hadn't come back. So before the girls had gotten up, Irena had put on her brave face and gone to the Gestapo headquarters to ask after her. When she returned she was shaky but hopeful that Hanni would be released at some point.

Two officers interviewed Irena for an hour, asking about Hanni's history and behavior, her loyalty to the Reich and club affiliations, like there was a chance Hanni might be a communist or something. The range of punishments for listening to an illegal radio station went from a few days in jail to death and everything in-between. The Gestapo wasn't friendly in the slightest and Stella heard what Irena related as a threat. "Had Hanni infected anyone with her radical ideas?" "Were any of the other girls rebellious or unhappy?" "The house wasn't completely searched. Perhaps there are more radios."

If they came back for a second search, they'd definitely go down to the cellar. Stella had to get that money out of her suitcase, but try as she might she couldn't find a way to get down there. She'd slept late and everyone was up when she came downstairs. She couldn't slip away and someone would see her if she tried to bring the suitcase upstairs.

They gathered at the dining room table with a meagre amount of food in the center, so meagre no one wanted to be the one who ate and they all picked at their half a roll with no butter or jam, drinking ersatz tea that had been steeped twice already. Thanks to Oscar, water was the only thing in abundance.

"Do you think they will come back?" asked Inge tearfully from under a cold compress on her eyes. She cried for so long her eyes looked like she'd been punched, lots of swelling and redness.

"They were very busy and annoyed about dealing with us, so I hope not," said Irena, hopefully. "The officer mentioned Hanni's beauty and Valkyrie more than once. I think that's a good sign."

"They must have more important things to do," said Maria.

"More important than the law?" asked Irma.

That got her a round of glares and she quickly said, "I meant that we know that we are loyal to the Führer, but they don't, not after Hanni, so we'll just have to prove it."

"It doesn't matter," said Irena. "They can search all they want. There's nothing to find."

Irma and Inge weren't looking, but Stella caught a worried flash between Maria and Irena. There was something to find. She was sure of it and that only made her more determined to get out as planned.

Cyril had originally said a week to get the necessary documents, but when she told him about Hanni, he changed it to Tuesday and he wasn't happy with that. Two more nights in that house made him nervous, but, they decided to get out clean and preserve the cover, she'd have to stay.

"As long as the Obersturmbannführer doesn't come back, I'll be happy," she said.

"His interest is good," said Irma. "He likes you and he's on his way up."

"It's not good."

"Just because he's not friendly is no reason to put him off."

"Rank isn't everything," said Stella.

"But it helps," said Irma.

"I'm not marrying him."

Maria set down her teacup with a clank. "No, you're not."

Sharp words from the quietest girl in the house and Irma asked, "Are you all right?"

She glanced at Stella, clinched her jaw, and said, "He doesn't want to marry her. He's like…what you said about Ashley, only…only nasty."

"Ashley?" Irena asked blankly.

Stella quickly explained about the book and Irma said, "He's nothing like Ashley. The Obersturmbannführer is making something of himself. He could be a Reichsminister someday."

"He's horrible," said Inge, lowering her compress. "I wouldn't marry him if he asked."

"Oh, you wouldn't, would you?"

Inge put the compress back over her eyes. "I know you think I'm silly and senseless, but even I can tell he'd be cruel and heartless to any wife. Don't marry him, Sophie."

"Aren't you listening?" Maria asked. "He doesn't want to marry her. He's going to make her move into Frau Durchdenwald's boarding house."

"That can't mean what you think it means," said Irena.

Stella nodded, her mind moving fast. This was good. A reason to leave that was plausible and the cover could be kept intact. "He said there was a separate entrance in my new room."

Irma clasped her hands to her chest. "No."

"Yes. I think…I think he expects me to be his mistress," said Stella, getting the desired reaction of gasps around the table.

"You can't do that," said Irena. "Frau Bothe wouldn't have it."

"I don't think he's going to ask her permission."

They went silent and then Irena checked the time. "You have to go, but Sophie, he won't be there tonight, will he?"

"I don't think so, but he's coming on Wednesday again."

Irena took her hand and said, "We will think of something."

Irma steepled her fingers and said, "Maybe you should think of it a different way."

"What way?" asked Stella.

"Like being in the Lebensborn. You're Aryan and he's Aryan," she said.

"What's Lebensborn?" asked Inge.

Irma explained what amounted to a breeding program for Aryans. Ideal women were matched to ideal men to produce ideal children. No marriage necessary.

"Do they take care of you?"

"Inge, how can you ask that?" asked Maria. "It's disgusting."

Irma turned on her. "It's for the Führer and the Fatherland. It is our duty to produce good Aryan stock for the future."

Stella watched the girls go back and forth, trying to figure out the world she'd landed herself in. Marriage. Morality. Nothing mattered but what the Führer wanted and they were perfectly happy with that. At least Inge and Irma were. Maria wasn't and Irena was subdued, unwilling to say anything for either side.

"Well," Stella said after a minute, "the Obersturmbannführer isn't perfect and he isn't going to be in the Lebensborn program."

"He's Aryan," said Irma.

"Not enough. You said the program is for the tall and blond. I'm not and neither is he."

Irena shooed them out into the hall to put on their coats, but she held Stella back whispering, "We will think of something. He shouldn't make you do that."

"He shouldn't," Stella said. "But he will."

With that, she went into the hall and put on her coat and hat. Maria was watching her closely, but Irma and Inge were discussing what the Lebensborn program would be like. The discussion lasted all the way to the club and the two of them decided it would be an honor to be included. Stella suspected that Inge was lured by the idea of not working, but Irma was a believer in breeding for the Reich. Stella couldn't wrap her mind around it. Irma hated what was happening to

Hanni and thought it unfair and unjust, but she still loved the Reich. The Reich was somehow separate from what it was doing to Hanni.

Letting Irma and Inge walk ahead, she hooked her arm through Maria's and they walked together in silence, listening to the insanity in front of them. Maria patted her arm and whispered, "I'm afraid for you."

"I'm afraid for all of us."

Their eyes met and Stella saw goodness in Maria's, but she couldn't trust it. Cyril had proved that to her in a most painful way.

FOR A MONDAY NIGHT, the club was buzzing with excitement more akin to a Friday or a Saturday. Frau Bothe was yelling questions at the girls that were already there and got only looks of confusion and denial in return.

"You!" she yelled when they walked up to the mirrors in the dressing room.

"Us?" asked Irma. "What did we do?"

"Did you talk to Clara?"

They shook their heads.

"I have it on good authority that she's gotten a job in the ministry as a secretary. A secretary!"

"Well, it's very good money," ventured a girl from Clara's boarding house.

"That's not the point!" Frau Bothe glared at them. "Did you know?"

They shook their heads and Irma said, "We found her dirndl on Saturday. She left it in the bathroom."

"And you didn't tell me?"

"We didn't know why she'd left it," said Maria quietly.

"You didn't know! You didn't know!" Frau Bothe focused on Stella. "You must've known."

"Me?" Stella asked.

"You are," she crossed her fingers, "like this with Obersturmbann-führer von Drechsel and his crippled brother."

Stella flinched at the word *crippled*. It was such a harsh assessment and it made her think of little Anna locked away in a prison or mental ward or somewhere equally horrid for being not perfect.

"Look at your face," Frau Bothe accused. "You knew."

"I didn't," she said. "I didn't talk to Clara at all."

"But you were kissing the Obersturmbannführer."

Horst walked in wearing a top hat and tails with an expression like he'd smelled something rotting. "Not by choice."

Frau Bothe blushed furiously. "What do you mean?"

"He kissed her and she couldn't get away."

"Oh, well. Why should she want to get away?"

"If you don't know, I can't make you understand," said Horst, looking around. "So we've lost the nasty redhead. Good riddance."

"Easy for you to say," said Frau Bothe. "I've got four tables without a girl."

Irma bit her lip, looked at the rest of them to see if they were going to say something. When it was clear they weren't, she spoke up, "Actually, it's eight."

"What?"

Irma explained that Hanni had been arrested and the whole place went crazy. Yelling, crying, and cursing, just for starters. Stella wondered what Clara would've thought if she could see it. No one expressed any regrets over her, other than the extra work, but Hanni was different. They genuinely wept for her. The performers thought her kind and beautiful. The other girls were shattered over whether she might be imprisoned for weeks or months over a little radio listening with no one to help her, cold and alone.

After the wailing calmed down, Horst spoke to Frau Bothe and she went to the door. "This night will not go down as a failure." She started assigning tables and everyone frantically changed shoes, tied aprons, and applied their approved Valkyrie lipstick.

The show must go on.

"Where do you want me?" Stella asked Bothe.

"Down in front. I have to use you while I have you."

"What does that mean?"

Bothe pulled her to the side and said, "I had word from Clara's house. You're to be taking a certain room there on the orders of Obersturmbannführer von Drechsel. That's how I found out about Clara."

"I'm not going," she said.

Frau Bothe grabbed her arm. "He has arranged it and you will do it. Word is that he will be Himmler's right hand man in a matter of days."

"Don't you understand what he wants?"

"I understand that we all must make sacrifices for the good of the Reich. Clara moves out tomorrow and you will move in on Wednesday."

"How can you make me do this?" Stella asked. "I'm a Valkyrie girl. We're supposed to get married, not…that."

Frau Bothe looked away and took a deep breath. "It was not my choice either. I was told, not asked for an opinion. You have gotten yourself under his skin."

"Well, I'll have to get out from under," she said.

"You will in time. He'll lose interest."

Stella pulled away from her. "Not soon enough though."

"No."

She turned around and caught Maria watching. She handed Stella her apron and then helped her tie a pretty bow on the left.

"No, no," said Frau Bothe. "The right."

They stared at her.

"You must show that you understand the Obersturmbannführer."

"He's not coming," said Stella.

"There will be plenty of SS here and they might tell him if you have it on the left." She pointed at the bow. "Change it."

Maria retied the bow and Inge said, "Maybe it won't be that bad."

"Take my place and let me know."

"You couldn't pay me to be you, but it could be worse."

"Could it?"

"You could be tying on the right for his hideous brother," said Inge.

"Inge!" said Maria. "He was wounded for our Führer."

She shrugged and pranced out. Irma came up and smoothed her hair. "She's silly as they come, but she's right. It might not be so bad."

"I'm not doing it," said Stella.

Irma looked sad for her and said, "Come on. We have to go up. It's a full house."

"It's always a full house."

It *was* always a full house and Stella's tables were packed with business leaders and Wehrmacht. She didn't know until later that she wasn't to serve the elite anymore, at least no other elite than Oscar. The other girls got the SS and Stella didn't envy the pinches and lack of tips. She served her tables, keeping her ears open for talk of Oscar, but no one mentioned his name. An SS officer dying of whatever was in that pill should've been big news and from what she could tell Oscar drank from the flask often. The L pill had been in there for over a day. Maybe she'd miscalculated. Maybe they'd given her a fake pill, although she couldn't see why they'd bother to do that. She could've picked the wrong pill and that thought tortured her. She had a chance to kill Himmler's right hand man and she failed. What would this mean for the war and for the Jews? Her stomach hurt when she thought about it and she could hardly remember her orders. Making small talk with idiot Nazis was an impossibility.

Frau Bothe had to keep reminding her to smile and she'd plaster a grin on her face, but it would slide right off. She'd failed and she had the worst feeling that something terrible was coming because of it.

"Smile," said Horst, catching her by the bar. "Herta is watching and this *promotion* of yours is important for her. She'd like to be a secretary, too."

Unbelievable. Secretary, mother, waitress, or wife. That's it. The most we can expect.

"I'm trying," she said.

"It's not a lost cause." He smiled. "You could run away and join the circus."

Plant the seed.

"Or maybe I'll just run away," she said.

"Let me see." Horst put his forefinger on the cleft in his chin. "Sleep with Obersturmbannführer von Drechsel or run away?"

"You sound like I have a choice."

"You always have a choice," he said with a tip of his hat.

Yes, I do.

STELLA LAY in bed listening to the sound of the old house creaking and watching her frozen breath stream out of her mouth, lit up by the moonlight coming in through the window. They'd gotten home at three and eaten the rest of the rolls and a couple of tins of sardines that Maria's Obersturmbannführer Krebs had gifted her. If Stella never saw another oily fish with beady eyes, it would be too soon. She'd been so hungry at the club she very nearly did the unthinkable and ate off the guests' plates, but she managed to hold out. Now she wished she hadn't. There'd be no food until she got to France. At the thought, she crossed her fingers under the covers.

Please let me do this. Let me save her.

An hour after the house had gone quiet, Stella slipped out of bed, still fully dressed, and crept down the stairs. There were a few creaks, but she was lighter than ever and they weren't loud enough to wake anyone.

Almost no light came in from the windows downstairs, but she managed to find a shopping bag in the kitchen and then feel her way down a dark, windowless hall until her fingers touched the door paneling. The lock made an unbearably loud click and she thought her heart would stop as it seemed to echo around her, announcing what she was doing. The door itself had rusty old hinges and they groaned and complained as she opened it the smallest amount possible to slide through the opening to step onto the cellar steps.

She pulled the door to and felt around for a switch. There wasn't one, so she waved her arm until it touched a bulb and cord hanging from the ceiling. She pulled the cord and the narrow staircase was filled with dim but warm light. Relief flooded her chest as she began down the stairs, picking her way past crates of empty canning jars, worn out pots, and stacks of newspapers. It was such a mess that she got worried about finding her suitcase in the clutter, but the cellar wasn't as bad as the steps. It had a rough stone floor and walls with pipes every which way. It smelled like dirt and decay. Off to one side were bikes, piles of boxes, the boiler, a sad little pile of coal, and more empty jars. On the other side was the laundry. Stella was familiar with that. She'd visit and help Mavis in the mansion's basement and it was basically the same with the large tubs, a mangle, and lines for drying. One tub was full with the girls white blouses, soaking in blue-tinted water. Behind that tub were the suitcases. If the SS were to search, they'd see them immediately.

Stella propped her suitcase up on the tub and popped open the clasps. The Reichsmarks were still there as were her fake papers. She never really doubted it, but it was soothing to know that, at least, was fine. She closed the suitcase and quickly carried it upstairs.

Peeking out the cellar door, she listened to the silence before turning off the light and going down the hall. Tiptoeing up, she held her breath until she was almost to her room. She exhaled and then she heard it. A creak and quite a complaining one. Was it a door or the floor? She hurried up the last five stairs, got in her room, and closed the door behind her.

Nobody saw me. Nobody saw me.

She didn't turn on the light in case someone was up and set about packing. A small job, it took less than ten minutes to get all her meagre belongings folded and inside the suitcase with lots of extra room. It was rather sad actually. She had almost nothing and no one thought it was odd. As pampered as the Valkyrie girls were, a few dresses and two pairs of shoes was normal. The old Stella wouldn't have gone away for the weekend with as little as that.

Her dirndl hung alone in the wardrobe and she felt inexplicably bad about leaving it, but it wouldn't work to take it. She had to seem like a good German and a good German wouldn't take the dirndl that belonged to the club. She closed the wardrobe and pulled a sheet of paper and her fountain pen out of her stationery set. The moonlight gave her enough light to write a short letter to Irena. She thanked her for everything she'd done for her and said she couldn't stay, blaming it on Oscar which was perfectly reasonable and could preserve her cover for use again. She signed it "Much love, Sophie" and left the letter on her pillow.

The empty frame where the Werner picture used to be was the last thing to be packed. She laid it on the top of the clothes and felt a fresh flash of anger toward Oscar, the first she'd allowed herself. Who did he think he was, taking her picture, ordering her to move as if she was nothing, not a person just a thing to be done with what he willed. He might've survived, but she would, too, and she'd tell the earl and Park-Welles, whoever would listen, what his nasty little mind was up to. And his brother, too. He was no better. He'd seen what his brother would do to her if he left, but he still went to Koblenz without looking back.

Go around the Maginot Line? Blitzkrieg? We'll see about that.

She double-checked the room and her eyes fell on the only remaining item in the room. Irma's copy of *Der Totale Krieg.*

"Total war," she whispered the first words she'd spoken in English in weeks. "If that's what you want, that's what you'll get."

CHAPTER 23

*P*erhaps it was the wrong thing to do, but Stella had done so many wrong things, adding one more to the list didn't weigh on her mind. She put Irma's book in her suitcase and closed the latches. Irma could have *Gone with the Wind*. Stella knew how it ended for Scarlett and the South. Soon it would be Irma and the Reich, if she had anything to say about it.

Stella slipped down the stairs, suitcase in hand, and put on her coat and hat. She turned around and took one last look, knowing that in a strange way she had belonged there, valued and welcomed. It wasn't real. Sophie Weber wasn't real, but it had felt real. Park-Welles had said, "Be sure to remember who your enemies are." She'd thought he was ridiculous. Her enemies were clear. The Reich, Peiper, the SS, but it wasn't clear in that house with those girls and Irena.

She turned the key in the lock and let herself out, closing the door on Sophie for the time being. The street was deserted at that time of morning. It was barely five. She hurried down the street, turning off into an alley and taking the long way to the U Bahn station. She wasn't the only one there to her surprise. Workers wearing soiled coveralls stood next to the tracks with glum, exhausted expressions. Stella couldn't tell if they were going to a factory or returning from it.

Men and women shivered in the cold, wearing multiple scarves and hats pulled so low only their eyes were visible. She couldn't guess where they were going. To bakeries or butcher shops maybe. Stella was the only one with a suitcase, but no one noticed her. They were too cold and, she suspected, hungry.

The correct train came and she left Irena's neighborhood, heading to the Hauptbahnhof. The station was bustling, but she found the bench Cyril described in an out of the way corner and sat down, setting the shopping bag, filled with the money and the instructions she'd taken out of her compact, next to her. She wasn't sure when Cyril would turn up and there was a little niggle of fear that he wouldn't show at all, or worse the SS or Gestapo would. She was done for if he'd turned her in. She couldn't explain that pile of money away and they'd soon find the false papers in the suitcase. There was nothing to be done if Cyril was as treacherous as he had been in Paris, so she occupied her mind with what she would do if nobody showed. She would go to Brandenburg, talk her way in with bribes or lies, and kidnap Anna if at all possible. It was insane and she was well aware of that, but she would do it. She couldn't look at herself in the mirror if she didn't.

"You're miles away," said a man in impeccable German.

He sat down beside her, wearing a natty suit, glasses, and a full beard.

"You look nice," she said. "The beard is a nice touch."

"How did you know it was me?"

She yawned and said, "You have a presence."

"That's not a good thing in our line of work."

"And yet there you are."

He put a fat shopping bag next to hers. "I got what you need, but I don't know if it will be enough."

"Why not?" she asked.

"Brandenburg is the first facility of its kind. Moving her might seem suspicious."

"But did you get everything?"

"I did and an ugly suit to make you look official, suitably stiff, and grim."

"Anything else?" she asked.

"It's all in the bag. You've brought the money?" he asked.

"Yes. I hope you will use it for what you're supposed to," she said with a glance at his disinterested, whiskery face.

"Don't worry about me. I know what I'm about."

"I wish I did."

"Don't be careful," he said, checking his watch.

"What do you mean by that?" she asked.

"Do you think a woman moving a child between facilities would be careful or discreet? Be a Nazi. Demanding. Entitled. But above all disinterested in the child. She's a thing. Unworthy of your interest."

Stella clenched and unclenched her teeth. "I will."

"They smell fear. Show no weakness."

She nodded, not trusting herself to speak, since fear was all she felt at that moment.

"Good luck, my darling girl." Cyril hesitated and she could tell he wanted to look at her or touch her hand, but he didn't. He reached over and picked up her bag and left his, walking away with a jaunty step to greet a group of Wehrmacht who'd walked up to a schedule board and were looking quite confused. He asked their destination and started telling them the appropriate lines without a single glance back.

Stella stood up, grabbing Cyril's bag and her suitcase, and went to the ticket counter. She quickly bought a second-class ticket to Brandenburg on a train that left in an hour and went to the track to wait on a bench in an unobtrusive corner. She kept expecting someone to show up and yell or arrest her, but no one so much as spoke to her.

The train arrived bang on time and she got on, leaving Berlin with Cyril's bag clutched to her chest and nauseated she was so nervous. She sat next to an exhausted woman with a fat baby, who wailed for the first hour, but he'd worn himself out for the rest of the ride and was slumped over, drooling on Stella's sleeve by the time they pulled in at the Brandenburg Hauptbahnhof.

She walked with the crowd off the platform into the unimpressive station and looked for a bathroom. Once inside, she locked the door, checking it twice, and then looked in Cyril's bag. He was thorough. She'd give him that. The little spy had given her two folders. The first plain brown folder provided her with two new covers. The first, a thirty-year-old doctor's assistant, Luise Schneider, who was born in Stuttgart and lived in Vienna, working at the Am Spiegelgrund clinic under Dr. Jekelius. She was a glorified secretary as far as Stella could tell and her picture was very close to Stella herself, just older and tired.

Her second cover was for a twenty-five-year-old Dutch woman, the married Adélaïde Weinzierl and her picture wasn't as similar to Stella, but the hairstyle concealed a lot of the face shape, and that helped. She was returning to Arnhem to visit her mother with her sick daughter, Adèle, who also had papers. Cyril had thoughtfully included an engraved wedding ring to go with her Werner engagement ring and a pack of makeup with instructions to age herself for the trip to the prison/hospital after she'd checked in at a hotel booked under her Luise cover. She was to go to the so-called hospital after five o'clock when Dr. Hans Heinze would leave for the day, so only a skeleton staff would be there. Cyril had included a full set of ration cards with an appropriate amount used up and some Dutch currency and a magazine.

She, also, had a very official-looking folder with a set of orders inside complete with signatures and the Nazi seal. Luise Schneider was to move Anna Wildholz to Am Spiegelgrund immediately upon receipt of the orders for research purposes for future expansion of the program. She had tickets for herself and Anna all the way through to Vienna.

Underneath all that was a complete outfit, a tweedy-looking suit like a secretary would wear. It had a brass and black-enameled swastika pin on the lapel for good measure and a pair of clunky black heels that were nicer than what she, as Sophie, had.

Stella put her Sophie papers with the new Dutch cover in the false bottom of her suitcase with her Charlotte Sedgewick papers. The new clothes and orders went in the regular part and she left the bathroom with a feeling lighter than she had since she'd heard Cyril say the word *prison*. A plan and it looked like a good one. She had thought she'd have to just see what happened and hope she could talk her way through. It'd been known to work for her, but she'd never tried to spring anyone from the Nazi system before. With their love of officialdom and paperwork, it was likely to get sticky.

She left the station after asking directions to the Hotel am Altstadt and found it was a short walk, which was a good thing since the weather was getting worse. She didn't have an umbrella and by the time she reached the hotel the cloudy sky was beginning to spit sleet at her. She rushed in the front doors of the hotel to find it surprisingly busy. It was a cheap hotel, but it was also a large one with five floors and a restaurant. There were quite a few men who appeared to be in the building trade, getting themselves together for a day of work. Women came rushing through, complaining of hours and wanting apartments. They were dressed as nurses. There were also men in uniform, like prison guards, and she wondered if the prison was expanding.

At the desk, she checked in with a harried clerk, who said her room wouldn't be ready for an hour.

"You can have a breakfast in our restaurant," she said. "You have your ration cards?"

"Of course," said Stella. "Is it always so busy here?"

"It is now. They are building at the," she lowered her voice, "prison."

"Must be expanding a lot."

The clerk wrinkled her nose. "It is not our choice to have so many undesirables here in Brandenburg."

"We must all do our part."

"That's what they say," she said and gave Stella her key.

Stella went into the restaurant and had the worst ersatz coffee of her life. She was sure they brewed it with moldy leaves. But the roll and jam she paid extravagantly for was delicious. After an hour, she went up to her room and found it to be a single but reasonable in size with a small wardrobe and view of the back of the hotel that bustled with people coming with deliveries. Off to the left, she could see the train station and it would be easy enough to get there the back way. She shook out Cyril's clothes so they wouldn't be too wrinkled and went out to explore.

She very quickly found a back staircase used by the staff to go down to the kitchens and laundry. Several people stopped her and asked her what she was doing and she played the silly tourist who was lost to great effect. They simply directed her back up the same stairs, but she kept on looking around when they'd turned their backs. Then she went out to buy an umbrella and went to the address Cyril had given her for what he called the old prison. She walked by the large but unremarkable building called the Brandenburg an der Havel State Nursing Home. It sounded quite innocuous and hopeful even, not a prison for life for small children. She passed the main entrance like she had somewhere to go and was pleased to see no guards in place. There was quite a bit of building going on, but Stella couldn't see what they were constructing.

Then she took a walk around the old town to admire nothing really and then returned to the hotel by the back way and went up to her room to wait until four o'clock when it would all begin.

FOUR O'CLOCK SEEMED to take six days to arrive and Stella was about to jump out of her skin by the time it finally did, but she forced herself to follow her plan. When her watch said four on the button, she got up and changed into Luise Schneider with her best stockings and the dreadfully uncomfortable shoes. Her long, film star hair wasn't right for a secretary and a Nazi one at that. She braided it the way Irena did and wrapped it around her head, but it somehow made her look younger. The hat helped but not enough.

She got out the makeup and did as Cyril instructed. She hadn't been given much training in disguise. It wasn't like she could put on a mustache or something. But she could make herself tired with dark circles under the eyes and shadow on her eyelids aged her a lot. She used a thin brown pencil to trace every future line on her face and then rubbed it in with a rubbery sponge. It was subtle, but she was definitely older. Her rosy cheeks gave her away and she covered them with a little beige pancake, careful not to overdo it so that she didn't look odd. The only thing that didn't fit was her lips. They were still plump and pink so she outlined them with the pencil making them smaller and narrow. A bit of pancake took out a lot of the pink and suddenly she had the dull face of a much older and more tired woman.

Taking a look in the mirror, she suddenly understood why her mother wanted her to use cold cream every night. Old before her time wasn't a good thing. She put her well-used dumpy hat back on and pinched the brim down to cover part of her eyes. Between that and the makeup even their pale blue was subdued and much less striking. She might even have called them green. Very interesting and some-thing to explore for later.

She took off her Werner's ring and hid everything back in the suitcase, pushing it back under the bed. After taking a deep breath, she put on her coat and double-checked her paperwork in the handbag and Anna's transfer orders in the official folder. Her watch said five and there was no reason to delay. She took a peek out of her door, found the hall empty, and walked casually to the back stairs.

That time no one was around to question her and she simply walked out the back like she was supposed to be there. The sleet had intensified and she put up her staid black umbrella, glad for its shielding presence. The walk was short and she got to the prison at exactly five twenty and the place was quieter than before. No hammering in the distance or shouts of irritated workmen. The sun was down and it felt much later, nine o'clock or even ten.

The enormous doors under the arched entryway of the hospital were locked and there was no bell or knocker, so she folded up her umbrella and pounded on it with the crook. Sleet was hitting her from the back and the irritation served her well when the door finally opened. A guard opened the door a crack and the smell of antiseptic drifted out. "What do you want?"

Stella glared at him. "I have orders from Berlin. Let me in immediately."

"Orders?" He didn't open the door for her and she started rapping on the heavy metal again.

He hastily opened the door and she barged in, stamping her feet and shoving the umbrella into his hands. "Who is in charge here? I have transfer papers."

"Transfer papers?"

Stella gave out an exasperated snort and slapped the folder on his chest. Bewildered he took it while she slipped off her wet coat and then gave it to him, relieving him of the folder. "Orders. Who do I talk to about a patient?"

"This is after hours."

"I'm aware of the time. That doesn't change my orders, does it?"

He straightened up and said, "Go down the hall and turn right to the nursing office."

She nodded curtly and marched down the hall, using her best Nazi walk. No swish of the hips. Ramrod straight and radiating irritation. The irritation part was a cinch. The back of her skirt, stockings, and shoes were soaked and highly uncomfortable. She could use that.

Turning a sharp right, she went straight into the office without a courtesy knock. "I have orders for a transfer. Who do I speak to?"

The young nurse sitting behind a metal desk reading a medical textbook nearly fell out of her chair in surprise. "What?"

Stella sighed. "I have orders for a transfer. Who do I speak to?"

"I wasn't told anything about a transfer," she said.

"I'm not surprised. I only found out this morning." She put the folder in front of her and crossed her arms. "How long will this take? I have to catch a train."

The girl sputtered as she flipped through the papers. "This is…it's never happened before."

"Never? This place has been in operation for years," Stella said, doubt dripping off her.

"Well, yes, but the…ward is new."

"You have procedures in place for the rest of the hospital?"

"Yes."

Stella tapped the folder. "Then let's go."

"Today?" the nurse asked.

Her irritation grew and Stella formed her lips into a thinner line. "Yes."

"Well, our orders are…we don't release patients from *that* ward."

I bet you don't release them period.

"The subject isn't being released. This is a transfer. You transfer patients don't you?"

"Yes, but why is she being transferred?" she asked.

"I don't question my orders. I follow them to the letter," said Stella.

A change came over the young nurse. Orders were orders. She understood that. "You'll have to sign some papers."

"Get them." She checked her watch for effect. "I have a train soon."

The nurse opened a file cabinet and started to look for the paperwork when an older nurse, looking as though she'd worked forty-eight hours straight marched in with much the same walk as Stella used and she knew she was in trouble before the woman opened her mouth.

"What's this?" she barked.

The young nurse backed away and told her the gist of the situation. The older woman snatched the folder off the desk and said, "We'll see about that."

Stella was quaking inside, but she said with narrowed eyes, "Whatever you're going to do, do it quickly. I have orders and I intend to follow them."

The older nurse looked her over and hesitated, "I will have to ask Dr. Heinze."

The quaking got worse. "Is he here?"

The woman's jaw clenched and she exchanged a glance with the younger nurse.

"Well?" asked Stella. "Is he or isn't he?"

"He is, but it would be better if you came back tomorrow," she said.

I don't need to see him. Just give me the papers. Please. Please. Please.

"I *will* be on a train tonight as you can see."

The older nurse looked through the papers and frowned when she saw the tickets and time frame. "Yes. Come with me then."

It took all the self-control Stella had to nod with disinterest and follow the nurse out of the office. There was no plan for this. What if Heinze called Berlin? It was late, but he might get ahold of someone. She found herself frozen, but a strange kind of frozen where she kept walking and couldn't find a way to do anything else.

The nurse stopped at a door, knocked, and receiving no answer, she let herself into a small reception area with two desks and no secretaries.

"Are you sure he's here?" Stella asked, surprised that her voice came out strong and certain.

"The doctor sometimes chooses to stay late." She crossed the room and knocked on another door. This time a voice answered in sharp irritation. "What is it?"

"I have a...a courier from Berlin with transfer orders," the nurse said.

"What?"

She moved her mouth closer to the wood. "Orders from Berlin!"

"Come in."

The nurse opened the door and handed Stella the file as she went in. She wasn't sure how it happened. It just happened. There she was standing in front of a large desk piled with paperwork and looking at a small man with very little hair on his close-cropped head. The doctor gazed at her through frameless eyeglasses with his tie askew and no white coat. It'd been tossed carelessly aside on a chair. He had one lit cigarette in his hand and another in the over-flowing ashtray next to a glass of amber liquid.

She glanced back, but the nurse hurried out with a worried look and closed the door.

"What is this about a transfer?" he demanded and Stella thought she detected a slur. She was a master at detecting impairment from years of being Uncle Josiah's keeper at her mother's parties. One hint of a slur and she was to whisk him away before he could spike the punchbowl or tell someone's husband he liked the man's mistress better than his wife. Stella had failed in this duty a couple of times with disastrous consequences, so the hint of drunkenness in Dr. Heinze filled her with courage.

She dropped the file on his desk and said, "I'm to take a subject by the name of Anna Wildholz to Am Spiegelgrund in Vienna immediately."

Dr. Heinze took a deep puff of his cigarette and leafed through the papers. "It doesn't say for what purpose." He looked up at her with dark, beady eyes.

She shrugged and said, "I wasn't informed of the purpose."

"Will I get a replacement?"

"I don't know."

He went through the papers again, squinting and listing a little to the side. "This comes from Dr. Brandt?"

"It comes from Berlin."

"What did Dr. Brandt say?"

"I didn't speak to him. I work for Dr. Jekelius. He gave me the orders and told me to go. That's all I know."

He took a drink of the amber liquid and then pointed at her. "I want a replacement."

"I'll relay your request," she said, holding her breath.

"See that you do." Dr. Heinze yanked open a drawer and pulled out a sheaf of papers. He signed them and directed her to do the same. Then he took a copy of the orders out of Stella's folder and put his paperwork in.

"Wilma!" he yelled.

The nurse opened the door, "Yes?"

"Take care of this. I don't want to be disturbed again."

Wilma looked unsure and stood in the doorway, looking back and forth between them.

You heard him. Just do it.

"I'm ready now," said Stella

"To?"

"I'm taking the subject now."

"But doctor," Wilma sidestepped Stella, "your work. You need this patient."

He snubbed out his cigarette and picked up the second one. "I do."

"Then we should keep the patient tonight and call Berlin in the morning."

No. No. No.

"My orders are for tonight. I'm not authorized to alter them," Stella said.

Dr. Heinze took another drink. "Does Dr. Jekelius know how important my work is?"

"I'm sure he does," said Stella.

"That's not good enough," said Wilma.

"This is the preeminent facility," said Dr. Heinze. "The first. The foremost."

Stella had to fight to control her breathing. How could this be happening? Germans that didn't follow orders? Park-Welles said that didn't happen. "I'm following orders as I suspect he is."

Dr. Heinze slapped a hand on his desk. "Call Berlin. See if there's someone at Tiergartenstraße 4."

"Yes, doctor," said Wilma and she left.

The doctor drained his glass and then rummaged through his desk to find a half-empty bottle. He poured another half glass and swirled it, eyeing her with increasingly unfocused eyes. "Tell me about Am Spiegelgrund?"

Stella knew practically nothing. She didn't expect to be questioned on it and Cyril didn't think she would either. "It's a children's clinic in Vienna."

"And reform school."

She hoped he wasn't trying to catch her out. Taking a breath, she said, "Yes."

"Dr. Jekelius will not be taking over my position."

Stella didn't know what to say to that and gave him a level stare, designed to make him uncomfortable, and it worked.

"Wilma!" He yelled.

There wasn't an answer.

"Go look," he ordered Stella and she opened the door.

"She's gone," said Stella.

He got unsteadily to his feet. "Tell her to hurry."

"I don't know where she is and I do not work for you, doctor."

Dr. Heinze glared at her, came around the desk, and stomped out, yelling for Wilma. Stella blew out a breath and made a decision. She closed the door and found the key in her handbag. The ill pill and the energy pill rolled into her hand. She selected the ill one, cracked it, and emptied the contents into his glass. She swirled it. The liquid was cloudy but not so that he'd notice. She set the glass down in exactly the same spot. Then she took out her cigarette case and dumped the camera into her hand. She looked over the desk and began quickly taking pictures, not really knowing what she was seeing. They were building something, but it didn't look like another ward. There were work orders and shipping receipts. She took pictures of everything she could until she heard the doctor yell, "Wilma!"

Stella dropped the camera in her handbag and reopened the door mere seconds before he came barreling back in.

"I can't find her." He dropped back into his chair. "Ridiculous what I have to put up with."

"I can imagine," said Stella, praying he'd take a drink, but he chose the cigarette instead.

"You can't. Nobody can. I need more staff and the building projects," he gestured to the papers on his desk, "they won't be ready in time."

It was dangerous to be curious, but she had to know. "In time for what?"

He squinted at her and pushed his eyeglasses up his nose. "You don't need to know."

She lifted a shoulder as if she couldn't care less while she roiled with frustration on the inside. "It's no concern of mine, but I wouldn't say no to a glass if you're feeling generous. I've had a difficult day and I will be traveling all night. This wasn't my idea, you understand."

The doctor's body relaxed. "Of course, it isn't your fault. *You* would never be making decisions at this level," then he laughed, "or any level."

Stella bit back a retort about what a disgusting little bureaucratic weasel he was and asked instead, "So do I get a glass or not?"

He gave her a lopsided smile that was meant to be a come-on but came out as idiotic. "Yes, of course." He found another glass in the depths of his desk and poured her a glass. "Sit. Sit. Frau…"

"Schneider," said Stella before raising the glass. "Prost."

"Prost." He took a healthy swig and asked, "How long have you been at Am Spiegelgrund?"

"A year." She faked a sip and he took the hint, draining his glass and licking his practically nonexistent lips.

"You have no plans to be married?" he asked.

"Not at the moment. I wish to serve the Reich as long as I can."

"You can serve the Reich by bearing healthy children. You're not too old, I think." He touched his stomach and frowned.

"No, I'm not," said Stella.

"You have the necessary paperwork?" he asked.

Stella had no idea what he was talking about but nodded as he poured another glass while burping and swaying.

"I shouldn't drink anymore," he said.

"You've had a long day, haven't you?" asked Stella. "This place seems very well run."

He smiled and took a big drink. "It is. I have put all of myself into it to serve the Führer and the Reich." He spasmed and his face twisted. "I…where is that Wilma?"

As if on cue, Wilma bustled in. "I've got a call through. They are looking for someone in authority."

He spasmed again.

"Doctor?" she asked and turned to Stella, who shrugged and took a sip of the alcohol which was like whiskey but harsh and smelled similar to paint thinner.

Dr. Heinze ignored Wilma and said, "They're going to expand the program, you know."

"I didn't know," Stella said carefully.

Wilma was watching with concern. "Doctor, she is not authorized to—"

"Don't tell me we are moving to adolescents and adults and we will do all the things that the things need to do," he slurred.

"Doctor, how much of this," she sniffed the glass and wrinkled her nose, "did you drink?"

He reached for the glass and she held it away.

"I need it," he said. "I don't feel good."

She sniffed again. "Of course, you don't." Wilma looked at Stella and said, "Don't drink that."

Stella put down the glass and said, "Fine. I need to be going. Are you done?"

"No. I haven't—"

Dr. Heinze lurched forward and grabbed at the desk, scattering papers and tipping over his trash bin. "I'm doing it all for the Reich."

Stella snatched her folder off the desk and frowned. "Doing what?"

"Doctor, don't say—"

"They will be put to use. No burden to the good working people."

"Please, doctor, there is no need to talk about this. The orders are clear."

He ignored her and said, "It is true. We must act. Life unworthy of life must be…oh I…" he trailed off and then vomited across the desk.

Wilma screeched and Stella jumped up to yell out into the hall for someone to come help.

"What's wrong with him?" she asked with disdain as he spewed again completely missing the trash bin Wilma held for him.

"He went into the prison today. Unsanitary conditions. I warned him," said Wilma. "Help me get him to the bathroom."

Stella recoiled and said, "What about that call? The ministry is waiting."

The doctor spasmed and the distinct odor of feces filled the room.

"I don't care!" yelled Wilma.

Three other nurses ran in and stopped short in horror at the scene or, more likely, the stench.

"But my orders," said Stella. "I have to catch my train."

"Look at him! He can't sign anything."

"He already did!" Stella waved the folder.

"Take her then, but we will be lodging a complaint." She waved at the other nurses. "Help me."

They weren't inclined to help her, but Stella didn't stick around to see what happened. She hurried back to the original office and found the young nurse back at her books. "The doctor has released the subject to me."

She sat up with a jerk. "But I thought—"

"Yes, yes. It's all taken care of." Stella showed her the signed papers and the girl seemed confused, but she got a set of keys and told Stella to follow her. They walked out of the office and heard the sound of retching echoing down the hall.

The young nurse turned to Stella and said, "I will be right back."

Stella grabbed her arm. "Oh, no you don't. I have my orders." She tapped her watch. "I can't miss my train."

"I have to—"

"Wilma and some other nurses are there," said Stella. "Let's go."

The sound of incredible flatulence replaced the retching and was followed by shouts of "Scheiße!"

"The doctor may have had too much to drink."

"Oh, poor Dr. Heinze," she said.

Stella nodded in sympathy for a doctor whose speciality seemed to be locking up helpless children and keeping them from their families. With any luck the combination of the ill pill and the liquor would have him vomiting himself to death.

"Well, since he signed the papers, I guess it will be all right to take you to the ward." She looked at Stella and tilted her head to the side. "You don't have a carrier?"

"A carrier?" she asked.

"For the child."

"No." It was Stella's turn to be bewildered. A carrier for a two-year-old little girl? Myrtle and Millicent weren't content to sit in a basket since they were six months old. They were always on the move and once they could crawl, they didn't even like their baby carriage and were forever escaping, scaring their nanny half to death.

"You'll need a carrier," said the nurse, glancing around nervously.

Stella lowered her eyelids to half-mast and asked, "Why?"

"Well, you know, the doctor's work. You'll need a carrier."

Oh, dear Lord. What have they done?

"Fine. Give me one." Stella's voice came out harsh and hateful and the girl looked startled. "I can't be delayed. I'm not losing my job over a carrier when no one said I needed one. It wasn't on the orders or my instructions."

"Oh, no. You shouldn't be fired," she said quickly. "I'll find you one. Right this way." She led Stella to a set of stairs and they walked up to the third floor. It'd been very quiet on the first floor, being filled with offices and other rooms labeled by numbers and letters, but there weren't any wards. Going up the stairs that all changed. The antiseptic was still in abundance, but under it, if you were paying attention, were hints of urine and feces. And maybe something else, earthy and metallic. Blood or unwashed bodies? Stella wasn't sure. She breathed as shallowly as she could and cleared her mind. She must get Anna and get out.

Focus on Anna. Just Anna.

On the third floor, they walked down a wide hall with the sound of crying children coming from both sides. There was one nurse at the end of the hall reading a copy of *Frauen Warte* and paying absolutely no attention to the wailing. She glanced up when they approached and yawned. "What is it, Hilda?"

Hilda explained the transfer and the other nurse, named Lisolotte, was incredulous. "Transfer? She can't leave."

Stella eyed her coldly. "Dr. Heinze has signed the paperwork. Perhaps you want to speak to him."

"No, no," said Hilda. "He is…indisposed. You can take the child."

Lisolotte just looked at Stella.

"I do not have all day. I must be on a train to Vienna in a short while. Get the subject and I will be on my way."

"It's not possible," said Lisolotte.

Stella heart sank. "Is she dead?"

"No."

The nurses exchanged a look that Stella took for something akin to guilt but not quite the same.

"Spit it out. Is she sick?" Stella asked.

Lisolotte sighed. "Yes, that is it. She's sick."

Very convincing.

"It makes no difference. Orders are orders."

Lisolotte put down her magazine and said, "She's too ill to be moved. She can't walk or anything."

"What does she have?" Stella made herself sound nervous, when, in fact, she didn't care if Anna had bubonic plague. She was getting her out of there.

"Don't worry. You can't catch it," said Hilda. "It isn't transmittable to us."

What does that mean?

Stella checked her watch. "I'm losing patience. You have the child. I have the signed papers. Get me a carrier and let's get this over with."

"You don't understand," said Lisolotte.

"Correct."

The nurses looked at each other and Hilda shrugged. "Take her in and show her. I have to go back to my station."

Hilda left, walking down that hall so thick with wails Stella felt she could almost see them. She kept her face a mask, thinking of Nicky and his cool composure. "Lead on."

Lisolotte reluctantly got out a fat set of keys and led her to a door labeled with a large 3. She unlocked the door and opened it to reveal a ward with rows of cribs and bassinets. "I need a carrier apparently," she said to Lisolotte.

"Yes." The nurse went to a storage cupboard and unlocked it, giving Stella a chance to look around. There were two rows of ten each. She couldn't see in the bassinets, but four of the cribs were occupied by small children who weren't moving or crying. That ward, unlike the rest of the floor, was eerily quiet and there weren't any of the smells that Stella associated with children. Myrtle and Millicent's nursery smelled of baby powder and warm pudding. The girls them-selves were nearly always sticky for reasons Stella couldn't figure out and smelled lovely. Florence loved to rock them and smell their heads. She called it baby smell and it didn't seem to have any other source but them. But that awful ward had none of that. It was antiseptic and starchy, cold and white without a single hint of warmth or care. Stella involuntarily shivered at the feeling of dread that came to settle around her heart as she looked at it.

"Are you all right?" asked Lisolotte.

"Fine. Thinking of the doctor. He's ill."

"Is he?"

"Yes. Very."

She made a face. "I'm glad I'm up here."

That says a lot about you.

"You're the lucky one today," said Stella. "Where is she? I have a train to catch."

"I think you'll change your mind." The nurse took a kind of hand-carrying bassinet out of the cupboard and led her down the row to a bassinet on the right. The hair went up on Stella's neck as she followed her and she felt a kind of panic come over her. She wanted to run out of the room. It was closing in on her. The eerie silence. The small, still bodies.

"Here we are," announced Lisolotte. "You're just in time."

Stella held her breath, locked her jaw, and looked down into the bassinet, prepared for anything, except she wasn't prepared for what she saw. Anna didn't have the flu. She hadn't been beaten or have any kind of illness that Stella had ever seen. The tiny little girl from the pictures the earl had shown her was almost unrecognizable. If it weren't for the curly brown hair, Stella would've thought Lisolotte had brought her to the wrong child. She was tiny and shrunken. Her head large on a spindly body with stick legs. One of her little arms was short and deformed, giving away why she was there. Her little lips were cracked and she was nearly as white as the sheet she lay on. Only upon looking closely could Stella detect the shallowest of breathing.

She balled up her fists and stared down, trying to think what to do.

"See," said Lisolotte with the satisfaction of being right.

Don't hit her. You can't hit her.

"I do, but it doesn't change my orders." *You're mad. Be mad. They respect anger.* Stella rounded on Lisolotte. "I can't take her like this."

The nurse stepped back. "I know. I tried to tell you."

"She'll die on the way and I'll be blamed."

"Give us a couple of days," the nurse made a fluffing motion, "we can fix her up."

"Fix her up now," demanded Stella.

The nurse's eyes widened. "We can't. This is…"

Unspeakable. Horrifying.

"I'm waiting," said Stella.

"This is an ongoing condition," said the nurse finally.

Stella crossed her arms. "Of what?"

Lisolotte looked around like there might be a place to hide that Stella wouldn't find her. "Well, you know."

Stella tapped her foot and continued to eye her.

"Of restricted diet."

They're starving children. To death.

"Then feed her," said Stella.

The nurse went pale. "It's not that simple. She's not…she can't eat now."

"A bottle then. You have bottles?"

"Yes, but—"

Breathe. Don't cry. Don't scream.

"But what?" The tapping of Stella's foot echoed off the hard walls and assaulted the nurse with its harsh impatience.

"She can't swallow," said the nurse.

"Fine. This is a medical facility. Give her fluids in the vein."

The nurse looked around. "Well, I don't know if that would really help much."

Stella kept tapping harder and harder. "Will it keep her from dying until I get to Vienna?"

"It might."

"Then do it," ordered Stella. "Now."

"I don't know if Dr. Heinze would want to waste our supplies on—"

Stella stopped tapping and stepped closer. "Are you saying you will not follow orders from Berlin?" She waved the folder at the nurse and she lost what little color she had.

"No, no. I'll do it." She hustled out of the ward and Stella called after her. "And get me a bottle, too. I'm not taking any chances."

Lisolotte nodded and left. The second she was gone, Stella began shaking.

Get ahold of yourself. This won't help anyone, least of all this poor baby.

She quickly walked to the door and peeked out with a stone face, catching the nurse turning the corner. Then she pulled the camera out of her handbag and went to the first crib.

Don't see. Document. It's all you can do, so do what you can.

Stella took photos of four children, ranging from a few months old to three. Every photo ripped at her heart, but it must be done so the world would see what was happening.

"What are you doing?" asked Lisolotte as she came back in.

"Looking at your other patients." Stella dropped the camera in her handbag and silently snapped it closed before turning around. "You are very effective."

"We believe so." The nurse went to Anna's bassinet and put a small box of supplies in it. "This will only take a minute."

"Good. That's all the time I have." Stella went to the bassinet and watched Lisolotte prepare a needle, attach it to a rubbery hose and a glass bottle with clear liquid in it. "You have quite an operation here and the doctor said you are expanding. The plans are impressive."

She nodded and searched for a vein on Anna's little neck. "When it's done it will be much more efficient than this."

More efficient killing. God help us.

"When will it be done?" Stella asked. It wasn't good to be curious, but the nurse was concentrating on the tiniest little vein in Anna's neck.

"Next month, I think." She stuck the needle in and Anna didn't respond. Her silence made Stella's heart ache. The nurse handed Stella the bottle and checked the flow before taping the tubing to Anna's neck. "Done."

"How long will this last?" asked Stella.

Lisolotte looked at Anna critically. "I've set it to slow because she won't take it fast, so maybe four or five hours."

"That won't get me to Vienna. You better give me another bottle."

"Can you change it?"

"If you show me how."

The nurse taught Stella how to change the bottle and Stella held the carrier as Lisolotte put Anna in. Even with the bottle hooked to the side, the tiny girl weighed nothing. Stella was used to Millicent and Myrtle's plumpness. Anna had to weigh less than ten pounds.

"There you go," said the nurse. "Good luck."

"I need blankets," said Stella. "She's only got a diaper."

She nodded. "Oh, yes. There will be people on the train."

Stella hid her amazement. It was the people seeing the child that was the worry, not sending a dying child out into twenty degree weather that was the concern. "Yes. I wouldn't want any undue questions."

"Come with me." The nurse led Stella out of the ward and her heart hurt more and more as she glanced back at the nightmare.

I'm so sorry. Please forgive me. God forgive me.

CHAPTER 24

The guard watched Stella walk down the hall with a doubtful frown on his face. It'd taken a good five minutes to convince Lisolotte that one thin blanket wasn't enough to keep Anna alive. The tiny girl who was barely breathing didn't do the trick. Stella had to remind her that all property of the clinic was Reich property and therefore the same as the clinic in Vienna where they were going. That got two more blankets, one of which Stella draped over the top to protect the child from the sleet. The carrier wasn't very big and with the blanket concealing its contents, it reminded her of a picnic basket. Immediately with that thought, a wave of self-hatred washed over her. Picnics were lovely things. Nothing about that basket was lovely.

She kept walking, breathing deep the plain old antiseptic air and wishing she could stop hearing the crying. It kept ringing in her ears, like that buzzing Great Aunt Rosalie complained about hearing all the time. The buzzing never went away. Stella hoped to God the crying would. She couldn't live with it. She really couldn't.

"I need my coat and umbrella," she told the guard without a smile or warmth.

He didn't move and asked, "They gave you…what is that?"

"A patient. She is transferred to another facility." She held up the folder. "I've got the papers signed."

"A very little patient."

"Yes. Coat and umbrella. I've got a train to catch," Stella said.

He looked curiously at the carrier and then went to fetch her things. She carefully and reluctantly set the carrier down when he came back so she could put on her coat.

"Where are you going?"

"Vienna," she said, buttoning her coat.

"In this weather?" he asked.

"It can't be helped."

Stella turned up her collar and reached for the carrier, but he was faster. "What does the child have?" He flipped back the blanket and gasped at the sight of her. "Good God! What happened?"

She hastily covered Anna again and picked up the carrier before looking in his horrified eyes. "Open the door."

"But, she, you can't take her out in that," he said. "It's freezing and ice everywhere."

Stella went for the door, but he blocked her. "No. You should wait."

"Orders are Vienna tonight." She softened her face and voice for a man who clearly had no idea of where he was working. "I've got supplies and a drip. She will be fine with me. I will keep her very warm on the train."

"But this is insanity. She looks…"

Stella nodded. "Yes, I know. The door, please."

He hesitated but went ahead and opened it. The storm outside had gotten worse and blew freezing icy rain inside, hitting Stella from the knees down. Now her front was as miserable as the back.

"Can you open the umbrella, please?" she asked.

"Are you really sure about this?"

"I am."

The guard opened the umbrella and thrust it outside to block Stella as she stepped past him. "I don't think you should. Orders aren't everything. It's not safe for her."

Orders aren't everything.

The guard wasn't the first German to express rebellious senti-
ments to her, but he was the first in a uniform. It gave her an unexpected jolt of hope as she looked up into his kind face.

"Do you have children?" Stella asked, surprising herself with the
question.

"Yes, I do," he said, growing concerned.

"Then you should visit the third floor, ward three."

"Why?"

"It will answer every question you have for me."

He shook his head. "It's just a clinic."

"It's not." She turned away and walked down the street with him
calling out after her. "Wait! What are you talking about? What is it?"

The storm soon drowned out his voice and she walked swiftly
through back streets and alleys to lose anyone who might have been
inclined to follow and finally ended up on her hotel's street. By that
time, her legs and feet were numb and burning. The blanket over
Anna was wet, despite her best efforts to shield the carrier.

The blackout curtains were all in place, but there was a warm glow
from under the canopy protecting the hotel's door. She'd begun
shaking and very nearly talked herself into walking straight into the
warmth instead of going around the block to go in the back. It was so
far and she was so cold.

At the last second, she didn't do it. Her training won out and she
walked past, keeping her head down and the umbrella low. The extra
walked seemed a lot longer than before and by the time she got to the
service entrance her teeth were chattering so hard she feared they
would crack.

"Hold up there," yelled a man in a doorman's uniform as she
reached for the door.

"I'm a guest," she managed to get out through clenched teeth.

"Maybe so, but this isn't your entrance. You have to go around," he
said.

She looked up at his young face and decided to go with charm.
"But I got lost and now I'm soaked. Can't I please go in here? I'll only
get lost again if I try to find the front."

He considered it and then tapped the carrier. "What's this?"

She lowered her eyes. "Personal things. For ladies."

"Oh, all right. Go in, but don't tell anyone I was the one who let you."

She assured him she wouldn't and rushed inside, stamping her feet on the rag rug and then dashing up the stairs, hoping he wouldn't rethink it and call her back.

He didn't and no one else said a thing to her. Maybe it was the dripping umbrella or the squishing sound her chunky shoes were making. Either way, she got to her room without a problem. She set the carrier on the bed and whipped off the soaked blanket, holding her breath. Little Anna lay inside, still as before, and, for a horrible second, Stella thought she'd stopped breathing. She pulled back the blanket and watched her sunken chest. It moved.

"Thank God," she whispered and started peeling off her coat, stockings, and shoes. "What you need is a hot water bottle, baby girl."

Stella took off her hat and was pleased to see her hair wasn't wet. She took out the pins and let it flow down her back, turning herself back into Sophie. Her wet stockings proved useful. She used them to wipe off all the makeup before draping them over the radiator with her hat and coat. A quick change of clothes and papers completed the transformation.

She slipped the Werner ring back on and turned to check on Anna. The saline bottle was still dripping and the child had soaked up a few milliliters in the half hour she'd had it. Her little eyes had opened a tiny bit and Stella rubbed her cold hands vigorously to warm them before touching the tiny face.

"I'm here and I've got you," she said. "I'm going to give you a little milk now."

Lisolotte had reluctantly given her a bottle of milk with a rubber nipple on it, but Anna obviously couldn't suck, much less swallow, so she used it like a medicine dropper and dripped four droplets of milk onto Anna's parched tongue. Maybe water was better. She didn't know. In any case, Anna didn't respond.

Stella got out her sweater and tucked it around her. "I'm going to put you behind the bed while I'm gone. Don't be afraid. I'll be right back."

She hid the carrier out of sight, checked herself in the mirror, and went out the door, locking it behind her. She smiled at a group of workers making their way down the hall with grimaces on their faces. They were soaked to the skin and making sloshing noises with every step, but they brightened up at her greeting and watched her walking away, something that didn't happen when she was Luise Schneider. It was amazing what a few years and a hairstyle could do or maybe it was the smile. Hard to say. She'd have to think about it when the crying stopped. It'd gotten better the farther she was from the clinic, but it was still there.

Once she got downstairs she was amazed at the amount of people in the lobby. Angry people complaining about the lack of heat or hot water. It'd been so long since Stella had had a reasonable amount of either she'd barely registered the cold in her room. Unlike everyone else, she calmly waited in line at the reception desk until a harried clerk got to her. The woman took a good look at Stella, noting her face and hair before saying, "There won't be any heat tonight. Tomorrow it will be back."

"I understand," said Stella. "Could I have a hot water bottle though? I got so cold coming here from the train I can't seem to warm up."

The lady relaxed and said, "Yes. That you can have. Do you have your ration card?"

"For a hot water bottle?"

She laughed. "No, for dinner. You will be eating with us?"

"I will, but can I have it in my room? I just want to stay in bed."

"I understand. I will send a tray to your room."

Stella made her order for dinner and the lady marked off her rations for meat, dairy, and bread. A kitchen boy brought her a hot water bottle wrapped in a heavy towel and the whole room started yelling about how no one said they could have a hot water bottle.

"I'm sorry," whispered Stella.

The lady rolled her eyes. "It is always something these days. Tomorrow it will be the bread or the blankets."

Stella nodded and turned around toward the stairs. She didn't get three feet before she was grabbed and nearly yanked off her feet. Ulrich von Drechsel was in her face, his eyes red and flaming with anger. "What are you doing here?"

She couldn't answer. Her mouth gulped like a fish out of water and she shook her head reflexively without any thought at all.

He shook her, causing several workmen to get concerned, so he dragged her off to a corner. "Sophie," he hissed. "What are you doing here?"

The shock vanished, replaced quickly by astonishment. How could she have such rotten luck? In all of Germany one of the very few people she knew just happened to be at that little workaday hotel? No. Luck had nothing to do with it. It couldn't.

"What are *you* doing here?" she asked.

"Looking for you."

"Why?"

Ulrich told her that he'd gone to Irena's house and found out she'd left. Run away as he put it. He wasn't wrong, but Stella put her nose in the air and said, "I didn't run away. I'm not a child. I left. I can leave if I want to. You did."

That took the wind out of his sails and he lowered his voice. "I didn't leave."

She pulled away from him. "Oh, really. You didn't go to Koblenz?"

"Well, I did, but just until…that's not the point," he said.

"What is the point? How did you find me?" Stella asked, fearing the answer. If he'd seen her going to the clinic, she didn't know what to tell him.

"I followed your little friend," he said. "It wasn't difficult."

"What?"

Ulrich pointed at a nearby column and standing behind it was Maria with a suitcase and tears running down her face. Stella said the only thing that came to mind, "Why bother?"

He grabbed her again. "Why did you leave?"

"I don't want to talk about it," she said, not wanting to bring up the dreadful Oscar. "I still don't know how you found me. I didn't tell Maria or anyone I was going."

Ulrich glared at her. "I know you didn't."

He told her that when he'd arrived at Irena's he'd spotted Maria sneaking out the back with her suitcase. When he discovered Stella had gone, he went directly to the U Bahn station where he found Maria waiting. He followed her to the Hauptbahnhof and, when she got on the train to Brandenburg, he got on, too.

"She wouldn't tell me where you were and we've been going from hotel to hotel looking for you."

"Well, you've found me." Stella started for Maria, but he yanked her back against his chest. "Stop that."

"How could you leave at a time like—"

She turned on him, remembering what Cyril said. She must be strong and never appear weak or frightened. They smell fear, he'd said. It makes them alert. "At a time like what? The time after you went to Koblenz and left me at the mercy of your brother? Is that the time we're talking about?" She waved to Maria so she'd come over, her mind jumping around trying to figure it out. How did she know about Brandenburg? Why would she come? What was she going to do?

What should I say? Why would I come here? Think, Stella, think.

"Hurry up," she said impatiently.

Maria came over slowly. Her hands shook as she said quietly, "I'm so sorry. I thought...I just thought—"

"How did you know I was coming to Brandenburg before I went home to Munich?"

"I don't know. I—"

"Did I give it away with that officer?" Stella widened her eyes meaningfully at Maria and the girl took note.

"Um...yes."

"I thought you overheard, but I was hoping you didn't."

Ulrich got stiff and formal. "What officer are you speaking about?"

Stella waved that away with irritation. "Hans or Heinrich or something."

"You don't know his name?"

"It wasn't important. I was paying attention to what he said about Hanni," said Stella.

"Who?" he asked.

Stella told him about Hanni's arrest, adding in a tale about an officer at the club that said she might be at Brandenburg prison. She'd come to say goodbye before going home to her mother.

"You came to say goodbye to a criminal, but you don't say goodbye to me?"

"You had already left and I didn't get any fond farewells from you," Stella spat out at him. "And Hanni isn't a criminal. It's all a mistake."

"Either way she's not here," he said, softening a touch. "She's in the custody of the Gestapo so she'll be in Berlin until trial."

Stella's face fell dramatically. "That's so cruel. I only wanted to see her before I went home. Why would he do that?"

Ulrich thought for a moment and then grew angry again. "Was it Heinrich Rehborn?"

She couldn't decide what the right answer was, so she shrugged. "He was a Wehrmacht."

He ground a fist into his palm. "He wanted to keep you away from me. He was a friend of Oscar's and no friend of mine."

Stella crossed her arms and said, "I'm keeping *myself* away from your brother."

Ulrich got a funny look on his face. His scars reddened and she asked, "What?"

"You haven't heard?" he asked.

Get angry. Be angry.

"I've heard nothing and I've had quite enough of your brother. It's his fault I had to leave a good job and go home like a failure."

He picked a piece of lint off her sleeve and said quietly, "You don't have to go."

"Well, I guess he didn't tell you that he ordered me to move to Clara's boarding house and I was going to have a special entrance to my room. Do you know what that means?"

He swallowed hard, his scars growing redder and twisting. "I know, but it doesn't matter now."

Maria stepped up with a warning in her eyes. "I was going to tell you. In case, you wanted to come back with me."

"Tell me what?" Stella asked.

She handed her a paper with a headline saying that Obersturmbannführer Oscar von Drechsel died of an undiagnosed heart condition minutes before a high-level meeting.

Stella clutched the hot water bottle to her chest. "I can't believe it."

"I know," said Ulrich. "He was very young."

"Did you know?" she asked.

"Know what?"

She looked up at him with big astonished eyes. "That he had a bad heart."

Ulrich shook his head. "He was always healthy."

If he knew something was off about Oscar's death, he wasn't giving anything away. Stella swayed slightly. It was almost like she was faking it, but she hadn't known how scared she really was of Oscar until he was dead. "I don't know what to say to you. He frightened me and he wasn't kind to anyone."

Ulrich took her arm gently and said, "He was my brother. That is the most I can say for him. My parents are very grieved though."

"Of course, they are," said Maria earnestly. "He would've done great things for the Reich."

"Yes," he said shortly.

"I think I need to lie down," said Stella, genuinely feeling shocked.

He made no move to release her as she'd hoped, but said, "I will walk you up."

There wasn't a way to say no, so she nodded and said to Maria, "You will get a room tonight?"

"I already have."

"Perhaps we could all have dinner later," she looked at Ulrich. "At eight."

He wasn't thrilled with company for dinner, but agreed that they should before walking her up. Stella's arms and legs felt stiff, like they weren't under her control. Ulrich was coming to her room. She had to keep him out. If Anna should cry or even whimper, disaster.

"Are you all right?" he asked as they walked down the hallway.

"I'm just not feeling well. That's why I got the hot water bottle. And now your brother," she said. "I don't know what to think."

"You'll come back to Berlin." It wasn't a question.

"I don't know if they will want me back. I left with just a note. Irena and Frau Bothe, they might not feel forgiving."

"I will put in a word for you."

Stella stopped at her door, panic pressed in on her chest as he held her arm. "Thank you for walking me up."

"Sophie?"

"Yes?"

"Aren't you going to open your door?" Ulrich asked, strangely flushing again.

"Yes, but I thought you were going to tell me something," she said. Any delay was a good delay.

"I was. I will still be going to Koblenz."

She nodded. "I thought so. It is your dream."

"I have many dreams now." He leaned over her and pushed a curl back off her forehead. "You reminded me that I am still alive."

Her heart pounded in her chest as she looked up at him. If she were Sophie, she would be very happy. "I'm glad."

He looked like he wanted her to ask him in and she yawned pointedly. "I will see you at dinner," he said taking the hint.

"You will," she said. "I hear they have good lentil soup."

Ulrich smiled for the first time. "That will be good on a night like tonight."

He clearly wasn't going to walk away, so she took a breath and prayed before unlocking the door. She opened it enough for him to be assured no one, in particular, a man, was in there and then said, "I must clean up. My things are everywhere." Her stockings were in plain sight and he looked away.

"I will see you at eight."

Impulsively, Stella went up on her tiptoes and kissed his good cheek. "I hope you will be all right." She meant it, truly, and it was an odd sensation to wish the best for the enemy.

"I know you do." Ulrich left and she closed the door, pressing her back against it as tears spilled down her cheeks. Then she pressed her ear to the door and listened. Men were walking by chatting about deadlines and she stuck her key in the lock, turning it quietly as possible. When nothing happened, she tossed her handbag on the bed and ran around it to look at Anna. The child's eyes were closed and Stella quickly checked her chest. She was breathing and another couple of milliliters of fluid had gone in.

"I can't give you any more milk, darling girl. We have to get out of here right now." Stella put her carrier on the bed and yanked her suitcase out to put it up beside it. She looked back and forth between the suitcase and the carrier, not to mention the umbrella. So much to carry.

"He could see you, darling girl," she said, touching a finger to Anna's forehead and the crying in her head got louder. "He'd send you back. He might not want to, but he would."

The carrier had to go. She simply couldn't take the chance of being seen with it. Even Maria might catch a glimpse and tell.

"I don't want to do this, but I must. You understand, don't you?" Stella gently lifted Anna out of the carrier and swaddled her the way Florence taught her when the girls were infants. Anna wasn't an infant, but she weighed as much as one. Then she rearranged everything in the suitcase. Not having much came in handy and there was plenty of room for the child. It certainly wasn't airtight being old and battered, but Stella got her fountain pen out and used it to pry the canvas seams apart. She set it on end and punched three holes in the top.

"It's not pretty, but it will work."

She stuffed the carrier behind the wardrobe where it wouldn't be found for a while and then tried to figure out how to get Anna in the suitcase at the top, nose up, so they could get out of there.

"All right. If I put you on your side like this," she said to the child, "and close it, you'll be okay."

Anna opened her eyes a bit as if she'd heard.

"I know, but it's only until I can get us on a train." She put the bottle attached to Anna above her head and the spare below with the milk bottle. She was just about to grab the hot water bottle when a knock rattled her door. She jumped in surprise and called out, "Yes?"

"Sophie," said Ulrich. "It's me. I want to talk to you a moment."

Oh, my God.

"Just a minute." She pulled some blanket out to prop up the lid for more air, closed the suitcase, and carefully pushed it under the bed. Then she rumpled the covers and shoved the hot water bottle underneath.

"Sophie?"

"I'm coming." She unbuttoned her dress and unlocked the door.

He opened it and she hastily buttoned herself back up. Ulrich averted his eyes, but he walked in uninvited. "I want to talk to you."

She found she couldn't speak for a second. He raised an eyebrow and she managed to squeak out. "I thought we would talk at dinner."

"I don't want to talk in front of her."

There was a rustling, a very tiny rustling. Could Anna be moving? Stella quickly stood between him and the bed. "What is it?"

He looked at her for a moment, frowning. It twisted the bad side and made him look a little like his brother. "I've decided I don't want you to go back to the club."

She crossed her arms. "Oh, you've decided, have you?"

"Yes. You should come to Koblenz. There is an officer's club. You can work there."

"I'll think about it," she said.

He drew back affronted. "What is there to think about?"

"Whether or not I want to go to Koblenz."

"That's where I will be."

For God's sake. Go away. Get out.

"I know. You told me," she said because she couldn't think of anything better.

"What is wrong with you?" he asked.

"Nothing. I told you I don't feel well."

"You should lie down then," he said and she obediently got in bed. The mattress sunk down and she pulled up the covers.

Please don't let me be too heavy. Please.

"You think I'm like my brother," said Ulrich.

All she could think about was Anna under the bed. "Um…"

"I'm not like him."

"I know."

He went to the door and looked at her with a frown before going out. Stella started to jump up but thought better of it. Something about the way Ulrich was acting. She picked up Der Totale Krieg from where she'd tossed it aside and opened it to a random page.

The door flew open again and Ulrich marched in, looking around like he was hunting. Stella yawned and asked, "Are you canceling dinner?"

He ignored the question and opened the wardrobe before walking around the bed. He looked around like he expected to see someone crouching there and then yanked open the curtains to look out. "No. I just thought…"

She flipped a page and said, "What? Are you jealous of my fine view?"

He gave her a hard stare and then dropped down to look under the bed. Stella clenched the book so tight she started to rip it in half. But then he looked up over the edge of her bed and said, "Oh, your suitcase."

"What about it?"

"I thought. There was a shadow and I thought, never mind." Ulrich stood awkwardly by the window, once again flushed and Stella forced herself to smile generously. "Are you ever going to let me rest?"

"I'm sorry. I'm just. It's been a hard day." With that he left and she waited another minute. With her heart in her throat, she slipped out of bed and turned the key in the lock.

She dropped to her hands and knees and looked under the bed. "Oh, my God."

Anna had poked her little hand out of the opening and it was in clear view. If Ulrich had been on that side of the bed when he looked —no, she couldn't think of that. It didn't happen.

She pulled the suitcase out and opened it to find Anna's eyes more open and she was moving her mouth. "I'll give you milk when we're on the train, darling. You'll have to wait."

She tucked the hot water bottle in below Anna, not too close, so she could be warm but not hot on the walk, and arranged her little body to be nose up. She snapped the latches closed and gingerly tilted the suitcase upright.

"It won't be for long. I promise." Stella took the swastika pin off the ugly Luise suit and popped it into the hollow heel of her Sophie shoes. Then she hid Luise's suit and shoes behind the wardrobe with the carrier since there wasn't any room in the suitcase before putting on her hat and coat.

"Here we go." She unlocked the door, picked up the suitcase, her umbrella, and handbag, but at the last second, tucked Irma's book under her arm. It was wrong to abandon a book, even that book. She opened the door a crack, listened for a moment to some inane chatter at the end of the hall, and then went out with her head held high.

Stella took a sharp right, going for the back stairs.

Almost there. Almost there.

"Sophie!" Maria's voice rang out behind her.

Stella glanced back at the girl looking out a door at the other end of the hall and then yanked open the door to the stairwell, ducking inside as Maria yelled, "Sophie! Stop!"

She ran down the stairs, practically running over a waiter and upsetting his tray. Metal cloches clattered down the stairs, hitting her ankles with hot soup and possibly sauerkraut.

"Sophie!" Marie yelled down the stairs, but she kept going. The suitcase knocked into a wall in her haste, but she couldn't stop. She ran out into the storm, sliding on the icy step and going down, but managing to keep the suitcase from hitting the ground as she fell. Pain shot through her back and elbow as they struck the concrete.

"Ma'am! What are you doing out here?" A doorman under the overhang smoking a cigarette came to her assistance. He hauled her to her feet and she tried to pull away.

"You're wet. You should—"

"My husband. Wounded," she shouted, not meaning to, but that's how it came out.

He pulled away startled. "Ma'am!"

"I have to catch a train. Now. Right now."

"Yes, yes. Of course." He grabbed the book, tucked it under her arm, and opened her umbrella. "Go, hurry, but be careful the…"

His words were lost in the sound of ice hitting the taut umbrella fabric and she ran, slipping and sliding to the train station. She fell twice more, banging her elbow so hard her fingers went completely numb, but she made it. Ducking into the station with other soggy, shivering travelers, she blended in with everyone else trying to catch trains that night.

In truth, Stella would've taken just about any train to get out of Brandenburg, but she was in luck. There was a train coming in ten minutes going to Duisburg. She could easily get from Duisburg into The Netherlands and then to Paris. The ticket booth was closed so she'd have to buy a ticket from the conductor. She quickly counted up her remaining Reichsmarks and was relieved that she had plenty— thanks to tips at the club—to get her out in first class.

People milled around, waiting and complaining about the weather and Stella counted up how many would be on the train to Duisburg. Not even half full and all looked to be second or third class travelers, looking to save a few coins on the cheapest fares possible. With any luck, she'd manage to get a compartment on her own or maybe a sleeping compartment. That would be ideal.

Stella went to the ladies room so she could check on Anna, but it was locked, so she stepped back into an out of the way corner and opened Irma's book. She got a few glances, but no one interrupted her reading, and it dulled the continual crying in her head. Books were so useful that way and when the train rolled in, she was pleased less people than she expected went to get on.

She chose a second class car that was nearly empty, except for a few men with sour expressions on their faces, and bought a ticket from the conductor who went down the aisle collecting fares and looking as sour as his passengers. He tried to be helpful and put the suitcase on the rack overhead, but she politely declined, getting her a disinterested shrug. Disinterested was good and it was quickly becoming her favorite expression in Germany.

The conductor headed back toward the other second and third class cars and a few minutes later the train began to move. Stella kept a sharp eye on the platform and doors for Maria, or worse Ulrich, but she didn't see either of them. Five minutes out of the station, she stood up and looked back through the glass into the next car. The conductor was nowhere to be seen, so she picked up her things and the suitcase, and went forward through the dining car into the First Class car. Only two of the compartments had passengers, more sour men sitting alone, and she went to the front compartment and coughed to get the conductor's attention. He was tucked in the storage area, obviously sampling the liquor, and spilled some on his lapel when she startled him.

"I'm sorry," she said, using the big eyes and poked out her lower lip. "I didn't mean to startle you."

Embarrassed, he told her it was nothing while hastily dabbing a linen napkin on his lapel. "I was…fixing drinks for my passengers. Can I help you?" He took in her clothes and battered suitcase and she could see he knew she wasn't First Class material.

"I hope so. I bought a second class ticket, but I need to move to first class."

"Well, I don't know. If you have a second class ticket, you should stay there."

What he meant was she should know her place and it steamed Stella through to her core, but she held her irritation in check and batted her eyes. "There was a man in my car that…well, I just can't stay there. My mother always says to move to first class if that happens. That's where I'll be protected. Men aren't allowed to bother girls in first class, are they?"

He drew up to his exceedingly short height and said, "No, they are not. Your mother is a wise lady."

"She is and I always try to do as she tells me. Can I buy a ticket in your car?" Stella emphasized *your*. Men did so enjoy being the protector.

"Of course, but I will have to charge you the difference."

She paid the difference and he opened the compartment she wanted, a very nice one with dark brown tufted seats in leather.

"Shall I put that up for you?" he asked, reaching for the suitcase.

"Oh, no." She stuck out her wet leg. "I think I have to change into something dry."

"Of course. If you need anything, just ring." He showed her a little button next to the door and left her alone.

Stella put the suitcase on the seat and pulled all the curtains, making certain there weren't any cracks so a potentially nosy conductor couldn't see in, and then turned back to the suitcase. She sat down and opened it with it facing away from the door.

Anna had shifted and was sideways, nose down against the bottom of the suitcase. "Oh, God," Stella whispered and gingerly rolled her over, terrified that the poor child had smothered, but she made a tiny squeak when Stella moved her and then opened her eyes. If Stella had been standing, she'd have collapsed to the floor instead of crumpling against the seat and wiping a tear from her cheek.

At the sight of Anna looking up at her, the crying in her head stopped. She put a light hand on her little chest and said, "You are a tough little thing, aren't you?"

Anna's mouth moved, but no sound came out. Stella propped her bottle of fluids up in the corner of the suitcase lid and tried to figure out how to hang it without anyone seeing. Then she took out the milk bottle and set it between the suitcase and seat with a sweater draped over so it couldn't be seen and stood up to take off her coat. She had it halfway off when the door lever moved. Stella lunged for it, but her arms were caught up in wet fabric and the door slid open.

Maria stood in the corridor with a large suitcase and a determined look on her pretty face. "I don't know where you're going, but I'm going, too."

CHAPTER 25

Stella yanked off her coat and tried to push Maria out the door, but it was too late. She got in and carefully put her suitcase down while simultaneously grappling with Stella, who was trying to get the door open enough to throw her out.

"I'm staying," Maria said.

"You're not," said Stella.

The conductor looked through the crack in the door and asked, "Is something the matter? I thought you knew each other."

Stella and Maria were face to face and Maria jetted up her eyebrows. "Is there a problem, *Sophie?*"

Oh, no. Oh, no. Oh, no.

"No, I was just startled…since I was changing," she said.

Maria closed the door and Stella backed away. Glancing down, she saw Anna open her mouth and she slowly closed the lid of the suitcase. "What do you want?"

"To go with you." Maria perched on the edge of the seat opposite the suitcase. "I know it's the right thing."

Stella couldn't think what to do. The train was moving. She couldn't jump off. It would kill Anna. The child was tough, but that was well over the line. "How do you know?"

She glanced at the door and lowered her voice, "You didn't turn me in."

"I don't know what you're talking about," said Stella, thinking she'd have to sneak off the train at the next stop. Somehow.

"Yes, you do. You heard us. You know."

"I don't know anything. Please leave."

Instead of leaving, she took off her hat and unbuttoned her coat. "Yes, you do and you didn't turn me in. Irma would have and so would Inge."

That was a chilling thought and the obvious question popped out of Stella's mouth, "Not Hanni?" She wanted to stuff it back in the second it escaped. It was a kind of admission and Maria saw it as such.

"No, not Hanni. She has a good heart, like you."

"You don't know that," said Stella. "I could be just like Irma and Inge or worse, I could be like Clara. Maybe I'd sell you out for a job as a petty functionary."

She nodded. "You could've, but you didn't. You wouldn't."

Stella started to feel sweat running down her sides. She didn't usually sweat much, but what was she going to do? The compartment was small. Maria was right there. "I would. I think I would."

Maria sighed and leaned back. "Then I would have to turn you in."

The breath whooshed out of Stella's lungs and she couldn't speak. Her first assignment and she'd been identified. Some spy she was.

"I won't though," Maria said quickly.

"You don't…you can't…" Stella whispered.

"Yes, I can. Those things you said about Herr Caron aren't true."

Stella came around the suitcase and sat opposite Maria, using the seconds to catch her breath. "It is true. He's been bothering—"

"Irena didn't believe you either."

Stella swallowed hard and started wishing she had another ill pill to slip Maria. "Why not?"

"Because he never came back. Don't worry I didn't tell her anything."

"Tell her anything about what?"

Maria sat up a little taller. "I followed you that night when you went in the back way to the club. I saw you together."

Who the hell are you?

"I don't know what you think you saw," said Stella, "but he accosted me. I told Bothe."

"You didn't tell her the truth. I saw it all."

Oh, my God.

"He grabbed me. I was terrified and I barely got away," said Stella, struggling keeping her composure while desperately trying to think straight.

Maria wasn't remotely persuaded. "He let you go."

"I escaped."

"You did tell the truth about one thing," said Maria.

Stella just stared at her, unwilling to hazard a guess.

"That man does love you, but he's not some odd stranger who's just following you around."

"What did you hear?" whispered Stella.

"Nothing really. I wasn't close enough, but I could tell you know each other well."

Stella shook her head. "No. Not well at all."

Maria let that go. "You didn't tell us the whole truth, so I knew for sure."

"Knew what?"

"That you're not who you say you are either."

The girls looked at each other until Stella whispered, "You don't know anything. I'm Sophie Weber and I'm going home to Munich."

"Then you're going the wrong way," said Maria.

"I'm going to see a friend first."

"Is she a Jew?"

Stella was dumbfounded. Whatever she expected, that wasn't it. "Why do you ask that?"

"Because you were looking for someone in Berlin and it wasn't your mother's friend," said Maria.

Stella clamped her mouth shut and began to pray that she'd find a way out. That somehow there was a way. Taking her silence as a kind of interest, Maria went on to tell her that when she went to the Maier Backerei, Irena sent Maria after her to see where she was going. They feared she might be turning them in to the Gestapo, but to Maria's surprise and relief she went to a ramshackle bakery and then to a doctor's house.

"I can go to bakeries and doctors," Stella said.

"You're hiding it, so it must be about a Jew," said Maria.

"I don't know why you think that."

For the first time, Stella's friend showed her nerves and quietly asked, "Who is the child you're looking for?"

Stella kept herself from looking at the suitcase, just barely. "Who says there's a child? Or a Jew for that matter?"

"The maid at Dr. Ehlich's house. You're looking for a child. It must be a Jew or you would've told us. We would help you find a missing child, an Aryan child, that is."

Why did you have to be so smart?

"She was mistaken. Just because I'm looking for someone it doesn't mean they're a Jew," said Stella. "I think you should go back to Berlin. There's nothing I can do for you."

"I think there is," Maria said and her hands trembled slightly.

"Please leave," said Stella. "Go into another compartment and leave me alone. I beg you."

"But you know who I am. Why won't you help?"

Her armpits were soaked and she could barely keep her voice from shaking. Anna needed milk. She might need air. "I don't know. Please." Stella was desperate. "I'll give you money. Do you want money?"

A tear slipped down Maria's cheek. "No. What can I say to you so you'll understand?"

There was a little rustling in the suitcase and Stella said, "Nothing." It came out harsher than she intended.

"You wanted to help that little girl. She's a Jew," said Maria with more tears.

Stella said nothing. Her heart hurt watching the sweet girl's face and she knew the situation, but Anna was the most important thing. The child was now her mission.

"I can pay you."

Stella put her face in her hands. "For what?"

"To get me out. Sophie, I'm a Jew."

The pain in Maria's voice was plain as she admitted the most dangerous secret. Stella looked up and Maria held out identification papers for herself under the name Ruth Winkler, a Jew.

"I was working as a gentile under a false name. If they find out, I'll go to a camp." Maria quietly told Stella who she was, the daughter of a German mother and a Jewish father. Rudolf Winkler owned a logging company in Tirol and was loathe to leave all he worked for when things went bad. When he refused to turn over his company and sign documents saying he was a traitor to the Reich, he was beaten to death on his own factory floor by the Brown Shirts. Ruth's mother had already taken Maria to her own family in Austria before the Annexation, thinking they would be safe there, but then the Nazis took over and her mother feared for her daughter's life. She arranged for false papers and sent Ruth to her dear friend, Irena, who agreed to hide her at great risk to herself until Ruth could be smuggled out.

Ruth put her papers in Stella's lap, both sets. "You can do what you want. You know all about me now."

Stella glanced at the door and tossed them back in Ruth's lap. "Are you crazy? Don't do that. Put those away. Hide them."

Ruth quickly put everything back in her handbag. "You're leaving the country. Can't you take me with you? You have connections. I know you do."

Stella looked in her eyes, searching for some kind of clue as to her intentions. She found nothing but naked honesty. Ruth and Irena had been suspicious of her for a while and they'd done nothing about it. They could have and it probably would've secured Ruth's position as a loyal patriot and kept her out of trouble.

"You want me to get you out of Germany?" Stella asked.

"Yes. You can, can't you?" Ruth asked.

She could possibly, but it would be a huge risk. All her Sophie papers were in order for her to cross the border. If Ruth used her cover and the border guards weren't looking too closely at pictures and eye color, they could get away with it.

"Maybe," she said finally.

"Who are you really?" Ruth asked.

Stella smiled. "I'm Sophie Weber."

Ruth smiled back. "I knew you'd help me. I knew it."

"You don't know what you're asking of me."

The girl straightened up and said, "I do. If you get caught with me, you'll go to a camp, too, but they would probably let you go after a while. You're not a Jew yourself, are you?"

"No, I'm not." Stella inwardly breathed a sigh of relief. Whatever Ruth knew, she still believed Stella was a German girl, but she had proved quite adept at keeping her own cover and finding out that Stella was up to something.

"What are you thinking?" Ruth asked nervously as Stella looked her over.

"I'm making a decision," she said.

Park-Welles would lose his orderly mind, if she survived to tell him about it, but she found she didn't care. Sometimes you had to make a decision on instinct, friendship, and, most of all, hope. "You may not want to come with me. Actually, you shouldn't. We should go separately."

Ruth clasped her hands together and she pleaded, "No, please, I can't do this alone. I understand the risks."

Stella shook her head. "No, you don't."

"Sophie, my father was murdered and I was in Vienna when the Brown Shirts attacked us. Our neighbor was thrown out a window. The synagogues were burned and people beaten for nothing in the streets. I know what they want to do to us because they're already doing it."

Ruth's words took Stella back to Vienna on that horrible night, to seeing the blood on the street, and Abel, always Abel, but she couldn't speak of it. She never spoke of it, not even to Nicky and he was there.

"You think you know, but you don't," Stella said.

"I do," said Maria. "We could sit separately."

"That's not enough. If I get caught, you don't want to be anywhere near me."

"Why? What did you do?"

"You know the little Jewish girl I was looking for?" Stella asked.

Ruth frowned and leaned forward. "Yes?"

Stella took a breath and said, "I found her."

Her friend's shoulders slumped and she let out a sad sigh. "Oh, she died. I'm so sorry. I know you tried very hard to find her."

"She didn't die."

Ruth frowned in puzzlement. "I don't understand."

Stella opened the suitcase and an incredibly fragile little hand reached up into the light.

STELLA BLED Lawrence considered herself to be a capable person, a person of talent and skill, and, as they say, it takes one to know one. Ruth Winkler was one. Stella opened the suitcase and Ruth, a terrified Jew with a murdered father, forgot herself and her precarious position. She didn't cry out in horror or uselessly sob. Ruth sprang into action. She used her enormous suitcase to wedge the compartment door closed and then helped take Anna out and examined her emaciated body with clinical but compassionate interest.

"How long was she without food and water?" she asked as she wrapped the child back up.

Stella told her what she knew, which wasn't much, and Ruth considered it while checking the drip. Anna had gotten about half the bottle and was now moving and blinking. She could swallow and they began giving her drops of milk every ten minutes for the next two hours.

"I thought I would be a doctor when I was little," said Ruth, yawning after the latest drops. "And then the universities stopped training girls. My father's father was a doctor and we had all his books." She smiled. "I read them the way Inge reads magazines about film stars."

"So in your professional opinion, will she recover?" Stella asked.

"If we can keep doing this with the milk, combined with the fluids, I think so." She opened Anna's mouth. "Look here. The membranes are looking better already and if she cries, she might be able to produce tears."

"She can't cry," said Stella. "Not on this train."

"I know. She's been in a kind of euphoria, but soon she will cry. It can't be avoided."

"We'll be getting off at Duisburg. It's not long."

"What are you going to do?" Ruth asked.

Stella considered the options and decided to go ahead and tell her about the plan to get off and change her identity to Adélaïde Weinzierl, a married woman with a sick child going to her mother in Arnhem.

"You have the papers?" asked Ruth.

"Yes."

"And I will use your papers to get over the border?"

Stella nodded. "That's the only way. I have the permission to cross as myself."

"Your eyes are blue though. I thought…could we get other papers? You have connections. You got the papers for you and Anna."

Stella took Ruth's hand and said, "It will be well after midnight when we cross the border into The Netherlands. We can only hope the guards will see a pretty, charming girl and look more at your face than mine in the passport."

"I will have to get lucky."

"Yes."

Ruth sat back in her seat. "You must get Anna out. They will kill her if you're caught."

"They will," said Stella, tucking Anna's malformed arm under the blanket. "The doctor said 'Life unworthy of life.'"

"'Life unworthy of life' and to say this about children. I can't understand it," said Ruth.

Stella thought back to what the doctor said in his drunken, drugged yammering. "They're not going to stop at children."

"What?"

The train made a slight lurch as they began to slow for Duisburg and Stella quickly repacked Anna in the suitcase. She closed the lid and told Ruth to move her suitcase so the conductor could open the door and inform them that they'd arrived at their destination.

Ruth moved the suitcase and they arranged themselves in poses of total relaxation, curled up on the seat with the provided blanket tucked around them. Stella began to pray that Anna would stay quiet a while longer. They just had to get off the train.

"Sophie?" asked Ruth. "What was that about not stopping at children?"

"Well—"

A voice boomed outside their compartment. "Duisburg! We've arrived at Duisburg."

The door slid open and the girls sat up, yawning for effect.

"We're there already?" Stella asked with a fluff of her hair.

The conductor smiled. "We are very efficient."

And then it happened. Anna squeaked, a tiny little noise, but plain as day and the conductor drew back puzzled. Stella froze, but Ruth didn't. She laughed with embarrassment and stood up, holding her stomach. "I should have gone to the dining car, but I was so tired."

He laughed. "I would've been happy to go for you. First Class passengers get the best service."

Stella stretched and yawned loudly. "My mother didn't tell me that."

"Mine, either," said Ruth.

They began chattering about mothers and their general lack of knowledge. The conductor moved on with a grin on his face, no doubt thinking about the silliness of young women.

The girls put their hats and coats on and waited until they were in the station before going out into the corridor. The male passengers hadn't waited and were off before the girls got halfway to the exit. They kept up their chatter and scraped their feet, making as much noise as possible as they passed the conductor. He only grinned and tipped his hat as they passed even though Stella could hear Anna moving and making little distressed noises.

Out in the station, her noise was still a worry. It was so late the place was practically empty and as cavernous as it was their voices echoed off the walls as they entered the station from the platform.

"Bathroom," said Stella.

"Yes," said Ruth. "There's a sign."

Happily, the station's designers put the ladies' bathroom in an out-of-the-way corridor where no one was at that late hour. It was empty and Ruth barred the door while Stella got Anna out of the suitcase, unhooked the drip for the time being, and wrapped her up so that only her eyes were visible. She gave her to Ruth and then exchanged her papers for Adélaïde's and Anna became Anna Weinzierl, complete with an Aryan certificate.

Stella repacked the suitcase, took back Anna, and gave Ruth her Sophie papers. Anna screwed up her mouth and Stella got ready for a full on caterwauling but all that came out was a kind of mew.

"It's all right. We're not putting you back in that dark place." Stella smiled and looked back at Ruth, who was looking at her new identity with consternation. "What is it?"

"We don't look very much alike. My hair is darker, too," she said.

"I know, but The Netherlands are neutral and it's late. I'm hoping they won't be very vigilant." Of course, Gertruda Hoppe, Anna's nanny, had been arrested for doing exactly what they were attempting, but it wouldn't help to bring it up.

"Do you think I can make it?" asked Ruth.

Stella had no choice but to tell the truth. "I don't know." She gave her the Werner ring and Ruth held it as if it were hot to the touch.

"Would you do it, if you were me?"

"I would get out in any way I could find." Stella put on her new wedding and engagement rings. They fit perfectly as she knew they would. Cyril had an eye for such things.

Ruth nodded, put on the Werner ring, and picked up the suitcases. "Let's find the next train to Arnhem."

Stella opened the door and took a look before walking out into the empty corridor. They went the opposite way and got a little lost, but that was useful as the train they'd arrived on had left and they didn't see either of the men from their First Class car. The schedule board said a train was arriving in a half hour from Cologne and it would go on to Arnhem. The ticket office was closed, so the girls found a bench to sit on for the wait.

When there was no one around, Stella got the bottle out of her coat pocket and put the nipple in Anna's mouth. That got a tiny frown, but she did try to move her mouth, she was just too weak to really get any milk from it. Stella clamped the bottle under her chin and squeezed the nipple for her.

"She swallowed," said Ruth. "And that was a larger amount, too."

"It was. I think she will be okay."

She continued to drip milk into Anna's mouth every ten minutes until the little girl drifted off to sleep and the train arrived. As they were getting up, Stella decided it was time. "By the way, from now on I will speak German with a Dutch accent."

"What?"

"I'm now Dutch married to a German. Understand?"

"I...I guess so."

"And you are Sophie from Munich. Be me, just smile and relax."

Ruth was flushed and nervous, but she picked up the suitcases and went with Stella to the platform. It was practically empty and suddenly that seemed like a bad thing. They were noticed, two pretty girls with a baby, getting on a train to Arnhem. The conductor watched them approach and she saw him glance over at a guard who was yawning and leaning on a wall. Stella went through everything she'd been taught about the Dutch. The Dutch trainer was forthright and friendly. She thought of Eva's walk and the way she tilted her head and looked everyone straight in the eyes. Thankfully, it was easy, more American. She hadn't practiced the accent in a while or used it on the way in, . She'd simply gone from Charlotte Sedgewick to Sophie Weber. So simple.

"Good evening," said the conductor as he evaluated their ability to pay for first class and found them wanting.

"Good evening," said Stella with her Dutch intonation a little stronger than she'd have liked. "Two tickets for Arnhem, please, and a child fare as well."

"This is first class."

"I know. My little girl is sick and we want to be away from the others."

He leaned forward to look at Anna and with her eyes closed and almost completely covered up, she looked better, not good, but not on death's door either. "What does she have?"

"I don't know. That is why I am taking her home to my mother. She is a doctor. I think she can help." Stella stepped forward to him and held out Anna. "You see how thin she is."

He stepped back as if she was contagious just the way she hoped. "Have you been sick?"

"No. Not me, my husband, or his family. The doctors in Berlin, they say she will die, but I must try. I am her mother," said Stella with tears forming in her eyes. It was easy. All she had to do was think of Ward 3 and her heart broke all over again. "I don't want her close to other passengers. She might catch something and she is already so weak."

The conductor nodded and looked at Ruth. "And is this your sister?"

"No, my friend. She's helping me. I can't travel alone and care for Anna."

"You have your papers in order?"

"Yes, of course."

"Your husband is German?"

"Yes."

The conductor switched his focus to Ruth. "You are Dutch, too?"

She shook her head. "No. German."

"You have papers?"

"Yes, I do," said Ruth and her voice was more steady than Stella expected.

The train whistle blew and he looked over at the guard who was watching but completely disinterested.

"How much for the tickets?" Stella asked.

"You can afford them?"

Stella looked him right in the eyes and said, "Yes, my husband told me to take the First Class car for Anna. He loves his child, too."

The conductor looked slightly abashed.

"Sophie," said Stella. "Can you open my handbag for me? I cannot do it."

"No, no." He stepped aside and waved her up the steps. "Go to compartment three. I will come to you once we are under way."

"That is very kind of you. Thank you." Stella climbed the stairs with his help and went down the empty corridor to compartment three. Ruth opened the door for her and they went in and dropped onto the seats in relief.

The train whistle blew and the train pulled out of the station. Ruth looked at her with wet eyes and mouthed, "Thank you."

Stella nodded and laid Anna on the seat, arranging her carefully so she couldn't really be seen well and then took off her hat and coat. Ruth reached for the door to close it, but Stella shook her head no. They were an hour to the border and couldn't afford to look secretive. Stella took off her sweater and draped it over Anna and fussed, trying to get her to take the bottle.

"Ladies?" asked the conductor.

She looked up and smiled. "You have the cost?"

He gave it to her and watched as she counted out the Reichsmarks carefully and handed them over. "Can I move your suitcases up for you?"

"Yes, but Sophie, can you get out your hot water bottle for Anna? She gets so cold."

Ruth had a bit of a shake, but she opened the suitcase and handed over the rubbery bottle. Then the conductor placed both suitcases on the rack and kindly asked, "Do you need anything?"

"We wouldn't like to trouble you," said Stella.

He smiled and quietly confided, "It is no trouble. I only have six passengers tonight and you are three."

She smiled warmly and asked, "Could you ask the dining car for hot water for Anna?"

He pointed at the milk bottle. "Do you have enough?"

"I think so. She won't eat much."

He took the hot water bottle and headed off. They left the door open and Stella began talking about what her mother would do, saying how happy she would be to have her take over. Ruth joined in and said that it would be a relief for Stella to have the burden taken off her shoulders for a while. The conductor came back with a boiling hot bottle wrapped in a towel. Stella thanked him and asked him to close the door so it would stay warmer in the compartment. He told them it would be an hour until they stopped in Emmerich for the border check and closed the door.

Ruth stood up to listen and then sat down. "You are very good. How do you know how to sound Dutch?"

Stella shrugged. "It's a silly talent of mine. I like to imitate people and my family liked it." She did a quick imitation of her trainer Magda Popper, including the little eccentricities like sucking her lips in on certain words and rubbing her eyes after having a little sneeze.

Ruth laughed and then grew serious as Stella started putting drops of milk in Anna's mouth. "I think we should hook up her drip again. She needs it desperately."

"She needs to get out of Germany more. The drip makes her look sicker. I don't want too many questions and it's only a little longer."

"I'm trying to imagine what that place was like," said Ruth.

"Don't. It will haunt me all my life and I wouldn't wish that on you," said Stella.

"How many others were there?"

"Please don't make me talk about it."

Ruth moved to the other seat and touched Anna's feet under the blanket. "It's really happening though. To children."

"Yes and I think it's a secret. The guard at the door was horrified when he saw her and the nurse tried to get Dr. Heinze to be quiet. She said I didn't need to know anything."

"What did you mean when you said they wouldn't stop at children?" Ruth asked with her voice funny and strained.

Stella tickled Anna's lower lip and was rewarded when her eyes opened a tad bit. "There you are, my darling girl. Drink for me now." She dropped in six big drops as an experiment. She swallowed. "Look at you. My big girl drinking."

"Sophie?" asked Ruth.

Stella looked up sharply. "Adélaïde."

"Yes, yes. I'm sorry. I just…what did you mean?"

She leaned back and laid the bottle next to Anna. "I don't think you want to know. I shouldn't have mentioned it."

Ruth looked at her with intensity. "I want to know. Please tell me."

Stella thought about it and something inside her said not to, for Ruth's sake, not her own.

"Please," Ruth asked again.

"This won't help you. It will only hurt you."

She swallowed and said, "I'm not worried about it hurting me."

"What do you mean?" Stella asked.

"Tell me."

Stella told her it was nothing specific, just that the doctor mentioned moving on to adolescents and adults and that there was building going on, but she didn't know what they were building.

"Did they know that Anna was a Jew?" Ruth asked.

"I don't think so. Why?"

Ruth started fidgeting and checked her watch. "Are you sure?"

"Well, the woman who took her to the doctor said she lost her papers so he wouldn't know she was a Jew. If he'd known, he wouldn't have seen her."

"I just thought…" She trailed off and stood up to look out the window.

"What did you think?"

"That that was why they did this to her. Because she's a Jew."

Stella tried to understand what Ruth was saying, but couldn't. She wanted it to be because Anna was a Jew? That didn't make it any better. "They did this to her because of her arm."

"Were the other children like Anna then?"

Stella couldn't answer. She could see them and the crying came back. One or two were probably already dead and she'd left them there. She would always have left them.

"Adélaïde?" Ruth's voice reached her, but it seemed far away. "Do you know what was wrong with the others?"

Stella wiped a tear from her cheek. "What does it matter? They don't deserve to die for it."

"It matters to me."

She looked up at Ruth's young face and found it etched in pain and fear. "I haven't studied medicine. I don't know what they had."

"Was it all limbs though?"

Stella could see them, sunken faces, withered limbs. "No. Anna was the only one with a missing hand."

"And the others?"

"Why do you have to make me remember?"

"Please tell me."

"One was disfigured with a birth defect of the face. Two looked perfectly normal and another had that disease children are born with."

Ruth was silent and Stella pushed the faces away, so she could see her, but she had turned back to the window. Her shoulders had dropped and she was digging her fingernails painfully into the rim around the glass.

"What is it? You don't have a child, do you?"

"No. I don't have a child," she said. "Was the last child a mongoloid?"

Stella could see the face. The child was very near death and her stomach hurt when she thought about it. "I think so, but I'm not an expert."

Ruth turned around, her face now resolute. "I have to get off the train."

CHAPTER 26

Ruth's aunt was born with the name Magdalena, but it didn't last. She was sunshine and soon got nicknamed Sonnig. She was what people called a mongoloid; although Ruth hated the term, she couldn't think of a better one. Sonnig had been cherished by Ruth's mother's family from the day she was born. They hadn't put her in an institution, insisting on caring for her themselves and they'd done a good job of it. Sonnig could read children's books and do a little math. The family had a cook, but she'd shown an interest and had learned to make bread and had a whole repertoire of things she could cook. As long as she had a simple recipe, she could cook anything and spent most days happily chattering away to the cook and her helper, who'd long since fallen under her spell of continual joy.

The family had managed to keep Sonnig out of the Nazi sterilization program with a hefty amount of common sense and money. Sonnig was forty years old and unlikely to get pregnant. That and some well-placed bribes did the trick. Ruth's mother had been desperate to keep Sonnig out of surgery. An awful lot of sterilization patients didn't make it out alive and that was suspicious. Ruth admitted that she thought her mother was silly for thinking doctors would let their patients die on purpose. Her many medical books told her that wouldn't happen. Doctors were sworn to preserve life, but Anna's condition had changed all that.

"I can't leave my family to save myself," said Ruth. "They have no idea what's coming."

Stella squeezed some drops of milk into Anna's mouth and waited to see if she would swallow. She did and then Stella said quietly, "There's nothing you can do for your aunt that your mother can't."

"You would abandon your family then?"

Stella couldn't lie. She wouldn't leave. "No, but I wish you would. We don't know for certain they'll expand to adults."

"We do," said Ruth. "We've known all along. I just didn't want to see it."

"What do you mean?"

She went on to describe the odd poster Stella had seen near the club, the one of the handsome German man weighed down by the misshapen people yoked on his back.

"Is that what that's about?" Stella asked.

"Haven't you seen the posters with the prices?"

"Yes, but I didn't understand them."

Ruth told her about the posters giving the cost of keeping people like Sonnig alive. Some gave the amount of food or cost of caregivers. All spoke of the burden on Germany.

"I thought those were about the sterilization programs. I never thought they'd actually kill people."

"We don't know—"

"Yes, we do. If they'll kill Anna, who's a perfectly normal child, except for her arm, they will kill my aunt. Sonnig isn't normal in any respect. They will kill her."

"They'll have to emigrate," said Stella. "You can write and tell them."

"You think they haven't tried? When my grandfather went to enquire about visas to America, my whole family was put under investigation for activities counter to the Reich. My grandfather never broke a law in his life. And they didn't get visas. The government blocked it."

"Why?"

"They didn't give a reason. What am I going to do? I can't go home to them as myself and I can't go back to Irena's. I ran. Everyone will know it by now and I'll be investigated. They'll find out who I am." Ruth started crying. Big gulping sobs enveloped her body and Stella jumped up in an attempt to quiet her.

"The conductor will hear," she said. "Stop."

"But I can't leave them. I have to do something. I have to…" The sobs cut off her words and Stella hugged her, rubbing her back as her mother rubbed hers when she was distressed.

"It will be all right. It has to be all right."

The door to the compartment slid open without a knock and the conductor poked his head in. "What is the matter? Is the child worse?"

Ruth buried her head in Stella's shoulder and continued to sob.

Stella wiped a tear off her cheek and said, "No. My Anna is the same."

Think of something. Think of something.

Ruth clutched her leg and the Werner ring glinted in the light.

Yes. That's it.

Stella made a decision. One she hoped she wouldn't regret, but it couldn't be helped. Someone had to decide. "She lost her fiancé in Poland and it is very hard to bear."

Sadness came over the conductor and he watched as Ruth sobbed. "Many of our finest have been lost to the aggressors."

Stella nodded as if it was all Poland's fault and then she gave Ruth a pinch, hoping she'd play her part. It was a gamble, but the distraught girl showed her mettle once again. She shook and looked up at the conductor. "I'm sorry for making so much noise."

He pulled out a handkerchief and gave it to her. "I understand. I lost my own brother in the Kaiser's war. I still miss him."

"I don't know how to go on. I can't stop crying. I'm trying, but I can't."

Stella took the opportunity and said, "You don't have to come with me to Arnhem."

Ruth sniffed and then blew her nose, giving herself a moment to think. "But I promised I'd help."

"You have helped. I couldn't have made it this far without you carrying my suitcase, but you can go back home to Berlin. You must grieve."

"But you have to get to your mother."

"I will. It's not far now." Stella smiled up at the conductor. "You'll help me, won't you?"

He assured her that he would help at the border crossing, if they had to get off the train. Sometimes the border guards insisted.

"But what about Arnhem?" asked Ruth.

"My family will be at the station."

"I don't want to let you down."

"You're not." Stella rubbed her back. "And there's nothing new in Arnhem. You've seen everything there is to be seen and the cheese hasn't changed."

That got a chuckle out of Ruth. "If you don't mind, I think I'd like to go home and be with Werner's mother. She is having trouble."

"I'm sure." Stella looked to the conductor. "How long until the border?"

He checked the time and said, "Ten minutes."

"You'll have to decide soon, Sophie. We haven't got all day."

She nodded. "I'll go home then."

The conductor said he'd come to help as soon as they pulled into the station and closed the door. Stella went over to listen and then said, "He's gone."

"Thank you for understanding, but I still don't know what I'm going to do," said Ruth.

"That's fine, because I do," said Stella. "You're going to pay a visit to Herr Caron."

"*Your* Herr Caron?"

"Yes. Do you want to stop them?"

"Who?" Ruth asked.

Stella took a breath. This was against everything she'd been trained to do, but Stella saw in Ruth what Mr. Bast saw in her in Venice. Someone with a cause and ability. "The Nazis."

Ruth looked at her and a light came into her eyes, an understanding that hadn't been there before. "Yes, I do."

"Then I have a plan."

Her friend dried her eyes and balled up her fists. "I will do it."

Without telling Ruth exactly who she was or who she worked for, Stella outlined what she was going to do. She would go to Leon Klaus and contact Herr Caron, exactly as Stella had done with the Shakespeare quotes and all. It was such a huge risk to Cyril and to Ruth, it nearly took her breath away, but as Park-Welles had once said about the business of spies, "This is how wars are won. We risk for the reward."

"What's his real name?" Ruth asked.

"Lester Nimitz."

"He's an American?"

"Yes. He works at the embassy and he will help you."

Ruth frowned. "Why? I'm nothing to him."

Stella squeezed her hand. "You were right about him and me." She slipped off the wedding ring Cyril had given to her and handed it to Ruth.

She read the inscription, "'Each time you happen to me all over again.' What does that mean?"

"It's a quote from Edith Wharton. He loves me. I don't know why. I've done nothing to deserve it, but because he does, he will help you."

She read the quote again and then said, "Every time he sees you he falls in love again."

"Yes." Stella put the ring back on and went to give Anna some milk.

"What if he doesn't believe that you sent me?"

Stella thought about it for a minute and said, "You will tell him something and he will understand."

"What?"

"'Now is the time for Bilbo to perform the service for which he was included in our company; now is the time for him to earn his reward,'" said Stella.

Ruth frowned. "Bilbo?"

"Yes and the quote is said by Thorin."

"Is this a book?"

"Yes, and it has to be exactly right, the name and the quote."

"And then he'll decide what to do and I'll be a…"

"Yes, you will," said Stella.

The girls never used the word spy, but they both knew that's what they were talking about. They didn't talk about risk or the war or what the cost might be. It was unnecessary. Stella had been lectured at many a time by Park-Welles and others. They seemed to think it made some kind of impression on her, but those words were meaningless and irrelevant in the face of what was happening in Germany. Stella saw in Ruth what she felt when those men talked at her. Nothing mattered but the fight and the win.

"Will you do something for me?" Ruth asked. "I know you've done so much already, but I have to ask."

"If I can, I will."

"Can you use your connections to try and get my family out? They have to leave Austria. I'll do anything to help. Anything."

Stella nodded. "I will do what I can, but these things are difficult."

"But you'll try?"

"I will."

Ruth gave her their address in Vienna and Stella memorized all the information as Ruth memorized the quote.

"There's one more thing," said Ruth, reaching up and pulling down her enormous suitcase. "I want you to take this."

She frowned. "You need your suitcase."

"No, I need it out of the country. My family needs it out. Will you take it?"

"Why? What's in it?" Stella asked.

Ruth put the suitcase on the seat across from Anna and snapped open the latches. "My family's most precious possessions." She lifted the lid and pulled out a piece of linen. Stella gasped as the contents were revealed. Inside the dingy suitcase was a Klimt. A gorgeous portrait of a young woman half-enveloped by a tree and books. Stella had never seen the work before and her father had insisted she be familiar with the great artist's work. He had books on the subject and Stella had read them all.

"You know Klimt?" Ruth asked with surprise.

"I do." Stella reached out. "May I?"

Ruth nodded and Stella quickly looked through the stack of paintings and prints. They'd been wrapped in white linen and taken off their original frames and tacked to light wood frames. Tucked in a corner was a velvet box filled with jewelry, coins, and a pair of lovely silver candlesticks.

"You were supposed to get all this out of the country," said Stella.

"Yes. It's what we had left after my father died. Irena knew a man who could smuggle me into The Netherlands, but he was arrested before we contacted him, and I was stuck. My mother told people I'd emigrated. I couldn't show up again. It would be very suspicious."

"Why were you doing this? Your mother's family isn't Jewish. They can't confiscate their property."

"And they can't murder children?" Ruth asked.

"Yes, of course, you're right."

"When my grandfather asked about the visas, the Nazis started sniffing around. We are a wealthy family. Another hint of disloyalty, they could take everything we have. My grandfather thought we should get at least some pieces out of the country, so if that happened, we would still have something to sell later."

"And you want me to take them?" Stella asked, astonished at the trust being shown her.

"I trust you. You've…revealed what you are and you would've gotten me out, I know."

"I would and you still can," said Stella.

Ruth shook her head. "No, it's decided. Will you take it?"

"I will, but this is a huge thing. Are you sure you know what you're doing?"

The girl closed the suitcase. "It is a huge thing, but I have no choice. How can we find you, when we need to?"

Stella named Bickford House and said that was where to inquire. She expected Ruth to ask if she was English, but she didn't. She just whispered, "Bickford House. The Earl of Bickford. Good. It's done."

"Not quite."

Stella got down her suitcase and removed all her other papers, the French stickers, Anna's extra bottle of fluids, and the Dutch money. "You'll have to take my suitcase or it will look strange."

"A secret compartment. Marvelous." Ruth put her real identification and Maria's, too, in the compartment. Stella took out Irma's book and put it in Ruth's suitcase alongside the bottle and money.

"I'm surprised you want that book," said Ruth.

"Me too, but I feel an attachment."

"What will you do with all your papers and the stickers? The art's one thing, but you can't be caught with all that. They'll know."

Stella had thought about that and quickly unwrapped Anna. She put all the papers under the tiny girl's back and then rewrapped her. "There. That's as safe as I get."

The girls sat in silence until the train slowed. Anna fretted, so Stella gave her some more milk in hopes of quieting her. She could move her mouth more, but not quite enough to suck. Stella slowly dropped individual droplets in her open mouth and Ruth came over to kneel on the floor and look in her mouth, gently lifting her upper lip and then tugged ever so slightly on her lower eyelid.

"Good," she said. "She's not so dry. Her membranes are beginning to moisten."

Stella leaned in and whispered, "I'll get her back on the drip as soon as I can."

Ruth cocked her head at the door and then said in a normal voice, "I'm going to miss you, baby girl."

"We'll both miss you, but who knows maybe we'll be back before Christmas," said Stella.

"Your mother does work miracles and I pray she can for Anna."

"She will. I know it."

The conductor opened the door and said, "We will stop in a

moment and I will tell the border guards to let you stay on the train. You shouldn't have to move the baby."

Stella heaved a sigh. "That's so much better than taking her out in the cold. Thank you." Then she looked at Ruth. "And thank you for coming with me. Such a kindness."

Ruth leaned over and kissed Anna's forehead. "I'll see you soon and we will read books and play with your blocks, sweet girl."

Then she and Stella stood up and their eyes filled with tears as they hugged fiercely. Stella could feel Ruth's heart pounding against her chest matching the rhythm of her own heart.

"You're such a good friend to me. I'm so sorry about Werner. I can't say it enough," said Stella.

"I know you are. No one could've been kinder to me."

Stella smiled and they exchanged cheek kisses. "And you to me."

Ruth picked up Stella's suitcase and stepped out of the compartment. "Which way?" she asked.

He pointed her to the right and said to Stella, "I will come back after I help the other passengers."

"You have been a godsend. Thank you."

The conductor puffed up as men generally did when being adored and hurried down the corridor. Stella closed the door and said a prayer to let Ruth get away safely.

Anna began squirming again and Stella broke the ten minute rule to give her some more drops. "You seem better."

The answer was a kind of mewing complaint and Stella thought for a minute she would break out into a wail, but she hadn't the strength. Stella gave her five more drops and the little girl fell asleep.

"There you go," Stella said. "Rest and you'll have more in a little bit."

She leaned back in the seat, feeling so tense she had to concentrate on not squeezing the bottle so hard. Her hand hurt. Actually, everything hurt and she had to get her muscles to relax. The border guards couldn't be allowed to see her fear so she put her head back, closed her eyes, and began counting sheep, slowly relaxing her feet, then her ankles and so forth.

By the time she got to forty sheep, she'd gotten all her muscles limp enough that the bottle nearly tipped over when the compartment door slid open. Stella sat up slowly as if she wasn't worried in the least. "That was quick," she said to the conductor.

"We've only got two new passengers," he said. "You have your papers?"

"Of course." She handed over one set. "Here are Anna's."

He passed them to a border guard who gave them a cursory look and said, "I need yours."

Stella passed them to the conductor who gave her Anna's back. The guard gave hers a harder look and she found it hard to breathe.

Calm but tired. Calm but tired.

"Do you need my ration cards?" she asked.

The guard frowned at her. "Why would I?"

"They were checked last time I went to my mother's."

"Oh, I don't know why." He looked through her papers again. "How long will you be staying?"

"At least two weeks, but I'd like to be home for Christmas," said Stella.

He glanced down at the photo. "Home is in Berlin?"

"Yes."

"Your husband is there? What is his position?"

"Yes. He works at Temmler, but he is going into the Schutzstaffel."

The guard and the conductor looked impressed. She got her papers back and a nice, "Have a good trip." The guard left and the conductor asked, "Can I get you anything?"

"I don't think so. Thank you."

With that, he closed the door and a few minutes later, the train began to move. Stella went to the window, peering out onto the platform. The train chugged out of the station and there she was at the very end. Ruth stood half-shrouded by a pillar, watching the train and her chance departing with her hand on her heart. Stella blew her a kiss and Ruth, who would prove to be one of the most courageous people Stella would ever know, was gone.

CHAPTER 27

$\mathcal{A}$nna let out a cry and Stella jerked awake, disoriented and bleary-eyed. The bottle had fallen on the seat and dribbled milk onto the cushion. Stella grabbed it and checked her watch. "Oh, my God."

She'd slept almost the entire way to Arnhem and Anna had missed two feedings. She grabbed the bottle and quickly dropped milk on Anna's tongue. It might've been Stella's imagination, but it seemed drier.

"I won't sleep again. Don't worry, darling girl."

Anna fretted and made motions like she was crying, but no tears came. Stella had to get her back on the drip as soon as possible. The train jerked and the conductor opened the door. "We have arrived in Arnhem."

She yawned and, for once, it was a real one, then said, "I fell asleep."

He smiled. "I saw that, but your child was sleeping, too, so I didn't wake you."

"I shouldn't have slept. I should be a good mother." Stella bit her lip for effect.

"You are a good mother and Germany needs good mothers. I hope you will have more children for the Führer."

"I very much want to and my husband agrees."

"Good. I'm glad to hear it."

The train ground to a halt and Stella stood up, reaching for the suitcase.

The conductor stopped her and picked it up, much to her dismay but she could hardly pry it out of his hands. He was trying to be kind.

"Thank you," she said instead, and tucked her papers into her handbag before gently picking up Anna, careful not to dislodge the papers still under her back.

"I will help you off the train and to find your family."

She nodded and they went down the corridor with her madly trying to think of how to get away. The conductor was determined to help her and she knew how determined a German could be.

He stepped down onto the platform, set down the suitcase, and helped her off. "There, you've made it to your mother."

She beamed up at him. "It will be a relief to have her take over with Anna."

"Good grandmothers know what is best." He glanced around the mostly empty platform. "Where are they? Don't they know your arrival time?"

"They do, but if it is my brother, he's always late." Stella looked around in exasperation.

"Soon he will learn to be on time."

Stella looked up puzzled, but with a sinking feeling in her heart. "How?"

The conductor leaned over and whispered, "When they are part of the Reich, they will be on time and do things as they should be done."

The crying erupted in Stella's head, but she managed to say, "Yes, that is what my husband says and the border crossings will be easier, too."

"Yes, the sooner the better."

She tried to push the crying away, but it wouldn't go and she could hardly think. "You don't have to wait."

"I will wait with you until he comes," he said, frowning, and she suspected he planned on giving her "brother" a piece of his mind for making her wait. She had to make a quick exit where he wouldn't follow and a man conveniently made himself available.

"Pieter! There he is." She pointed at a man leaving the platform. "He forgot I was going to be in first class." She quickly picked up the suitcase, went up on her tiptoes, kissed the conductor's cheek, and dashed after the man, calling out, "Pieter!"

"Grüß Gott!" the conductor yelled after her as she darted as fast as she could with Anna in one arm and Ruth's enormous suitcase in the other hand into the station. She looked around and went for the bathroom down a corridor way at the far end of the station, happily far from the conductor and any possibility of nosy interference. Because it was the middle of the night the bathroom was empty and Stella was able to change all her papers out for her French ones, slap the French stickers on Ruth's suitcase in peace, and breathe. She breathed and breathed until the crying lessened. Then she took off Oscar's hated necklace, considered throwing it in the toilet, but put it in the heel of her shoe instead. She wasn't going to cut off her nose to spite her face as her mother would say, and twenty minutes later she emerged as a French woman going to Paris, accent, lipstick, and hip swish in place. She checked the departures board, and, unfortunately, there were no express trains to Paris until the morning and she was unwilling to wait. Stella and Anna got on a local train and chugged out a half hour later.

There was no first class and it would take over ten hours to get there through Amsterdam, but it would still be hours before the morning train. She laid Anna on the bench seat at the front of the car and glanced back. There were five other people in the car and they looked as miserable as she felt. Anna was fretting and she needed her drip. Stella gave her a little milk, more than before, and she swallowed but didn't stop fretting.

There was nothing to do but hook up the bottle again and hope no one caused a fuss and got her noticed. She waited until the car had settled into sleep and then put Ruth's suitcase on the opposite seat.

She got out the mostly empty bottle and closed it without anyone seeing what was inside. Then she hooked the rubber tube back to the needle in Anna's neck and held up the bottle so it would drip properly.

After fifteen minutes and more milk, Anna calmed and fell asleep. Then a conductor entered the car and Stella tucked away the bottle and covered Anna's neck before he came up the aisle to her. She showed him her papers and paid for their tickets. That conductor, a Belgian, was completely disinterested in the two of them and left the car, never to be seen again.

Yawning, Stella looked at Anna's little face, distressed even in sleep, and picked up the bottle. She was so tired, but she couldn't go to sleep again. Someone could get curious and take a look at Anna or steal the suitcase. Anything could happen and there was no way she could keep going on her own without sleep. She couldn't trust anyone. If she took Anna to a hospital, they would rightfully question what had happened to her. How had she gotten into such a terrible state? Who had done it? Stella couldn't answer those questions. She couldn't tell people that Anna came across the border with false papers after being stolen out of a death clinic. They wouldn't believe such an outlandish story and think she did it. Stella could be arrested. What would happen to Anna then? They had to go. Straight through to England where Stella would be believed and Anna safe.

So she made a decision and opened her handbag, rooting around until she found the key down at the bottom. She glanced back at the other passengers, who were sleeping, and she unscrewed the top of the key, letting her last pill drop into her hand. The energy pill. She was supposed to use it during an escape. Park-Welles thought that meant hiking over the Alps, but this was her Alps so she popped it in her mouth and swallowed it dry before picking up the bottle again.

Park-Welles had been non-specific about the length of time the pill would last, but if it was anything like Pervitin, it would get them home. It had to because Stella Bled Lawrence wouldn't settle for anything less.

IT WAS RAINING when Stella stepped off the train in Bickford, but she didn't feel it. She didn't feel much of anything at all, except tremendous pain through her entire body. It surged through her muscles and pierced her brain, gaining intensity as the hours wore on. Great Grandmother Leonie spoke of such pain before she died and Stella took that as a bad sign as she stood on the platform barely able to put one foot in front of the other.

She had to get to Bickford House. She just couldn't think how. The energy had left her in London. It took the rage with it and that she wouldn't miss. Stella had never felt such aggression, even considering everything she'd done in the past. If someone had dared to get in her way, she would've cheerfully strangled them and savored the experience. Now all she was left with was a burning need to save Anna. She'd finished the bottle on the boat and the second drip bottle in France. Stella couldn't think how to get more. She couldn't think of anything but getting the child to safety. Safety meant Bickford.

The estate had always sent a car for her before and she'd never had to get herself there. She wasn't even sure of the direction. She'd have to ask. The station was crowded with people, but Stella didn't know them. To be fair, she wasn't sure she could really recognize anyone anyway. Her vision was blurry and sometimes got distorted in a way that reminded her of an Edvard Munch painting.

She started walking, getting jostled by passengers rushing to get on her train and she lost her balance a couple of times, nearly going down but catching herself at the last second. It took away from her slim reserves and she was gritting her teeth by the time she saw the ticket office and its usual line. She got in the back and queued for what seemed like an hour until she got to the booth. The stout lady behind the glass asked her something, but Stella couldn't understand her. What language was she speaking? It wasn't German. All Stella had in her head was German.

Then a man behind her yelled. "Go on and buy your ticket, girl!"

English. He's speaking English. I think he is. Maybe.

Stella started speaking, but it sounded like gibberish to her and to the lady who frowned and leaned forward, puzzled.

"Get out of the way." A man pushed her aside and she stumbled into a wall, trying to say, "Help," but unsure if she actually was.

"Mrs. Bled Lawrence?" a man asked.

She looked up at a weathered face with a short-brimmed hat pulled low over the blue eyes that peered at her with concern. She answered. It could've been gibberish or the wrong accent. She didn't know.

He tilted his head and looked at her like he wasn't sure if she was sane. "Are you all right?"

Do I know him? Speak English. Speak English.

"I had…an…accident."

He pulled out a thick cotton handkerchief and wiped her face gently. "Mrs. Bled Lawrence, who is this baby?"

He knows me, but do I know him?

"She's ill. We had an accident."

He took her by the arm, trying to lead her away from the booth, but she had to get a car to the house. She pulled away and turned back.

"Mrs. Bled Lawrence, it's Tom. Don't you know me? I'm Lord Bickford's farm agent."

She nodded. She did know him. Of course, she did. "I have to go."

"To the house?"

Stella nodded.

"I'll have Em call the house. You wait here."

"No, no. Can't you take us? I have to go. Right now."

Tom looked down at Anna, cringing slightly. "I only have the wagon. I brought some—"

"Where is it?" she asked, starting to walk with no direction in mind.

"All right, ma'am. I'll take you." Tom called over his shoulder, "Em, send Dr. Reynolds out to the big house."

"Right now?" the woman yelled back.

"Yes!" Tom pried the suitcase out of her hand and Stella looked down in surprise. She hadn't realized she was still carrying it. "This way, ma'am."

He gently led her out of the station past curious onlookers whispering her name and saying things like, "Whatever happened to her?" "She must be terribly ill."

Then they were at an old rickety farm wagon. Tom put the suitcase in the back and boosted her up onto the seat behind one of the estate's enormous workhorses. Tom climbed up beside her, shifted a lever, and made a clicking noise to the horse. "Walk on there, Geraldine. Walk on."

The wagon moved slowly out of town and onto a road Stella recognized.

"Can't we go faster?" she asked as Anna began to fuss.

He slapped the reins and the big horse reluctantly broke into a trot, making the wintery countryside more blurry than it already was.

"What happened to you, ma'am?" Tom asked.

"I…we had an accident."

"You said, but that child, she's very ill. I have five of my own and I never saw—"

"She had the flu." Stella was only able to put those words together because she practiced them over and over again during the twenty-four hours it took to make it to Bickford. She knew she would have to say something and it was the best she could come up with.

"Must be a new flu," he said.

"Yes, the worst kind."

Stella couldn't tell if he believed her or not. It didn't matter. The earl would handle it and he would make Tom believe.

"There we are," he said as they left the woods and came into the open area around the house. The view, as always, was incredible. The stately home in front of its lake, perfectly serene and untouched by time.

The wagon clattered onto the stone bridge and Anna broke out into a whimpering wail that made her sound every bit as sick as she was.

"I hope Doc Reynolds gets here quick," Tom muttered.

Anna shuddered in her arms and Stella said, "We have to go faster. It's right there. Hurry."

"We are, my lady."

Stella reached for the whip. They had to get home. She had the whip, ready to lay it on the horse's broad back.

"No, my lady, she's an old horse. We can't whip her."

She gave up the whip and clung to the rough wooden seat as they cleared the bridge, following the lane to go around the house away from the closest door. Her vision got blurrier and the house started to blend with the lake. Her arms were giving out. She couldn't hold Anna much longer.

I have to get her there. I have to.

Stella leaned over and tried to climb off the seat.

"My lady, don't!" Tom yelled and pulled back on the reins.

"I have to get there."

Anna began to wail. She was in pain. So much pain.

Tom jumped off the wagon and ran around to Stella. "Let me help you."

He got her down and she stumbled off down the path to the grand front entrance of Bickford House.

"I'll bring the suitcase!" yelled Tom behind her, but she'd forgotten all about it. All she could think of was that door. The door to the earl and to Agatha.

She clambered up the wide stone stairs where Uncle Josiah had told her Abel was dead. For a second, she thought she saw him there, smiling with roguish approval, but she kept going up and pounded on the big door. Anna was slipping. Her legs began to buckle, but she kept pounding until the door was yanked away from her fist to reveal Smith the butler, glaring out at her with his usual imperiousness.

"Smith," she whispered.

Then his mouth dropped open. "Mrs. Lawrence?"

She pushed past him into the great hall, stumbling and going down on her knees. "Agatha! Agatha!"

People came running from every which way and then Agatha, the

Countess of Bickford, was there, down on her knees. "Stella, darling, what happened—"

"I got her. I got her." Stella pushed the wailing Anna into Agatha's open arms and a huge weight lifted away from her chest. She fell backward, her arms and legs splayed on the cold floor. Above her the ornate ceiling swirled into a circle, a tornado of color and wood. Stella sank into the floor, into blackness, and then it was all gone.

CHAPTER 28

A loud crackle and thump woke up Stella, but *up* was really an exaggeration. Coming into consciousness was like swimming through mud in a lead jacket, but slowly her eyes opened and focused on a panel of green silk twisted into a sunburst pattern high above her. It seemed vaguely familiar, but she wasn't at all sure of where she was.

The scent of a wood fire hung in the air, along with roses and lavender, all comforting and familiar, but the comfort confused her. Stella couldn't remember being comfortable or clean. And she was clean. Her hair flowed over her shoulders in fat, shiny curls and smelled of rose water.

Stella pushed the thick covers off, but was unable to sit up. She had to roll onto her side and push herself up with her arms. Her head was foggy and her eyesight blurred slightly as she looked around at a lovely room with blue-green walls, tapestries, and pastoral scenes painted on canvas. The crackling fire blazed under an Italian marble fireplace that had several framed photos of herself and Nicky. Bickford. She was in her room at Bickford. Everything was fine, but she wasn't sure what she was doing there.

Her eyes roamed around looking for an answer and landed on the chair next to the fire with its needlepoint cushions, probably stitched two hundred years ago but used like it was everyday furniture. On the cushion was a lumpy black handbag that didn't look like anything she would have, but the sight of it lit up a flame of fear inside her chest. Something was wrong. She was supposed to do something.

Then she saw it. On the floor behind the chair was a large suitcase with French stickers pasted to the side. It was Ruth's suitcase. She'd left Germany with Ruth's suitcase and Anna. Where was Anna?

Stella frantically looked around the room as the crying began in her head. No crib. No Anna. Where was the child? How long had she been asleep? Had she told Agatha what happened? She didn't remember anything. Not bathing. Not getting in bed. Nothing. They didn't know the situation or how much Anna had been fed or about the fluids. What if they gave her too much? What if they didn't give her enough? What if? What if?

Tumbling out of bed, Stella got tangled up in an old-fashioned nightgown with heavy lace at the neck and wrists. The soft cotton fell past her ankles and tripped her as she stumbled toward the door. She gathered up the voluminous fabric and ran into the hall. The nursery. Anna would be in the nursery.

The hall was empty and no one was there to see Stella weaving her way past the main gallery, bumping into walls and tripping over her own feet. She managed to get herself to the Queen's Wing, through trial and error, and yanked open the nursery door, fully expecting to see a nurse and a nanny in residence and hovering over a crib. But the nursery was empty with no sign that a child had been there recently.

She spun around and frantically ran back toward the main gallery, calling for Anna. Servants emerged as if from nowhere and tried to grab her, but she pushed them away as she looked in multitudes of bedrooms, all empty, and her cries for Anna got louder until she was screaming.

When she reached the grand staircase, she took a tumble, rolling down five stairs before landing on her rear. Hands lifted her up, but she shook off their help and clung to the railing as she hurried down.

"Anna! Where is she?"

"Mrs. Lawrence! Stop!"

"You have to lie down!"

"Please, Mrs. Lawrence! Dr. Reynolds says you must rest!"

The voices and hands came at her, but no one answered her about Anna. She wasn't going to rest. She couldn't rest. Anna needed her.

And then Agatha was there, grabbing her by the shoulders. "Stella! Stop! How are you out of bed?"

"Where is she? Where is she?"

"Who?"

"Anna! Where is she? I have to tell you."

"She's not here. She's gone," said Agatha.

Gone.

Every muscle in Stella's body tensed and she was screaming. She couldn't tell when she started. She was just screaming, like she'd always been screaming and always would be. Her own voice was matched by the children wailing. Their voices crescendoed and she clapped her hands over her ears.

"No! No!" yelled Agatha. "Listen!"

Stella couldn't listen and she couldn't stop screaming. Anna gone. Gone. Like all the others, she was lost to hate and ignorance.

Then someone whipped her around and a face more familiar than any other in the entire world looked at her. The eyes were her own, except with deep chocolatey brown instead of her pale blue.

Francesqua Bled pulled Stella's hands off her ears and said in her sternest voice, "Quiet!"

Stella's jaw snapped shut and she began violently shaking and her knees started to buckle. Strong arms wrapped around her back and Agatha said in her ear, "She's not dead. Anna is fine, Stella. She's fine."

"Fine?" whispered Stella. "How?"

Francesqua pressed her daughter's hands between her own. "Perhaps not fine, but she's being cared for by the very best doctors."

"I have to tell you what happened. You don't know what happened."

Agatha squeezed her tight and said to someone, "Where is Lizzie? She was supposed to be sitting with Mrs. Lawrence."

"I believe Mrs. Hart asked her to change Mrs. Lawrence's linens," said Smith. "She must've gone below stairs to get a fresh set."

"Listen," said Stella. "I have to tell you what I did. Anna was in—"

"Fetch his lordship," said Agatha loudly. "Immediately."

"Yes, ma'am," said Smith.

"Run!" Agatha squeezed her again. "Anna is fine. You don't need to tell us anything."

"But I do," said Stella. "You don't know what happened."

"Francesqua, please help Stella up to bed."

"But I—"

"Shush." Agatha pushed her gently toward the stairs. "I'll call Dr. Reynold's and order a tray for you."

"I don't need a tray."

Francesqua put an arm around Stella's waist and started walking her to the stairs. "We'll get you into bed and then you can tell me everything."

Everything.

That got Stella's attention. She'd never told her mother *everything* in her entire life. Her mother. Francesqua Bled was there. In England. It was incredible, unlikely, and, quite frankly, impossible. By the time they got to the top of the stairs, Stella had almost convinced herself she was dreaming. Or was it a nightmare? The difference was hard to discern.

They went into Stella's bedroom and with assistance she climbed into bed and servants swarmed in. The curtains were opened. The fire stoked. A hot water bottle underneath her covers was removed and replaced.

Francesqua stepped back and let them do their work, primly sitting down next to the suitcase and picking a bit of nonexistent fluff off her lavender day dress. That more than anything else convinced Stella that her mother was real, not a figment of her imagination. That and the serenity that Francesqua exuded as she watched the activity. She wasn't considered to be a saint for nothing. If she thought anything about the situation and made a judgement, Stella couldn't tell. Stella could *never* tell. People said God worked in mysterious ways and so did Francesqua Bled.

When the maids stopped fussing, one turned to Francesqua and asked, "Can I get you anything, Mrs. Bled?"

"Yes, a tray of tea and biscuits for my daughter, please," said her mother in the calmest of voices.

The maid bobbed a curtsy.

"Would you please close the door on your way out?"

"Yes, ma'am." The maids scurried out and closed the door, leaving Stella alone with her mother. She wanted to protest, but her mouth was dry and no words formed in her head. She tried to find something else to look at, but her eyes wouldn't stop returning to her mother, who sat there looking at her like she had so many times before, showing nothing but knowing everything.

"Who is she?" Francesqua asked.

Stella took a breath and asked, "Who?"

"The child."

"Anna." She hoped the earl hadn't given her a false name because that particular cat was well out of the bag.

"I know her name. Who is she to you?"

Stella felt considerably better now that she was back in bed, but her brain was still muddled and she didn't know what to say. "We had an accident."

"An accident?"

"Yes."

"An accident where you lost ten pounds and that poor child was at death's door?"

Stella folded her hands together and mimicked her mother's calm voice. "What are you doing here?'

"I came to see you," said Francesqua.

"How long was I asleep?"

"Two days."

"How did you get here so fast?" Stella asked astonished.

Francesqua crossed her legs and said, "I've been here over a week."

"A week?"

"Over a week."

Stella heard the words. She even understood them, but comprehending them was another matter. "But *why* did you come?"

Francesqua raised a brow, very much like she did when Stella's father would announce that he was going to the brewery on Christmas morning. Who knew so much disbelief could be conveyed in one eyebrow?

"I'm serious," said Stella. "Why would you come all this way?"

"I knew something was wrong."

"How?"

"Your last letter was…odd."

Stella frowned. She'd carefully composed it precisely so Francesqua wouldn't be suspicious. "There wasn't anything wrong in my letter."

"Clearly that is untrue," said her mother. "What happened to you and that child?"

Stella couldn't answer that, so she said, "That's still fast. How did you get here a week and a half after I sent my letter?"

"You sent it airmail, which in retrospect might have been a mistake."

"It wasn't a mistake. It was just a letter."

"Shall I get you a mirror?" asked Francesqua.

"No, thank you," said Stella.

"What happened to you?"

Stella smoothed her blankets to give herself something to do. "I still don't understand how—"

Francesqua stood up and came to the side of her bed. A curl escaped from her carefully composed hairdo of swoops and coils. "I packed a suitcase, called a cab, and went to the airport."

There were so many things wrong with that sentence, Stella didn't know where to start. Francesqua Bled didn't pack. The maids did that and they certainly didn't pack *one* suitcase. Call a cab? She'd never known her mother to ride in a cab. She considered it unladylike and Stella had been warned against hailing cabs forever.

"Where's Papa?" Stella asked.

Francesqua checked her watch. "At the brewery, I presume."

"What did he say?"

"About what?"

"You leaving."

"Nothing. I didn't tell him," she said evenly.

It was unimaginable. The perfect wife, a widely acknowledged saint, didn't tell her husband she was leaving the country? Who was this person who packed and acted?

"I can do things, Stella," said her mother. "I'm quite capable of doing a great many things."

Stella had heard the stories of her mother's youth, driving to Florida with her sister and a few other choice tidbits, but those incidents didn't seem real, just fun anecdotes, not really about the prim woman who looked down on her with calm restraint.

"I know that," said Stella because what else could she say.

There was a knock on the door and Lizzie dashed in with a tray laden with a plethora of food. "I'm so sorry, Stella. I should've been here when you woke up."

"I'm fine. It's nothing."

Lizzie smoothed her faultless apron and asked, "Shall I pour for you?"

Stella nodded and Lizzie quickly made her a cup of tea just the way she liked it and carefully placed the cup in her hands.

"Is Albert here?" Stella asked.

"I believe he's on the estate, looking after Mr. Harrow, the pig man. He took a fall yesterday."

"If you see him, can you tell him I'd like him to pay me a visit?"

Lizzie blushed and said she would before she curtsied and left. Stella was glad to see her love of Albert hadn't diminished, even if he wasn't aware of her devotion.

Her mother came over and put a chocolate biscuit in Stella's hand before retreating to the window to be bathed in warm light that accentuated the frown on her face.

"You should have some tea," said Stella before she took a bite of the biscuit. It was so full of butter and sugar she instantly got lightheaded from the influx of calories.

"What happened to you and that child?" Francesqua asked. "I'm your mother and I have a right to know."

"We had an accident."

"Like the accident you had with Mr. Fuzz?" she asked.

Stella's eyes went wide and she sputtered, trying to come up with a reply. She hadn't thought about that in ten years and hardly at all, even then.

"Well?" Francesqua asked.

"Mr. Fuzz?"

"You do remember Mr. Fuzz?"

"Um…"

When Stella was eight, she'd had a pony named Mr. Fuzz. Stella was small for her age and not allowed to ride any other horse. Of course, that didn't stop Uncle Josiah from sneaking her out to her grandmother's house, Prie Dieu, and putting her on his favorite jumper, Top Hat. She took three jumps splendidly and fell on the fourth, breaking her arm in two places. They told her mother that she'd fallen off Mr. Fuzz when he shied after seeing a fox, which was ridiculous. Mr. Fuzz was elderly and could barely see his trough, not to mention that he was so low to the ground that Stella could fall off a thousand times and not break a nail. But Francesqua never showed any sign that she doubted the story and Stella thought herself quite clever to get away with it. Now, under her mother's wilting gaze, she wondered if she'd gotten away with anything at all. One day before her cast was to come off, Uncle Josiah was sent to Australia for six months to look into bringing Bled beer into their market. It was a miserable six months without Uncle Josiah to spring her from her mother's boring educational goals. Stella had to take etiquette lessons and learn the proper way to walk, sit, hold a wine glass, and put a napkin in her lap. It took up an amazing amount of time and the broken arm was pleasurable by comparison.

"I thought so," said Francesqua. "Tell me what really happened."

Stella clamped her mouth shut and the door of her room flung open. The earl rushed in, panting and smiling from ear to ear. "My dear girl, you're awake."

"She is," said Francesqua, "and I was just asking about what happened to her."

"She had an accident," he said, meeting her mother's eyes without a hint of deceit.

"Ah, yes. The much ballyhooed accident," she said. "I'd like to hear about this accident that caused starvation in a little child."

The earl straightened his tweed jacket and said, "They never should have been sent to that clinic. It was unacceptable. I will lodge a complaint."

"Yes, please do that," said Stella.

"I will need the details and the address."

"Of course," said Stella. "It was terrible there. Like a prison."

"So now it's a clinic that caused this," said Francesqua without a hint of irony. If Stella hadn't known better, she'd have thought her mother bought it, but apparently Francesqua didn't buy much.

"Yes, my dear. Quite a terrible place." The earl came over and ushered Francesqua to the door. "Agatha is waiting with Mrs. Wallace. They're trying to decide what Stella should have for dinner today. They would like your input."

For a second, Stella thought her mother would balk, but true to form, she simply nodded and left. The earl closed the door behind her and whipped out a handkerchief to wipe the sweat off his balding head. "What did you tell her?"

"Nothing. I had an accident." Stella sipped her tea and let the warmth steady her.

He pulled up the needlepoint chair. "Agatha said you were quite… indisposed when you came downstairs."

"That's putting it mildly."

Instead of sitting down, he began to pace. "I don't know what to say to you. When I saw Anna…"

Stella stared down at the amber liquid and said, "I'm sorry. I know I shouldn't have brought her here."

"What?"

"I connected her and me and Bickford. I wasn't in my right mind. What will he say?"

The earl sat down, but she didn't look at him. "Who in the world are you talking about?"

"Park-Welles. The new 'C'. I didn't follow orders and people will talk. They always talk."

"People will talk, but as always *we* will steer the conversation. You, my dear, were in a dreadful accident and ended up in a country hospital with abysmal results, so you came to Bickford, both suffering from pneumonia."

She hazarded a glance at him and found the earl smiling. "Pneumonia?"

"Double pneumonia. It's a terrible disease. As a foreigner, you rightfully didn't know where to turn, so you came to your home away from home. Bickford. The papers have reported these facts."

"And people believe it?"

"Of course, they do. Tom says he heard you wheezing. He's telling everyone within five miles how he brought you home when you were out of your mind with fever."

Stella smiled back. "Well, I was out of my mind. He's got that right."

"Tom has been very helpful and amply rewarded for his assistance," he said. "Furthermore, to answer your question, I've informed SIS of your return and they won't say anything until they know the actual facts."

"Did you tell them I have pneumonia?" Stella asked.

"I did not. They were merely informed of your status. You will be debriefed at your earliest convenience."

"When I can drag myself to London?"

"Correct."

"Is Anna really all right?" Stella asked, her chest tightening.

The earl looked away and ran the handkerchief over his head again. "Yes. I can't thank you enough for bringing her home. Henry and his wife send their heartfelt gratitude. He is forever in your debt and a man like that doesn't take vows lightly."

"I wasn't sure she would live. She was so very weak when I got her."

"The doctors say you did the right thing with the fluids and milk. She was, I believe, very close to death, but they say she will recover fully."

"Thank God."

"Stella, when I saw that needle in her neck and her…condition, I've never felt more angry in all my life and that includes seeing my son in hospital after the Kristallnacht. What happened? Surely her nanny didn't do that to her."

"No. Gertruda Hoppe was arrested for having false papers." She reached for the lumpy handbag and he quickly handed it to her. "Should we wait for the official debrief?"

"I'm partial to unofficial myself." The earl sat back and listened to her story of tracking Anna, his face growing more grim with every word. She opened the handbag and found the cigarette case.

"Park-Welles didn't give you that," said the earl.

"No, he didn't," she said.

"You have a friend. Could it be the mysterious Mr. Bast?"

"Could be." She popped open the case and the little camera slid into her hand. "Pictures of the paperwork on the doctor's desk and children in the ward."

"This program is expanding? You're sure?"

"I believe so and it's a secret. I have a feeling that parents are turning over their children without any idea what's going to happen to them," said Stella. "The guard at the clinic didn't know and I suspect the doctor who sent Anna there didn't either."

The earl sat back and steepled his thin fingers. "I have to tell London about Anna, if this information is to be of use."

I'm done then. They'll give me the boot.

"Do we have to? Maybe I accidentally ended up in the clinic. I sprained my ankle and I went there. That's how I found out."

"No. We have to come clean. Tell me that you gave your contact the money."

"I did, but only because of Anna," said Stella.

"I think you may have left something out," he said. "Start from the beginning and tell me everything that happened."

Stella told him everything. Well, almost everything and then took out the key, handing it over. "I killed Oscar von Drechsel. The papers said it was a heart condition, but it was me."

"You used all three pills on one mission," he said, shaking his head in disbelief.

"I got the job done."

"Several jobs actually." He dropped the key and the camera, securely in its cigarette case, back in her handbag. "No regrets?"

"About Oscar? No. I told you what he was up to with the Jews and he had a way about him. It would happen. He had it all worked out. Extermination."

"I can't believe they would go that far. Hitler is a vicious little twerp but surely even he wouldn't go along with that"

"We have to stop thinking things are impossible. If they'll starve children to death, they're capable of anything," said Stella.

"Yes. That changes a great deal of my thinking," he said. "And you're certain about the Manstein plan?"

"Absolutely. They're not going to do what they did last time. It's going to be a lightning war. Blitzkrieg. Forget about the Maginot Line."

"Stella, my dear, no one thinks they can breach the line. France believes they are secure."

"I'm telling you they're going to go around it and they'll use Pervitin to do it."

"It sounds…rather fantastic," said the earl.

Stella sat up straighter. "You sound like you don't believe me."

"I believe you."

"What happens now? What will they do?"

He smiled at her. "We never know what happens next. It's not our job to make those decisions."

Stella crumbled the remains of a biscuit into dust. "That's ridiculous."

"All you can do is give them the intelligence. What they do with it isn't your concern."

"Isn't it?"

"No."

"Then what's the point?" Stella crossed her arms and glared at the fire. "They might decide to do nothing at all."

"Don't lose sight of what you've accomplished." The earl moved the needlepoint chair back to its usual position. He didn't mention the suitcase and neither did she.

"And what is that precisely?"

"In addition to saving a child's life and bringing in Ruth as an asset, you proved you could do the job and dare I say," he gave her a wink, "better than any forty-year-old Etonian. Lady Churchill will be pleased and she will make sure Winston is pleased."

"Do you really think so?" Stella asked.

"Don't doubt it for a minute. Your information about the Siemens factory alone should secure your position."

"Do you think we'll bomb it?"

"I think we should." He gave her a rare grin. "That you probably will know, if it happens."

"I hope they take it out," she said with a smile. "I'll feel like I've done something."

The earl poured her another cup of tea and said, "You've definitely done something and it occurs to me that Agatha owes Clemmie a letter. She should mention your impending visit to London. Don't you agree?"

"I do, but how much does Agatha know?"

"My wife, like your mother, can be trusted with most everything that matters."

"My mother? I don't think so. She would take to her bed for a week, if she knew one tenth of what I've done."

"And yet, here she is. Your mother came across the Atlantic during a war to get to you and she came on instinct alone," said the earl. "I now see where you get your nerve."

"From my mother? You must be joking," said Stella. "Uncle Josiah taught me everything. How to fly. How to—"

"Some things can't be taught. She likes art, doesn't she?"

Stella stared at him in confusion. "What?"

"Art. Francesqua's a connoisseur, isn't she?"

"I suppose so."

He went to the door and stopped with his hand on the knob. "I like your mother. You should like her, too."

"I do."

"Then it's time you tell her."

"She knows," said Stella without any idea of what Francesqua Bled knew. "You don't understand. Uncle Josiah was the one that said I could do anything."

"But he isn't here, is he?" With that, the earl slipped out the door and closed it firmly behind him.

CHAPTER 29

Dr. Reynolds gently leaned Stella forward and pressed an ice cold stethoscope to her back. She coughed and held her breath on command as the doctor made unhappy noises and then leaned her back on her pillows.

"How long were you without food and water?"

Stella smiled at the ancient doctor. "Not long."

"Mrs. Bled Lawrence, you can tell me the truth," he said in his wheezy tired voice. "I'm sworn to keep your secrets."

"Have you signed the Official Secrets Act?"

"I have not."

"Then I was never without food and water," said Stella.

The doctor sighed before shining a light in her eyes and examining her arms. "My guess is that you were without food and water for at least twenty-four hours, but probably closer to forty-eight, during which time you took a medication that raised your heart rate and kept you awake for the entire period. Your heart was affected and you require complete rest for at least two weeks."

"I had pneumonia."

Dr. Reynolds packed his black doctor's bag and said, "I have been the head of his Lordship's cottage hospital for over forty years. I know you and that poor child were not in York getting pneumonia after a car crash. I need all the information to treat you properly."

"You have it," said Stella.

"I saw you at Abel Hershmann's memorial and I may be old, but I'm not a fool. You've lost a considerable amount of weight in a short time. You must see to your health. Make no mistake, what you have done has affected you."

"This is my private information?"

The doctor snapped his bag shut and eyed her through small wire-rimmed glasses. "It is."

"Good. I expect you to keep it that way," said Stella.

"Your mother is in the hall waiting."

"What will you tell her?"

He stood by her bedside and thought about it so long that Stella was afraid that he'd lost the tether of her question, but he hadn't. The doctor, who'd survived two wars and multiple epidemics, was merely weighing his options. "You signed the Official Secrets Act?"

Oh, no.

"No," she lied, knowing it was too late. "I was only asking."

He nodded and picked up his bag. "I will tell your mother that you're young and unaffected by the pneumonia. You're quite recovered."

Stella hadn't expected that. "Will you?"

"We all must do our part for king and country, even an old country doctor," he said. "But take this seriously. You must not push yourself for a good while."

"I'll do my best."

Dr. Reynolds shook her hand and said, "I have the impression that your best is quite something."

"Thank you."

"I feel like I should thank *you*, but there's nothing to thank you for, since you've done nothing but contract pneumonia."

"That's right," said Stella, beaming up at him.

"I will be back in a couple of days to check on you," he said as he went to the door.

I will not be here.

She waved. "See you then."

Dr. Reynolds shook his head in resignation and walked out.

A minute later, Francesqua stalked in with a tea tray, looking as agitated as she did when a neighbor came to report Uncle Josiah's latest misdeed and she was required to do something about his drunken urinating in highly-prized rose bushes or hiring a polka band to play at three o'clock in the morning on his porch. Still, it took a practiced eye to see that she was bothered at all. Only the set of her slim shoulders and a pair of lines between her brows gave her away.

"What did he say?" her mother asked, putting the tray on the end of Stella's bed.

"I'm young and well recovered."

Francesqua crossed her arms. "That's what he told me."

"See, everything is fine," said Stella.

"He lied." Francesqua straightened her covers. "Everyone is lying."

"No one is lying. I'm fine. Everything is fine."

Her mother went over to the door and closed it. "Everything is not fine."

"I don't know what you mean."

"You're not coming home, are you? Even after this," she said.

"After what? Nothing happened," said Stella.

Francesqua balled up her fists and raised her voice for the first time in Stella's life. "Stop. You're as bad as Josiah. Lying to my face and saying he hasn't drunk a drop while reeking of whiskey and vomit. Just stop."

"Mother, really I'm—"

"You were supposed to be my child."

Stella drew back. "I am."

"You're not. You belong to your father and Josiah. They could've taken the boys, but it had to be you. *My* daughter. *My* child." Francesqua's eyes spilled over with tears and she wiped them away furiously, leaving her cheeks red.

"The boys work at the brewery."

"It's not the same with them and you know it."

Her mother was right. It wasn't the same, but Stella couldn't say just why. Her brothers worked and learned the brewery business, but their interest was more required than desired. Uncle Josiah never snuck them out of lessons or taught them how to fly. Her father didn't put them in charge of limited edition brews to test their knowledge or open the books to them so they could see exactly where the money came from or where it went. Her brothers knew and seemed to accept on instinct that this was the way it was. They were smart and capable, but they weren't Stella. No one minded the way her father took over the brewery as a younger son instead of the oldest, Nicolai. At least, Stella had thought no one minded until the moment her mother finally spoke. Stella found she couldn't lie to her like she had so many times before. Her mother's pain changed everything. And as the earl said, her mother was there. She came when no one else did.

"It is different," said Stella.

"I know what you're doing," said Francesqua.

Stella shook her head. "I'm not doing anything."

Her mother plucked the lumpy handbag off the chair and said, "This is your handbag?"

"Er…yes."

"The heiress to the Bled brewing fortune and wife of the heir to the United Shipping and Steel fortune carries this handbag?"

"I don't have to have fancy things all the time."

"Shall I open it and see what's inside?"

Stella's hands clutched at the covers. "It's private."

"I just bet it is," said Francesqua.

"I'm not doing anything, Mother. Please don't be upset. I don't want to upset you."

Francesqua dropped the handbag and went to the tray, picking up a folded paper and slapping it on Stella's lap. "I picked this up four days ago. Page 8."

Reluctantly, Stella opened the paper and read the article. It mentioned her attending a dinner party at someone's house that she'd never heard of. "Well, it's a mistake."

"Stella, please. You weren't at some dinner party in Nottingham *while* you had double pneumonia in the Midlands. I doubt you were even in England."

Stella looked at her mother's flashing eyes and for the first time saw the intelligence in them. She'd never thought of her mother as dumb, nor had she though of her as smart either. Stella realized that for nineteen years she'd rarely thought of her mother at all. Not really. Not as a person, who felt, loved, and hurt the same as everyone else. Francesqua Bled was an obstacle and an ideal. A problem, in other words.

She bit her lip because these words couldn't be said. They were so horribly unfair and her mother, her perfect saint of a mother, was crying at the foot of her bed.

"I understand we are at war," said Francesqua, once she'd composed herself.

"*We* aren't. America isn't."

"I meant, *we* as a family. You and Nicky were the first to answer the call. Your father and uncles are planning a retooling of the second line in the factory to produce war supplies. I'm raising funds for the Red Cross with Florence. All those bazaars, teas, and clothing drives you think are so dull and pointless are going to keep St. Vincent's Hospital open, feed the orphans and ill, not to mention give our troops beds and medicines. I can fight, Stella. Maybe not like you or Nicky, but I can and I will. But I can't do anything for you, the most precious thing in my life, and I can't help."

"Mother—"

"Don't lie. I can't stand it. Nicky's mother is at least allowed to know where he is and what he's doing."

Stella tossed back her covers and slipped off the bed. Francesqua rushed over, trying to push her back. "What are you doing?"

"Proving you wrong." Stella grinned at her. "It's my favorite thing."

"How am I wrong this time?"

"You can help me."

"Do tell," said Francesqua. Stella didn't know her mother could sound sarcastic, but it suited her well.

"See that suitcase?"

"Your suitcase? The one the *real* Stella Bled Lawrence wouldn't be caught dead with?"

"That's the one."

Her mother insisted she get back in bed and got the suitcase, placing it next to the tea tray. "How is this suitcase going to help me help you?"

"Open it," said Stella.

Francesqua looked doubtful, but she opened the case and her doubt was replaced with astonishment. She went through the canvases, jewelry, candlesticks, and coins. "Stella, where in the world did you get this suitcase?"

Stella tilted her head and rolled her eyes.

"Oh, right," she said. "This must be someone's collection or, at least, the best of their collection. I've never seen this Klimt in any book or catalog."

"It's never been sold. It was a private commission and kept within the family."

"A Jewish family?"

"No. Well, not exactly," said Stella. "It doesn't matter. I've been entrusted with keeping the collection safe and I need your help to do it."

Francesqua smiled at her and that look of joy sparked a memory of her mother smiling at her that way when she was little, before the brewery, before the flying and everything that came with it.

"I'm not sure what to do," said Stella. "I gave her the earl's name and told her about Bickford House."

"So she can locate the collection when it's over."

"Yes, but I didn't tell the earl." Stella thought about his comments on her mother's love of art and smiled. "I think he knows though."

"The earl doesn't miss a trick and I like him in spite of his getting you in up to your neck," said Francesqua as she gazed down at the Klimt.

"It's not his fault," said Stella.

"I'd rather blame him than you," she said. "First things first. This suitcase must leave England immediately."

"I was thinking the same thing. There could be an invasion."

Francesqua got quiet and poured Stella a cup of tea before saying, "I'll be right back." She dashed from the room, making her daughter smile. Dashing wasn't ladylike at all. When she came back, she had a tray with a little pot of glue, a brush, labels, string, and a fountain pen. "Here we are. Just what we need."

"What are we going to do?" Stella asked.

"Everything must be labeled with all the information you have about the family, so there's no chance that it could be mistaken for anyone else's property."

"I'm not sure if I should."

"You should. This is that family's fortune and we're taking no chances with it," said Francesqua, giving Stella a label. "Start writing."

Together they labeled every piece in Ruth's suitcase with a list of family members and their address in Vienna. Francesqua did an inventory and a copy of the inventory. One went in the suitcase and she gave Stella the other. "When I've gone, you will give that to the earl for his records."

"When are you leaving?" Stella asked, feeling oddly bereft.

"Immediately. We can't take the chance that I won't get out before this Phoney War ends."

Stella impulsively hugged her mother and asked, "What will you tell Papa?"

"Nothing. He doesn't know about you and he's not going to," said Francesqua.

"But what will you do with Ruth's collection? He's bound to notice a new Klimt in ours."

Her mother jutted out a hip and tapped her lip. "You're right, of course. He will. Very nosy, your father." Then she smiled. "I'll give it to Florence. She knows and she'll be happy to help."

Stella's mouth dropped. "She knows? What does she know?"

Francesqua patted her cheek. "That you, Stella Bled, are not wandering around England gazing at obscure literary sights like some retired librarian. Anyone who really knows you, knows that's ridiculous."

"What about Uncle Nicolai?"

Her mother snorted. She actually snorted. Another first for Francesqua Bled. "Nico notices nothing. Don't you remember? When Florence had Millicent, he was completely shocked. He never noticed she was pregnant."

"She was enormous," said Stella.

"Exactly my point. Florence it is and while we're at it, you should come up with a code."

"A code?"

"For communicating with us when you send things. Just in case."

Stella closed the suitcase and secured the latches. "I'm not going to be sending you anything else. The world isn't full of Ruths."

"Our world is. And this *was* the plan."

"What plan?"

Francesqua rolled her eyes at Stella. Would wonders never cease? "The plan Josiah gave you for Vienna. Surely you remember. You were supposed to contact the Block Bauers and the Kronsteiners to help them, give them funds, take out pieces, whatever they needed. Those families are still there. So are dozens of others."

"You knew about that?" Stella asked, unable to contain her amazement.

"It was my plan. You didn't think Josiah came up with that on his own, did you?" Francesqua asked.

"Well…"

"Oh, darling. The only thing Josiah would think to smuggle out would be pretty girls."

"Why didn't you say it was you?"

Francesqua put her little nose in the air. "I'm your mother. I'm supposed to be a good example."

Stella threw her arms around her mother's neck and kissed her cheek. "You are."

"My girl."

Francesqua left bright and early the next morning and she wasn't alone. Bickford House was saying goodbye to two sons, several workers from the estate, and one footman, Toby. The entire estate had gathered to say goodbye, a crowd much like Abel's memorial, although boisterous instead of sad with forced cheerfulness and broad smiles.

Stella stood off to the right with Francesqua, their arms around each other's waists. They'd never been like that before. Of course, they'd hugged and kissed cheeks, but it wasn't comfortable. Stella had always been waiting for criticism and it made her keep her distance from her mother who wanted no distance at all.

Standing there, comfortable and close as they hadn't been since Stella was small, she couldn't understand why it happened with Francesqua when it didn't happen with her father or Uncle Josiah. They gave her plenty of criticism, endlessly correcting her in the brewery or in the air. She had to be perfect and that was fine by her. With Francesqua, it wasn't so. It seemed the smallest cut from her mother left the biggest scar.

"I hate to see this," said Francesqua. "They're so young."

"They want to go," said Stella.

"And they must. What's in the little packets?"

The earl and Agatha stood at the end of the line of well-wishers with Albert, whose face was pained for more reasons than just the goodbyes. He and the earl shook the men's hands and wished them good luck. Then Agatha gave each man a packet wrapped in brown paper and tied up with string. Their sons were given the same packet with no special treatment. "They're not special," the earl had told her earlier. "Because every man is special to someone."

Albert's brothers accepted their packets with the very same cheek kisses as Toby the footman or Joe the farmhand and they got in one of the family cars, squeezing in with the other men to be driven to the station in style.

"Twenty pounds, stationery with envelopes and stamps, and a bar of chocolate," said Stella. "Albert, also, wrote a note to each one."

"We should do that when it happens," said her mother. "The brewery will be sending a lot of young men."

"And women," said Stella.

"Do you think so?"

"We'll need nurses and other positions filled. Women will be needed."

"Mavis will want to go to the front lines."

Stella laughed, thinking of her feisty Irish friend. "She'd give 'em hell."

Francesca stiffened and then relaxed. Stella waited for a rebuke but none was forthcoming. "She would without a doubt. You know, she wanted to come with me on this trip."

"Why didn't you bring her?"

"Well, you know how sassy Mavis is. She's the only one that can bully your father into eating properly."

"You left the laundress in charge over the whole house?"

"Only over your father. Mrs. Dunn was relieved."

They smiled and put their heads together as the last man received his packet and kisses.

"It's time," said Francesqua.

Stella hugged her and said, "I'll miss you."

"It was worth the trip just for that." She opened her handbag and pulled out an envelope. "Here's a list of families we know that haven't been able to emigrate. If you can help them, please do."

Stella pressed the envelope to her heart. "I'll find a way."

"In that, you are just like Josiah, and I mean that as a compliment."

"Don't lose my envelope," said Stella.

"I'll protect it with my life," said Francesqua, making it sound like a jest, but she was dead serious.

Stella had given her a code that she'd devised during training. She and Florence would use it for communicating about people like Ruth who were escaping the Reich and needed help from the Bleds. Park-Welles had given her a rare compliment on the code's ingenuity and Stella felt good about the security.

Francesca and Stella exchanged cheek kisses and Francesqua got in the second car with Toby, who looked somewhat terrified of riding with Mrs. Aleksej Bled of the Bled Brewery. Stella waved and turned to go up the stairs, although it was daunting. Coming down was hard enough. Going up would be a trial.

"Can I help?" Albert was at her shoulder. "I'm good for something. Occasionally."

Stella took his arm and they went up the stone stairs. She was a little wobbly, but Albert was steady and they made it up and through the house to the front steps in time to see Francesqua's car drive onto the bridge. A bicyclist emerged from the woods amid a flurry of honking as it was nearly hit by the cars going to the station. The rider stopped and waved until Francesqua's car was out of sight and then started pedaling furiously for the house.

Albert chuckled. "Ah, Chester. It's a wonder that boy wasn't flattened two weeks ago."

"What happened two weeks ago?" Stella asked.

"He started delivering telegrams and a logging lorry ended up in a creek on his first day."

"Not good on the bicycle?"

"He doesn't pay attention. My mother got the butcher's telegram last week and Sir Richard at Everwood got hers."

Stella put her head on Albert's shoulder and said, "Well, I was going to go in, but now I'm curious to see if he makes it all the way to the house."

"You joke, but there's a strong possibility he won't," said Albert. "Smith caught him going to see the pigs a couple of hours after you arrived instead of delivering the telegram from the Viscount Alanbury telling us that they were on their way to get Anna."

They stayed on the steps and watched the boy turn left to follow the road around the house.

"Success," said Stella.

"Wait for it," said Albert and a minute later the boy was heading out across the park into the trees.

"Where's he going?" she asked.

"Not to the pigs this time. Sally Grey lives at Broken Bow farm and it's out that way. They're in the same class at the village school."

"You know everything about everyone, don't you?"

Albert heaved a sigh. "Not much else I can do, but remember details." He pointed with his bad hand. "There he is. Someone must've turned him around."

Chester rode pell-mell back toward them but then didn't turn left to go to the back of the house. He headed toward the bridge.

"For crying out loud," said Albert, raising his hand and yelling, "Chester! Chester!"

His hand, although not as bad as Ulrich's in Berlin, made her think of his scarred face and his pain so similar to Albert's and she felt a surge of love for the thin man beside her who watched his brothers go off to war and thought himself useless.

A few more yells got Chester's attention and the boy turned around to race back to the house. He started to go to the back again, but then turned to pedal up the walk to the front, panting and smiling at the same time as he skidded to a halt in front of them. "I have a telegram, your lordship."

"Thank you, Chester," said Albert and he waited while Chester eyed Stella with interest and showed no sign of handing over a telegram.

"Are you the Yank that were sick?" he asked.

"I am," said Stella. "Do you know a lot of Yanks?"

"Not many of them around. Are you married to a cowboy?"

"No. Not many of them around either."

Chester snorted and waved that idea away. "Psst. They're all over the West. I go to the movies. I know."

Stella smiled at him and said, "I'm from Missouri, so I wouldn't know."

Chester wrinkled his freckled nose and looked like he doubted that Missouri was a real place. "I got to go. I deliver telegrams. My brother's off to the Navy and me mam cries all the time."

He flipped his bike around and Albert said, "Chester."

"Your lordship?"

"The telegram?"

"I gived it to you."

They shook their heads and the boy dug in the bag slung over his shoulder. "Would ya look at that?" He handed it to Stella. "It's from London. Mr. Foster was excited. Do you know Winnie?"

"Who?" Stella asked.

"Lord Churchill," said Albert.

"Does he really drink whiskey all day?" Chester asked.

"That's enough, Chester."

The boy frowned. "Enough of what?"

Albert sighed again. "Why don't you go around to the kitchen and ask Mrs. Wallace for a treat. Tell her I sent you."

With a happy whoop, Chester peeled out and headed back toward the road.

"Do you think he'll make it?" Stella asked.

"Eventually." Albert eyed the envelope. "Would you look at that. It's actually addressed to you and it's from the Admiralty. Chester remembered something."

Stella held the telegram away from her as if it might burst into flames. It could be a rebuke. With her heart so heavy from seeing her mother off, she couldn't bear the thought of it.

"Go on," said Albert. "Get it over with."

She opened it and read the sparse lines from Lady Churchill and relief flooded over her. An invitation to tea in the lady's private boudoir. She'd done well and Clementine knew it. She tapped the telegram against her lips. It had to be worth something.

"Well?" Albert asked. "What is it?"

"Nothing. Just an invitation for tea," said Stella.

"So no hurry," he said.

"Not at all."

Albert gave her a sly smile. "Shall I help you pack?"

Stella laughed. "Already done."

"If you hurry you might make your mother's train," he suggested.

"I have a better idea." She turned him around and opened the door. "You should drive me."

"All the way to London?" Albert asked.

"Yes and to tea with Lady Churchill today at four."

They walked into the great hall and watched the hive of activity as the remaining servants bustled past, carrying tea trays to the families bereft of their sons, who were gathered in the big library to commiserate.

"So now I'm to be your chauffeur instead of planning wheat fields," said Albert, smiling. "It's a promotion and I'll take it."

"You'll be going to tea *with* me," said Stella.

"What for?"

"A job."

"With Lady Churchill?"

"With someone and the Admiralty is a good place to start," she said. "Strike while the iron is hot as they say."

"And you're hot, as it were?" he asked.

Stella grinned up at him. "Let's find out."

"My parents won't like it."

"That's why we aren't going to tell them," she said.

"Did you get this from your mother?"

"Maybe?" Stella gave him a nudge. "To London?"

Albert smiled back and he seemed to fill up, becoming someone akin to who he'd been before Vienna. He, too, would come back from the sorrow. "It will be my pleasure."

Stella took his arm and said with a smile, "I'll make sure of it."

The End

PREVIEW

DARK VICTORY (STELLA BLED BOOK FOUR)

There wasn't a thought in his head, not a single one. Abel Herschmann walked across roll call square with his previously active mind curiously quiet. He saw the new prisoners entering Dachau in his peripheral vision but didn't bother to give them a good look. He hadn't any curiosity left.

Several dozen men sat with their bony bottoms on the gravel, hammering nails into boards and then pulling them out again. Abel threaded his way between them, not meeting their eyes or hearing the weeping. Some guard had come up with the idea, genius in its insidious evil, as a punishment. At first, Abel had thought this simple hammering was benign and it was, compared to having your hands bound behind you and being hung by them from a pole. But the senseless activities were a special kind of torment that affected the mind terribly and Abel had seen more than one man come apart at the seams after spending a few thirteen-hour days hammering or digging a hole only to fill it back in.

Jakob had told him hopelessness was the enemy and that's where those punishments excelled. The old man was the wisest person Abel had ever met as well as the bravest. He kept his wits about him, despite illness and injury, to give Abel a name to help him survive in Dachau.

"Adam," whispered a man as he passed.

Abel gave the slightest of nods to acknowledge the voice of a bookkeeper from the Jewish barracks, but he didn't hesitate or answer. The guards were watching and it would do neither of them any favors. He'd learned a lot in his eighteen-month internment, but the most important was not to think. It was a rare time when Jakob had been wrong. His sweet and naturally hopeful nature leaned toward happy distracting thoughts. He'd advised dwelling on pleasant memories of childhood or friends or holidays, but those thoughts only tormented Abel. They were so far away that he was no longer quite sure they had happened. He'd discovered during a particularly long punishment of moving sand from one pile to the next and back again that not thinking was the key.

So a man given to thinking in vivid imagery and full complex sentences in multiple languages learned to turn it off and found the specter of insanity that had been barking at his door disappeared entirely. Now the guards ignored him and it was considerably easier to pretend to be a communist bricklayer named Adam Stolowicki when he didn't think about Oxford, his beloved books, his friends, or, most importantly, Stella. That beautiful young woman had to go, pushed into a corner of his mind, where her smile and charming naïveté didn't twist his soul with longing. That was the kind of thing that showed on a man's face and made him a target. Abel was blank and obedient. He'd become a master bricklayer and memorized a mountain of useless facts on communism, making him both convincing and useful.

Abel would do what he had to for survival's sake. It was only a matter of time. He'd given his name, his real name, to Michael Haas a second before his friend's release and Michael would save him. It would happen. He was so sure he'd even stopped thinking about that. Wondering if today was the day was pointless and inefficient. Let the others waste their time. He'd told them his secret to survival and counseled them on their pain as Jakob had done for him, but some couldn't or wouldn't follow his advice and there was nothing he could do about that. Some would whisper and plead as the bookkeeper was just then. They could not be led away from it. Abel heard a boot connect with flesh and a howl burst out in protest, bringing more guards and more pain. Some survived with hope like Jakob and Michael, a path much harder in Abel's opinion. The guards didn't like hope. Blank was better.

In silence with his quiet empty mind, Abel Herschmann approached the guard standing next to the Jourhaus door. He'd eyed Abel critically, looking for something to target or suspect.

Finding nothing, he asked in a guttural kind of German accent most often spoken in factories or fields, "What do you want?"

"I was ordered to come to the Jourhaus," said Abel without any interest at all.

"What for?"

"I was not informed of the reason."

"Do you deserve a reason?" asked the guard slyly.

There was a time when Abel's heartrate would've skyrocketed. He'd have flushed and broken out in a sweat, but now he merely stared straight ahead and said, "I follow orders. I do not question them."

Mollified, the guard stepped aside. "Weiß is waiting for you in his office. Don't make him wait." He said it like Abel had some kind of control over his situation and might just decide that angering the assistant to the camp commandant was a swell idea. Both notions were ludicrous, but neither one made the slightest impression on Abel.

"Yes," he said. "May I open the door?"

The guard shoved his shoulder. "Unless you want to walk through it."

"I will open the door."

"Do that."

A nearby prisoner sweeping the gravel tensed up and backed away. Abel saw the move. Once he would've been dismayed, but, for him, this wasn't a tense exchange. He had no interest in the outcome because he couldn't do anything about it.

"Do I have permission?" Abel asked simply.

The guard was puzzled but said, "You do."

Abel opened the door and walked inside the Jourhaus, feeling the warmth of a heated building for the first time since the time he was there with Michael. Jakob had somehow arranged to have their designation changed from Jews to communists and it had been a terrifying experience. There was no terror now. He explained himself three more times before standing at Weiß's door and giving it a single knock.

"Come," barked the SS officer and Abel walked into an office with a large window overlooking the men hammering and the beating that was still taking place. The SS Weiß sat behind a cherrywood desk that was at least a hundred years old. Its neoclassical elegance was completely out of place in the white-walled office replete with metal filing cabinets and photos of Der Führer, the high command, and Nuremberg rallies covering the walls.

Weiß sat on a rolling office chair and signed a series of papers, stacking them in a basket next to a bronze-colored SS desk eagle. It looked like an oversized paperweight and if Abel had been thinking he'd have wondered what on Earth it was for and why anybody would put such a hideous symbol on such a beautiful desk, but he wasn't thinking and he merely stood waiting in silence.

The SS signed three more papers, tossed them in the basket, and finally looked up saying, "Who is she?"

Abel's blank mind had nothing. He hadn't seen a woman for five months, not since Michael stumbled into the arms of one just outside the gate and he didn't know who she was.

"Sir?"

"There's a woman here asking for you," said Weiß as he leaned back in his chair and steepled his fingers.

"I don't know who that is," he said with complete honesty. He thought he felt a flicker of interest inside himself, but it was quickly gone.

"You don't?"

"No."

"She knows who you are." The SS shuffled around the desk and found a folder. "Adam Stolowicki."

Abel remained silent. There was no right answer.

"You don't know any women?"

The answer to that would seem obvious. Of course, he did. All men knew women at least in some capacity, but in Dachau the simplest answers could be death. Three months ago, a new arrival had been asked during a work detail what color the sky was. The prisoner had said without hesitation that the sky was blue. The guard had beaten him into unconsciousness because the sky was currently grey as it was an overcast morning. The man was lying and he died for it. Abel had been working near him and he'd seen it coming. They all had. That guard roused them that morning and they knew him well enough to know he was spoiling for a fight, but they hadn't said anything to the new prisoners. Abel bitterly regretted it, but in the end, it made his silence more profound.

"Not since I've been here."

Weiß watched him with dark eyes. He was a brutal man, but not the kind that beat men to death over the color of the sky. He would, however, have no difficulty sending Abel to the medical block for what would be called treatment.

Read the rest in
Dark Victory (Stella Bled Book Four)

ALSO BY A.W. HARTOIN

Afterlife Issues

Dead Companions (Afterlife Issues Book One)

A Trunk, a Canoe, and all the Barbecue (Afterlife Issues Book Two)

Old Friends and Fedoras (Afterlife Issues Book Three)

The Trouble with Tinsel (Afterlife Issues Book Four)

Fun Ivy (Afterlife Issues Book Five) coming soon

Mercy Watts Mysteries

<u>Novels</u>

A Good Man Gone (Mercy Watts Mysteries Book One)

Diver Down (A Mercy Watts Mystery Book Two)

Double Black Diamond (Mercy Watts Mysteries BookThree)

Drop Dead Red (Mercy Watts Mysteries Book Four)

In the Worst Way (Mercy Watts Mysteries Book Five)

The Wife of Riley (Mercy Watts Mysteries Book Six)

My Bad Grandad (Mercy Watts Mysteries Book Seven)

Brain Trust (Mercy Watts Mysteries Book Eight)

Down and Dirty (Mercy Watts Mysteries Book Nine)

Small Time Crime (Mercy Watts Mysteries Book Ten)

Bottle Blonde (Mercy Watts Mysteries Book Eleven)

Mean Evergreen (Mercy Watts Mysteries Book Twelve)

Silver Bells at Hotel Hell (Mercy Watts Mysteries Book Thirteen)

So Long Gone (Mercy Watts Mysteries Book Fourteen)

<u>Short stories</u>

Coke with a Twist

Touch and Go My Book

Nowhere Fast

Dry Spell

A Sin and a Shame

Stella Bled Historical Thrillers

The Paris Package (Stella Bled Book One)

Strangers in Venice (Stella Bled Book Two)

One Child in Berlin (Stella Bled Book Three)

Dark Victory (Stella Bled Book Four)

A Quiet Little Place on Rue de Lille (Stella Bled Book Five)

Her London Season (Stella Bled Book Six)

Double Duet (Stella Bled Book Seven)

Paranormal

It Started with a Whisper (Son of a Witch Book One)

Angels and Insects (Son of a Witch Book Two)

Young Adult fantasy

Flare-up (Away From Whipplethorn Short)

A Fairy's Guide To Disaster (Away From Whipplethorn Book One)

Fierce Creatures (Away From Whipplethorn Book Two)

A Monster's Paradise (Away From Whipplethorn Book Three)

A Wicked Chill (Away From Whipplethorn Book Four)

To the Eternal (Away From Whipplethorn Book Five)

A.W. HARTOIN'S NEWSLETTER

To be the first to hear all about the A.W. Hartoin news and new releases click the link or scan the QR code to join the mailing list. Only sales, news, and new releases. No spam. Spam is evil.

Newsletter sign-up

ABOUT THE AUTHOR

USA Today bestselling author A.W. Hartoin grew up in rural Missouri, but her grandmother lived in the Central West End area of St. Louis. The CWE fascinated her with its enormous houses, every one unique. She was sure there was a story behind each ornate door. Going to Grandma's house was a treat and an adventure. As the only grandchild around for many years, A.W. spent her visits exploring the many rooms with their many secrets. That's how Mercy Watts and the fairies of Whipplethorn came to be.

As an adult, A.W. Hartoin decided she needed a whole lot more life experience if she was going to write good characters so she joined the Air Force. It was the best education she could've hoped for. She met her husband and traveled the world, living in Alaska, Italy, and Germany before settling in Colorado for nearly eleven years. Now A.W. has returned to Germany and lives in picturesque Waldenbuch with her family and two spoiled cats, who absolutely believe they should be allowed to escape and roam the village freely.